Praise for
A Bride for K

"*A Bride for Keeps* treats readers to an engaging prairie romance when God's will and love collide, delivering a heartwarming, satisfying read."

—Maggie Brendan,
CBA bestselling author of *The Heart of the West*
and *The Blue Willow Brides* series

"Melissa Jagears is a stand-out talent! Her fresh new voice is strong, stylish, and makes *A Bride for Keeps* a page-turner for anyone who fancies a stirring love story. Vivid description and unforgettable, heart-tugging scenes between hero and heroine transform the ever-popular mail-order bride storyline into something much more real and three-dimensional. In this appealing novel, Ms. Jagears demonstrates beyond doubt that the aplomb of the writer determines the quality of the story."

—Rosslyn Elliot,
author of *Fairer Than Morning*
and *Sweeter Than Birdsong*

"Melissa Jagears has penned a tender tale of a mail-order bride who takes both the groom—and herself—by surprise when love comes softly . . . quietly . . . to heal their broken hearts."

—Julie Lessman,
author of *Love at Any Cost*

"*A Bride for Keeps* is just beautiful. It put me in mind of Janette Oke's sweet prairie romances but with a bit more edge, which I found compelling. . . . I loved it."

—Mary Connealy,
author of *Fired Up*

A *Bride*
FOR KEEPS

A Bride
FOR KEEPS

A NOVEL

MELISSA JAGEARS

BETHANYHOUSE
a division of Baker Publishing Group
Minneapolis, Minnesota

Published by Bethany House Publishers
11400 Hampshire Avenue South
Bloomington, Minnesota 55438
www.bethanyhouse.com

Bethany House Publishers is a division of
Baker Publishing Group, Grand Rapids, Michigan

Printed in the United States of America

Library of Congress Cataloging-in-Publication Data
Jagears, Melissa.
    A bride for keeps : a novel / Melissa Jagears.
        pages   cm
    Summary: "After three failed attempts, Everett Cline is not happy when another—uninvited—mail-order bride steps off the train in his Kansas farming community. But is she the wife he's been waiting for?"—provided by publisher.
    ISBN 978-0-7642-1168-3 (pbk.)
    1. Mail order brides—Fiction. 2. Farmers—Fiction. 3. Frontier and pioneer life—Fiction. 4. Kansas—Fiction I. Title.
PS3610.A368 B75 2013
813'.6—dc23   2013023264

Scripture quotations are from the King James Version of the Bible.

Wedding vows in chapter seven are from *The Book of Common Prayer*.

The hymn in chapter fourteen is *Fairest Lord Jesus*, translated from German to English by Joseph A. Seiss, 1873.

Cover design by Dan Pitts
Cover photography by Mike Habermann Photography, LLC

Author represented by The Natasha Kern Literary Agency

13 14 15 16 17 18 19   7 6 5 4 3 2 1

To my husband, who puts up with
a lot so I can write and believes in me
when I don't believe in myself.
I wish I was more like you.

Chapter 1

KANSAS
SPRING 1876

Everett Cline loosened his grip on the mercantile's door-knob and let the door shut behind him. Kathleen Hampden waddled straight toward him, the white feathers in her hat dancing like bluestem grass in the late March breeze. In the three years she'd been married to the store's owner instead of him, couldn't she have bought a new hat?

He hadn't talked to her alone since the day she arrived in Salt Flatts with those identifying white feathers he'd been told to expect, but he hadn't anticipated her being married to Carl before she stepped off the train. Why hadn't she thrown her hat out a passenger car window and pretended she'd never been his mail-order bride?

"Afternoon, ma'am. Is your husband around?"

He glanced behind the long glossy counter cluttered with candy jars and sundry items and saw that the door to the empty back room stood ajar. The two overflowing shelves that cut the store into thirds kept him from being able to see into every corner. The fabric table was a jumbled mess, and a few potatoes lay on the floor in the corner, escaped from their bin. Were they the only ones in the store?

Mrs. Hampden stopped three feet from him, the tang of the wood polish on her rag warring with the leather and tobacco smells permeating the room. She was such a tiny thing, even large with child. Perhaps it was a good thing she had married Carl. If she worked outside as Everett did every day, the wind would have blown her away sooner or later.

"Mr. Hampden's away on business, otherwise he'd have rushed out at the bell. Especially since it's you." Her cheeks pinked.

Carl needn't worry about him. Stealing someone's mail-order bride was different from stealing someone's wife.

Everett fidgeted. "He has no reason to be concerned."

"I know." She rubbed her swollen stomach. "But he's still worried your good looks might make me wish I'd chosen differently."

The skin under his collar grew warm, and he pulled at the strangling fabric. He might be a decent-looking sort of man, but a lot of good that did him.

"I hope you have better luck today than you did with me, and you know . . . the others." She bit her lip. "I'm sure this time it will be for keeps."

He swallowed hard and eyed her. What was she talking about? Surely another rumor about him ordering a bride again wasn't circulating. "I'm afraid I don't understand."

"It's all right. Rachel told me." Her voice was hushed, as if someone might hear.

He leaned down and whispered back. "Told you what?"

"About the lady coming on the afternoon train. She said you'd need prayer."

Rachel.

He ran his tongue along his teeth and nodded absently. Surely his best friend's wife wasn't pulling another one of her matchmaking schemes. She'd tried to set him up with every girl in the county since the day her sister, Patricia, had left him for someone else. When matchmaking failed, she'd pushed him into mail-order bride advertisements.

If she'd gone and ordered another one for him, by golly—

"I hope I haven't upset you." Mrs. Hampden's concerned tone reminded him of her presence. "I haven't told anyone since . . . well, you know how they are."

Yes, the townsfolk. Everett clenched his teeth. Every unescorted woman who stepped off the train was asked if she belonged to Everett Cline. When she answered negatively, some young man in the gathered crowd would drop to his knee and propose.

He stared at the saddle soap on the shelf beside him. What had he come in here for?

"I wish you luck." Mrs. Hampden's eyes looked dewy.

Everett squashed the felt brim of his hat in his clammy hands. *Third time's a charm* hadn't worked for him, and he'd never heard anything like *the fourth's a keeper*. There wouldn't be a fourth time for him. Well, fifth, if he added being jilted by Patricia so long ago. Was there a saying akin to *five failures prove a fool*? He was a hairsbreadth away from confirming himself a dunce. "You have nothing to wish me luck for."

"Oh, Everett, surely this time it will work."

"Really, Mrs. Hampden, I don't know what you're talking about."

"I can understand why you don't want to say anything, but I'm the last person in Salt Flatts who would tease you."

He'd let her believe whatever she wanted, because nothing

would happen. "Thanks just the same." He smashed his hat back on and hightailed it out the door, down the steps, and toward the weathered wagon belonging to his neighbors. Was this why Rachel insisted they needed him in town even though any train porter could have helped her husband load the shipment she was waiting on?

He wouldn't believe it. She wouldn't do that.

"Come on now, Everett," she'd said. *"You can't avoid town forever. Surely you have supplies to get."*

He reached into his pocket, clasped his scribbled list, and stopped in the middle of the road. Rachel wouldn't have gone so far as to invite another woman to Salt Flatts to marry him without even telling him. Would she?

A horse sidestepped beside him, the boot of its rider grazing his arm. "Hey, watch what you're doing." The cowboy glared down at him, the stench of bovine overpowering the scent of the cheap cigar wiggling between his lips.

Everett turned and scurried across the dusty road and onto the boardwalk. He glanced at his list. Should he return to the mercantile and face Kathleen again or confront Rachel? Neither would be pleasant.

"Got me a letter to send, Everett?" Jedidiah Langston stepped out of the false-front post office and stood next to his son, eighteen-year-old Axel, who perched on a stool, absently whittling a stick. A smirk twitched the corners of the younger man's mouth.

Everett's hand itched to swipe the boy's lips clean off his face, but he shook his head instead. He hadn't personally posted something for over a year—always sent his mail in with the Stantons—but it seemed as if Rachel had decided to mail some correspondence for him.

"Surely you're hankerin' for another bride by now. Helga's

been Mrs. Parker for plumb near a year. Seems to me it's about time you up and tried again."

Axel chuckled at his father's joke, and Everett scowled at the mention of his third—and absolutely last—mail-order bride.

He crammed the shopping list back into his pocket. "No letter, gentlemen."

"Axel needs a wife about as bad as I need him off of my porch." Jedidiah glared at his lazy son, who only rolled his eyes. "Maybe your next one can marry him."

Axel sliced the tip off his pointy stick. "Only if he orders a stunner this time."

Any woman dumb enough to marry that boy would have to work to support them both. Everett tipped his hat. "Good day, gentlemen."

He'd been Axel's age eighteen years ago, but he'd at least had some gumption, a promising future, and an adoring girl on his arm. Yet he was still single. A mail-order bride was probably the boy's only hope, though Everett doubted he'd ever try for one. Axel's ma had once been a mail-order bride, and when her marriage plans hadn't worked out, she'd wooed Jedidiah over real fast.

Mrs. Langston was hardly ever seen in town, and Jedidiah never talked about her but in disdain. Axel's parents' animosity toward each other didn't help the boy's disposition—as prickly as a cocklebur and as useful as one too.

Everett marched over to the train platform and scanned the crowd. Rachel was nowhere in sight, but her husband, Dex, reclined on his wagon's bench seat, hat pulled over his face. His soft snores jostled the brim resting on his nose. He couldn't know his wife had hatched another scheme. That joker wouldn't have been able to keep a straight face when

Rachel insisted they needed help. And he'd be too antsy to tease the daylights out of Everett now to be sleeping.

Perhaps Mrs. Hampden had made a mistake and assumed too much. The town loved to conspire, and though Dex was a joker, the Stantons wouldn't plot against him like that. No, Mrs. Hampden had to be mistaken.

Everett stopped at the depot's window and perused the station's chalkboard schedule. Thirty minutes until the train arrived. The bunch of wild flowers he'd picked before leaving home lay piled in his wagon bed. He snatched them and headed for the cemetery.

"Everett!" a voice called out, and he turned to see Carl Hampden hotfooting it from the livery straight toward him. The tilt of his head and the look in his eyes reminded Everett of a charging bull.

He stopped and tensed, half expecting the man to reach for a sidearm. "Carl?"

"Where are you going with those?" He pointed to the flowers.

Everett released his stranglehold on the prairie bouquet and kept his lips from twitching up into a smile. He stood but ten feet from the mercantile entrance. "They're not for your wife, if that's what you're worried about."

"Who are they for, then?" Carl backed up, but the heat hadn't left his gaze.

"I don't exactly believe that's your business."

Carl leaned closer. He'd evidently had garlic for lunch.

What did it really matter if Carl knew? "They're for Adelaide Gooding."

"Who?" Carl cocked an eyebrow.

Everett sighed. "My first bride."

"Ah, I see . . . I guess." Carl relaxed. "Well, carry on."

As if he needed the man's permission. He snatched Carl's sleeve and dug out his list. "Would you gather these items for me? I'll return within an hour."

Carl folded the note and tipped his hat.

Everett strolled through town, keeping the jonquils tucked by his side. Why did he keep taking her flowers anyway? He looked at the sad, flaccid mess in his hands. Because no one else would—and that was his fault.

He stepped through the gap in the waist-high stone wall, marched straight up to Adelaide's grave, and laid the flowers at her feet. "I'm afraid they're wilted, but they're better than what you have." Which was nothing. He lowered himself to the ground and stared at her headstone. He hadn't even known what birth date to engrave for his first mail-order bride, but he'd done his best. Even wrote an epitaph: *Long-awaited and Missed*.

Everett glanced around to make certain no one else was near. "Have you heard any talk about me lately? Seems Mrs. Hampden thinks I'm crazy enough to try marrying up again." He grabbed a twig and scratched at the dirt. "I wish you'd held on for a few more hours. At least so I could have told you that I . . ." He tossed his stick. Had he loved her? He would have. But he no longer had any stir of feelings for this woman he'd never met.

Closing his eyes, he conjured up the one image he had of Adelaide. Wrapped in a rough woolen blanket, her face white as clouds, hair dark as a raven's wing, and her mouth, crooked and stiff as a fence post. The fever had stolen her breath and his hope.

The low hum of metal wheels against iron track rumbled from far off. With the toe of his boot, he shoved a stray jonquil back into his jumbled pile. "Maybe if I'd lived along

15

the Mississippi, I'd have had better luck ordering brides by steamboat." He snorted, and a gray-green pigeon above him fussed. "So you don't think so?"

A whistle sounded. "Rachel's always wanted a pianoforte. Please let it be a piano." But she'd asked Mrs. Hampden for prayer . . . and surely nothing she could order would be so heavy she'd beseech God's assistance. The tremor of the approaching train pulsed through the soles of his feet.

What if there was another woman on that train coming for him? He clenched his trembling fingers. Patricia had jilted him. Then Adelaide arrived dead, Kathleen disembarked married to the shopkeeper, and Helga left him for another man with a better farm within a week of arriving. He couldn't begin to imagine what a fourth mail-order bride might do. But he wouldn't allow another bride to make a fool of him again.

She'd made a mistake. A huge, irrevocable mistake.

Julia Lockwood stared out the train's window, watching the flat Kansas land sail behind her, mile after mile. Nothing but waving grasses, clumps of trees, and a few outcroppings of rocks. The vacant prairie lands wouldn't conceal the past she ran from, and the man awaiting her wouldn't make it better—only worse. What had possessed her to believe this was a good idea? She set her bag aside to stand.

"Young lady, you are making me queasy with your ups and downs, to-and-fros." The buxom woman across from her swished a fan violently. "Please, for once sit still."

Julia hesitated, hovering above her seat. Her nerves wouldn't obey the woman's pinched-mouthed decree. "I'm sorry. When I return, I'll try not to get up again."

The woman huffed. "Yes, do."

Holding in her split pannier overskirt, she swayed easily through the center aisle of the railroad car. A few days of travel had made her an expert at walking in a moving train. She grabbed a strap hanging from the ceiling to make room for a young frizzy-haired girl to pass.

The porter at the front of the car straightened. "May I do something for you, miss?"

"Nothing, Henry. Unless you can make this car go faster . . . or slower." She bit her lip. "How much longer until Salt Flatts?"

"Not too long. Just a hop and a skip. We'll be there before you know it." His smile stretched across his face, slicing his dark skin with a glimmering white. "I reckon you'll be just fine, miss."

Just fine? When she'd agreed to marry a man with whom she'd never even exchanged a single letter? No. Not fine. The thought of being close to any man again made her stomach churn.

"But one thing I'd be doing is stop playing with that there brooch. You're going to be wearing off its shine."

She released her mother's portrait clipped to her collar, her fingers red from rubbing the gold filigree frame. "Perhaps I am a bit nervous."

"I suspect you don't have to be anxious for nothing."

If only that were true. But there was nothing to be done now. She couldn't very well jump off the train. Oh, why hadn't she gotten off at the last stop? Stiffly, she returned to her seat.

The large woman across from her glared from behind that ever-swishing fan and sighed.

Her husband leaned forward. "You worried about meeting someone?"

Julia nodded, wishing her whole life didn't depend on a

man she'd never met. Why had she handed some stranger a hold over her? She wanted to see Rachel Stanton, the woman she'd corresponded with for the past few months, but she should have come simply to visit Rachel. Instead, she'd panicked and promised her life away in matrimony when Rachel had mentioned her husband's friend would be interested in a mail-order bride. Would Rachel and Dex Stanton offer their hospitality if she didn't follow through with marrying Everett Cline? The sourness in her stomach crept toward her throat.

"A fella, I suppose?"

Feeling color invade her cheeks, she shrugged.

"Stop worrying. No fella'd be sorry to see a girl like you step off this train."

No. No lonely fellow would. That was part of the problem. Maybe she should have worn her day dress instead of her best silk.

Henry walked the aisle, touching headrests as he passed. "Next stop, Salt Flatts."

Her heart doubled its rhythm. A friend awaited her . . . but so did a man. Last chance. Stay in the seat or meet her potential husband? He'd want an intimacy from her she wasn't ready to give anytime soon. She wrapped her arms about her waist and suppressed a moan. What choice did she have?

The locomotive's gleaming chimney loomed. Its acrid smoke rolled over the prairie land surrounding Salt Flatts, marring the gray-blue sky. Everett paced on the crowded train platform, wondering if Rachel had indeed set him up. He scanned the crowd. No sign of her yet. Surely she'd be waiting for the woman she intended to foist upon him if there were one. He blew out a breath and ambled toward the Stantons' wagon. He'd know soon enough.

The train's whistle scattered the birds pecking in the grass next to the tracks, and the hissing iron monster slowed. Rachel scurried across the road and up the plank ramp. Her three-year-old, Emma, bounced on her hip and waved wildly at the train.

The pullman's door opened, and Everett stared at the line of silhouettes behind the passenger car windows. Several men disembarked before a skinny woman stepped onto the rough wooden platform, her curly orange-red hair trailing across her blemished face.

Rachel looked straight at the tall girl, and Everett tensed, but Rachel didn't hail her. The young woman scurried to a waiting wagon and embraced an elderly man.

Everett rubbed at the tension in his neck.

More men poured out of the passenger car, and finally the porter exited and sauntered toward the depot. Everett released his pent-up breath and chuckled at himself. He'd allowed Mrs. Hampden's foolish notions to mess with his head.

"There you are." John, Rachel's youngest boy, rushed toward him. "Are you ready for the surprise?"

A surprise for John or a surprise for him? His breath grew shallow, and he squatted to the boy's eye level. "Do you know what it is?"

John shook his dark head. "No. Ma won't tell me. Would you ask her?"

"You're too impatient. We'll find out soon enough." He rubbed the boy's head and forced himself not to walk straight toward Rachel and ask. If John was anxious, then the surprise had to be for the family, not him. Rachel wouldn't have hinted to the children about a scheme to match him up with a stranger.

"There she is." Rachel's call ended in a high feminine squeal. She handed Emma to Dex and darted into the crowd. Dex threw him a glance before covering up a grin with his free hand. Too much amused twinkling danced in his best friend's eyes.

He'd been hoodwinked.

Everett slowly pivoted toward the train. A petite, fashionably dressed lady wrestled an oversized valise through the pullman's door and climbed cautiously down the stairs. Her ivory skirt was extraordinarily full in the back. A red sash cinched her waist, enhancing its tininess. She fingered a brooch at her neck and brushed at the veil whipping against her forehead in the wind. Dark wavy hair fell from under her straw hat, framing her perfect lips and tiny nose. He had never seen a more beautiful woman. Not even Patricia, the prettiest gal who'd ever set foot in Saline County, could compare.

The woman gestured toward Rachel with a wad of papers in her hand and a question in her shoulder shrug. Rachel's hands flung out, and she swallowed the woman in an embrace. Though one was dressed in worn homespun calico and the other in ruffles of shimmering stiff fabric, they started chattering like long-lost sisters.

He pushed down the jolt that traveled up from his toes. This stunning friend of Rachel's would never need to become a mail-order bride. She was not here for him.

Julia pulled away from Rachel's third warm hug, which couldn't calm the storm of emotions swirling within her chest. Though she rejoiced to hold this dear friend in her arms for the first time, she couldn't help looking around the crowd for him. Her heart thudded at the base of her throat. "I can hardly believe I'm here." If she hadn't seen Rachel waiting on the platform, almost bouncing with anticipation, she would have slouched in the leather passenger seat, dug out the last of her money, and rode the tracks a little farther.

"Me neither." Rachel hugged her again. "I never realized how much I missed having a bosom friend until I started writing you. We'll take you home and talk all night and meet the neighbors and . . ."

Rachel's banter was infectious, but her friendliness didn't stifle the need to know what her future husband expected. "Won't Everett want to, uh, start things right away?" A few hundred feet away a white steeple loomed over rows of buildings, making her feel faint. She tried to imagine riding straight to the church and marrying, but she just couldn't do it. "Do you know what he has planned?" Julia gripped Rachel's arm, anchoring herself from rushing back to the train.

"About Everett . . . I'd not bring up the marriage plans until he does, and he'll probably give you plenty of time." Rachel rubbed her lip and averted her gaze. What was she keeping from her? "My advice is to act as if you've come to court rather than run him to the altar."

"Who's your friend, Mrs. Stanton?" The sound of undisguised male interest caused a shiver to run across Julia's back. She wet her lips and turned toward a group of young men, the one in front a tall, scrawny thing with blond whiskers and very pink lips. He looked down at her with an amused glint in his blue eyes. Was this Everett? He was younger than she had imagined and not entirely unpleasant to look at, but his body appeared fragile for a farmer, and the flash in his eye matched his unsettling roguish tone. "You wouldn't happen to be here for Everett Cline?"

What an awkward way to greet her. "I, um . . . yes. And are you he?"

Rachel crossed in front of her with hands jammed on her hips. "Now, you all go on and get."

The young man's face changed from amusement to bewilderment. "Don't tell me she really is here for Everett." The four young men behind him snickered.

"None of your business, Axel. If you please, find somewhere else to be." Rachel pointed toward the depot, but the group had fallen dumb and stiff.

Axel cocked his head. "Then she is?"

Rachel didn't answer, and he let out an impressed huff.

Was there something so appalling about Everett that Axel couldn't believe a woman would marry him? Maybe that's why he needed a mail-order bride. But surely Rachel wouldn't have matched her with a dreadful man.

Rachel stared at Axel as if he were only knee-high instead of towering over them both.

Julia rubbed her arms, suddenly cold and hot at the same time. Every eye in the small group of men focused on her. Men had ogled her before, but this was ridiculous.

"Excuse me, gentlemen." A man taller than Axel pushed through the group, a girl with fluffy blond ringlets hooked on his arm. "You heard my wife—find somewhere else to be. I'm sure you have better things to do than detain our guest."

The men behind Axel poked each other, talking under their breath. Everett's name was the only word she caught. Was he here? Why hadn't he shown himself?

Axel smiled wide. "I hadn't any faith in you, Everett, but you pulled through. She's a beauty."

Julia stepped to the other side of Rachel and tried to see to whom Axel was speaking. Oh, why did she have to be so short?

Axel tipped his hat toward her. "I look forward to getting to know you better . . . Miss . . . ?"

She gave a tiny nod. "Lockwood, and I'm sure we'll have plenty of time to get acquainted."

"Of course you will." Dex patted the boy's shoulder dismissively and then turned to her. "It's nice to meet you at last, Miss Lockwood. I'm Dex."

"At last?" The incredulous murmur of a deep male voice sounded behind Dex.

Julia looked straight up at Rachel's husband. The top of her hat didn't even reach the bottom of his chest pocket. "Pleased to meet you, Mr. Stanton."

"Call me Dex. And I'm assuming you're rather interested in the gentleman behind me."

She thought her cheeks had been hot a minute ago.

"The finest neighbor any man could have."

A tall shadow of a man walked toward her, but it was no stranger who lifted his hat. *Theodore*. No. It couldn't be. All heat drained from her face and pooled on the platform at her feet. The ensuing shock of cold stopped her breath.

He'd said he'd find her no matter how far she ran, but she hadn't believed him.

She pressed her hand against her heart, galloping in vain against her chest.

"Pleased to meet you, Miss Lockwood. I'm Everett Cline."

She blinked hard at him and reached for Rachel to keep herself from falling, from running.

He frowned. "Is everything all right?"

His voice was wrong and his hair parted on the left and the front tooth didn't overlap. She worked to wet her mouth enough to speak. "Mr. . . . Mr. Cline?"

"I believe so." His tickled smirk released the breath stuck

in her lungs. The set of his jaw was similar, but not when he smiled. Not Theodore. She released her vise grip on Rachel, who looked at her as if she'd lost her wits.

Like Theodore, Everett had beautiful dark blond wavy hair, a prominent brow, and laugh lines around the eyes. He was certainly handsome—just like the man her father had chosen for her to wed.

How could she marry someone whose appearance reminded her of a man she never wanted to lay eyes on again?

Chapter 2

Miss Lockwood's hands scrunched the fabric of her rustly skirt, her knuckles as white as the petticoat peeping out from beneath. Everett forced his eyes off the inch of undergarment and tried to find a place to rest his gaze, but each place distracted him just as much as another. She sucked in a steadying breath and smiled—the same kind of fake smile he was attempting to keep plastered on his face.

"I'm sorry, forgive me. I just wasn't expecting . . . well . . ." She nodded. "It's nice to meet you, Mr. Cline."

Perhaps he wasn't as pleasing to the eye as Mrs. Hampden had led him to believe. He forced a curve back into his lips. "I'm pleased to meet you as well, Miss Lockwood. But I can't say that I knew you were—"

"Coming today." Rachel gripped his arm, her fingers gouging his muscle. "We hadn't told him exactly that you were coming *today*."

Everett cut his eyes toward his neighbor, her hairline dotted with perspiration, her cheeks flushed. She aimed a heavy-lidded glare at him, the same one she gave her restless children during church services.

Miss Lockwood fingered her brooch. "Oh, I see."

Everett pressed his lips together hard. He'd not call Rachel out on her ruse in front of Miss Lockwood, as it would only embarrass her. But how could his best friends continue the town's joke at his expense? And at Miss Lockwood's as well?

But this wasn't a game. He'd heard her talking to Axel, and he wished he hadn't. Judging by the look she'd given him—was still giving him—she'd likely leave on the next train. Another woman within his reach only for a moment, and this one so attractive it hurt to look at her.

How could he extricate himself—right now? "I, uh . . ."

Rachel pulled her younger sons in front of her and thrust the older one in between him and Miss Lockwood. "This is my son Ambrose, and this one's John." Whether enthralled by Miss Lockwood's angelic features or confounded by the awkward adult conversation, the ten- and seven-year-old spitting images of their mother were abnormally quiet. "And the boy behind me is William. He'll be sixteen on Monday."

"Howdy do, ma'am." William pulled off his hat and stared as if he'd never seen a woman before.

Emma squirmed from Dex's grip and launched herself into Miss Lockwood's arms.

"My goodness! You must be Emma." She caught the three-year-old and maneuvered her onto her hip. "Your ma told me about your gorgeous blond curls, so I brought you this." She pulled a pink ribbon from a hidden pocket.

Exactly how long had these women been exchanging letters? Everett glanced at Dex, who seemed more fascinated by a ribbon than a man ought to be.

Emma grabbed the hair thing and leaned to put it within her mother's reach. "Mama, put up."

"What do you say, Emma?"

"Say pwease."

Rachel cleared her throat. "Yes, you should say 'please,' but what do you say to Julia for giving it to you?"

Julia. His mouth silently tested out the name.

Emma placed the ribbon inches away from Julia's nose. "Pwease, put up."

Julia chuckled. A beautiful melodic laugh. Was there anything about this woman that wasn't dazzling?

"Tell Julia thank you."

"Sank you."

Julia tapped the little girl on the nose. "You're very welcome. But we'll wait to put it in your hair until we get home, all right?" She smiled down at the child. A real smile. His breath caught.

She looked over at him quizzically, and he straightened. Did she expect him to say something? Surely with how she gawked at him with those fright-filled, lash-fringed, intoxicating dark brown eyes she'd decided to have nothing to do with him. But then what was she staring at him for?

Rachel wrapped her arm around Julia's shoulder. "I'm sure your trip has made you bone-weary. No sense standing about the depot. We should start for home immediately."

"I have to admit train travel wasn't as pleasant as I'd hoped. For a while there, I thought I'd never make it."

"Good thing you survived"—Dex coughed over a laugh— "unmarried."

Julia threw a questioning glance at Dex, then Everett. Heat rushed into Everett's ears, and he held back the desire to box his friend's. So help him if Dex made Julia curious enough to ask what he was talking about.

The look Rachel turned on her husband would have stopped a stampede of cows. She huffed, then pulled Julia toward the platform stairs. "Why don't we head to the mercantile and leave the menfolk to load your trunks? Your dress is simply stunning. You'll have to inform us of all the latest fashions."

Julia glanced back at Everett for one mesmerizing second before they crossed the street. Her curls bounced under her small straw hat with each step, and her tiny body swayed with the weight of the toddler on her hip. Never had he seen anything more visually pleasing in his whole life. No lady who lived and worked on the Kansas prairie should look like that. She was meant to be on the arm of some politician or businessman, not a struggling farmer.

William whistled. "She's the prettiest lady I ever did see."

"Perhaps my woman's meddling was better for you than I thought." Dex's voice was far too glib.

Once the women crossed the street, Everett glanced toward Julia's three trunks piled on the platform. What did a woman need with so much? "If you don't mind, William, I think you and Ambrose can handle her luggage. I need to talk to your father—alone."

William tore his eyes away from Julia and threw a quick look at his father before nodding and catching Ambrose by the shoulder.

"Before you go shaking your finger at me, in my defense, I didn't know about this until last night," his friend blurted.

"Then you had time to tell me something."

Dex shrugged. "Well, with your record, I wasn't all fired out certain I'd have to tell you anything."

Everett throttled his hat to keep from throwing it at Dex.

"Besides, you're without a wife, and she's looking to become one."

"And why's that?"

"Something about falling on hard times."

"By the look of that dress, I'm not sure I'd agree."

"Personal type, not financial."

"And . . . ?"

Dex shrugged again. "She's from Boston?"

Everett waved his hat at the eastern horizon. "So I know where she's from, that she has some vague personal problem, and her name. Which, by the way," Everett said through gritted teeth, trying to keep his voice down, "I didn't know until five minutes ago."

"Well, you've also learned she's not too bad to look at."

His mind flashed to her pretty face and dainty stature, but Rachel's sister had been a stunner too, and how his heart had burst when Patricia pushed him aside for another. "That's no reason to marry someone."

"Oh yes, you're finally being sensible for once. No need to seriously consider an attractive woman who wants to start a new life out here with you." Dex rolled his eyes. "For crying out loud, Everett, Helga could barely speak English, and you were going to marry her."

Everett crossed his arms and glared at him.

"You're simply worried she'll leave like the rest of them."

"And shouldn't I be?"

Dex rubbed his hand along his jaw, staring at him as if he could see into his soul. "I suppose if any man should worry, it would be you. But Rachel—"

"I'm not sure I can forgive Rachel for this."

"You've forgiven Mrs. Hampden and Mrs. Parker."

"They were strangers. You're my friends."

"Perhaps what she's done is meddlesome—"

"And foolhardy and embarrassing and underhanded—"

"But done out of love."

Everett huffed. Rachel loved him all right. If only she

A Bride for Keeps

didn't love him so much she thought she could control his life. Couldn't she keep to running Dex's? He shook his head, and a breathy chuckle escaped. Poor Rachel. Dex wouldn't let her run his life either.

"She regrets not asking you about Julia."

Everett narrowed his eyes, and Dex held out his palms.

"I'm not joshing. She came to me last night wringing a dish towel so hard I thought she'd start a friction fire. She knows what she's done is wrong, but maybe, in God's way, He'll make this crazy situation right."

"He hasn't chosen to do so with any of my other mistakes."

"Maybe you haven't yet made the right mistake."

Everett pressed his lips together and kept himself from shaking his head. No matter what Dex said, he wouldn't let an ounce of hope wiggle in.

"Look, a year ago Rachel decided she'd match you up with a wife from the advertisements since you were doing such a poor job. You know her saying, 'If you want a thing done right, ask me to do it.'"

Everett would've given him a courtesy chuckle had he been calm enough.

"But I made her quit after I saw the strange influx of letters. But something about Julia kept her interested—as a friend. And there aren't many lady friends to have out here. Rachel wasn't going to set you up with her, but something in her past letter made her think Julia needed to escape. And evidently she did. She thinks she's here because you want her to be."

Everett stared at the store as if he could see Julia behind its weathered planking. Did he want her to be here? He'd had life figured out. Or at least he had told himself he could live with the direction it seemed to be going. But this wasn't a curve in the road, this was a fork.

"If you don't marry her, I'll question your sanity."

But he wasn't her only option—and he shouldn't be. "If I don't marry her, someone else will offer."

"Lots of someone elses."

William and Ambrose bounded over. But there was no use discussing this anymore. Wishing she wasn't there wouldn't make things any better. But then, what man in his right mind would wish to have never seen such loveliness?

"Come on, boys, let's go meet up with your mother." Dex nudged Everett's shoulder as he passed. "Go with it. See where the Lord leads."

The Stantons headed toward the platform stairs, and Everett forced his feet to follow. This really wasn't too much different from the last time, right? She could change her mind just as easily as Helga after one good look at his farm.

Except he'd written to the other women prior to them coming to Kansas. They'd known hard labor, grown up in squalor or on a farm. But Julia's tiny gloved hands and little waist bespoke of a much different past. Homesteading wasn't fun; it wasn't easy. It wasn't sitting in a parlor and serving tea.

But Julia would be better than no one at all. Wishing he could stifle the thumping sensation in his heart, Everett sped up. No, she'd be exorbitantly better than no one. To embrace her, have children with her—Everett kicked at a rock on the dusty street. If he let those thoughts turn into emotions, he'd look like a fool the day she left him behind.

The next rock he kicked hit Ambrose in the calf. Ambrose turned to glare at him.

Everett raised his hand. "Sorry."

The boy bounded up the stairs and followed his father inside the store.

Everett stopped at the edge of the road and swallowed, staring at the closed door. Dimple and Curly really ought to be checked on. He walked to his team, ran his hand along Curly's neck, then bent to inspect the ox's leg, staring at the mud patch above its fetlock. Looking at his animals wouldn't make the woman inside go away. And he didn't really want her to go away.

And that was the problem.

"Are your oxen all right?"

Everett nearly fell backward at the sound of William's voice inches from his ear. "They look fine."

"Mr. Hampden says your supplies are ready."

Everett sprang up and tugged at Curly's halter. "Be inside in a minute."

William loped up the stairs, and Everett watched him go inside. He had to face her. Despite his stubborn refusal to order another bride, he did need a wife. Around here, a girl of marrying age had a handful of eligible men to choose from. He wasn't the only man stuck on a lonely farm needing someone to take care of the house and animals in order to have a chance at making his farm profitable.

Maybe when he'd written his mail-order brides he'd come across as too eager and desperate. No woman wanted a man so weak he acted as if he needed her in order to survive—though some days out on the wind-scourged prairie he certainly believed he'd go plumb crazy without one. This time he could exude confidence from the very beginning. Maybe if he was more aloof, more self-possessed, Julia would be attracted instead of repelled. He whispered near Curly's ear, "Heaven help me," then pulled at his shirt, marched up the stairs, and straightened his shoulders before entering.

A crowd surrounded Julia. He walked to the front of the store and leaned against the counter. Where had all these people come from? The womenfolk seemed to be oohing and ahhing over Julia's fancy pleats, but the four men on the outskirts of the group stared more at the woman wearing them.

Carl's attentive gaze rarely strayed from Julia as he helped her sort through bolts of cloth on the table. Everett drummed his fingers. Must he inform the shopkeeper to pay attention to his other customers? The twenty people surrounding Julia could surely help her move fabric.

He could march straight over to Kathleen and smile at her. No, too bold. Carl'd have his head.

A tap on his shoulder and the smell of moonshine pulled his focus off Julia.

Ned Parker stood behind him, looking toward the crowd. He spit at a spittoon without taking his gaze off her. His spittle landed six inches from the rim. "Mighty fine-lookin' woman, eh? Don't think we're going to get any help over here unless we pull Hampden off her."

"I think you might be right, but—"

"I'm just sorry Helga don't look like her. But then again, the wife's good enough for housework if nothing else."

The skin on his neck crawled. Everett's third mail-order bride most likely wished she hadn't left him for Ned. The man worked her like he worked his oxen—into the ground. It would have been better for Helga if Everett had learned his lesson after Kathleen and not sent for another bride.

Ned spit, this time making it in the bucket. "You don't know anyone I can hire, do you?"

"No." He'd not advise his worst enemy to work for Ned Parker.

Ned rapped on the counter bell. "What do I got to do to get some service?"

---·◦·---

"What do you think about this one, Miss Lockwood?"

Julia fingered the fine pink-sprigged lawn, silky and untextured. "Combed yarns. Very nice feel to it. I think it would make you a fine dress, Miss Lenowitz."

"Wish I could have something as fancy as yours with those ruffles all the way to the top. Maybe you could help me with my sleeves?" The young lady looked as if she were debating on fabric for her first ball gown, not a light summer dress. Was the girl old enough for a debut? Did they even do that in Kansas?

Julia swallowed hard. Even if they did, she couldn't help this girl—she had no idea how to sew. Looking around at the men and women surrounding her in homespuns and dyed calicos, she knew that her dress probably cost the equivalent of their entire closets. Every dress. She had nothing like what they were wearing—and all their work dresses and shirtwaists showed signs of wear. Her silks and sheer lawns most likely wouldn't last a month out here. Should she even be encouraging this woman to buy this? It was the most expensive bolt of fabric on the table. "I'm afraid I'm not good at sewing something this intricate. Perhaps I could lend it to you for a pattern."

The girl's eyes flashed, and several of the ladies sucked in air and started murmuring. But Miss Lenowitz shook her head. "I couldn't ask you to part with a dress for so very long. We don't come into town but once a month, and I live in the opposite direction from Mrs. Stanton."

What Julia really needed was to give Miss Lenowitz this

dress in exchange for one of hers. But she wouldn't dare bring up such a thing and embarrass the girl in front of this crowd. Nor had she the courage to admit she'd come west with not one work dress. But she'd need several if she was staying, wouldn't she?

If she were staying . . .

Julia absently played with a bit of lawn. Everett hadn't looked her way since he'd walked in.

At the counter, Everett strode away from the man who'd leered at her since she'd entered the store, grabbed some candy, and walked toward a stand of hats. "Put two molasses chews on the tab, Carl," he called over his shoulder.

"Miss?" A man with a ragged beard and huge eyes swiped off his hat.

She pulled her attention from Everett and tried to keep from wrinkling her nose at the farmer's stench.

"I'm here to buy my wife enough fabric for a shirtwaist, and I don't have a good eye. Would you mind picking one? These women seem to think you have a knack for it. She's got green eyes with specks of gold in them and red hair, well more orange-like, but she don't like me saying so."

"Hmm, I'm sure a deep green or blue—"

"And I can't spend too much on it."

She nodded and fished out a teal calico with white-sprigged daisies. "This ought to bring out her eyes and complement her auburn tresses."

"A fine choice, Lincoln." The store's proprietor grabbed the fabric and escorted the farmer to the counter, where the leering, impatient man threatened to ring the bell a second time.

"I don't believe the Hampdens have sold this much fabric in a week," Rachel whispered. "Watch out or Mr. Hampden will be offering you a job."

Julia smoothed a creased corner of gingham. A job in the mercantile? Now, that she could do. But not in Salt Flatts.

From this distance, Everett did indeed look a lot like Theodore, except he didn't have the same arrogant, self-assured posture—more like stiff and agitated. He chewed candy and stared out the window as if he had all day to watch the clouds go by. Or was that just his way of reacting to how she'd treated him at the depot? She'd never been so rude to someone in all her life. Had she ruined all chances with him? If her mother had been alive, she'd be mortified.

"I can get his attention." Rachel slipped a bolt of mauve fabric out from the bottom of the pile.

Whose attention? Oh! "I don't think we need to—"

"Everett!" Rachel's call snapped him away from staring at his reflection.

With everyone looking at him, he left his sad image behind and kept his focus on Rachel as he snaked through the crowd. "Yes?"

"We were discussing whether or not Julia should buy this rose-colored calico. I think she should since it brings out the color in her cheeks."

His mouth dried into crumbles as the crowd turned to stare at him. His quick peek at Julia showed that her cheeks were indeed blooming with color.

Rachel grabbed the fabric and placed it next to Julia's jawline. "It'll be gorgeous on her, don't you think?"

Julia's gaze dropped to the floor. Whispers sounded behind him. . . . "Another one?" . . . "Can't be that lucky" . . . "Surely she didn't come out here for him."

They were right. He couldn't be this lucky, being that he'd never had any luck at all.

Julia's dark brown eyes met his with a halfhearted smile.

Did she actually smile at him? "Yes," Everett's voice squeaked, "looks just fine." He cleared his throat. "I think you ladies have a better opinion of what one should or shouldn't wear." He looked toward the back of the store. "My stuff is gathered. If you don't mind." He strode toward the pile Carl had stacked on the counter and grabbed his first crate.

Of course she'd look gorgeous in the dark pink fabric. She'd look gorgeous in a feed sack. That image caused heat to rush from his head to his toes, so he pushed it away.

"Carl, would you mind helping me with these? I have to get over to the mill." He was very afraid he'd prove the town right. If he followed her around like a goose and she chose one of the men in the store making moony eyes at her, he might as well abandon his farm and move farther west—so far west no mail-order bride would answer his advertisement if he were daft enough to write another.

Julia paid a few dollars for the rose calico and hugged the soft package as she walked outside with Rachel.

Dex and his boys loaded the Stantons' goods around her trunks. He played with his sons as they threw things into the back of the wagon, and Rachel absentmindedly covered Emma's head in kisses as she barked orders for packing the supplies so nothing would break. A lump throbbed in Julia's throat. The Stantons seemed wonderful, too good to be true.

But these were not the people she'd be living with forever. As nice as they were, the brooding Everett held her fate in his hands. She didn't want the man physically interested in her, so why did she care that he stayed as far away from her as possible? Because he had to need her. At least for work;

otherwise she'd have to go with another plan to support herself. And she had no other plan.

She chewed on her lower lip and looked around the small, dusty town. She didn't see him. Where was he? Had he left? Maybe that would be best. Marrying a stranger wasn't a good idea at all. At the Stantons' place, she would have time to think of another option.

Everett exited the sawmill's large front doors at the end of the road, his hands tucked in his pockets as he strode her way. Besides the roguish shock of dirty-blond hair falling across his forehead, he seemed to grow less and less like Theodore with every minute. Had her imagination grasped at straws earlier in an effort to sway her from saying vows to a stranger? If her mind was that desperate for an escape, perhaps she would be wise to reconsider.

She staggered down the stairs. What wagon should she head toward? Although Rachel's company thrilled her, Everett was her opportunity to make a life here. She'd not given him any time to prove himself, and she wouldn't let fear rule her, no matter how hard it tried. With her heart pounding, she intercepted him.

"Mr. Cline?"

He stopped short, his eyebrows held in question. The muscles filling his shirt and the scruff along his jaw gave him a rugged, handsome look that caught her breath.

She cleared her throat. She should have thought of something to say *before* she stopped him. "I bought the rose calico."

He gave a slight nod, and she rambled on. "I think it would make a good work dress. Something more . . . more suitable than this one." She picked at the lace at her collar. "Do I ride with you?"

His eyebrows shot higher, but then descended, smashing

his eyes into slits. "Uh, I didn't think to ask what we're doing this evening. They're the ones making the plans." He strode away without even offering his arm.

"Everett's coming for dinner, right?" Dex hollered to his wife.

Rachel held Emma's hand as the little girl jumped down each stair. "Of course."

Everett kept his stiff back toward her. "She wants to know if she's riding with you or me."

Did he not want her to ride with him? A young couple walking along the boardwalk looked toward the three of them hollering and then at her. Did Everett have to speak so loud?

Rachel cocked her eyebrow. "Well, of course, it'd be best if she rode with you. Wouldn't be ladylike to throw her in the back of our wagon with the supplies and trunks and all."

Everett pivoted and returned to her, his eyes bland. "You're with me."

As if she hadn't just heard that much. Everyone on Main Street knew she was with him—and that he'd had to be browbeaten to take her. Had she misunderstood the proposal he'd had Rachel send? Maybe there was no hope he'd marry her, even if only for a farmhand. Granted, she wasn't built like most of the ladies she'd seen in the hour she'd been in Salt Flatts. But size shouldn't matter. She bit her lip.

Dex cleared his throat and glared at Everett.

Everett pulled his hat off and offered her his arm, a slight redness creeping up his neck. "I'm this way." Maybe he was just nervous. She could sympathize, since she'd been trembling since she woke up that morning.

She tightened the hold on her package and slipped her free arm into his. The man radiated tension, from the flexed muscles in his forearm to the set of his jaw. If something in her letters to Rachel had been disagreeable, he wouldn't have asked her there, right? Maybe she'd found a man who didn't find her attractive. She took in a steadying breath. That would be a good thing.

He tossed her package in the back and handed her up onto the wooden plank seat, his hands tarrying at her waist for less than a second.

John yelled at her from the back of his wagon. "See you at home!"

She waved at him as Everett slid onto the bench, keeping a large gap between them. Farther than decorum dictated.

The wagon jerked forward, and she nearly slid off the seat. She righted herself and clenched the rough wooden plank beneath her. She'd never ridden on a farm wagon before. How was she to keep her seat in a ladylike fashion? As the Stantons' wagon passed them, she dared to wave at Emma, who peeked over her mother's shoulder. Their wagon left a cloud of dust, the children's gay laughter mixed in with the powdery earth.

Glancing behind her, Julia caught several men staring at her from the boardwalks, a few pointing and laughing. She smoothed her bunched skirts with only one hand while glancing at Everett's stony face. Why was the man she'd come to wed the only person who refused to look in her direction?

They hit a rut, and she grabbed for her hat as she bounced off the seat. Everett's arm shot around her side and pulled her back beside him. His touch left an icy hot imprint about her waist. She slid to the opposite side of the bench seat. She didn't want to feel anything like that again.

"Yah!" he shouted at the oxen without giving her the slightest glance. He kept his gaze trained forward. She waited for him to talk first, but his jaw stayed rigid. Maybe he'd talk after they'd gone a distance. She tried to calm herself by watching the tall green grasses wave in the forceful wind, rippling this way and that, chasing each other to the lines of trees scattered in the distance. The tremors in her chest settled with the swaying of the seat as she picked imaginary lint from her skirt. More prairie disappeared behind them.

She couldn't stand the silence any longer. "So, Mr. Cline. Where's your property?"

He pointed ahead of them at a line of trees. "My land is adjacent to the Stantons, about an hour and a half southwest of Salt Flatts. The Stantons live to my east and the Parkers just to the south."

When he didn't elaborate further, she examined his face. His lips, though hard-pressed, kept moving around, like words wanted to come out but wouldn't. Silent tension, hard as a block of ice and about as movable as the man beside her, filled more time than she could bear. She didn't want to start rattling off about herself since he didn't seem at all interested.

She watched the oxen and Everett's movements, waiting in vain for him to talk again. More quiet minutes ticked by. She had to make him talk. She didn't know how long the Stantons' hospitality would last, but she couldn't waste several days in silence with the man. In fact, she wasn't sure she could handle another hour of it now. "What do you use your land for?"

"I've several acres of grain and corn. Looking to get more cattle once I get more hedgerow readied. Have a dairy cow and her heifer at the moment." After another period of silence, he said, "I do a lot of hunting on the property."

"Will you teach me to drive the oxen?"

Everett's head snapped her way. "I suppose you could learn."

She smiled. Looked like he did want a worker. "When do I get to see your place?"

"Soon, I suppose. I'm having several neighbors over in a few days. They're going to help me put up a barn."

"That's nice."

He flicked the reins and glanced at her dress. "I'm sure our get-togethers can't compare to anything you're used to back in Boston, but they're fun nonetheless."

"I'm sure it will be exciting." When they abruptly dipped into a wheel rut, her grip on the seat slid, and she gained a splinter. Thankfully, her gloves kept it from lodging deep into her skin. "I know this isn't the city."

"No, it's not. It's a rough life and requires hard work."

"I can work."

He eyed her, and she shot him her most winning smile. Pulling his collar away from his neck, he looked her straight in the eyes. "I'm sure you can do whatever you set your mind to, but I have to warn you, it's not easy." He glanced at her from under his heavy eyelashes. "I'm sure you had servants or cooks or some manner of paid help back in Boston, but I haven't the money. The women here have to do everything from mending to cooking to cleaning to farm chores. Sometimes, with big projects like a barn, neighbors pitch in, but homesteading is all about self-sufficiency because everyone needs to survive. And if you don't sow enough, harvest enough, can enough, stockpile enough . . . you may not.

"You may not like that. And that's—" He cleared his throat. "That's fine. And I can't promise I can help you adjust since I'm racing the first frost like everyone else around here. And if you marry me, so will you. I want you to know that I hold you under no obligation if you decide that's too much. Just . . ."

He squirmed, and she gripped her seat tighter. Was he trying to convince her to forget this whole arrangement? She wasn't too comfortable with the idea of marrying a stranger. Getting married at all, actually. But maybe a man not wanting a wife was exactly what she needed.

"Just, well, there's no need to drag on anything if it's not what you want." He looked off in the distance, and she could barely make out his words. "But if you want to work hard and marriage is why you're here, then I'm willing to offer that. For God knows I need a helper."

Chapter 3

Julia swayed in the wagon seat next to Everett, her gaze glued to the waving prairie, her hands clamped onto her wooden seat. Marriage. Funny how hearing him vocalize his proposal made her heart skitter in fear—she'd come here for this very reason, known that's what he wanted, but somehow it hadn't seemed real. But now he'd asked, and she'd have to answer—aloud. But words wouldn't come.

"You don't have to say anything now."

She let the tension in her body flow out with a slow, controlled exhale. She'd never been so thankful to have someone read her thoughts.

Everett pointed to a faraway stand of trees so close together they entwined with one another. "Dex and Rachel's place is just beyond that hedgerow."

She nodded, the only answer she was capable of giving.

The wagon swayed at an agonizingly slow pace until they finally passed the line of hedge. Julia watched as William hefted her largest trunk from the back of the Stantons' wagon and hauled it toward the barn. The peace of knowing she had a place to stay while she worked up the courage to discuss Everett's proposal in more detail washed over her.

Everett's wagon jerked to a stop, and she clenched the seat to keep from hopping down unassisted. She could see the question she hadn't yet responded to lingering in Everett's eyes as he held out his hand. He supported her elbow as she navigated her way down. Her feet found solid ground, yet she felt as if she were sinking as she stared up into his cold blue eyes, a touch of heat in his cheeks.

"Thank you, Mr. Cline."

He swallowed and dropped her hand, yet stood staring at her. She quickly clasped her hands together. He'd said she didn't have to say anything now; had he not meant it? But how much more time did she need to frame a reply? He'd not wait forever.

"I can't stay for dinner. I have to get home."

"Oh." Julia sighed with relief. She'd at least have tonight.

"Good-bye, Miss Lockwood." The tone of his voice descended, sounding final and resigned. He hoisted himself back into the wagon and was off before she could think to bid him farewell.

Rachel walked up beside her and jammed her hands on her hips. "Where's he running off to so fast?"

"He said he wasn't staying for supper."

"Hmm." Rachel wrapped her arm around Julia. "It will just take some time. You'll be talking marriage any day now."

Yes. Already. A half hour ago. How she wished she never had to talk about marriage. But that wasn't an option.

The cool night wind threatened to blow out the lantern in Rachel's hand, though she shielded the light with her body.

She held the door open with her backside and tilted her head toward the barn's dark interior. "In here."

Julia pulled her skirts up as she crossed the threshold but didn't release the fabric. The smell of manure, hay, and mice cautioned her against letting her dress drag on the floor. She could imagine Theodore's look of disdain if anyone had even suggested that he were to sleep in such a place. She tried to discreetly cover her nose.

A circle of illumination around Rachel closed in around them. "I'm sorry to have to put you here. We've had guests find these accommodations not to their liking." Rachel sighed. "But unlike the boys' loft, you can stand up without hitting your head. I do so hope you can bear it for a while."

"Rachel, you told me I'd be out here, and I came anyway. I can handle it." Julia squeezed Rachel's upper arm to assure her. To assure herself. The sudden lowing of a cow caused her to jump.

Rachel giggled. "Sure you can."

"I can." She had no choice. She loosened her grip on Rachel's flesh.

Rachel headed to the ladder at the back of the barn, then hitched her skirts and climbed, keeping the lantern extended from her side. "Mornings are still quite brisk in March. It'd be best to sleep in the loft. The air is warmer. Plus, there's no chance Daisy could wake you with a wet tongue to the face up here."

"Is Daisy the dog?"

"No, the cow. Dixie's the dog."

Julia gathered her skirt material with one hand, stepped up to the first rung, and stopped. "Did the boys put my trunks up top?"

Rachel peered over the edge of the hayloft. "Goodness,

no. I forgot. You'll want to get yourself a nightgown. It's there in the corner. But I see Ambrose brought the quilts up here like I asked."

Rachel's lamp dangled over the edge of the loft, giving Julia enough illumination to find her trunks. But she had to feel the fabrics to find her nightwear. Something small scurried over her shoe, and she rushed back to the ladder, suppressing the childish squeal that bubbled in her throat. Would there be more rodents up there? She had whapped quite a few mice with a broom before, but never in her bedding. A shiver shook her entire frame as she clung to the ladder's rungs. At the top, she pulled herself and her voluminous skirts onto the straw-littered floor.

"This is the best I can do." Rachel gestured to a corner. Several quilts spread on top of a flattened pile of hay formed a bed. Shards of moonlight filtered through cracks in the exterior wall.

Julia removed the straw clinging to her skirt. "Really, you needn't apologize anymore."

Rachel set the lamp on a box. "I'm sorry." She covered her mouth, but not quickly enough to conceal her amused smile. "I'll bid you good night, then. Make yourself at home. But don't fall asleep with this lit. Don't want a fire." Rachel walked off into the darkness, but at the ladder, she stopped. "Just so you know, Everett's coming in the morning to help Dex and William round up calves for branding."

A few minutes later, the barn door creaked open and slammed. The lamp's feeble light couldn't reach the four walls of the barn, and a mouse, perhaps, scampered across the beam above her. Gooseflesh formed on her arms, and she hugged herself. Undressing quickly, Julia laid her crumpled clothing across a pile of hay and slipped into her nightgown.

Thinking it unwise to bring the lamp any closer to her sleeping area, she blew out the flame and felt her way to the pile of quilts.

The sound of animals moving and making noise would take getting used to, but they didn't disturb her sleep—her brain did. How many disparate feelings had coursed through her within so few hours? The feeling of belonging while chatting with Rachel, immediate love for the children, discomfort as she rode beside taciturn Everett. Unrest in her soul. She relived everything she'd done today since she'd awoken, replayed everything she'd had the nerve to say to Everett and the few words he spoke in return, how he sat stiffly on the wagon seat, his sun-darkened face intent on his oxen and his square jaw clamped shut. His dark blond hair flopping with the ruts in the road, intermittently giving her a peek at his eyes, the color of roiling ocean waves during a winter storm. She sighed and rolled over.

Could his disturbingly familiar looks be a sign that she shouldn't pursue marrying him? She trusted Rachel hadn't encouraged her to marry a disagreeable man, but what did she really know of him? He didn't seem drawn to her, he barely spoke, and his proposal sounded more like a work agreement than a marriage.

But wasn't that exactly the kind of man who would agree to her own proposal?

———•◦•———

The corners of the hayloft came into focus with the dawn as Julia shivered under the quilts.

A rooster crowed. Again. She swore he'd been aiming his morning vocal display at her for the last half hour. A dog's bark made her jump. The barn door creaked.

"Julia?" Rachel's voice called softly. "Are you awake?"

She moaned despite her teeth chattering.

"I came in as late as possible to let you sleep."

She pulled the quilt tight around her shoulders before scooting to the edge of the hayloft and leaning against an upright beam. After rubbing her eyes, she focused on Rachel's cheery face below. "Yes, I'm up. Your chicken woke me."

"Big Red's quite good at crowing—won't let you forget it either." She walked over to Daisy and seated herself at the cow's side. "If I'd waited any longer, Daisy here would have woke you with some pitiful lowing."

Julia tried to make her gravelly voice heard over the sound of liquid spraying metal. "I need to learn how to do that." No better time to start learning to be a farmer's wife than now.

Rachel stopped to stare at her. "You've never milked a cow?"

Julia shook her head. "City girl. From Boston. Remember?"

"Right." Rachel returned to her chore. "Didn't stop to think you hadn't milked a cow before."

Julia stood, stretched, and then rushed through changing clothes. She had no brush in the loft to fix her hair, so she settled for finger combing. "I'll help you." Climbing down the ladder carrying a lantern and not stepping on her skirts was tricky.

"If you don't mind, go ahead and take the lantern to the porch. It needs refilling."

"Of course." She'd wait and let her help, wouldn't she? Rachel couldn't milk a cow that quickly, but the barn door refused to budge. Julia kicked at the bottom corner. If she couldn't open a simple door, how would Everett believe she could do the work around the farm that needed to be done? Using all her weight, she rocked the door back and forth.

With a final push, the bottom hopped over a dirt rut and flew open. Her feet entangled with each other and she tumbled to the moist dirt outside, the lamp rolling from her grasp.

"Whoa, there!" Dex's hands encircled her upper arms.

She bit her lip as he hoisted her to standing. His face, aglow with suppressed laughter, appeared through the hair obscuring her vision.

With a big puff of air, she blew the errant strands away. "The door was stuck."

Switching the placement of his hands, Dex turned her to face the door. "I saw that, but . . ." He reached around her and took hold of the handle. "If you lift it ever so slightly," he pushed up a bit and pulled the door toward him, "no tumbling in the mud required."

She laughed, but her face still burned. "I'll have to remember that." She bent over and grabbed the lantern handle.

"Good." Dex glanced over his shoulder. "I'll be right back, Everett." Dex let himself inside the barn, the door giving him not even a modicum of a problem.

A violent chill traveled the length of her body. She didn't have enough time to wait for her raging hot face to cool before she would look rude for not acknowledging Everett's presence.

Prepared to see him laughing at her, she turned, but was surprised at his expression—almost like he was in pain. "Good morning, Everett." Was he afraid she'd hurt herself? "I'm all right."

"Good morning, Julia. Good to hear."

She ducked her head and hurried past him, intent on setting the lamp near the house and then running back to Rachel. She'd known he was coming today, but she thought she'd have plenty of time to ready herself to see him. Ready herself to talk to the man she'd decided she'd marry if he agreed to her terms.

But she wasn't ready, not yet. Or was she only fooling herself into thinking that she'd ever be ready?

Everett stayed outside the barn, his mild gaze clinging to her back, sending more heat to her face. Would that her reddened cheeks were already hidden on the other side of that barn wall!

She put the lantern on the porch and returned to the barn, hoping she was strong enough to push up effortlessly on the door. She gave him a slight nod and headed past him.

He took a step in front of her before she grabbed the handle and pulled the door open for her. "Let me."

Rachel's voice reverberated from the dim interior. "Everett? Here already? I hope you haven't eaten breakfast."

"We both know whatever I scrambled up back home wouldn't keep me from eating whatever you're offering."

Julia ducked under his arm and into the barn. She might not know her way around a farm, but she could cook. Perhaps making him breakfast might cause him to think better of her.

Rachel stood, beckoned him in, and pointed to the milk bucket. "I haven't finished milking. Julia wanted to learn how. Mind showing her so I can start cooking?"

Shaking her head was impossible, for Everett would see her, so she widened her eyes and mouthed a big "No!" She was sure Rachel understood the gesture, but the woman's smile only grew.

Dex came around the stall corner with a few harnesses in his grasp.

Rachel laced her hand through her husband's nearest arm. "Come, Dex. They're getting the milk. I'll have breakfast done shortly so you two can get to work."

He grunted in affirmation and exited the barn beside her.

51

Julia swallowed hard and kept her hands tucked into the folds of her skirt. She stepped forward and then turned to face Everett.

He bit his lip.

"You don't have to teach me now if you don't want to."

"Do you want to learn, or is Rachel pushing you into it?"

"Oh no." She shook her head. "I want to learn."

"All right, then." He walked over and settled himself onto a three-legged stool and leaned into Daisy's side. "Come here, and you can watch."

Julia squatted next to him.

He dropped his gaze. "You place your hand up top here and walk your fingers down like this. Aim the milk into the bucket." He alternated squirting milk from two teats. His swift movements filled the bottom of the pail. It didn't look difficult. She was embarrassed for asking.

He stroked Daisy's flank and stood. "Your turn."

"That looks easy."

"It might be harder than you think."

Julia settled herself beside the cow and reached under. Daisy sidestepped. The cow was a giant compared to her. Fear of doing something wrong and being stepped on crept in.

"She just startled. Your hands are probably cold."

They were, in fact, icy. Julia rubbed her hands together before creeping back to Daisy's side. Tucking the bucket between her knees like Everett had, she attempted to keep the material of her skirts covering her bare feet. Why hadn't she taken the time to put on boots? She reached under to grab a teat and pulled. A dribble plopped into the bucket. Pulling harder with her other hand, the same amount of milk came out, and the trickle hit the ground.

She turned to Everett for advice.

"Kind of walk your fingers down. And watch where you're aiming."

She tried again with more success and then applied herself. She would fill the bucket. But after a few minutes, her hands ached, yet she hadn't gotten close to the amount Everett had milked in less time.

He stooped and felt the cow's udder. "Feel. It's not soft. You go until the udder's soft."

Julia blew the hair from her face.

He let out a sharp exhale. His eyes shut, and he ran his hand down his face.

Why hadn't Rachel shown her how to do this? The man was exasperated with her in less than a few minutes. Was he as embarrassed for her as she was herself? Her lips were dry, so she licked them. A swallow couldn't wet her parched throat. "I'll get it done." She went back to the cow with a vengeance.

He coughed and stood. "Easier. Smoother."

Finally figuring how to use her thumb to the best advantage, she let go of her trapped breath and filled the bucket at a slow, but steady pace.

"Doing good."

A smile crept onto her lips. She was doing well. The steadily rising liquid's warm earthy smell made her empty stomach rumble. She looked to see if Everett heard, but he was no longer standing beside her.

She kept at the milking until the udder felt soft like he said it was supposed to. Standing to stretch her back, she waited for her arms to recover enough to heft the bucket to the house.

She patted Daisy. "Thanks, girl, for putting up with me." She scratched at the cow's spotted side. Why had Everett left? Rachel's incredulity at learning that she didn't know how to milk a cow came back to her. "Maybe he thinks I can't do this."

Daisy answered with a low cry that ended with a "bleh."

Julia tickled her behind the ear. "You think so too, eh?" She hefted the bucket. "But look here, I've got a full pail. I'll get better, if you're patient with me, that is."

But would Everett be patient enough? He said he wanted a helper, but he didn't seem eager to have one.

———

Everett shut the barn door behind him without a sound. Didn't she know she was indecent? Hair tumbling about her shoulders. Not even wearing stockings. When she blew that strand of bed-mussed hair from her face, he'd been wildly tempted to tuck it behind her ear to see how the brown wavy strand felt between his fingers.

He'd been too close to her. Had she heard his heart thumping when she'd licked her lips? It was unfair how her looks messed with his head. He'd stood and waited until she seemed to milk well enough that she'd drain Daisy tolerably. Then he had to get out of there. Though before he left with Dex to round up the calves, he'd have to come back to make sure she'd milked the cow dry.

Smoke rose from the Stantons' chimney, and the smell of fried pork called to his near-empty stomach. Inside, he sat across the table from Dex, who was twisting dogbane plant fibers into rope, his booted foot propped on the wall beside him. Rachel hummed as she piled crisp bacon on a plate, slapping little hands attempting to grab slices while they still sizzled.

"What's wrong with you?"

Everett's head snapped up at Dex's question. "Nothing."

Dex grabbed more fibers to splice into his cord. "Then why are you already in here?"

Rachel set the plate of meat in the middle of the table. "Talk to her. She won't bite."

Couldn't Dex have brought this up outside? "I reckon I just don't have much to say."

"Honestly?" Rachel put her hands on her hips. "You're all of a sudden reserved?"

To prove it, he kept his mouth shut. He wouldn't remind Rachel in front of the children how all of this was her fault.

Rachel stood, waiting.

Dex waved his cord at him. "Find something to say to her."

Rachel returned to the cookstove and cracked eggs into a bowl. "It's not like she's stupid or repulsive."

Wishing there was a way to close his ears, Everett settled for closing his eyes.

Dex cleared his throat. When he gave in and looked at his friend, a glint in Dex's eye flashed. "Well, maybe just a bit repulsive."

He groaned. It would help if she were.

Rachel brought a stack of plates and silverware to the table. "John, please set the table. Ambrose, get the napkins." She turned to Everett. "You're staying for dinner tonight—no arguing. Won't hurt you none to talk to her over dinner."

"I'm sorry, Rachel. If I'm still here I'll take lunch, but I'm expecting my lumber this evening or tomorrow. Want to make sure they put it in the right spot."

Dex left off fiddling with his rope. "So you done bought everything? Enough for a house?"

Everett nodded. "Yes. But next week, we'll just put up the barn. I'll do the house myself."

"Why not let us help you put up the frame while we're there?"

"Not sure what I want yet." Everett glanced around the

Stantons' three-room home. The living area felt large until the entire family crowded in. The kids' loft above and the bedroom behind the table weren't much in space, but nicely done. To make a house as nice as this one, he'd need time. If Julia did marry him, they'd have to make do with his rickety cabin—not that she'd be willing to live in such a place, especially since his animals would have nicer housing.

The door creaked open. Julia entered, fancy leather shoes on and hair coiled at her neck. Her face glowed as she set the bucket by her feet, sloshing milk on the floor. "I did it, Rachel. What do I do now?"

Rachel instructed her on how to strain the milk. Something any child in Kansas knew how to do without being told. Julia didn't belong here, but rather in some fancy house, in a big city like New York or Boston—where she came from.

Why had she left? No matter what the answer, it wouldn't change facts. Julia might find a few farm chores exhilarating, but they would turn into drudgery all too soon. He'd find out how committed she was to the idea of being a farmer's wife at the barn raising. One glance at his farm, and she'd surely run.

Chapter 4

The Parkers' wagon pulled in a few hours late for the barn raising. Too bad Ned decided to show up at all. Had the echo of hammers floating across the gully guilted him into coming over? Everett hadn't forgotten the look in his neighbor's eye the day Julia arrived. And he still wanted to pummel him for it. He jogged to the stopped wagon. "Good morning to you."

Ned's face remained expressionless as he leaned his tall, thin frame away from the very plain woman with wide shoulders next to him. He spat on the ground. "A good morning now that the wind's died down."

Everett shifted his gaze. "Mrs. Parker, how do you do?"

Giving him no answer, Helga stepped onto the wagon wheel and to the ground without assistance. Though Everett smiled at her, she didn't return the favor. Her eyes simply met Everett's for a second before she ducked her head.

Everett jerked his head up at Ned and narrowed his eyes at the man's indifference to his wife. "Hope you brought your hammer."

Ned jumped in the back and picked up a few tools. "That and a plane." He hopped off the wagon.

Mrs. Parker bit her lip, her arms wrapped around a small basket.

Ned left them and headed toward the construction site, where the postmaster and his sons, along with Dex and William, had already helped put together two walls of the barn.

Everett offered his arm to Helga. "I'll take you to the other women."

"I bring bread." She gestured to the covered basket. Her head tipped down so low he couldn't see her face.

"I appreciate it." Even if the bread was as stale as ten-year-old crackers, he'd not tell this woman for the world. She surely received enough criticism. Why had God blessed a man like Ned with a wife that had been meant for him? But Everett no longer felt hurt when he thought of how she'd left him for Ned, only compassion.

He opened his shack's door for Helga. Julia lay sprawled on the uneven floor, reaching for Emma under the table. Her pointy boots kicked out from under her petticoats as she pretended Emma was too far to reach, causing the toddler to giggle uncontrollably. Rachel, John, and Ambrose echoed the laughter.

He cleared his throat.

Julia bumped her head on the underside of the table. "Oh!"

The boys snickered before their mother's warning glare shushed them.

Julia's hair was a mess, half of it fallen out of her updo. Why couldn't she keep herself properly made up? A prim woman would help him keep his thoughts where they ought to be. Especially since she'd never answered his marriage proposal, not the day he asked, not the three days since. He had no right to think so warmly about another woman who'd decided against him.

He cleared his throat again. "Miss Lockwood, this is Mrs. Parker. I'm not sure if you've met."

Arms splayed, Rachel strode over and hugged Helga. "I hope you've brought needlework or something to keep your hands busy."

At Helga's nod, Everett headed back to the men.

The image of Julia sitting on the floor rubbing her head, lower lip pouting, taunted him.

"Everett!" Julia's lilting voice stopped him midstride.

He turned and waited for her.

"I was hoping to help outside."

"What?" It was hard enough seeing her in his cabin, but for her to be outside with him the entire day? He took a breath to calm himself.

"Well, I don't really do needlework, and Rachel can teach me some other time. I'm not needed until lunch. So I thought I could help out here." Her hands rested on her hips as she surveyed the working men. A bright smile settled on her face.

He assessed her dress, which was barely serviceable, and the bonnet in her hand wasn't the least practical. Why'd she think he needed her help when seven men were there to do the carpentry? But then, he couldn't steal glances at her loveliness if she remained inside. He bit the inside of his cheek. He didn't need to spend any more time absorbed in her looks than he already did. If he couldn't enjoy them later, then he shouldn't enjoy them now.

He cleared his throat. "You aren't a skilled woodworker by chance?"

Her lips bunched to the side. "No, but I can work hard, do whatever needs to be done." She shrugged. "Maybe hand nails to the men?"

"John or Ambrose could do that. Wouldn't you rather talk with the women?"

Her cheeks flushed. "I'm not saying it wouldn't be nice, but I am here to . . ." She shrugged. "To help you."

His insides churned. Had he been wrong? Maybe her silence hadn't been an answer. But she still sounded undecided. Well, maybe he was undecided too. He needed a woman who could do farm chores as well as attend things in the house. Could she prove today that her tiny frame was up to the task?

She tipped her head toward the barn. "I'd like to help."

What would the men think if he allowed her to help? She distracted him more than he was comfortable with, and perhaps the men would not welcome her in their midst. He followed her gaze toward the construction site, where the sound of work had receded. The Stantons were still pounding nails, but the others had stopped and formed a ragged line in front of the woodpile, their gazes fixed on Julia. Ned's slanted smile and Axel's sly grin made Everett want to send them home. "I don't think—"

Caleb Langston, a gangly fourteen-year-old, swept his hat off and nodded past him. "Good morning, ma'am."

Everett glanced back at Julia. Her dazzling smile as she answered Caleb sucked the wind from his chest. Her lit face could not fail to have the same effect on the young lad.

No more time to waste deciding—they needed the whole day to get the frame up before nightfall. He waved his hand toward her. "Miss Lockwood, this is Caleb Langston. His brother, Axel, and father, Jedidiah. This other man is my neighbor, Ned Parker."

Axel's hungry eyes beamed. "It's nice to see you again, Miss Lockwood."

Everett swallowed before delivering the news. "She wants

to help us out here, so let her know if you need anything." He expected to see apprehensive faces, but smiles played on every set of lips.

"That'd be mighty nice, ma'am." Caleb tipped his head at her before flipping his hat back on.

Julia rubbed her hands together. "All right. What shall I do first?"

Axel stepped in and offered his arm. "Father told me to cut that wood over there. You could help me hold it steady."

She turned pleading eyes toward Everett as Axel dragged her away.

"Perhaps she might rather help us, um . . ." Everett looked around for something, anything to get her back.

"You said she could help us with anything we needed, and I need her." Axel threw a challenging look over his shoulder, then cupped Julia's elbow, giving her a charming smile. "I don't know how I could manage without you, ma'am."

Everett stood, clenching and unclenching his fists. Why had he given in to Axel? The whippersnapper was hardly older than William. And Everett was just old enough to be the boy's father.

He should have sent her back in or insisted he needed her, rather than tie her up with Axel for the rest of the morning. He had thought she'd distract him out here, and would she ever. Especially now that Axel was fawning over her. At least she didn't look thrilled to be with the kid.

The harmony of hammer, nails, and saws buzzed around him. He couldn't just stand and stare. Stepping over the arranged lumber on the ground, he joined the Stantons but kept his eye on the group working on the other side of the barn's floor. Imitating Axel, Julia hefted a board and carried it to his set of sawhorses—impressive for a person that small.

Maybe she could survive the work his farm and the Kansas earth threw her way.

Julia brushed sawdust from her face. Axel had stolen her again to steady the wood he was cutting.

"You know, Miss Lockwood." Axel swiped the sweat from his brow with his forearm, exposed below his rolled-up sleeve. "You're just the right-sized counterweight: featherlight, but made of something stronger, like you've got pinions of silver and gold."

How long had it taken him to piece together that line? He should have thought longer . . . much longer.

"Thanks." She sighed and leaned her weight against the board as Axel's saw ripped through the wood. She muttered under her breath, "I guess." Flying wood shavings attempted to take up residence in her eyelashes, so she turned her head aside.

Everett's body braced a wall frame not ten feet away from her. Ned and William nailed the wall to the adjacent frame Dex held steady.

If she wasn't to be a part of Everett's group, she really should have stayed inside and learned to sew, though she wouldn't admit just yet to Everett that she didn't know how. But she'd said she was willing to help however she was needed, and she would prove true to her word despite the sawdust flying in her eyes.

Everett whooped and twirled a hammer in his hand. He patted William on the back before both men positioned themselves along a series of long boards lined evenly across the top of another. Dex lowered his arm and shouted, "Go!"

Everett and William both pounded nails into the boards

furiously. With each step Everett took, he pulled a nail from his mouth and pounded it in with ease and quickness. He looked over at William and shouted around his mouthful after every finished nail.

The sullen Everett she'd encountered was not the one she was observing now. The playful gleam in his eye made his face more attractive, and the muscles under his shirt rippled with every hammer stroke. He was jovial and cooperative with the other men; why would he be so different with her?

Everett threw his hammer down at the end of the row and flexed his arms while William nailed in his last nail. After ruffling William's sweaty hair, Everett glanced at her.

"Julia?" Axel tapped her shoulder from behind.

She whirled toward him. "Yes?"

He wiggled the board under her fingers. "You can let go. I'm done with this one."

"Oh." She took her weight off the board.

"I'm done with this stack. Maybe I'm working you too hard? I know I'm getting tired myself." He walked up close.

Julia looked back toward Everett and saw him frown.

"You still thinking about marrying him?"

"Why wouldn't I be?" She narrowed her eyes at Axel.

"Just seems like a woman of your qualities would go for a man ladies flock to, not run from." His smirk unsettled her stomach. Everett might look like Theodore, but Axel's egregious manners were more like him. His allure was weak in comparison, though, and he surely was several years younger than her.

Axel had more guts than Everett did with all his flirtatious teasing, but he simply churned her stomach. "I suppose you have plenty of girls."

"Quite. But you, Miss Lockwood, dazzle them out of the

sky." He stepped closer and reached for her arm, but she sidestepped him at the last second. His affected charm might have worked on her a year ago, like Theodore's had, but she could now spot bitter poison hidden under spoonfuls of sugar.

His finger slid down her arm. "Perhaps we should set a spell?"

"If you're tired, you ought to sit, but I can't—lunch preparations."

It was Axel's turn to frown.

Holding her skirts, she moved as fast as she could toward Everett without running. "How's the barn coming?"

"Fine," he said. A smile broke out on his lips, small, undesigned.

She smiled back. "I saw you won the competition."

He nodded. And then he reached for the side of her face.

She jumped back out of his reach, wrapping her arms about herself. A chill burned a pathway where he'd almost touched her and lodged in her chest.

Frowning, he clamped onto her shoulder. "Hold still. You have sawdust about to fall into your eye." He brushed a thumb along the corner of her right eye, then dropped his hand. He crossed his arms and looked askance at the ground.

She released her grip on her arms and tried to act normal. She couldn't blame him for looking so baffled. She didn't even understand her own reaction. One second she'd been smiling, the next reliving a day with Theodore she never wanted to remember. "Sorry. You scared me." She wanted to forever banish those thoughts, not share them. Stuffing them inside would keep them away—from her, from him, from everybody.

"I apologize . . . for whatever it was. I need to go." He sidestepped her, but she moved with him.

She couldn't let him go, not when it'd looked like he was about to open up to her before she'd ruined it. "Could you show me around your place before I head in to make lunch?" She tried to look exceptionally eager, pretend nothing odd had happened. If those feelings resurfaced, she'd have to refuse to react. "Just a quick tour, since you're taking a break?"

"I don't have much time."

"I understand." She flashed her sweetest smile.

He abruptly looked away and moved off to the side of the house. "Here's the well if you ladies need water for lunch."

Julia relaxed and walked over to him. Maybe she could draw him back out . . . if she could control herself and the troubling flashes of memories.

Everett pointed toward the construction site. "That, of course, will be the barn for the animals that now shelter in the soddy."

"What will you use the soddy for?"

"I'm thinking of using it for tanning and storing furs."

"What do you do with the furs?" Furs. Surely he wouldn't do business with Addison Fur Company out here on the plains. But what if Theodore's family business made rounds in this part of Kansas? Would he be involved with the transactions? A shiver wound up her spine.

"Sell them."

Her mouth went dry. "What company do you sell them to?"

He looked down at her. "No company, just Carl Hampden at the mercantile. He might sell them to a particular company. You could ask him if you're interested."

"Oh, I'm not interested." Her heart slowed its pace, and she could breathe again. Julia pointed to a pasture, its ground ripped with black seams. "What's over there?"

"That's where I'll plant corn." Everett turned to face her.

"I'm sorry, but I have to get water for the men. If you'll excuse me."

"Why didn't you ask me to get it?" Was he trying to ignore her?

"I didn't want to bother you."

She laid her hand on his arm. "But I'm out here to help you."

His wide eyes swung to her fingers. Julia dropped her hand.

He grabbed at his forearm where she had touched him. Was he trying to get the feeling of her touch off him? Everett looked at her askance. "So you'd get us some water?"

"Yes—"

"Thank you." Everett tipped his hat and strode off.

She stamped the ground. Fine. Forget about talking. She tromped to the shack and flung open the front door. The top hinge let loose and the wooden door thudded against the jamb. She gasped. "I broke Everett's door!"

Rachel laughed. "Don't worry about it. He's had to fix that door a hundred times. You ought to suggest better hinges for the new house."

She stepped into the leaning, filthy structure. "He's building a new house?"

Rachel nodded.

The desire to sigh with relief overwhelmed her. She grabbed a few onions and worked at tearing off their skins next to Helga, who peeled potatoes.

"Done playing outside?" Rachel's amused voice made her cringe.

She shrugged. "It was time to help with lunch."

Rachel dropped her needle and the pair of pants she was mending into a basket and stretched. "Guess I can't let you two do all the work readying the food and drink."

"Drink!" She dropped her onion. "I'm supposed to be getting water."

Julia rushed out with a bucket, filled it, and hurried over to the men, sloshing water on her boots.

Everett stopped laughing when she reached the outskirts of the construction area. Was she that disappointing she killed his mood the second she walked into view? What could she do to prove she could work hard enough to be of worth?

He took the bucket, refilled the men's jugs, and returned the empty bucket to her. "Thank you."

"You're welcome." She placed her hand on his arm again. It tensed under her fingers. They both stared at her hand.

Everett's glance moved to her face for a few seconds. His eyes reminded her of the frightened jackrabbit she'd scared from its hiding place by the privy this morning.

His arm disappeared from under her hand, and he left her alone. At the barn's frame, he turned sideways to walk through the wall studs. Within seconds, he had climbed to the top of the roof.

Julia pursed her lips. Scared and not talkative.

Well, perhaps her future husband was simply shy. That had to be good—a man who was skittish was not a man who'd force her against her will. She heaved a sigh. He had to be her answer.

With one hammer blow, Everett drove another nail through both boards.

"What have those nails done to you?" Dex scooted along the roof's beam. Behind him, the fading light of day shrouded his friend in shadow.

"Just trying to get as much done as possible before the sun sets."

"Or you're pretending each nail's head is shaped rather like Axel's."

Everett glanced over to his shack, where Ned was yelling at Helga to get moving and Axel had found a need to chitchat with the women, leaving his father and brother lounging in their wagon. Normally, Axel would have been dogging William's heels, but his childhood friend obviously paled in comparison to Julia. Of course, Everett agreed with his assessment. "He wasn't so bad. I'll have to go over every joint and beam Ned worked on, though."

"That's not what I was talking about and you know it."

"Then why don't you talk plainer?"

"You're giving her up, then?"

"In order to give something up, you have to have it in the first place." Everett wasn't even going to ask God for anything this time—he had before and gotten nothing.

"She came here for you."

"She came here for Rachel."

"And you're going to let Axel have her? He's a scant two years older than William."

"No, I'm not going to let him have her." Everett wondered how old Julia was. He was afraid to ask. Would she rather marry closer in age, despite the boy being younger? "I'd rather she be allowed to choose who she wants rather than feel obligated to fulfill a make-believe arrangement."

"She doesn't know about that. Rachel hasn't told her."

"And all the more reason to give her room to decide." Would she choose him? Today she'd seen the whole miserable mess of a farm he claimed as his own—the same one that caused Helga to look elsewhere. Though Helga probably rued her decision more than he.

Axel's thick, throaty laughter snaked its way from the cabin and squeezed at Everett's guts. This time a man closer to Julia in age—and charming to boot—openly pursued his mail-order bride.

He'd proposed marriage to her on the first day, and she'd yet to accept. Everett wouldn't push her, but with each day, his faint hope faded. How many times could this happen to him before he felt like less than a man?

"You could lose her to Axel."

Everett sat back and looked at the moon in the pale blue sky. With each bride he'd brought to Kansas, the more fearful he'd grown of being jilted and the more humiliated he'd felt when he was. He had to completely let Julia go and let the Lord direct their paths. If Axel won her, Everett would have to learn to deal with it, just like he had with the others. "Then he'd be a lucky man."

Now all he had to do was prayerfully fight the urge to follow Dex's tempting suggestion of imagining Axel's face on the head of every nail.

Chapter 5

Julia sat in the rocking chair, sewing. She was doing tolerably well after nearly two weeks of Rachel's instruction on stitching, but she'd learned nothing more about Everett. He'd only stopped by once since the day of the barn raising.

"Ouch!" Julia stuck a bleeding finger in her mouth.

Rachel chuckled. "That dress is going to be dotted with blood the way you're going. Perhaps you should start stamping your fingers on the cloth to make a pattern. Won't notice the stains that way."

Julia crumpled the bodice piece in her lap. "I'm no good at this."

"You'll get better. You've no choice." Rachel stacked some freshly washed plates on the shelf behind the stove. "No tailor around here."

Ambrose opened the door for Dex, who was carrying a load of wood, before climbing the loft's ladder.

"I'm tired of having to take my seams out." She took her tiny scissors and chomped them through the stitches she'd undone three times already. "It's taking forever." She shoved the blades through a knotted piece of threading. The scissors slipped through and right into Dex's torso.

"Woman!" Dex dumped his handful of logs and grabbed his side. "More antics like that and see if I let you sit around all day while I slave away, bringing in your wood."

"Sorry." She worked at keeping a straight face. She never knew if he was serious or not. If he wasn't, he'd make a to-do over her amusement when he was in pain, and if he was, well, it wasn't kind to laugh, even if he was overreacting

Rachel inspected Dex's shirt. "He's fine. Not even bleeding. Barely a hole."

"An unpleasant little hole." Dex rubbed his side.

Julia leaned back into the chair. A yelp caused her to jump from the seat. Emma turned on the waterworks, clutching her little hand against her chest.

Rachel scooped her up. "Mama's told you not to play behind the rocking chair."

"Dolly!" Emma's hands reached for her doll, whose porcelain fingers lay precariously under the chair's rocking edge.

Julia handed the doll to Emma. The little girl clutched the toy to her chest, and a big drop of moisture fell onto its painted face.

"I'm sorry, Emma. I didn't mean to hurt you." Taking care to look behind her first, Julia lowered herself into the rocker. "Seems I'm intent on drawing blood from everyone tonight."

"That's why we're staying up here!" John leaned over the loft edge.

Ambrose's curly fair head appeared next to John. "Yeah, it's dangerous down there."

Giggles burst from the two boys dangling over the living room as Dex walked around, hunched over and moaning, his hand clutching where she'd stabbed him.

Julia yanked her dress bodice from the basket and pulled out the rest of her seam. She took her time, making sure the few family members who'd yet to receive a wound from her tonight remained unscathed.

"What I don't understand is how a woman can know how to cook, but not know how to sew." Dex lowered himself into a chair, with a wince for good measure. Then he winked before pulling out a paper and pen.

Julia sighed. "I didn't know how to cook until about six months ago. That's when I answered Everett's ad, or rather Rachel's. I'd run away from home—"

"You're a runaway?" The eyes of the two boys above her turned as large as their ears. And it seemed that little boys had big ears.

"Yes, I ran away from home."

"Why?"

"I'd rather not discuss that." She squirmed in her seat and frowned at another misplaced stitch. "But I couldn't find a job as a clerk. So I started working at . . . at a tavern. But only in the kitchen, mind you. Seems a saloon as shabby as Halson's doesn't care too much if the cook has no idea what she's doing."

Rachel turned to frown. "They let you stay in the kitchen?"

Julia hung her head. "They were desperate, and no. Once the other cook was no longer sick and could handle cooking again, they wanted me to serve in the front. But that only caused problems. . . ."

Dex hummed in disapproval.

"But I learned a lot from Marie. But I wouldn't say I'm a good cook." Her thread wasn't pulling out very easily. As she turned over the fabric, the knotted mess underneath made her growl. "Just like I'll never be a good seamstress."

"You'll do just fine. We might never fully overcome our problems, but God never gives us more than we can handle."

Dex smiled, then turned to Rachel with a frown. "Like spelling. How do you spell *calves*?"

William trudged in reeking of barnyard animals. Pulling a chair from the corner, he leaned over to take off his boots. The sound of his yawn filled the room.

While William gave his parents a rundown on the cattle's condition, Julia worked steadily. But she couldn't focus. All she could think about was how much of a burden she was to this family and her need to relieve them of her presence. After folding her material, she dropped her scissors into the basket. "I'm going to go to bed. 'Night, everyone."

"Good night," the boys' voices chimed in above her.

"Good night," Rachel said, grabbing Julia's shawl to hand to her.

Julia opened the front door. The night air was a welcome relief on her sweaty skin. She let her eyes adjust before stepping off the porch and scurrying across the yard.

She never thought she'd be thankful for getting to sleep outdoors with animals, but when she entered the barn, the draftiness was a welcome change from the cabin's smoky stuffiness.

Daisy mooed when Julia gave her a quick pat. "I'll see you in the morning, old girl." Then she climbed the ladder and scurried over to her pallet of hay. After changing into her nightdress, she flopped down across the quilts and sighed. Emma's wails reached her ears from the house. Julia smiled. Emma hated going to bed, and she couldn't blame her. She didn't want to be in bed either, but she couldn't stay in the house. There simply wasn't room for another adult.

Julia knew it was time she stopped eating their food and interrupting their routine. She couldn't remain a permanent houseguest no matter how much she'd miss Rachel's daily company. The thought of never seeing Rachel again hurt. How sad that a woman she'd known for such a short time was the only person in the world she could trust. And going back to writing Rachel letters was unappealing.

She mentally tallied her money. Half remained. She could go somewhere else if she wanted to—travel as far as her money could take her—and hope there was something there for her. It could be better, but it could be so much worse. She'd had worse, and she didn't want it again. With Rachel's recommendation of Everett and his own respectful distance, she didn't think he'd ever hurt her like Theodore had.

But would he marry her? He'd been over once this past week but had said nothing to her beyond what was necessary. Yet she'd seen that spark of male interest in his eye. She wasn't too thrilled about that spark being there, but it meant that this option might not be lost.

No matter how much she thought over each alternative, she couldn't choose. So Everett would have to decide. Tomorrow.

———•◦•———

After breakfast, Julia and Rachel waved good-bye to Dex and the boys, who were going to Everett's to mend a fence and then were bringing him back with them for supper. She'd decided to ask Everett today and now she'd get to, but the certainty of doing so made her jittery. She threw herself into performing her allotted chores. If he saw how many things she'd learned in two weeks' time, wouldn't he be more receptive? Hadn't that been his qualm, that she couldn't do the work necessary to be of service to him?

Later that afternoon, while Rachel cared for Emma and worked inside, Julia fed the livestock and cleaned the animal stalls. Nerves quickened her pace so she had time to try her hand at chopping the stack of golden hedge wood, surely a good chore to work out nervous tension. Thankful the others weren't around to see her first pitiful attempts at swinging an ax, she hacked until her shoulders ached. The pile of wood grew, and her pent-up aggravation eased. In no time she'd be able to do farm chores without difficulty.

The creaking of a wagon and voices of men alerted her to the Stantons' return. It was only a matter of time until she'd speak to Everett.

Balancing a pile of wood in her arms for the supper fire, she turned the corner of the house and thumped into his chest. The wood fell, and she tried to pull her feet from the kindling's trajectory. One piece managed to thwack her toe anyway. She grimaced.

Dex came up behind Everett. "You got enough wood?"

She nodded. "Chopped it myself." Why was Everett always around when she looked like a fool?

Dex stacked the wood pieces in the crook of one arm. "I'll take these in. Doesn't look like there's much left to teach you, so why don't you stable the oxen?"

"Do you need me to do that now?"

Dex shook his head. "I was kidding, Julia. The boys'll do it."

"No, teach me if you don't mind." Looking directly at Everett, she squared her shoulders. "I'm plenty capable of doing whatever's needed. You just have to show me."

Dex mounted the stairs behind his boys. "Everett can show you."

Looking unhappy, Everett spun and headed toward the team. "Come. It's not hard," he called to her over his shoulder.

She pursed her lips. She knew it wasn't hard; she just didn't know exactly what needed to be done or where things went.

Everett went about stabling the beasts, handing her the

tack and telling her where to store each piece. "Over there you'll find their feed. One scoop for each." Everett rubbed down the oxen.

After hanging the bridles, Julia grabbed the scoop and distributed the food. She knew she should talk to him now, while they were alone, but her tongue glued itself to the roof of her mouth. How could she be sure his decision would be based on wholesome reasons when she knew so little about him, when so few words had passed between them?

"Everett . . ." She stopped him before he exited the barn.

His silhouette turned at the door and brought its arms in, fusing into the blackness.

"How did the fencing go?"

"Good."

"Did you get anything else done?"

"No."

She played with the button at her collar. "Are you staying for supper?"

"Yes, I brought my horse."

She let out a breath. Maybe he'd loosen up at the supper table surrounded with his friends. "You have a horse?"

"Yes."

"I wonder why I haven't seen it before." If he wasn't going to give her more than a word or two, she was going to have to drag him into a conversation. "What color is it?"

"Black."

"I always wanted a pony. One Christmas Father promised me anything, but when I asked for a pony, he didn't keep his word." She shrugged. "Always wanted a white one."

Everett strolled in from the doorway and toward the glow of the lantern. He leaned against a post. "So your father didn't get you a pony?"

She shook her head. Was his tone mocking her? Maybe ponies were looked down upon here. Her heartbeat placed pressure against her rib cage. "Do you think I might . . . be able to find a white horse?"

"You need a horse?"

"I don't know if I need a horse." How could she know what was a want and what was a need on the prairie? "Maybe I need a horse." Her dry throat demanded moisture before she could push out her next words. "Wouldn't your wife need a horse?"

Everett's eyes closed. He opened one eye before the second one revealed itself. "Um . . . that is to say . . . maybe a second horse would be needed. Would make the trip to Salt Flatts faster. And smoother." He rubbed his chin. "Anywhere, in fact."

"Julia?" Rachel's voice called through the doorway. "Everett?"

"In here." She returned the scoop to the feed bucket. Just when he'd let go of a complete stream of words, they got interrupted. But hopefully, that feeble start would untie his tongue at the dinner table and in turn her own.

Rachel walked in wiping her hands on her apron and stopped beside Everett. "Are you two finished yet? Dinner's ready."

"Yes, but I want to bring in Blaze first." Everett let his gaze wander over Julia's face for a second before leaving the barn.

Rachel turned to examine her, a sparkle in her hazel eyes. "Were you two talking?"

"Sort of."

"Sort of?" Rachel tilted her head to the side.

He was about to talk until you appeared. "Well, he doesn't exactly talk much. It's difficult to get more than two consecutive words from him."

Rachel's right eyebrow went up. "Two words?"

"That's what I said." Julia huffed. "Are you having difficulty hearing today?"

"Sorry." Rachel set her hands on her hips. "I just haven't known Everett to be quiet before."

"That's all he is with me."

"His tongue's just knotted up over your pretty face." Rachel's features softened. "I'm sure with time his words will come. Well, as much as a man is capable of talking. Sometimes I wish Dex would talk more, but it just doesn't happen." She squeezed Julia's shoulder. "That's why I have enjoyed your company so." She stooped to look into her eyes. "There isn't anything else bothering you about him, is there?"

Julia played with her dress's shoulder seam. "If I could just be assured we'd get along and he'd . . . I need to make up my mind one way or the other. I'm grateful for your hospitality, but I've got to decide what I'm doing. I can't stay here indefinitely."

Rachel's smile flipped down. "It is a bit crowded."

She mentally surveyed her assets again, hoping she'd missed something. "I don't have the money to go home even if I wanted to. And I can't stay here much longer."

Rachel laid a hand on her shoulder. "You're welcome here as long as you need."

"Thanks." She squeezed Rachel's plump hand. "But I know it's time to go, like I knew it was time to leave home. I just need to do it." She pushed dirty hay around with her foot, then looked into Rachel's soft eyes. "You sure he'd do right by me . . . be kind? Do I even know enough to help him run a farm?" She shook her head. The Stantons had only assigned her a bit of the farm chores, and all of them normally reserved for the children.

Rachel's face turned tender. "I'm positive. You two will do just fine."

"It's just . . . never mind. I've never been wanted for anything other than my looks. Theodore . . . only found my face worthwhile for his wants." She thumped her chest. "I didn't want to be a pawn for profit or some man's whim. I couldn't stay there and work for nothing and be some man's toy. I want so much more from life." Tears spilled over her cheeks. How she wished she could tell Rachel all that had happened, but the shame when those images returned made her hold her tongue. If she couldn't tell Rachel, she couldn't tell Everett. What would he think of her when she laid down her stipulations for getting married?

Rachel slipped her arm around her slumped shoulders. "No use dwelling on something that won't happen. Put it behind you and look forward." She smiled.

The barn door opened. Everett tipped his hat and led his horse around them.

While he talked to his horse in soft tones, Everett brushed out the animal. Julia's heart squeezed in time with his quick rhythm. Soon, she'd see if he'd have her. If not, where would she go?

Everett had left the women in the barn so he could grab his horse, Julia's words bouncing around in his skull.

"Wouldn't your wife need a horse?"

Everett patted Blaze's neck, the wind blowing the gelding's mane into his face. "How would you like a buddy, ol' boy?"

The horse nickered as it swung its neck around to sniff him. "I might have to buy you one for my wife."

My wife.

His heartbeat soared like the clouds racing across the dull

sky. He'd distanced himself, waiting for the inevitable pain of being abandoned once again, but it looked like God wasn't bound and determined to make him live his whole life alone. And with a girl prettier than any he'd ever dreamed of. Patricia had been pretty, but not gorgeous, and she'd never really wanted to be his wife. It ended up that she was stringing him along, waiting for a wealthier fellow to marry.

He unwound the tether and tugged on Blaze's harness. "Let's get you inside and stabled so I can have dinner with my intended." His lungs emptied. He stopped for a second and took in a cool sip of fresh air. No more needing to guard his feelings in case she left. Tonight he'd get to know her as well as possible, for it couldn't be long before she'd want to marry and move out of the Stantons' barn.

He pushed on the barn door, but stopped at the sound of Julia's expressive voice.

". . . the money to go home even if I wanted to. And I can't stay here much longer."

"You're welcome here as long as you need."

"Thanks. But I know it's time to go, like I knew it was time to leave home. I just need to do it."

Everett retracted his hand as if the door had singed his fingers.

He turned to a nearby bucket, his foot poised to kick it across the yard, but he stopped mid-swing. That would alert the women to his nearby presence. He ground a patch of grass into the dirt instead. "Fool!" he hissed. "I should have stuck to my guns and said 'no more' to this wife nonsense."

Blaze nuzzled him.

He exhaled slowly before he calmed enough to talk to his horse. "Wanting oats, eh? Well, you'll have to wait until we get home. I've got to suffer through dinner with her first.

But I won't be long." He strangled the leads in his hand. "I want to get home as quickly as you do." At least he wouldn't be the only one disgraced this time. Perhaps Axel and his crowd wouldn't increase their mean-spirited teasing since their leader would share in the humiliation.

He stepped to the door and pushed it over the dirt bump, wishing he had ignored the invitation to dinner.

"I couldn't stay there and work for nothing and be some man's toy. I want so much more from life."

"No use dwelling on something that won't happen. Put it behind you and look forward."

How humiliating to listen to Rachel encourage the friend she'd set him up with to leave him.

Julia's face searched his for a moment before he forced his eyes away. The less he looked at her the better. Another teasing woman. Why did God bless some women with mouth-watering features if they only used their looks to get men to do whatever they wanted with no intention of reciprocation? He felt like a chewed-up dog bone.

He took his time tethering Blaze in an empty stall, giving the horse a good rubdown until he heard both sets of footsteps exit the barn. He patted Blaze's neck. "I'll be back soon. I promise, boy." But his feet wouldn't move. He couldn't stay for dinner. He had to make an excuse.

Chapter 6

Julia gripped the reins of the Stantons' wagon as the wheels crunched over the dirt tracks on the outskirts of Everett's property. The man was either shy or noncommittal, and she intended to find out which. He'd left the Stantons' with barely a good-bye minutes after she'd mentioned becoming his wife. Was he going to marry her or not? She had bullied Dex into letting her tag along with him and the boys this morning. Today would either be her last trip to Everett's or the first of many.

"Give them more slack," Dex said.

She relaxed her trembling grip.

"I do believe we've made it safe and sound. You sure you haven't driven a team before?"

Her smirk twisted. The animals did most of the work, but she doubted she could handle them without his help if they got upset. "We have a ways to go before we reach the house."

"You'll do fine. You've done perfectly so far."

A satisfied bubble filled her. Almost crowding out the jitters. The Stantons thought she was ready for farm life, but did Everett?

"I'm glad you came to cook." William popped up from

the back and let out a groan. "But I can't wait. The smell of that apple pie is calling to me something fierce. My stomach's been grumbling the whole way over."

"Me too." John grabbed his stomach and hunched over the front seat. "I'm near starving."

"You're in bad shape, then." Dex pushed John's head full of thick hair playfully to the side. "We've got hours of mending fence before lunch."

"And I won't be serving that pie until dinner."

William and John moaned, causing her to smile.

Everett's barn, barely illuminated by the dim morning light, loomed in front of them. Wonder washed over her. The new structure dominated the landscape. And she had played a part in that construction. She examined her gloveless hands, no longer white and soft. How right to use them for creation and artistry, the construction of buildings, the making of garments. A little rivulet of pride tingled down her back. The male conversations she'd overheard in her father's store flowed in from memory. The desire to go west and build an existence from nothing made sense now. It was a heady thing.

Everett pushed backward through the barn doors, a bucket in each hand.

"Good morning, Everett," Dex bellowed. He placed a hand on her shoulder. "Stop the wagon next to the barn. We'll put the oxen in the new paddock."

Nervous that the huge animals wouldn't respond to her light feminine voice, she kept the team headed in Everett's direction with a firm hand.

He turned toward the wagon, set a bucket down, and shaded his eyes from the sun, which was growing brighter every second. "Good morning, Dex."

If her hands weren't busy holding the reins, she'd cross

her fingers. Now it was time to see if the creatures would obey. "Whoa!"

"Rachel?" Everett squinted up at the wagon seat.

The team halted nice and easy, and she let out her breath. "No. It's me, Julia." She couldn't see his eyes, but sensed he wasn't pleased. The same glare he'd given her last night when he said he couldn't stay cut through her.

"You drove?"

"Yes, it was great fun." The oxen tugged gently on the reins as they ate the grass within reach. She released the leather straps.

Everett ran his hand through his hair. "But . . . what—"

"I'm here to cook. Dex said you could finish today, so I came to serve lunch." She jumped down, not waiting for him to assist her, and took a step toward him. "I want to help."

"It's worth it, Everett," William said, rubbing his belly. "She made an apple pie." The young man handed her the basket, but when she tugged at it, he wouldn't let go. She shook her head at his grin.

Everett cleared his throat. "I've got to get these inside. Excuse me." He picked his buckets off the ground and scurried toward the cabin.

John jumped over the wagon's side and ran after Everett's black-and-white dog, Merlin, while Dex and William took care of the oxen.

When would be the best time to ask him? Perhaps she should take advantage of the fact that he was alone. Who knew how often that would happen today? She entered the cabin and peeked around the open door, its hinge still loose.

Everett put his buckets down and walked to the window. He leaned his forearm against the pane, followed by his forehead.

She cleared her throat.

He jumped, then straightened to his full height. "Sorry, I best get back out there."

Her heart kathumped at the sound of his dejection. She tried to catch a glimpse of his eyes as he passed, but he'd pulled his hat brim low, and the cabin shadows kept her from seeing anything.

She reached out her hand and grasped a bit of his shirt sleeve. Now might not be the best time, but now was what she had. "Can I have a word with you, Everett?" Seeing his form stiffen, she let go. "Later, I mean. Would later be better? After lunch?"

"Sure." He fidgeted with the door handle as if he were only waiting for a starting gun to fire before racing to the fence line.

When she nodded, he slipped out the door.

She grabbed a bucket and followed him out but veered off toward the well. How could he be afraid of her? She wasn't even tall enough to see over his shoulder. Maybe he wanted to back out and didn't know how to tell her. Well, he'd have the chance this afternoon.

The men laughed as they headed off into the pasture, their implements and posts loaded in Everett's smaller wagon. They disappeared in the direction Dex had told her they'd be working. She pushed a sense of foreboding away.

Heart tangled in knots, she debated again the wisdom of her choice.

She pulled in a steadying breath. Living near Rachel trumped her other alternatives. And she'd trust her friend not to lead her astray. And a man who wanted to run any time she appeared would be less apt to bother her for marital favors. At least not right away.

Her fingers played with the loose strands of hair at her neckline. Could she face that in her future? With him? She looked at the horizon, but the men had already disappeared behind a stand of trees. His behavior might be odd, but something in the way he looked at her made her confident he'd respect her wishes, unlike most men she'd met. Tremors still coursed through her limbs when she sensed his admiring glances, but neither did she fear for her safety. He was the kind of man she would have chosen, before Theodore. . . .

She needed something to do. Right now.

At the table, she unpacked the basket. A pile of dirty plates and an empty kettle lay haphazardly on the small bit of counter space. Cobwebs clung to the feet of the few furniture pieces in the tiny one-room shack. The small four-paned window would let in more light if she removed the caked-on dirt. She cinched her apron strings tight about her waist. If this would have to be her home until a new one was built, it might as well be clean.

Julia stopped quite a distance from where the men worked and set the milk jug and basket on the ground. Scrubbing Everett's cabin had left her arms aching, and they begged for a rest from the weight of food. Her heart needed the rest too. It pumped so fast she was afraid it would burst.

Breathe, Julia. She forced herself to take in air. *Nothing odd about bringing marriage up in conversation. That's why he invited you to Kansas.*

She hefted her items and moved toward John, who finished setting a wooden rail before running around William to push up the other end.

Why had she asked Everett to talk after lunch? Her cheeks burned. The Stantons would guess what the conversation was about when she asked him to take a walk with her. But it had to be today. No time to plan a more private interview.

She took a final big breath and marched within hearing distance. "All right, boys. I've brought lunch."

"You brought us that pie?" John ran to her, his face glowing.

She couldn't stop the tickle of a smile on her lips. "We should wait for dinner to eat pie, don't you think?"

"I sure could eat it up right now, Miss Julia. Two pies, even."

She handed him the food basket and ruffled his hair with her freed hand. "I don't doubt that for a second." She snatched the blanket off the top and scanned the area for shade. "But I'm sure you'll survive on whatever meager portions I brought you."

She flicked out the blanket as much as the wind allowed, then stomped on the dull red fabric to bend the grasses underneath. John jumped on it next to her and used his body as a rolling pin. When he deemed the blanket flat enough, she settled herself at a corner. He rolled over to her and stopped on his belly, his head resting in his hands.

"I wish they'd hurry, Miss Julia. I'm awful hungry."

She rolled her eyes. "You're always hungry."

The others were finishing a section of fence. Everett wasn't as tall as Dex, which was a good thing. She didn't want to spend her life with a crick in her neck talking to her husband.

"Still wish they'd go faster." John rolled over onto his back and caterwauled, his little hands gripping his shirt at the stomach.

She jabbed tickling fingers into his armpit. His high tenor giggles burst forth way too easily.

The men sauntered over and lowered themselves to the

ground. Julia adjusted her posture to sit more ladylike. Her body's awareness of Everett's closeness tripped her heart into a chaotic rhythm. Deep breaths did nothing to steady the tempo.

Only John's eyes held a sparkle of merriment. The others simply looked weary. And something more in Everett's intent gaze unnerved her. Julia poured milk into tin cups. "Have you had a good morning of work?"

Dex took the first cup. "I'd say so. I think we can get it done before supper."

"That would be good." Everett took a cup from her, his eyes meeting hers for only a second.

William downed his milk as soon as she set it in his hands and then returned it for more. She shook her head at his bottomless stomach and refilled. "I'll have supper waiting whenever that time comes. But for lunch, I've got bacon, buttered rolls, cheese, and . . ." She brought the basket to her face with an exaggerated look of astonishment. "What is this I have in here? I think the pie jumped into my lunch basket." She pulled the apple pie out and smiled at the joyous look on John's face. "Maybe it ought to be eaten for lunch after all."

"Yes!" John's two big front teeth poked through his face-wide smile. He held out his hands.

She laughed. "After we eat."

"That's all right." He rubbed his tummy. "I'll still have room enough to eat it all up."

"You'll be sharing that, boy." Dex clamped his hand over John's head, hat and all.

Chuckling, Julia glanced at Everett. A tiny smile graced his face, but when she caught his gaze, his mouth tightened. He took a sip from his cup and looked out over the land.

Despite the sun overhead, she shivered.

The adults ate while listening to John talk about his recent fishing exploits, the fun he was having fencing, and anything else the boy's mind lighted upon.

Her heart beat harder as the food disappeared and the grown men grew restless. Dex pushed off the blanket and thanked her for the meal. Everett tipped his hat to her while the boys' chorus of gratitude echoed their father.

Now or never. "Everett?"

He stood, head cocked to the side as the other three headed to the fence.

How in the world could she make her galloping heart calm itself? "Might we talk?"

"Sure. Said we could." He didn't move.

She glanced behind him toward the Stantons. They'd hear at this distance. And with Everett's reactions, she was pretty sure she was going to get turned down. She didn't want them to hear that. Her fingers found her brooch. Not sure she wanted to hear that either. Not now that she'd reconciled herself to the decision. "Would you mind walking with me? My legs need stretching." Actually, they were about to collapse, but she'd get them to move.

He pointed to a nearby pond. "That's a good place to walk if you've a mind to." He smashed his hat on his head and set off with long strides.

She gathered her skirts and followed him. Evidently, talking while walking was not something Everett did.

At the edge of the pond, he gestured toward the willow tree's long branches sweeping the water's surface. Its tiny light green buds shone against the still-brown grasses of the bank. "Prettiest tree on the place."

She nodded though he wasn't looking at her. "It's lovely."

Her teeth chewed on her inner cheek. An army of tiny frogs jumped into the rippling water.

"So?" He turned to her. His biceps bulged where his arms crossed.

If only he was less distant, she wouldn't feel like she'd plucked this subject out of thin air. But if he had been eager for this arrangement, she would have run away the first day she'd arrived.

Now, Julia, or you won't do it.

"Do you attend the same church as Rachel and Dex?"

"Yes."

"They made mention your preacher comes out here once a month."

"He's scheduled to preach this week. Salt Flatts holds services every Sunday, but I can't justify the time and expense. Did you want to attend?"

She colored. More than attend. "Well, seeing that the preacher won't be here again for quite some time . . ." The phlegm in her throat caught. "If we were to do this marrying thing, it'd probably be best to do it this week."

She forced herself to look at him. His face hadn't changed.

The warmth of blood rushed from her face. "That is, if you're still agreeable to the arrangement. I know I don't know much about farming, but I've learned a lot from the Stantons these last two weeks."

His features didn't waver. He didn't even blink. She almost reached over to poke him to see if he was still alive. She rubbed at the gooseflesh forming along her arms. If he refused, her life looked more than bleak. But she wouldn't beg him to say yes, lest he get the wrong idea.

"So—" she coughed—"that's what I wanted to talk about." She stole another glance at him. Her gaze lowered to the squashed grass at his feet. Time to get the hardest part over with. "It'd just be, you know, for companionship . . . nothing more. I know you want help, and that's what I can offer."

"A companion?" He blinked.

Now she'd have to rip apart his dreams just like Theodore had hers—but at least Everett got to choose. "We are nothing more than strangers. And we need to acknowledge that one or both of us might never be comfortable with each other beyond friendship." Namely, her.

Did he take a step back? "You'd be all right married to someone you have no feelings for? To give up ever having that?"

Julia shrugged. "I've given up on a lot of dreams." She plunged on. "I thought with the new house you were building, you could build us separate rooms for us to use until . . ." No, she wouldn't offer him any hope.

She went on. "You told me the first day you didn't hold me under any obligation, and I think it only fair to give you the same deal." She dared a peek up from under her lashes, but his face was still unreadable. "In other words, don't feel bound to your proposal. But I know how it is to live with no one to talk to, so surely we can be friends. But . . . but of course, you may not want to be tied down to me given I'm not interested in . . . having children." What if he did want kids? She scrambled around for an alternative. "Maybe an orphan . . ."

His expression hadn't changed, but his gaze intensified. "An orphan?"

Julia picked a long stem of grass and started to peel it. "That's if you want children. I'm not opposed to raising orphans once we settle into a routine."

"You don't want any of your own?" His face was so hard. Had his lips even moved?

What little girl didn't dream of children? But that dream was dead. Perhaps Theodore had done her a favor—she'd never become like her mother. "My mother had eleven miscarriages and stillbirths, plus one baby that didn't live through his first day. I was the first and only child to live. My grandmother had about as many children but only two survived. And her mother before that . . ." She wrapped the stem tight around her finger. It broke. "I watched my mother's heartbreak hollow out her insides until she had nothing to give me. She was too busy mourning and pining for the other twelve." Especially the last one who'd been born alive. But he'd died because she'd been too inept at caring for her hours-old brother. "I can't live through that again."

"You're afraid you'll have the same trouble?"

"A doctor pretty much confirmed I would." She dropped the spent grass to the ground. "Of course, in light of . . . my conditions . . . I don't expect you to answer right away." He'd told her the same thing two weeks ago. Would she have to wait weeks for him to respond in turn?

"But you want to marry me?"

"Yes," she whispered. For what else could she do? If he agreed to her conditions, then he was the right man for her.

"Why?"

She stared at her hands. "I have nowhere else to go. I could get a job as a cook, maybe a clerk somewhere, but I did that once, and . . . and . . ." Her mouth grew so dry, she wasn't sure she could form any more words.

"And?"

She glanced up at him for a second but couldn't hold his searching gaze. "I'm a small woman. Once a man with ill intentions realizes no one will call him to task over how he treats me, what'll stand in his way?" The tears in her throat threatened to shut off her voice. She'd written to Rachel the night she was cornered in the tavern stairwell. Thankfully, her boss heard the scuffle, but she'd realized how precarious life was as a hired girl. She'd hoped Rachel could advise her on how to find a better situation.

Well, Rachel's suggestion stood before her now. But would Everett want to provide for her this way? She shook her head a bit. She wouldn't blame him if he didn't, but she had to try. "A girl usually looks to her father for that kind of protection or has money to stay away from the riffraff—but neither of those are true for me. An understanding husband is my only choice."

After hearing nothing but the whooshing sound of her heart in her ears for what seemed like forever, she watched him turn his back on her. She wished she could run. Wished she'd run earlier, but the lack of reply cemented her to the ground.

———

Everett swallowed and turned from Julia's fidgeting form. With his back to her, he let his face contort to mirror the confusion inside. He ached to talk to God aloud, but she'd hear.

Lord, I don't understand. She said she'd hoped to get away as soon as possible. Said she didn't want this life.

Her cough sounded behind him.

He had to give her a reply. Throwing a glance over his shoulder, he said, "Give me a minute."

She gave him a sharp nod. "Take as many as you need."

He stepped farther away, swiped his sweaty hair off his forehead, and took a deep breath.

I said I wasn't doing this again. And I wasn't kidding. Not one more time. Figured you done made it clear I'd remain single my whole life. I'd reconciled myself to that.

He looked up at the fluffy clouds hanging low overhead, bright and cheery, the antithesis to the storm rolling in his gut. Whatever plans she was talking about last night must have fallen through. But he'd given his word. He'd said if she wanted to marry, he would. Despite her ramblings about not holding him to it, would he be able to live with himself if he didn't?

And if I don't take her up on this, Lord, I'm not trying this torturous wife-acquiring business again. That's for sure. No matter what you say.

He kicked a rock into the pond. The wind blew across the water, causing the ripples to cascade across its surface.

She can cook and do farm chores well enough, and that's what I need. I'd be mad to think love comes without time. It's not her fault I was immediately attracted to her.

He looked back at her. She was staring out over the prairie, arms clasped across her waist. She might think marrying for protection was worth the commitment, but what would happen when she decided she had enough of this life? She could sneak away, leaving him unable to marry ever again.

But then, he'd already vowed never to get tangled up with another bride.

The rippling grasses undulated in the breeze all around her, tall enough to whip around her slight hips.

How could he live with her platonically? He looked up at the clouds as they breezed past. *Would you truly ask that of me?* No answer sounded from the sky, but he felt a peace. How he kept his thoughts pure when looking upon other attractive women would work . . . for now.

Julia was right, though; they were strangers. But they

wouldn't be strangers for long. And with time, caring—if not love—would come. He'd not force her faster than he'd force any woman he might court. They were just going through the marriage ceremony first for convenience.

"Julia?" He crossed the distance between them.

Her glistening eyes turned to him. Pink tinged her cheeks. Never before had he been so tempted to comfort someone. He grabbed both of her elbows and held on, though she tried to step from his hold. "I can build an extra bedroom. It can always be a nursery later on." He kept his gaze locked on her to see her reaction.

Her arms pulled in closer to her body. "For . . . for an orphan?"

"You don't have to be afraid of me." He tried to talk as soothingly as possible. "We'll go slowly. Goodness knows we've known each other for less than a month. But I'd never force you to do anything until you were ready."

"And what if I'm never ready?" Her chin tilted up in the air, and her words came out strangled. "Would you keep your word?"

He examined the faraway look in her eyes and the sheen of wetness that had taken up residence across the big, beautiful brown centers. Her tremble reverberated through his fingers. Scared. He wanted to pull her into his arms, but he knew that would not help. "Did someone hurt you?"

She quickly looked down to the side and swallowed several times in a row. He kept his hands from gripping her any harder. Someone had hurt her. Thinking of a man harming her made him want to punch something. A lot of things.

Her lips stayed pressed against each other. She wasn't going to talk about it.

Tugging ever so slowly, he finally convinced her to take a

step toward him. When she was close enough, he pushed her head against his chest.

Could he help her overcome her hurt? Once she realized she had nothing to fear from him, she'd come around. He'd have to be sensitive. And patient.

"You have my word."

Chapter 7

Julia toweled her hair while looking at herself in the glass in the Stantons' cabin. No wonder Dex and Rachel hadn't said much when she'd asked them to witness at her wedding. Her face looked like she'd met with death itself.

She picked up the mother-of-pearl brush that had belonged to her mother. Losing count of her strokes, she absent-mindedly continued until her hand tired. It was hard enough keeping her eyes open.

The feel of Everett's arms around her had disturbed her sleep for three nights in a row. Being enwrapped in a man's arms whom she never intended to get close to was wrong.

But it felt right.

And the mental churning of what was right and wrong had stolen the sleep she'd needed to look beautiful on her wedding day. She examined her reflection. Puffy eyelids. Red-streaked eyes. Pale, blotchy skin. No bride should look like this.

Maybe her face was trying to tell her something.

Everett tried not to squirm in the rickety chair in the back of the church. The preacher spat and hollered. Hard to imagine this fiery man performing his wedding ceremony. Reverend Vale favored the same rant, scaring his parishioners enough to lace their consciences with guilt if they didn't return to hear him spew the same thing the next month. Everett assessed the preacher's speech and identified repeated bits of monologue. The sermon was almost over. His pocket watch said 11:38. He'd be marrying Julia anytime now.

Next to him, old Lady Fritz cleared her throat and glared.

He stopped his jiggling feet.

His ears tuned out the rest of the sermon, and his gaze sought Julia sitting up front next to Rachel and Emma. He had paced outside church before the service, so the chairs near them had filled before he calmed enough to sit still.

He halted his restless feet again.

Julia sat ramrod straight in the dress she'd worn when she stepped off the train. An ivory dress full of little flowers. He remembered a huge red bow around her waist, though he couldn't see it. Her hat seemed alive, topped with feathers that moved in the drafts blowing through the structure that doubled as a school during the winter.

He'd been afraid she wouldn't come to church. He'd been afraid she would.

"Our Father, which art in heaven . . ."

Everett bowed his head and crushed the hat in his hands. He tried to focus on the prayer, but his mind refused.

"It is with great pleasure that I announce the engagement and nuptials between Everett Cline and . . ." Reverend Vale glanced at a piece of paper in his hand, "Julia Lockwood following the service. Before you leave, please stay and witness the first wedding I have the pleasure of performing among you."

Everett choked and covered it with a cough. Murmurs

floated around him. He didn't know where to look. He'd not asked for the congregation to witness.

"Congratulations, Everett!" Mr. Fritz clapped him on the shoulder. "Couldn't find a prettier girl this side of the Mississippi, I reckon."

A whisper rasped behind him. "She's actually going to do it?"

Sweat formed on his brow.

"The last mail-order bride that pretty was Jonesey's wife." Another low male voice responded to the previous man. "And you know how long that lasted."

A snigger popped out. "She wasn't anywhere near that pretty. I give her three months."

Everett's hat was an unrecognizable wad in his hands. Had he fooled himself? He'd never met Jonesey's wife, but he knew the man had fallen for the pretty mail-order bride he'd married. Then half a year later, she'd left him with no warning.

The abandoned man had advised him not to trust a mail-order bride after he'd heard about Kathleen marrying Carl, but Everett had dismissed Jonesey's counsel.

And then Helga came . . . and chose Ned Parker.

Everett gripped the edge of his seat. Julia was different. She'd asked to marry him. She wanted to marry him. But then again, not a real marriage. His stomach flopped.

"Would the couple please proceed to the front?" Reverend Vale's smile beamed. The gaiety seemed odd after his fierce preaching face.

Everett clamped his hand on the back of the chair in front of him. He pushed himself to his feet, testing their steadiness before unclamping his hand. Though every muscle told him to flee, he moved forward. The faces of most of his neighbors displayed well-wishes as he moved to the front.

He'd given his word, though it might hurt him in the end. His mind shut off thinking. It was time for doing. Tugging on his coat, he tried to make it lie flat. His hands shook in the attempt.

Julia arrived before him, front and center. She didn't look at him, just the preacher.

He stopped next to her. Her rosy-cheeked face turned his direction for a second before returning to the pastor. The quiver in her lip told him she had pushed herself up front too.

Holding his *Book of Common Prayer*, Reverend Vale trailed his finger across the pages as he read aloud.

"'Dearly beloved, we are gathered together here in the sight of God, and in the face of this Company, to join together this Man and this Woman in holy Matrimony; . . .'"

Everett forced himself to stand still.

"'. . . which is commended of Saint Paul to be honourable among all men; and therefore is not by any to be entered into unadvisedly or lightly; but reverently, discreetly, advisedly, soberly, and in the fear of God.'"

Everett trembled. What had he done? His eyes shut.

God, forgive me for rushing into a sacred union.

Reverend Vale, perhaps hungry or impatient, let only a small sliver of silence interrupt his reading upon asking whether the congregation, bride, or groom had an impediment to the marriage. His voice boomed straight into Everett's face. "'Wilt thou have this Woman to be thy wedded Wife, to live together . . .'"

Everett couldn't concentrate on the words. Fortunately, at the pause he knew to say, "I do."

Julia echoed the same a few seconds later.

Did she really? Until death parted them? He took in her tiny nose, long neck, and petite form. Would he have to live with her and not touch her? Or would she end his agony and run off like Jonesey's wife? Was there a shred of hope he'd be able to overcome her fear of men so he could take her in his arms and feel her melt into his embrace, instead of resisting?

He stared at the top button of the preacher's shirt. He'd go crazy if he didn't stop thinking.

"The ring, Everett?"

He scrunched his eyebrows at the minister.

Reverend Vale ducked his head and whispered, "The ring?"

"Oh." Everett felt his pockets before remembering he didn't have one. "It's . . . I don't have one with me."

The minister frowned. He glanced at his book for a few seconds. "Then take her hand."

Everett clasped Julia's equally clammy fingers in his.

"Repeat after me: With this pledge, I thee wed."

Everett spoke the words verbatim.

Julia's slipping hand stole his attention. He gripped tighter lest her sweaty hand break free from his.

"Amen." The whole congregation startled him with the end.

"You may now kiss the bride."

Her wide eyes turned to face him. Pretty as a doe startled in a dewy flower-filled meadow.

His smile disappeared. The thought of her lips touching his, her skin against his own, ratcheted up his heartbeat. How had he been so ignorant to believe he could behave himself with this woman under the roof of his one-room cabin? The words they'd repeated before God meant he could take her into his arms and hold her all night long. Every night.

Every bride had hurt him, but this one . . . this one would trump them all. And he'd just agreed to allow her to do so for the rest of his days.

How could he kiss her?

The murmur creeping about the room grew louder in his ears.

She peeped up at him through dark lashes. His gaze wandered down to her mouth. A mouth he'd been commanded to kiss. Her sharp intake of breath drew him in. And for a second, nothing but the feel of her lips existed.

"Congratulations, Miss Lockwood." An older woman Julia had met at the mercantile the day she arrived in Salt Flatts quickly covered her mouth with a gloved hand. "I mean, Mrs. Cline."

I'm Mrs. Cline.

The next man in line stepped forward. "Nice to meet you, Mrs. Cline. I'm Mr. Stewart and this is my . . ."

An older man in a patched coat penetrated the haze and took her hand. "Congratulations on your marriage. What a happy day."

"Yes, thank you." Her mind whirled at the attempt to remember the names of people introducing themselves. Julia's cheeks ached. Perhaps more from the falsity behind the smile than the smile itself. And her lips buzzed. She'd rubbed them with her hand, but the feeling of Everett's kiss wouldn't disappear.

At the end of the line, Rachel hugged her neck. She called over to Everett a few feet away. "Come, you two. Let's eat."

Rachel's quilt lay under a tree away from the rest of the congregation. A young lady with strawberry-blond hair frizzed about her forehead sat near William, but other than her, Julia was relieved no more strangers wanted to see her happy face. She lowered herself to the ground and let the smile drop.

Dex placed a basket beside her. "Rachel made two lunches. With Nancy's basket, we should be able to fill William's stomach." The girl next to William blushed prettily. He stopped rifling through his mother's basket and made a silly face at his father.

Everett lowered himself next to Dex, but stopped halfway down. He straightened and looked at Julia. She tilted the basket in his direction to indicate they should share, and he moved to sit next to her, the basket between them.

Dex prayed, and Julia pulled the food from the basket Rachel had packed. She hadn't thought about eating after church. Filling her trunks had been all she was capable of doing last night.

John, of course, chatted away, oblivious to the adults' silence. Nancy and William were in their own world, and soon he assisted her to her feet, and they walked off hand in hand. Ambrose ran off to play after stuffing one last bite into his mouth. Emma busily stuffed grass and rocks into her pockets.

Julia fiddled with her fried chicken. Her basket overflowed with special foods. Her heart pooled in a puddle of warmth at her friend's gesture of making such a special meal for her. And all she could do was pick.

She reached in for more, but instead of food, her fingers bumped into Everett's. She withdrew her hand as if she'd found fire. He held her gaze for a second before lowering his eyes and pulling out two biscuits. He handed her one, his focus resting on her mouth again.

Turning away, she tore the flaky pastry apart before nibbling on it. Her nerves were out of control; she hoped the awkwardness would leave after a few days.

John's conversation waned with the amount of food he ate, and Rachel tried to fill the silent gaps with funny things the kids had done that week. Stories everyone had already heard or witnessed. Julia tried to chuckle at the right places, but all she could do was think of Everett sitting beside her. And try not to think of Everett at all. His even breathing kept her from succeeding.

They all fidgeted, ready to go. Except her. Maybe she'd never be prepared to go. He'd promised her he'd wait until she was ready, but the shudder that went through him at their kiss frightened her. What if he didn't? What if he . . .

Her stomach twisted with nausea. Staying forever in the churchyard was not a luxury she had. She'd committed herself to this path.

Everett stood and brushed off his slacks. "I need to catch Mr. Jackson before he leaves." He strode away.

Dex grabbed the baskets. "I'll gather the boys."

John followed in his father's wake.

Rachel stared at her with an empathetic turn of her brow, pulling Emma onto her lap. "Are you feeling well, honey?"

Julia tossed her biscuit toward a bunch of robins and swiped at the crumbs on her skirts. "No."

Rachel reached over and squeezed her hand, stopping her attack on the biscuit particles. Scooting over, she hugged her from the side. "I know Everett. You'll be just fine. I'd never have matched any woman with a man unless I would have happily released my own daughter into his care."

Julia watched him in animated conversation with a short, stocky man. His flash of a smile was so charming. So like Theodore's. She groaned. "I shouldn't have married him."

Rachel squeezed her tighter. "Even people madly in love get a little frightened at the lifelong commitment."

Without a care for propriety, Julia unbuttoned the collar bent on strangling her neck.

After clearing her throat, Rachel grabbed her hand. "I have to apologize." Rachel squirmed. "I never should have meddled in Everett's affairs." She turned and smiled. "But I so badly wanted you to come. I'm glad I interfered this last time for selfish reasons. I'm sure you two will find your way."

Rachel pulled a package from her basket. "A wedding present."

"This last time"? Julia took the slim package. "You didn't have to."

"Of course I did."

Julia tore off the white wrapping paper and exposed an embroidered housewife, stocked with needles and thread. "Ugh. Sewing."

Rachel laughed. "Like marriage, you'll get better at it as you go along. I'll come over and help you finish your dress. And I'll teach you the rest of what I know, but my guess is you'll be plenty occupied with mending. A bachelor's wardrobe is hardly ever in good condition."

She took in a deep breath. Mending Everett's clothes. So many things she hadn't even thought of, though they should have been obvious.

Like her name being Mrs. Julia Cline.

She glanced across the yard to see Everett watching her. His eyes looked sad. He bit his lip and turned his attention back to the men patting him on the back and laughing.

If he didn't hurt her, she'd most likely hurt him.

Chapter 8

Everett pulled into his homestead, his wife at his side. A strange, unsettling thought—his wife. He'd wanted one for years, and now that he had one, it felt odd.

Her eyes had avoided his after the service, and Julia had looked so pale when he'd helped her onto the wagon that he'd decided to let her talk first. But she never had. He stopped the oxen in front of his shack, and before he could say a thing, she started climbing off the wagon. He clambered around to her side before she hit the ground. His hands betrayed him by trembling at her tiny waist, as if he were a boy caught stealing from a store's penny candy jar.

Though her feet touched the ground, he couldn't make his hands let go. It was no sin to have his hands wrapped around her. She kept her eyes level with his chest, and he was glad she wasn't tall enough to look straight into his. She wouldn't like what she saw there. The boning under her shirtwaist felt strange and somehow totally absorbing. His arms struggled, then finally succeeded, to let go.

She peeked up from under her bonnet, a stain of red clouding her cheeks. "I'll go inside."

He swallowed and moved to pull her trunks from the wagon, his hands tingling with the sensation of the shape of her waist impressed upon his palms.

She disappeared through the front door, which still hung loose on its broken leather hinge. Why hadn't he fixed that? Looking over the rest of the cabin, his shoulders slumped. How unworthy of her. But after the locust plague of '74, it had taken longer than he'd hoped to afford the lumber for a new house.

Not that this shack wasn't one of the better ones around these parts. At least it wasn't a soddy, dripping mud every rainstorm. His other brides had come from poor backgrounds, and he'd expected they'd be content with a glass window and a cookstove for a while.

Hefting her largest trunk, he followed Julia inside. She'd seen his tiny house before agreeing to marry him, and he couldn't do anything about it now. He set her luggage on the table and quickly brought in the other two, then swiped the road dust off the trunk's tops. "I'm afraid we don't have room to store all three of these in here. You'll need to choose what you want to keep in one trunk. I'll store the other two in the barn." How different this must be for a city woman. Would throwing her beautiful dresses out with the animals be enough to send her fleeing?

"All right." Her hands clenched tightly in front of her as she stared at the bed, the single bed.

So sure the marriage wouldn't happen, he hadn't even prepared for her arrival. How would he handle tonight? How would she?

He should have done this whole marriage thing conventionally.

"Unfortunately, I've got animals to feed, and well . . . plenty

107

of work to be done." He slapped his hat onto his head. "Like always." He headed for the barn, but turned his head before stepping outside. "I'm, uh, grateful for you coming and helping me. Thank you."

She nodded and then sat on the bed, hugging herself. He closed his eyes. She needed someone to reassure her everything was all right. But somehow, he was certain it couldn't be him. He'd give her time alone. God knew he needed some.

In the barn he shed his jacket and went to work. The novelty of her beauty would wear off, and soon his natural desires would subside. But how long would it take? Could he keep himself busy enough that he wouldn't be thinking of her every hour? Thinking how she was only steps away, but far out of his reach? He chucked a forkful of hay and drove the tines into the compacted dirt floor.

The vision of her large eyes in a china-white face as they stood before the preacher floated before him. Why did she have to be so attractive? The memory of her lips quivering after he'd kissed them floated before him. Why did she have to taste so good?

Why oh why had he agreed not to touch her?

———•———

After he disappeared from sight, Julia relaxed and surveyed the room. An errant curl dropped into her line of sight. Her hair must look awful. She rummaged for her mirror packed at the bottom of her trunk, but stopped halfway through the pile and smiled her first real smile of the day. Pulling her hat off, she yanked out all her hairpins. A simple hairdo would suffice on a farm. No need for perfection and style or worrying about how she looked. She fashioned her hair into a simple bun and took another look in the mirror. Would

Everett mind? Even if he did, being less attractive would be a good thing right now.

She changed out of her fancy dress, found her cap, and placed it over the bun. Tying the strings under her chin, she fingered her jam-packed trunk and wondered where she could put the contents of the other two. No wardrobe. No shelving. No other rooms. Where did Everett keep his clothing?

The interior of the cabin was serviceable, but not homey. Cookstove, washstand, bedstead, table, two chairs, and two sawed stumps for extra seating. A small cupboard above the stove provided the only shelving in the room. Could she get used to this unsightly house? She shrugged. Better than the Stantons' barn.

She looked in the last possible spot—below the bed, a strange contraption of boards wedged high in the wall with one stout post anchoring the corner. Two dusty trunks and a pile of linens were crammed underneath. She dragged the linens out, some folded, most threadbare.

The smaller trunk was the easiest to grab first. She unlatched the top and leaned it against the bed frame. A bit of unease filled her while rummaging through his things, but this was her home now. She'd be expected to take care of his stuff.

Mostly Everett's clothes, crammed in haphazardly, many in need of mending. Matches, soap, and a few other sundries sat along the side.

She shoved the first trunk back and tugged out the larger one.

A sneeze tore through her as she wiped the dust off the top. After wiping the grime off the brass plate with her apron, the faint etching of the initials AGG appeared. Whose trunk was this? His mother's perhaps? She unlatched the case. On top of the contents lay a white linen tablecloth with grapevines embroidered on the edges.

She stood and spread the fine cloth over the table. This dreary cabin could use all the help it could get. Smoothing it with her hand, she scowled. "Needs ironing."

She returned to her knees to see what else might be of use. A large flowered piece of fabric turned out to be a woman's ruffled nightgown.

Odd.

A chemise, bonnet, drawers . . .

Why did Everett have a woman's unmentionables stuffed away under his bed?

Two work dresses, a coat—a whole store of women's effects. At the bottom lay a beautiful quilt of white, pale blue, and orange. It looked and felt new.

Sitting on the bed, she ran a finger over the beautiful even stitching on the blanket's wedding ring pattern. Bending over, she dropped the lid of the trunk back down. AGG. There would be no reason for him to have saved his mother's clothing down to her stockings.

At the picnic, Rachel had mentioned she'd messed with his affairs one last time. What did that mean? Had he lost a wife? Yet most of the items looked new. Julia had only worried about hiding her past, but what was his? So focused on feeling certain she could trust him to act according to her wishes, she hadn't asked him anything about himself. The pain and sadness in his eyes at the church picnic—had that not been directed toward her, but toward this AGG woman? Maybe that's why he said nothing on the way home. He was so still, she hadn't wanted to disturb him.

Julia wasn't sure she wanted to know who these things belonged to, wasn't sure she should pry—might lead him to ask his own questions. Would he compare her to this woman from his past? Of course he would. Her fingers fiddled with the jewelry at her throat. She'd never measure up to a woman who had become his wife in every sense of the word.

Maybe she could get him to talk without saying a thing. Having the quilt spread over his bed and the tablecloth on the table would give him the chance to explain when he saw them. Would it embarrass, irritate, or grieve him to have these things lying about?

Not wanting to see the feminine garments any longer, she repacked the clothing and shoved the trunk under the overhang of the quilt. Her largest trunk would have to remain at the end of the bed.

Her mind and body itched for something to do besides think. She gathered cleaning materials and started scrubbing. She finished scouring the floor, washing the windows, and beating the tick before her stomach told her it was time for dinner. After a simple meal of leftover chicken and bread was prepared, she called out to Everett, but he didn't come, nor was he in the yard or barn. She should have asked him what hours he kept before he left.

An hour later, she threw the scraps into the chicken yard. The moon blazed white in a sea of purple and pink, yet Everett had yet to return.

Would he bed down in the barn? It wasn't right for him to give up his bed for an animal's stall, but she didn't want to think about what would happen if he didn't. The one bed was excessively narrow. Why hadn't he told her when he'd return or what he expected? Was he regretting his decision as much as she was?

The only thing she could work on in the dim lantern light while she waited was his mending. Her muscles ached to recline, but the straight-back kitchen chair did not oblige. Her eyes strained to keep tabs on her stitches as she darned her first sock.

No telling how her patch job would look until the sun rose, but she continued until the toe felt serviceable. A few lonely stars hung in the deep navy sky peeking in through the single windowpane.

She threw the sock in tomorrow's laundry pile. Her back screamed for relief, and her eyes had been at half-mast for the last hour.

Was sleeping on his bed appropriate? Lying across the soft quilt, she enjoyed stretching the muscles in her back. If he didn't bed down in the barn, he could wake her when he returned and tell her where she should sleep. Let him make the decision. She didn't want to talk about it.

Everett rubbed his black horse's neck. "Good night, Blaze. I can't stay outside any longer."

All afternoon and evening he had worked hard. Off in the fields, the barn, the spot where he would build the new house—all to stay away from the cabin. But the flicker of the lamp through its window both called to him and repelled him.

A lump stuck in his throat. No more dawdling. He didn't feel right making his wife sleep in the barn like she had at the Stantons'. And he wouldn't be caught sleeping in a stall if a neighbor came by for help. As he had every few minutes of the day, he imagined sleeping next to her, waking next to her. He couldn't handle that.

He grabbed the old straw tick he'd just finished restuffing and marched to the house.

Of course, he knew what the opinion of some men in town would be about his sleeping on the floor. They'd laugh at him for not taking what was rightfully his. He couldn't deny the temptation of the idea. Though a piece of paper joined them as man and wife, nothing else of substance connected them. What was she really like? Everett gnawed on his lip. He hadn't worked on building a relationship with her, believing she wouldn't stick around.

But she had. Yet no love existed between them. Not even friendship.

His fault.

The broken door made little noise as he closed it. A soft snore permeated the room. Julia's frame lay catty-corner across the bed. Her shoes were still on, their tiny soles poking out from under several layers of skirts.

Her face looked weary, though she was sleeping soundly.

He dumped his tick in the corner and made his way over to her. Squatting beside her, he tried to remove her shoes, but the little buttons stymied him, so he left them alone. He wouldn't be able to slip his pillow out from under her without waking her. She'd bunched both under her head.

He grabbed her tablecloth off the table and folded it for a pillow. He tromped outside and grabbed the horse's blanket.

Though the door opened and closed numerous times, she didn't so much as move. He lowered himself onto the floor and tried to make the blanket cover the majority of his body. Her rhythmic breathing was both unsettling and comforting. He was no longer alone. But he didn't feel any less lonely curled on the floor across from the bed.

Once his vision adjusted to the dark, he tried to make out her face.

Her generous lips and the dark rim of eyelashes curving on her cheeks were barely discernible. Her hair, loose and wavy, blended with the shadows. The desire to twirl her hair around his fingers would keep him awake, so he turned to the wall and willed himself to sleep.

⁕

Julia stretched and turned toward the light. Rays of morning sun illuminated the dingy room. The door stood ajar. She pulled the quilt over her head.

Bolting upright, she squinted beside her, then around the room.

The tablecloth lay wadded up in the corner atop a small tick she was sure hadn't been in the cabin yesterday. So that's where he'd slept. If her feet had complained about their sleeping arrangements, she was sure Everett's muscles hollered at him for how they'd been treated. How could one sleep with no coverings on a plank floor with large drafty gaps?

No food smells filled the room, only whiffs of coffee.

She wiggled her toes against her boots, her feet angry with how they'd been kept all night. She wrapped the quilt around herself for warmth and walked to the door.

At the well, a single crow perched at its edge. The oxen tore grass in the nearby pasture. No Everett. Surely he wasn't going to try to pretend they didn't live together. She made more coffee, scrambled some eggs, and waited.

She ate her food before it grew cold and stared at the tick and tablecloth on the floor in the corner.

A few hours later, she threw Everett's cold eggs into the chicken yard and tromped to the barn. "Ready to go, boys?" she murmured to the oxen while fumbling with hooking them to the wagon. "I sure am."

Chapter 9

Everett's stomach growled. He'd been stupid to leave without breakfast, but he hadn't wanted to wake his wife. Her sleeping face looked happier than before he'd blown out the lamp last night.

She'd have plenty of days in the future to wake ahead of the rooster's crow. One day off wouldn't hurt anything. She'd have their whole lifetime together to work.

Whistling a tune in time with the horse's steps, he turned Blaze up the familiar path. The rabbits he'd shot hung from his saddle and bounced against his legs. He might not feel like he could fully handle being around her, but he could start the process of showing Julia she didn't have to dread a relationship with him. He would begin with gifts—what could be gleaned from the prairie, anyway. Nothing he could afford would impress a city woman. Not one who wore a traveling dress that cost more than Rachel Stanton's entire wardrobe.

Hopefully Julia knew a good way to prepare rabbit. He'd skin them for her before heading out to the fields. At the paddock he let Blaze in to graze and walked into the shack.

The small room was empty, her quilt twisted in a heap at

the foot of the bed. She'd made eggs for breakfast, but there were none leftover. He put his shotgun above the door and laid the rabbits on the table. Heading to the well, bucket in hand, he glanced around, listening for her.

He quit whistling. Was she in the barn?

He pulled the overlarge door open. The interior's stillness caused the hair on his neck to stand at attention. His empty hands clenched, and he wished his gun still resided within his grip. Dimple and Curly were not in their stalls. The wagon no longer waited against the north wall. Everett chewed on the side of his cheek and checked his desire to swear.

She'd left him. Just like the other brides. But this one had the audacity to take his team with her.

He glared at the straw-littered floor and gritted his teeth. His savings weren't enough to replace the team, tack, and wagon and still have enough to see him through the winter if his crops failed. She could have left him without causing so much trouble. Sure, he'd be made fun of, left unable to marry again, and without help. But how dare she take his livelihood with her?

He raced over to Blaze. "Sorry to cut your break short, boy, but we've got a woman to chase down."

Everett kicked Blaze to a gallop. Ahead, Julia's bonnet ribbons flitted behind her as she drove the team toward Salt Flatts. Thankfully, she hadn't tried to forge off in another direction, or he might not have found her. Relief, crippled with anger, surged through his body. He pushed Blaze faster.

Had she planned to leave his team unattended at the train depot? Any number of drifters or boomers would have stolen them once they realized no one claimed the wagon.

Blaze's hooves thundered as he neared Julia. She yanked on the reins. The wrong thing to do. But thankfully, Dimples and Curly barely changed speed.

Everett's body tensed as he called, "Whoa."

His well-behaved team settled to a stop. He turned hard in his saddle to glare at her. "Why take my oxen? Didn't you realize I would need them?" Blaze pranced under him, so he relaxed the pressure his legs exerted on the horse's sides.

Her eyes grew rounder. "I didn't know. You . . . didn't have them with you, so . . . I figured it'd be all right."

"You figured that would be all right?" He tempered his voice, not wanting to yell at a woman. "I can't work without them."

"But you didn't use them yesterday." She played with the neckline of her dress. Couldn't the woman leave her collar alone?

"And so if I don't use them once in a while, I don't need them anymore?" Blaze sidestepped again. Everett pulled on the horse's reins with more jerk than necessary. "Did you not think someone would steal my team if you just left them hitched to a post? You could have at least ridden to the Stantons' and had them take you to town instead of abandoning my animals in Salt Flatts."

"Why would I abandon them?" Her face had lost its pretty pink color.

He almost wanted to apologize for causing her to pale, but he wouldn't, not when she ought to feel bad.

"I don't know what you're talking about. Wouldn't they be fine for a few minutes in front of the general store?" Her brows met in the middle, and she cocked her head. "Or did you think . . ." Her face relaxed, and she placed a finger to her lips.

117

His heart sidestepped with Blaze. Hot shame crept up his neck. "So you weren't going to ride away with my team?" He swallowed hard. "You . . . weren't going to take the train?"

She tilted her head and laid both hands in her lap. "Did you think I was leaving? With no trunk?" One eyelid was lower than the other. Adorable and maddening.

He glanced in the back. Nothing but dirt and straw filled the corners. "Uh . . ."

She turned her head to look toward the team. "You were not around yesterday, and you didn't let me know where you were going this morning." She played with the leather straps in her hands and continued in a soft voice. "I figured I needed to be about my work. I would have asked you, if I knew where you were, but . . . We needed supplies, but I didn't . . . think." She fiddled with the reins. "I shouldn't have taken the wagon."

He squirmed in the saddle, wishing he hadn't run after her in a fury. "I'm sorry that I thought—"

"I wasn't running, Everett." Her head shook decisively, and she took a slow breath before turning to him. "But now that you're here, would you like me to purchase supplies with my own money or your credit? I would have asked earlier, but . . ."

Could he feel any more of a fool? She was doing as he wanted, looking after his homestead without being asked, and in a blind rage, he'd called her a thief. Giving her more reason to find him contemptible. Good start at curing her fear of men.

"My credit, of course. Carl will do that for you, no questions."

She nodded and collected the reins. "Will you be joining me in town?"

He ached to flee her presence more than his stomach yearned for food. "No, thank you. I have work at home."

"I made a list. Would you like to check it over and see if you need to add anything?"

"Uh . . . no." He coughed and attempted to pull his voice down an octave, back into its normal range. "You just get whatever you think we need." Even if she used more credit than his crops would bring in this summer, he wouldn't say a thing.

"Thank you, Everett."

He couldn't even look at her. "No need to thank me." She had nothing to thank him for. He swallowed hard. "I'm right sorry that I assumed you were leaving. It's just that . . ." She didn't need to know how many other women had found him not good enough to stick around for. "I'm sorry."

He tipped his hat at her nod and kicked Blaze's flanks for home. He ought to go with her into town for supplies, but he just couldn't.

When Julia returned home yesterday, Everett had apologized again, but the second the words were out of his mouth, he'd fled to the barn. Whatever had possessed the man to think she'd run away? Didn't he realize she'd not have become a mail-order bride if she had tons of options for her life? She had married and given up her last name for his. She was stuck.

She flipped her potato cake over, the hot oil popping out of the skillet and burning her hand for a short second. Maybe *stuck* wasn't a very good word to use around Everett. It would play to her advantage for him not to know she had nowhere to go and that her continued presence relied on how he treated her. That would keep him from pushing to become intimate anytime soon. Then once a pattern of nonphysical friendship became routine, they would simply continue the habit. She hoped it would be that simple.

She set the table and sliced some bread. A quick glance out the window revealed no Everett.

He said he'd return for lunch. Was his promise empty? Empty promises were not good. If he couldn't keep this small one, why would he keep the one she'd wrangled out of him when she agreed to marry him?

Shouts in the yard snatched her attention, and she stepped out the door. A wagon pulled around the barn. It wasn't the Stantons.

Her teeth bit into her lip. She didn't feel comfortable welcoming people into the house without Everett. The shack didn't feel like her place yet. More like she was intruding upon the dilapidated structure. She wiped her hands on her apron and forced herself outside.

"Ho there, neighbor!" A vaguely familiar skinny man stood and jumped off his seat. A shiver ran down her spine; this man's slimy leer had given her gooseflesh at the barn raising.

"Hello, Ned." Everett's voice boomed from her right. He came around the corner and swiped off his hat. "Helga, good morning."

Julia heaved a sigh of relief. The silent woman had been hidden by her husband on the bench seat. Welcoming her into the house would have been fine, but her husband . . . Julia stepped into the sun and smiled, but the smell of burning potatoes stopped her. "Food! Excuse me." She ran back in to scrape the cakes off the pan. She frowned at her two slightly charred lumps of potatoes.

The group of three stepped through the door.

"I'm sorry, I don't have enough for everyone, but give me a

moment and I'll make more." Scowling at the two blackened disks she and Everett would be eating, she grabbed another few spuds and began peeling the skins off in long curls.

"We've already eaten, ma'am." Ned held his hat in his hand, his mouth in a crooked smile.

She stopped halfway through the potato. Like the eyes of the patrons at Halson's bar, where she'd learned to cook, Ned's squinty eyes roved over her body while he talked. "But I could always use more lunch if you're offering. I bet you couldn't help but make everything taste sweet."

The panic swirling in her gut was the exact reason she'd decided to get married. Ned could look, but if he touched, her husband would teach him a lesson. She glanced at Everett. His frown was definitely directed at Ned, but he indicated with his head that she should offer the Parkers food.

She smiled at the heavy, drooping woman. "Helga? Shall I make you some?"

"No, thank you. You're very kind."

The group settled about the table while Julia scrambled potatoes together.

Ned leaned back in his chair. "I had to shoot two coyotes this morning. They were after my sheep. They killed a lamb before I could even get out of bed and grab the gun." At the sound of his spitting on the floor, Julia turned and saw the dark stain near his boot. Everett shook his head slightly, his eyes pointedly telling her to refrain from speaking. She gritted her teeth, turned, and dumped the potato mixture into the pan. How dare Ned spit on her clean floor.

"You're the best tanner in these parts," Ned said. "Hate for the furs to go to waste. Haven't ever taken care of one." He let the chair legs thump to the ground. "I know this is awfully inconvenient, but thought you might help me before the sun goes down. We'd leave Helga here." His tone of voice clearly indicated he regarded his wife as a nuisance.

Julia scraped the pan and glanced at Mrs. Parker in the corner shadows. She looked more vulnerable and defeated than she had the day of the barn raising. Julia suppressed the indignation the hefty woman didn't display. Since Ned made her skin crawl with his very presence, maybe she couldn't read the situation correctly. Perhaps he did right by Helga and she was simply reserved.

"You didn't bring them with you?" At Ned's shake of the head, Everett's face darkened. "You skinned them already?"

"No, but they ain't but a few hours old."

"Next time, you ought to skin them as soon as they're dead. The skins come off easier."

The group ate in silence. As soon as the men's plates were clean, Everett followed Ned out the door. So much for talking over tonight's plans.

Helga's fingers fiddled with the button on her shabby blouse. "I sorry, Mrs. Cline, if I am inconvenient."

Julia placed a hand on her shoulder. "Actually, it'll be nice to have someone to talk to while I sew." Or try to anyway.

"I know how it is to have no one to talk. 'Tis a lonely prairie."

"Yes, the sound of the wind here sometimes sounds like the ocean, though. I like that." Julia stacked the dishes.

Helga made a sour face, making the lines around her eyes and mouth more prominent. "I remember the ocean. Made me sick."

"You mean on a boat?" She'd always wanted to sail.

"Yes. Long hours in a boat cabin. Sick all day. Sick three days after off the boat."

"How long ago was that?"

"Two years." Helga crossed over to the stove. "I should help you."

Julia washed while Helga dried and talked about her trip from Germany. The description sounded like a nightmare. Maybe losing the opportunity to sail across the sea was nothing to be depressed over. Helga's thick accent was hard to get used to, but after an hour, Julia barely noticed it anymore.

Julia leaned on her broom. "So . . . you came to America to marry Ned?"

Helga glanced up at her, a puzzled look in her eye. "No, I came for work, but I not find cooking job, and I not want factory. Worked in factory my whole life in Germany. I come to America for better. Then I came to Kansas . . ." She grabbed a dry pot and wiped it again.

She hadn't meant to disturb or pry. Marriage to Ned couldn't be easy, and it wouldn't make good conversation anyway. Julia took the pan from Helga. "Why don't we sit? Did you bring any needlework?" Julia grabbed the new pillow she'd finished stuffing with the feathers she'd bought yesterday morning in town. Everett's pillows were too thin, and she couldn't let him continue to sleep without one.

The makeshift pallet still lay in the corner. Their neighbors would have figured out the sleeping arrangement as soon as they had stepped in the door. Was Helga and Ned's relationship as distant as hers? Was what she asked of Everett out of the ordinary for brides in similar circumstances? Julia bit her lip. Would the woman look down on her for where her husband slept?

Helga looked into her eyes. "Hard to live with strange man, yes?"

A cold shiver trickled across her scalp at the question so closely echoing her thoughts. She dropped her gaze.

Helga tugged the unfinished pillow from her grasp. "I will help you."

She stared at the feathers floating from the open seam. "I guess I'll start on the pillowcase."

"I feel sorry. I am in the way."

"No apologies. I have, uh, many things I'd like to ask."

"Like will marriage to a stranger become easy?"

Julia didn't turn to look at her but nodded.

Helga shrugged. "I know not. I think I have a difficult man. He is very . . ." She stared at the wall across from her and said no more.

Julia didn't want to intrude on the thoughts that pulled Helga's mouth further into a frown, so she concentrated on cutting her material straight. Did Ned beat her? Was he involved with other women? Could Helga get away if she desired? Julia chopped at the material as if it were Ned.

After a few minutes, Helga turned. The sides of her mouth drooped, resisting the smile her lips attempted to form. "Yes, Ned is difficult. But Everett is not so difficult . . . a smart woman would marry him."

Julia sniffed. "But he's difficult to talk to."

"But he talks nice." Helga bobbed her head. "Talks like he likes you. Much better than Ned."

"You've heard Everett talk about me?"

Helga's eyebrows scrunched. "No."

"Then who does he like?"

"Everybody. He is nice to all people. Even ugly, no good ones. Like me." Helga's voice ended in a whisper.

"You shouldn't say such things."

Helga attacked the ticking in her hands with a vengeance for a few minutes before slowing. "But Everett, he will like you. Ned likes you."

That last part Julia refused to take as a compliment. The leer he'd trained on her at the barn raising had made her skin prickle. And worse, today he had assessed her boldly while his wife and Everett stood beside him. Did Everett see how Ned looked at her?

She began the pillowcase's hem before turning the conversation away from their vexing husbands. "We should get together often. Work would be more pleasant with you around." Though that might bring Helga's husband around more often. She grimaced. But how could she ask her not to bring Ned along?

A glimmer in Helga's eye accented the tiny smile on her face. "I would like that, but I not know if I can." She sighed.

Julia reached over and squeezed her hand. If she could be an excuse for this lady to have time away, she'd welcome her over anytime. "Well, whenever you get the chance, you come. Even if you haven't asked. Come when you can."

"Thank you," Helga whispered.

Her neighbor seemed to be finished talking, so Julia kept her remaining questions to herself. In the neighborhood where she grew up, a lady down the street had been harmed often by her husband's heavy-handedness. When a couple next door tried to have a talk with the man, the poor woman's bruises multiplied.

She would have to tread lightly.

But one thing was answered: things could have been a lot worse. She could still be unmarried and unprotected from men like Ned. Or she could have succumbed to the pressure back home and married Theodore—smoother than Ned, richer than Ned, but probably no different inside.

If Helga could endure her lot, Julia had no reason not to as well. She would focus on the fact that her situation was much better than some. And that Helga's opinion of Everett was high. Surely she'd married a good man, even if he was a bit inhibited.

———•◦•———

Merlin raced the wagon to the barn as Everett and Ned rolled into the yard. Preparing the coyote pelts had been easy. Easy for Ned, anyway. He seemed content to let Everett do all the work. Everett had tried to lead him through the steps, but Ned said he learned better by watching.

Everett scowled at Ned's turned head and halted his team in front of the barn. Somehow he doubted Ned needed that much watching to get the hang of things. If he asked again for help, he'd tell him there was no more visual teaching left, reiterate the steps, and send him on his way.

The few times he'd worked with his closest neighbor, he'd hoped his ill feelings toward the man were baseless. But he'd never appeared to be anything but incompetent and shady. And now entirely too interested in Julia.

The smell of cake floated from the house's open broken door. He should get to fixing the hinge, but that required time around Julia. His body told him to take advantage of the time he had with her, but his heart told him to stay away.

But Everett couldn't help but wonder if his streak of bad luck with brides was over. Julia had basically called him a fool for thinking she was leaving yesterday morning. And he had been, but with no other attachment to him than a signature in the church records, could he be certain she wouldn't leave him later—like Mrs. Jonesey—especially when she'd decided to have no true marital attachment to him?

Ned followed him into the cabin. Helga's nearly cheery face receded into her ever-present frown. He'd never seen the woman smile before, but the hint of her half smile was already gone, along with Julia's.

Not happy I'm home. Julia looked toward Ned, who sported the smile the two women had lost. *Or maybe Ned makes her uncomfortable. He's definitely making me so.*

"Smells good in here, ladies. Good eatin', I'm sure." Ned planted himself in the same chair he'd sat in at lunch.

Hopefully Julia figured on him staying.

"It will be a little while, Mr. Parker." She gave him a pained smile before heading to the stove. "These sweet cakes Helga whipped up need a bit more time."

Ned leaned back and surveyed the room. Everett watched his eyes take a second look at the pallet on the floor. Ned's mouth twitched, and then he craned his neck around in Julia's direction. "So, how you enjoying Kansas?"

"All right, I guess. The wind takes getting used to."

"Sure looks like you're agreeing with the weather to me. Right pretty in that fancy getup."

She glanced down at her clothing and then at Ned.

Everett's blood boiled at the man's compliment. Of course, one would have to be blind not to notice how well she filled out her dress, but the oily smoothness behind Ned's voice rankled.

Julia returned to her cooking and barely looked at Ned. "Thank you, Mr. Parker."

"No need to call me Mr. Parker. Being neighbors, we can go by our Christian names. I'll call you Julia, and you can call me Ned."

"All right." She put down her spatula with more force than necessary.

Ned's gaze moved from Julia's head down to her toes. A smirk formed on his lips.

Everett's fists balled under the table as he glared at Ned's profile. In front of him, in his own home, this man was leering at his wife. Unlike Helga, Julia had married him. No man would steal her. Everett stood and knocked over his chair.

Helga squeaked.

Helga. How could he dress down her husband in front of her?

"Excuse me, I have to check on the livestock in the few minutes we have to spare." Everett turned to his neighbor, whose cocky grin had disappeared. "Mind helping me with the choring?"

The man lazily unfolded himself from the chair. "'Spect that's fair."

Everett stalked off to the barn, taking a glance over his shoulder to make sure Ned was following. First inside the barn, Everett slammed his fist into a stall door, wishing the wood swinging away from him was Ned's face. Maybe he ought to punch the man's pointy nose deep into his pock-marked skin.

He took a calming breath. Though he was sure Ned wouldn't do anything unseemly with his own wife beside him, the man needed supervision and a talking to. And if his neighbor didn't back down, he'd use him as an excuse to exercise his fists.

When Ned stepped inside, Everett threw a milk bucket at him. The man caught it and eyed him.

Everett tipped his head in the direction of his house. "I'm thinking you need to be keeping that look you gave my wife for your woman alone."

Ned's eyes narrowed. "Don't know what you're talking about."

Everett tested the weight of the rake in his hand and gritted his teeth. "You know what I'm talking about. Don't look at Julia that way again."

Shrugging, Ned leaned against a stall post. "Not much you can do about a man admiring a lady. Simply nature. And you happen to have finally snagged one of the prettiest gals in Kansas. Can't blame a man for noticing."

He gripped the rake harder. "Keep your noticing to yourself from now on."

"Sure." Ned drawled. He raised his bucket. "I'm supposin' you're wanting me to do the woman's chore?"

Actually, he'd rather have him leave, but perhaps now that he knew he was being watched, the man would shape up. A neighbor was too valuable of a commodity during harvest and other times of emergency. "You want milk with your sweet cakes, right?"

Ned rolled his eyes. "If Helga made them, we'll each need a gallon to wash them down." He moved to the cow and settled himself into her side.

Sorrow for Helga quenched his anger. Though she'd jilted Everett, she didn't deserve a man like Ned. No woman did. Ned was lucky to have a hard-working woman. But he was also blessed that no gorgeous lady had married him, moved into his house, and sent his mind places she didn't want it to go—at least not yet. Or maybe never.

Taking a deep breath, Everett mucked the nearest stall. Julia was his wife, and those thoughts were fitting. But if she didn't love him . . .

Despite the madness she would put him through, she didn't deserve to be ogled by that miserable excuse for a man. Maybe the best thing would be to send the Parkers home with sweet cakes in hand.

Chapter 10

Ned banged open the door and thumped a bucket of milk onto the table. "Pack up your cakes. We're going."

Helga plunked her tin cup back onto the table and was gathering her sweet cakes before Julia could even walk over to the stove.

"I am sorry, Julia. I must go."

Julia took one look at Ned, who raked his eyes over her like she were something to be consumed and thrown away. Though she felt sorry for Helga being hustled away, she would not insist they stay. "Good-bye, Helga. Please come again when you can." She forced herself to nod at Ned.

"Thanks to you for having me. I enjoy very much." The lady's shoulders drooped as she scuttled out behind her husband, who hoisted himself up onto the driver's seat.

After their wagon disappeared over the ridge, Everett stepped out of the barn and took a few steps toward the house. "Did you have a good talk with Helga?"

"Yes." Why hadn't he seen their guests off? She moved to the railing. "I . . . I'm a bit worried about her. Do you know them well?"

He shook his head. "No, but I'm glad you put a smile on her face this afternoon. I don't think she smiles often. Maybe you ought to invite her over. Just her . . . you know, for female companionship. She'd probably enjoy your company. Give you someone to talk to." He dropped his gaze to the dirt. "Well, I've got animals to attend."

"Would you like a cake? Helga left us a couple."

"Thanks, but I'll have to eat them later." Everett pivoted and walked right back to the barn.

Did he dislike talking to her so much he had to leave the second he found himself alone with her? Julia wanted a love-less marriage, not a friendless one.

Loveless. Was that really what she wanted? With slow steps, she returned to the house and readied for bed, no longer inter-ested in dessert. She sat on the bed and stared at the wall. To feel love would be nice, but with a man, that would mean . . .

Pulling off her cameo, she watched the glow of sunset from the open door. A full white moon nestled in a peach-and-magenta-swirled sky. The bottoms of the clouds on the horizon glowed from below as if they were afire. This land wasn't as beautiful as the land surrounding Massachusetts, but the breadth of the horizon and the openness held its own charm.

A bath sounded good. Maybe she could get the feel of Ned's perusal off her. But she couldn't have Everett coming in while she bathed.

Julia rearranged the chairs and grabbed the quilt off the pallet, where she'd thrown it that afternoon. The tick on the floor wouldn't be any more comfortable than the Stantons' barn loft, but she'd have a new pillow stuffed to the perfec-tion of plumpness. She draped the blanket across the chairs' backs for a makeshift screen and pulled the big stock pot over. Cool water would be welcome in this cloying heat, but she'd have to sit on the floor to stay out of sight. She'd need to figure out a better setup for the future.

Julia walked to the barn. Everett's swift strokes with the horse's comb accentuated the muscles moving under his shirt as he brushed.

"Everett?"

He popped up and whirled to face her.

She cleared her throat. "I'm going to wash. Do you want me to save the water for you?"

"A bath would be a good idea. I smell like a coyote."

He did indeed. Smelled awful all the way across the barn.

He returned to his brushing. "But it would be easier to bathe in the creek. I don't have a tub." He stopped his frantic movements and turned. "Unless you bought one in town."

She hadn't thought to. "No." They couldn't bathe in a creek during the winter though. "Could we put that on the list?"

He hung up the animals' brush. "I'll have Hampden order one." He stopped in front of her, his Adam's apple bobbing. "Actually, why don't you order it? Get whatever you want."

She took a step back. The dead meat smell mixed with sweat made her nauseous. Why hadn't Ned smelled so bad? "Anything I want?"

He took a step back as well. "Within reason. But tonight, we can use the creek. Do you know where it is?"

"No." The moon would provide enough light to bathe by, but she didn't know the land well enough to follow directions. He'd have to take her. She swallowed. "Could you show me?"

"Sure." He turned her around and placed a hand at the small of her back. His unexpected touch created a buzz between her shoulder blades. "We'll go together."

She dug her pointy-toed boots into the dirt floor. "To-gether?" Surely he wouldn't force her to do something so unseemly, since he'd promised . . .

His hand slipped off her waist. "Not . . ." He cleared his throat. "Not bathe together. I'll take you there and wait my turn since it's a long walk, and there are animals to watch for."

"Oh." Her voice squeaked. "Give me a minute." She hurried to the cabin, deciding on what to take.

Animals? What kind of animals? And where would he wait his turn?

Everett opened the door Julia had slammed behind her.

She spun around, her nightgown crumpled against her chest.

Everett met her gaze for a second. "I need to get my things too." He pulled out his trunk and grabbed his long undershirt, towel, and a bar of soap.

Her eyes widened when she turned toward him. "Maybe this isn't a good idea. I've never bathed in a creek before."

"No, it's a fine idea." They had to live together. Might as well figure out how to go about this now. "At night, no chores can be done, so it's a good time. Are you ready?"

Her eyes closed, and he could tell she was debating. Did she think no honorable men existed in this world? "I won't watch, if that's what you're thinking."

Redness crept onto her face. "All right."

He headed out the door, and Merlin bounded up. "C'mon, boy. Let's go take a swim in the creek." He needed something to occupy his mind while Julia bathed, and the dog would be just the thing. Everett beckoned her and walked toward a stand of brush. "This way."

When they stepped off into a path overhung by foliage, the shadows deepened. Her voice, barely discernible, trembled behind him. "Maybe we should've brought a lantern."

Although she'd jumped at his touch earlier, he tried again. Finding her arm, he lightly encircled it. "Once we get through this brush, the moonlight will be plenty."

Julia tripped a couple of times on the tree roots his feet skimmed over. After one close call, they slowed.

"I need to get a pair of sturdier boots. Something to work in. Maybe a man's boot."

Her dainty feet enclosed now by myriad buttons were hard to imagine swallowed in a man's shoe. "Put it on the list."

For a while the chirping of crickets, Merlin's panting, and Julia's tiny breaths were all he heard until the sound of hundreds of tiny frogs filled the air. He let go of her arm when they stepped onto the small dirt bank. "This is it." In the daylight, she probably wouldn't be overjoyed to see the muddy water she was about to bathe in.

A broken twig poked out from her hair, so he flicked it away. A wisp of her hair tickled his wrist. He had to stop touching her.

"How are we going to go about this?" She sounded like she was shivering.

"I figured you could go first, and after my bath, I'd escort you home." Sounded odd to be calling his dinky place her home. "I'll head up the bank and find a tree to sit against. Facing the other way, of course. Just make sure you swish around first. Scare off any snakes." He turned, but her hand grabbed his bicep, fingernails digging into his flesh.

"Snakes?" She tugged at him. "I won't bathe with snakes."

He smiled. Definitely a city girl. "They won't want to bathe with you either. They'll swim off if you're there."

"No. You're going first. You shoo them away."

"Fair enough." He helped her climb the embankment and sat her against a tree. "Merlin, you stay here with Julia." He slipped down the embankment and quickly bathed—the cool water exactly what he needed. Once he dressed, he'd have to work hard to keep his mind from envisioning what Julia would be doing in a few minutes.

"It's your turn." Everett's wet hair glinted in the moonlight. The round silver orb reflected in the big black circles of his eyes. She turned and caught a glimpse of his bare legs from the knee down, and her face flamed. He held out his hand. "Let me help you down."

Keeping her gaze off him, she stepped onto the embankment, her heel sinking into mud. How was she going to keep herself clean after she bathed? "I'll wait until you say you're at that tree." Slow-moving ripples glistened on the creek's surface. "You sure there aren't any snakes?"

"Shouldn't be."

Hardly comforting. She took a deep breath. Evidently, she'd be bathing here until a new tub could be ordered. She'd better get used to it. When Everett called that he had turned away, she dropped her things and undressed, trusting he'd respect her enough not to watch. The slimy mud between her toes as she entered the water made her cringe. Could one really get clean in a mud-bottomed creek?

She walked in far enough to stoop and cover herself in water to her shoulders and quickly scrubbed with the bar of soap. She wasn't going to share the water with the snakes any longer than necessary. What if she got bit? She had no idea what to do. How much she needed to learn to survive here. It was overwhelming.

As soon as she left the water, Julia realized she had forgotten a towel. The clothing she'd shed near the creek was soaked through. She growled in frustration. Why hadn't she paid better attention to her things? She had nothing to dry herself with, and she couldn't ask for Everett's towel. She couldn't walk beside him in a thin wet nightgown or don her muddy clothes again either. She'd have to stand and let the night air dry her off. "I'm going to be a little while. Why don't you go home?" she shouted to him from the bank.

"Not a problem. I can wait."

"No. Don't wait. I'll just head home when I'm done."

Animals. Were the snakes all he meant when he mentioned animals?

A long silence followed. Surely he would have said good-bye before he started off.

"I won't do that."

"Leave Merlin with me. He knows the way."

"Sorry, but if you got lost, I wouldn't be able to find you before morning, and I'm not sure Merlin would stay with you. You're still a stranger."

His last sentence couldn't be truer. Well, he'd have to wait. She wrung water from her hair.

"Julia, what's wrong?"

He evidently wasn't going to wait in silence. She sighed. "Nothing. I just forgot my towel, so I'm going to have to wait until I air dry."

"That will take a while in this humid air."

"Right."

"Let me bring you my towel."

She spun in his direction and held her nightgown in front

of her. "No! No need. I'll be dry any second now." Twigs cracking from his direction caused her to don her nightgown with haste. "Don't come near me. I'm coming." After gathering her muddy clothes in a tight bundle, she started toward the tree where she'd sat earlier. "Just you go first. I'll walk farther behind."

"As you wish." His outline showed him waiting, with his hands on his hips.

Merlin whined.

"You can lead now. I see you." How crazy must she sound to him? But even she could hear the thick panic in her breathy voice. He slowly turned. It didn't matter what he thought. She couldn't let him see her in nothing but a simple summer nightdress, clinging to her skin. She'd slept in her clothes the last two nights without meaning to, but what should she wear to bed, two feet away from him? It would soon be too hot to hide under a pile of blankets.

She sniffled. Her thoughts were absurd. She was married, but she felt vulnerable—exposed and weak—like that horrible night she'd learned Theodore was only marrying her for her father's business. That she was simply a toy for him to play with.

"Are you all right back there?"

He stood motionless several feet before her, and she stopped in the path. Clamping the bridge of her nose, she dammed the flow of tears. "I'm fine." She wasn't. Maybe he could protect her from stubbing her toes or being whacked by tree limbs, but he couldn't fix anything. Nothing could repair her soul.

Falling to her knees twice on the walk home, she remained ten feet behind him until the lamp in the window flickered ahead. "You go in. I'll wait until you turn off the light."

When the lamp's flame disappeared, she climbed onto the

porch and dropped her muddy clothes inside the darkened doorway. She felt her way around the table and knelt in front of the tick. Everett's hands grabbed her shoulders, and she shrieked. "You're supposed to be on the bed!"

His grip remained firm. Her eyes adjusted enough to see his head shaking. "I won't allow you to take the floor."

"But that's where I intended to sleep now," she whispered. His nearness did crazy things to her insides. Fear and something strange crippled her breathing.

"Not unless you're sleeping with me."

She struggled against his grip. He released her, and she fell against the small stump that served as a bedside table.

"Calm down." His voice was soothing, not sultry or slick. "I meant I will not, for any reason, let you sleep on the floor."

She scrambled onto the bed, her heart thumping wildly. The thought of being in his arms made her want to cry, but not simply from fear. Crazily, she wished he'd hold her. But she knew where that would lead, and that definitely was not what she wanted. What she really wanted was someone's arms she felt comfortable enough to curl up in and sob buckets of tears.

The low rumble of his voice filled the room. "Thank you for making this pillow for me. It's much nicer than my old ones."

Of course it was nicer. That thing had enough fluffy white down to tar and feather a gang of thieves. Folding up his thin pillows, she chastised herself. Being upset over a pillow was ridiculous, especially since he was kind enough not to force himself upon her. But she couldn't stop her shuddering breaths. Why had she thought this marriage would work? The only way to escape crying was to fall asleep, so she turned to do so. She focused on a dark knot in the wall and worked to breathe at a slow, steady pace.

When her heavy eyes ceased producing tears, he spoke.

"I'm sorry about yesterday, Julia, when you were going to the mercantile. I shouldn't think so poorly of you to assume you would steal from me."

- A hiccup of a giggle escaped. What a minor thing. "It's forgiven. Next time, I'll tell you when I plan to leave."

Everett clasped his hands behind his head against the thick cushioning. He flipped over and plumped the down, then blinked at the dark, blank wall, his eyelids not the least bit heavy.

Julia's slight snore distracted him. Her very presence distracted him.

When I plan to leave . . .

She only meant for town, but each past bride's jilting played with his head. Without a physical bond between them, what would hold her here? Was a legal document enough?

A promise wasn't enough for Patricia Oliver.

Paid traveling expenses weren't enough for Kathleen Templeton.

His farm wasn't enough for Helga Scholz.

What would be enough for Julia? All she'd asked for was provision and protection. And he would give that, but through the long Kansas summers and winters, would she be happy with nothing more?

He wouldn't be happy. The vision of her silhouette in front of the moonlit creek popped up before him. He'd caught a glimpse before he led her home. Her nightgown clung to every curve of her body. No, he wouldn't be content. He'd be tortured. Years of living in close quarters with a woman would inevitably lead to more accidental visions of things he didn't want to see if they were to be nothing but companions.

Everett raked a hand through his hair. He sounded like

a spoiled child—he'd gotten exactly what he'd asked for, a willing worker, yet wouldn't be happy unless he got more.

When she'd crawled next to him in the dark, her sweet-smelling hair and soft body had made it difficult for him to let her go. Every bit of him wanted to pull her closer. Much closer.

But his stupid mouth spoke without consulting his brain. Her nearness turned his brain into mush. He hadn't meant to insinuate sleeping together, but his words gave him a window into her thoughts. The fear, revulsion, and shock on her face as panic overtook her made him wonder if his resolve to win her heart might very well be a delusion.

Chapter 11

Everett crossed to the well, buttoning his shirt. Too hot to be wearing it, but he knew leaving his shirt off would bother Julia. She was always uncomfortable around him; no sense in making her more so.

"Would you mind bringing a bucket of water over here?" She stood behind the garden fence, brushing dirt from her hands.

After taking several long swigs from the dipper lest he die of thirst, he filled a bucket for her, then plopped it over the fence. "Here you are."

"Could you make sure I need this? At least, I think this area needs more water." She pointed to a section that caught most of the sun throughout the day. He hadn't helped her with the garden much these last three weeks, though he should have. He sighed. They were worse than two strangers: they were friendly combatants, neither wanting to get close to the other, yet having to.

Grabbing a clod of baked dirt, she crushed it, the dust falling from her hand onto a few carrot and turnip seedlings wilting on the ground. Did she pull them up on purpose?

He grunted. "I would say so."

"Do you think one bucket will be enough?" She peeped up at him, streaks of dirt crisscrossed on her forehead. How could dirt make a woman more attractive?

"Depends on the soil. Check it after an hour." He walked off before she could ask anything more lest he hop the fence and tell her to forget about the garden, the woodpile, the fields, the animals, the whole blessed farm.

But he couldn't do that. He didn't have time for anything but his own work.

That was an excuse, and he fooled neither God nor himself.

Everett licked his dry lips and rubbed his sore shoulders. He could use a break, a moment to sit with a glass of cold water on his porch and watch the chickens scratch and pick at each other. But that would have to wait until he finished the woodpile. Yesterday, he'd returned from the fields to find her hacking at logs. She did enough already; he didn't want her to take on firewood too.

Moving his flapping union suit to the side, he passed under the clothesline. The thought of Julia cleaning his underclothes made him grimace.

Cooking his food, mending his clothes . . . she did too much for him and took as few breaks as he did. He should slow them both down, but he couldn't spend that much time with her right now. He set another log, his mind focused on nothing but hitting the striking point, and chopped with vehemence. Concentrating on hitting his mark proved difficult with images of Julia cleaning, sewing, and gardening floating in his mind.

He set the next log and whacked it good. Throwing the pieces on the pile, he looked over at her talking to herself in the garden. He thwacked the next log, splitting it in one frustrated motion.

Last Saturday in town, he'd talked to Jonesey, who was ready to quit and head farther west. Just a year ago, Jonesey's joy had been infectious, but now . . .

If Julia followed in Jonesey's woman's footsteps, how would he keep himself from descending into the depression Jonesey found himself in? Especially if he gave in to his feelings? Julia was more than a pretty woman—she was a hardworking, uncomplaining one. She deserved to be more than ignored and forgotten. She wasn't forgotten, though . . . not when thoughts of her made him forget what row he'd just sown and where he'd left his hoe.

What could he offer her that she deserved? Nothing.

When she realized he was not worthy of her, she'd disappear, just like the rest.

His blow glanced off the wedge, sending wood one way and the blunt edge of the maul into his shin. Words that normally did not pass his lips spilled forth, and he threw his maul on the ground. He sat down hard and squeezed his shin, as if adding more pain to the area would make the stabbing leave more quickly.

He looked over at the garden, but she was no longer there. The little green lines of new seedlings marched in crooked paths on the other side of the white fencing.

Weeks. He'd only offered her weeks of loneliness, yet she'd never mentioned anything about leaving. But then, Jonesey's wife didn't leave until half a year passed.

The seedlings that she tended in the garden taunted him, along with the quilt she'd pieced together, now draped on the line next to the work dress she'd sewn from the dark pink material she'd bought her first day there. She appeared past the chicken coop, wearing a serviceable green dress Rachel had helped her alter last week from her stash of fancy clothing.

Julia's persistence indicated she planned to stay, but could he trust her to do so? Could he believe she wouldn't discard his heart if he gave it to her?

Does it matter, Everett?

He clasped his hurt leg and looked through the puffy clouds racing by. "I give up, I get it. In order to protect myself, I've been terrible to a woman who's done me nothing but good." Slumped, he stared at the grasses between his knees. How could he begin to live joyfully with her with the precedence of silence he'd started? Going in, lounging with a mug of coffee and talking about the weather sounded unappealing, fake. What would he say? They'd had a handful of conversations since she married him. And all of those about the farm's needs.

He pushed himself up with the maul's handle. He needed to feel normal. Get away and take a break. And stop thinking. Stop pining.

In the barn he grabbed the tack he needed to return to Dex and saddled Blaze. He cinched the girth strap. "Let's ride over to the Stantons, talk farm stuff, and I'll sneak you carrot cake if Rachel's got any. How's that sound, boy?"

The gelding stomped his front foot.

Everett hoisted himself into the saddle and readied to prod his horse when Julia's silhouette appeared in the barn's doorway.

"Where're you going?" Her voice sounded lifeless.

Everett pulled on Blaze's reins, the gelding's eagerness barely contained. He wished he had something major that needed attending, but all he really wanted was to chat with Dex, to be in an environment that relaxed instead of strained. He pushed away the sudden thought that all the strain was of his own making.

He couldn't lie. "I'm heading to the Stantons."

A basket containing wild flowers hung on her arm. "How long do you think you'll be?"

"All day, most likely."

"Does Dex need help with something?"

"No. I just . . . just planned on visiting."

The pain etched on her face was almost as raw as the blow to his shin. Rachel was as much her friend as Dex was his. He'd not even thought to ask her to come along. He'd only been worried about getting away from thoughts of her, though he knew that was impossible.

Unfeeling. Selfish. More reasons for her to hate him. He could hardly stand himself. "I'm sorry, I should have asked you. No. I should have told you to get ready to go with me. I . . . I forgot." He slid off the saddle. "Why don't you get whatever you need for a visit with Rachel, and I'll hook up the wagon."

She nodded before exiting the barn.

The horse stamped his disapproval.

"Sorry, Blaze, but I've got to hook you up. I'd much rather ride, but there's no way I can have her in the saddle with me."

Too close, much too close.

The horse clipped at a good speed, creating a breeze that felt refreshing against her perspiring skin. But Julia wasn't comfortable, not with a grouchy man sitting beside her. If Everett refused to talk the first time they'd had a break from choring in several weeks, then she'd cram in as much conversation with Rachel as possible today.

John's ill-combed head popped through the doorway as soon as they drove past the Stantons' barn. He smiled, waved, and ran straight for them.

She let a half smile slide onto her face as she stepped down onto the dirt-packed yard. Though just turned eight, John could make any girl feel welcome and wanted. Unlike her husband, who had busied himself with grabbing bridles from the back of the wagon.

"Juuuliiiiaaa!" John sang her name and bounded over to her. "Ma's got a secret! But I'm not supposed to tell. No. Can't tell. Anyone. But she said she'd tell you whenever you got here." He grabbed her wrist and tugged. Heaven help his future bride. Whereas she wished Everett would utter three words together, John's wife would need three sets of ears and plenty of spunk to keep up with his jibber-jabber.

"I have to keep it a secret. I'm not supposed to tell no one. Not even you. Or Everett. Not one single person, and I promised. You'll have to keep it a secret. Just like me."

John dragged her up the stairs, followed by Everett, and stopped in front of Rachel, who dropped her mending into her lap and rolled her eyes at him. Dex was whittling at the head of the table.

John bounced in place. "Go on. Ask."

Rachel held out her palm and stood. "No need to ask, but I'd better tell you the secret before John bursts." She turned to the squirming boy. "But it isn't polite to forget to greet your guests. I hope you greeted Julia before you dragged her in here."

John's face scrunched.

Julia laughed and chose to save him. "I think his spirited waving would constitute a greeting. Good morning to you, Rachel."

"Pleased to have you drop in." Rachel flattened her skirt over a slightly bulging stomach. "I'll give you a chance to guess the secret yourself." She flashed a grin at Everett.

146

"I presume there's a little one to be born in the Stanton household?" Julia forced a smile, though all she wanted to do was frown. Rachel would expect her to be happy at this news, and so she would be—at least on the outside. "Why didn't you tell me before?"

Rachel shrugged. "I've lost a few."

That familiar feel of cold ran up her arms. Losing babies was one thing, but losing mothers was another. Would she lose the one person in the county whom she could talk to in just a matter of months?

"I'm excited this time though, because I'll have someone to help attend *me*."

"Is there another midwife in the area now?" Everett leaned against the wall in the corner, hat in his hands.

Julia wished he'd leave so she could talk to Rachel alone, but it didn't look like either man planned on moving anytime soon.

Rachel grabbed Julia's hand. "No, but I have her."

Julia stepped back. "Me? No." She waved her hands in front of her. She wouldn't ever go into a birthing room. Not again. Never again. The last time she had done so with her mother, she'd forever turned her father against her. But she couldn't blame him; it was all her fault. She swallowed hard and worked out a reply that sounded intelligent. "I'm no midwife, no nurse. I barely know how to bandage a wound."

Rachel chuckled and whispered, "I've given birth four times and attended countless others. All I need is a helper. I can tell you what needs to be done."

That wasn't the problem at all. She knew what needed to be done—and what things should never be done. She hugged herself to staunch the qualm in her middle. "I can't."

Rachel bent to look in her eyes. "It's not that horrifying."

She shook her head. The image of her dead baby brother painted itself onto her arms. She squeezed her eyelids until darkness overcame the image. If Rachel's baby died, she'd be stuck in Kansas with a friend who would hate her and a man she wasn't comfortable with.

"Really, you'll be great help. Seeing a birthing will help you get over any fear of going through it yourself."

Julia would never voluntarily go through the agony her mother did, losing child after child. Rachel had said she'd lost a few. How could she be serene about it? Her mother had never gotten over a single stillbirth. She barely cared that she had a daughter. But the last baby was a boy, a son, a living son, who died in his sister's hands only minutes before his mother followed him into heaven.

The Stanton boys' shouting in the yard bespoke that Rachel had indeed been more successful in bringing children into the world than Julia's mother, but she couldn't bear the thought of holding another dead baby—and definitely not her own. Her grandmother had the same problem as her mother, so why would it be any different for her? It was best to never try. And Theodore had swiped away any desire she'd ever had to become a mother.

But how could she not help if no one else was around to do so? "I guess I can help."

"And I'll send for you when Mrs. Hampden has her baby. She's due in a few weeks. That way you'll have a good idea of what to expect."

Could she for once expect something good? It wasn't like children didn't exist. Children and mothers did survive the process.

John tugged on her hand. "And she forgot to tell you about the kittens. We have kittens too, so we know all about babies around here. I was there with the mama cat, I was. I can help with birthin'."

"Sure you can." Rachel poked his side. "You'll do your chores when the time comes without complaining. Now, get with you."

Julia sat beside Rachel in the rocker and unwrapped the knitting needles she'd brought with her. Feeling watched, she looked up.

Everett was staring at her with the most peculiar look on his face, but then grabbed a discarded wooden piece off the table and tried to spin the misshapen piece like a top. "So glad to find you home. Need any choring help this afternoon?"

Dex leaned over to spit before answering. "Naw, I'm inside for a while. Broke the ax handle." He brandished his carved stick of wood. "Nothing left to do with the handle but whittle. Rachel wants me to carve a whistle while I'm at it."

"Ambrose's eleventh birthday's tomorrow," Rachel said.

Everett grabbed a different chunk of wood. "You using this piece for the whistle?"

Dex nodded.

"I'll help you start. What's the plan?"

The men conversed about dimensions and angles for cutting. Julia took a deep breath and released it. Just because Everett remained inside didn't mean she couldn't talk. If she didn't converse with someone, she might explode. But maybe she could get Rachel to do most of the talking. "So how far along are you?"

"Five and a half months—not too much longer to go."

A few times, the men's laughter interrupted their conversation. Throughout the next hour, she often stopped to stare at Everett as he rocked in his chair with laughter or teased Dex or the boys. He even chucked wood pieces at

John, who attempted to catch them by contorting in crazy positions.

Everett stood and hiked his knee onto a bench, crossing his arms below the crook of his leg, a hand wiggling on either side of his knee. "Put your arms like this, John. I'll throw two at a time."

Upon John's success at catching the wildly thrown sticks, the men roared in approval.

"Hush, boys. You'll wake up Emma." Rachel wagged her finger at them, and they at least tried to keep it down.

Julia fidgeted in her chair. This was not the Everett she knew. He had not stopped smiling for the last twenty minutes. The camaraderie between him and the children and Dex sliced at her. He had an enjoyable personality. Just not one he wished to share with her, apparently.

She was nothing more than an intruder. The Stantons had been friends with Everett for years, and their easy company revealed she didn't yet belong. He'd reiterated many times the past few weeks how summer work was too important to put aside for things like sleep and food, yet he didn't seem a bit on edge about spending hours here wasting time. Hanging her head, she tried to concentrate on her stitch count.

"Glad to see him act like his old self." Rachel's soft voice cut into her tally. "I knew it wouldn't take him long to warm to you. Thought his tongue had froze off right after your wedding. In a stupor over your beauty and his good fortune, I suppose. Never seen him act like that." Rachel leaned over to catch a wayward spool of thread. Her constricted voice floated up from between the chairs. "Not even around my sister." She settled back into her seat and waved her needle. "Though she's quite pretty, Patricia can't hold a candle to you. I felt terrible for him when she left him for Duncan, but Everett'll make you a better husband than Duncan has Patricia. I can read between the lines of my sister's letters. He's a scoundrel.".

Patricia? Everett had been courting Rachel's sister? Scrambling through her mind, Julia envisioned the extra trunk's engraved latch. No *P* in the monogram. He'd never said a thing about the items from the trunk she'd spread throughout the room. Maybe the reason he remained distant lay in this new information.

Pining for a lost love, perhaps? Seems he had two women to choose from.

A repressed sob reached into her throat, threatening to strangle her. She stood, and the beginnings of an infant's cap in her lap dropped to the floor.

Rachel looked at her, puzzled. "Are you all right, Julia?"

"I . . . I ought to, need to, uh . . . go outside."

Rachel stood and caught her shoulder. "By all means, go. But you'd tell me if you were in pain, right? If something's wrong?"

If only she could tell her. She moved her head with an ambivalent shake before turning to escape out of doors.

Rachel followed her onto the porch. "Julia?"

Afraid Rachel would pry into emotions she didn't understand, she sucked in air and put on a cheery face, hoping to mask the tears about to spill over. "Just need to, you know . . ."

When Rachel nodded, she headed in the direction of the privy and once out of sight, tramped into the woods quite a distance before letting go. The onset of tears heightened the stabbing pain behind her eyes, yet she sobbed all the more. She was clearly overreacting. She wasn't supposed to care what Everett had done, who he'd known. Of course something terrible in his past had pushed him into a marriage of convenience—just like her. But why did it bother her that he'd most likely loved two women when she'd already suspected he'd most likely been jilted by one?

She swiped at the nonsensical tears. She shouldn't care. Why did it matter? She didn't want to be his wife in the traditional sense.

It rankled her that he'd had the capacity to love more than one woman, that he loved the entire Stanton family—but didn't care for her, not even a smidgen. No one had ever loved her, and now, no one ever would.

When the tears ceased, she leaned her head against the mossy trunk of a nearby tree and fixed her eyes on a small flock of songbirds pecking near a puddle.

Everett wasn't thrilled with her, but she was no stranger to that. Father had never been pleased with her. And it turned out Theodore had never been enthralled with her either, just the business opportunity she represented . . . and just like every other man she'd met, he considered her nothing more than a delicate ornament to crush if it suited his fancy.

She closed her eyes. She'd wished many times to be more than an attractive face useful for conning her father's customers into purchasing something they didn't need, and she'd finally gotten her wish. Her husband cared nothing for her looks.

But he also cared nothing for her. Might never care. She was competing with women in his past she didn't even know.

There had to be a bright side to this.

She had the opportunity now to make a man who hadn't fallen for her physical charms to think well of her. She'd always wanted to be respected for the woman she was on the inside.

Yes, this was the good of it. She would work so hard, she'd make him proud. If all he did was see that her beauty was only one of many good things about her, she'd be happy.

Her mouth grew dry and new tears pressed on the back of her eyes. That was a lie. What she really wanted was to make the Everett back in the Stantons' cabin like her. Maybe even something more. The thought terrified her, but she couldn't deny that the desire toyed with her heart. Could she really end her days content, knowing that no man had ever truly loved her? The image of Everett cutting wood shirtless swam unbidden before her. Could she truly allow a man to love her like a man loved a woman?

No. A friendship like the one he enjoyed with the Stantons was a worthy enough goal. And a lot less scary.

Whimpering in the woods wouldn't help. She dried her tears and threaded her way back to the Stantons' cabin. Their door opened, and Everett's lithe form bounced down the stairs. Whistling, he headed to the barn and threw open the whitewashed door. Children's laughter rolled out of the dark interior. The kittens were probably in the hayloft. At least she'd have Rachel to herself now.

Pulling the front door open, she envied the sound hinges. Perhaps she could figure out how to fix the hinge at home herself. Inside, Dex was standing in front of Rachel, his hands resting on the arms of her chair, their lips only a breath apart.

Dex glanced in her direction, a shaft of sunlight illuminating his face.

"I'm so sorry." Her face flamed. "I'll just step back out."

"Not a problem, Julia. I was just leaving." Dex turned back to his wife. "But I needed something before I left." He lowered his lips to Rachel's.

Julia threw her glance to the floor. After the sound of their kiss ended, she couldn't help but peek. Dex cupped the back of Rachel's head and kissed her hairline. "Love you, Rach."

A lovely blush settled upon Rachel's cheeks, and Dex gave her a tender look before straightening.

Dex winked at Julia and sidestepped her for the door.

Rachel coughed. "Sorry for that."

"No reason to be sorry." At least one woman she knew could enjoy kisses. If only she could look forward to them without fear.

Julia bit her lip. She would not cry a second time today.

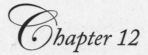

Chapter 12

Several days later Everett straddled the last beam of his new cabin's roof.

"I can stay and help get the rest up," Dex called up from below in what would one day be the main bedroom. But would it forever remain just his bedroom? Everett almost didn't want to finish the house since separation was exactly how Julia wanted things.

"If you're sure the boss won't mind."

"She's rather anxious for this to get done so she can have my slave labor back. She won't mind—too much." Dex sidled over to the fence. "If we work hard enough, I think we can have the whole roof on by tonight."

Everett dropped down out of the rafters and joined Dex, taking the canteen he offered and pouring the lukewarm water over his head before taking a swig. "As long as you leave well before nightfall."

"The moon will be bright enough to keep my team on the path."

The moon was visible even now, a chipped silver dish in the bright blue sky, but the flicker of Julia's bright green skirts swimming in his peripheral vision distracted him. He rubbed the bruise on his left hand and forced himself to stare at the grasses bending in the breeze in front of him. He'd missed the roofing nails one too many times, his purpled hand testifying to how many times Julia's green skirts had stolen his attention today.

"Let's eat and get back to it then." He grabbed a biscuit for each hand from the plate Julia had set on the crate near the well and returned to the fence, hopped onto the other side, and slid down the post. She couldn't steal his attention from his food if he couldn't see her. Dex brought the plate over, but stayed on the other side.

The biscuits were flaky and buttery, and he wanted another, but he couldn't take Dex's. "Toss me an apple if you would."

Dex ignored him and turned to scratch his back against the fence post, facing the cabin.

Did he have to get up and get the apple himself? Everett turned and noted Dex's frown, a frown that scrunched his whole face. Everett followed the man's gaze to the old shack's roof, where Julia was traipsing atop the peak. He worked at keeping his hands in his pockets. How did she get up there?

Dex pointed. "What's she doing?"

"Don't know. I didn't ask her to do anything up there."

"What did you ask her to do?"

"Nothing."

"What do you want her to do?"

What did he want? She didn't want to know what he wanted. It was enough she was there. Or at least it should have been enough. He stood and snatched up an apple and tore a bite out of it. "I let her do whatever she wants."

Dex's eyebrows lowered. "Do you ever talk to her?"

He turned to look at him. What was he getting at?

Dex coughed. "I saw Ned yesterday. He came by my place."

Just the mention of that man sent a wave of heat through his chest.

"He had Helga with him, poor woman."

He nodded. No one would argue with Dex there.

"He takes her for granted, doesn't speak to her unless he wants something." Dex shifted. "But she works hard. Long and hard, trying to do anything that will please him. But it won't do any good." Dex picked a blade of long grass next to the fence post and snapped it off. "He's a sorry old cuss. Treats her like she's less than human. He doesn't share a life with her—he simply shares his space with her."

True. But talking about it wouldn't change anything. What could they do for Helga? Ned wasn't the kind of guy to take unsolicited advice.

Dex turned to face him. "She might do something as dangerous as climb onto a rooftop. And Ned wouldn't care. Just as long as she didn't bother him."

He frowned and kept his vision fixed on Julia fiddling with the roof's shingles.

"But he's got a beautiful wife. Not beautiful like yours, mind you, but like Julia, beautiful on the inside. Proverbs says 'Whoso findeth a wife findeth a good thing.' But sometimes I have to wonder why God casts His pearls before swine. Sometimes."

Everett worked his lips apart in order to speak. "Are you saying I'm no better than Ned?"

Dex leaned over slowly and spit over the fence. "What I'm saying is, from what I've seen, nothing about your behavior toward your wife looks any different than Ned's behavior to his. In fact, I've seen you treat Helga better than Julia."

Every muscle in Everett's body turned to stone.

Dex shook his head. "Never thought I'd say I felt sorry for one of the most beautiful women I've ever seen."

Everett hung his head. His stomach felt like lead.

"Now, I know you. And I don't want to believe what I'm seeing is a true reflection of your character. But if it is, I hope you have enough brains to change." Dex threw the strap of the canteen over his shoulder and pushed himself off the fence post. "Now, I can finish helping with the roof if you like, or I can leave. But it had to be said."

Everett wanted to punch Dex in the nose and tell him he had it wrong. But Dex didn't have it wrong. He'd known he was being a blockhead, but to be called on it smarted. He stifled his desire to snap at his friend. His friend had said nothing amiss. "We'll work."

Dex nodded and headed back to the barn.

God, how do I start something I know is going to hurt me even more if I fail?

Everett walked slowly behind Dex's wagon. He needed to walk a long, long way, sit down in the middle of nowhere, and think and even make himself pray a little. Before too long, his friend drove over the ridge and disappeared just like the sun, and Everett kept on walking until the path to the far creek materialized. He fought through the bluestem and sat on a mound of grass next to the muddy bank so he could dip his hand's purpled flesh into the cool moving waters. The back of his hand throbbed under the big bruise growing across his knuckles.

Dex's lecture had proven just as distracting as Julia waltzing around the farmyard, and he'd hit himself more times than someone with a brain and pain perception should have been capable. He'd been surrounded by the cacophony of hammer versus nail for the rest of the afternoon, but all he'd heard was Dex's words over and over with each whack.

"I have to wonder why God casts His pearls before swine."

A few minnows nibbled his swollen hand. He swished them off, lay back, and stared at the stars and bright moon.

Was he truly no better than Ned? He'd never laid a finger on Julia. One day, his attraction to the woman under his roof would wane and he could be her friend.

Who was he kidding? Why had he ever promised that? He'd only grow crankier and more malcontent until one day he did indeed turn into Ned.

He stared at the silver rippling on the pond surface while crickets sang him a monotonous lullaby, but he couldn't succumb to their call. Even if his mind hadn't been all jumbled, he wouldn't want to worry Julia by not returning until dawn. Not that she should worry about a fool like him.

He was wrong to be running from her still. If he stayed away from her, he'd have no chance at winning her, which he couldn't do alone on a creek bank. He pushed himself off the ground with his bad hand and flinched. Would she still be awake? The moon's travel indicated an hour or two worth of movement. He hadn't meant to stay out so long.

At home, he inched open the shack's door and saw a lamp burning low on the stump next to the bedstead. He let his eyes adjust, waiting for her to barrage him with questions, but soon he heard sleeping sounds. She lay across the bed, fully dressed, one stockinged foot dangling off the side. How was she handling the lack of company? Did she even miss him?

He stifled a groan as he lowered himself into a chair to pull off his boots. After donning his nightshirt, he crossed over to turn off the lamp. He stumbled over her dangling foot, wrenching her leg back. He tensed, but she only groaned, curled up, and rolled over.

Surely he'd hurt her. Yet her breathing quickly returned to the sound of restful slumber. He bent over and looked into her face. Not restful. Her face seemed pinched and worried. He brushed hair off her furrowed brow. Not even an eyelid fluttered.

He sat beside her on the mattress, careful not to sit on any of her hair. Even with circles under her eyes, she was gorgeous.

Her tiny hand lay relaxed, poking out from under the blanket. Cracked skin around her nails and a huge gash on her hand gave him pause. She worked for no thanks. Not even liniment for the open sore on her hand. He didn't know she had need of it, and the bottle probably sat in the barn where he'd last used it, where she wouldn't know to look.

In an attempt not to hurt himself, he'd hurt someone far more precious.

Precious.

That word caught him off guard.

If she stayed only one more day, she was precious. If not to him, then most certainly to God. But as his wife, that's how he should be viewing her anyway. What had Dex said? Something like *He who finds a wife finds a good thing.*

Everett pulled his Bible off the stump next to the bed and thumbed through Proverbs until he found the verse: *Whoso findeth a wife findeth a good thing, and obtaineth favour of the Lord.*

"I obtained your favor," he whispered. The circles under her eyes haunted him. "And squandered it."

Julia moaned in her sleep.

No, he'd ground it into the dirt.

His throat constricted as he looked at her in the flickering light. How could he ever face anyone who'd seen how he'd treated her? Did they talk about him around their dinner tables, how he cared for his animals with more love than the woman who shared his home?

Careful not to wake her, Everett slid his fingers beneath her own and caressed the rough skin that had been silky-white and smooth the day they'd met. Despite being left to fend for herself in a land and occupation foreign to her, she'd worked without complaint. And he'd watched her struggle and hadn't had the decency to come alongside her to teach, help, or encourage. He was a rat.

Would you forgive me, Lord? I'm not sure she should.

He put the Bible on the table and fingered the dark hair framing her pale face. He could feel his pulse thudding in his throat.

I'm afraid to feel, Lord.

How I've treated her . . . Even if this is a temporary blessing and she leaves tomorrow, I should treat her better. I know that. I've known that. I've allowed my pride to turn me into a scoundrel and keep me from befriending her. Just because Patricia married a stranger the morning I was going to officially propose doesn't mean Julia is going to run away with another man the minute I start being nice to her. Nothing the other women did to hurt me means Julia will follow their footsteps.

The memory of Miss Gooding arriving after her untimely death stopped his breath. *Please, Lord, don't let Julia die before I make this right.*

His heart felt as bruised as his hand. He wanted her to stay. More than he had ever wanted anything in his life. More than even making his homestead a success.

Everett blew out the lamp's flame, crossed over to his pallet, and settled under the covers. Though Julia was only a black silhouette, he continued to watch her.

If she weren't beautiful, I'd still want her to stay. She's what I need.

He sighed. He'd probably ruined any chance he had with her, but his desires and God's commands pushed him to give in and do as he ought. His brain wouldn't let him sleep, as if allowing him to do so would erase this revelation.

But there would be no forgetting—he'd start tomorrow. No matter how much being rejected by his wife might hurt, he couldn't remain a coward forever.

———◆———

Everett woke before Julia. The early morning sun only highlighted the creased lines of exhaustion surrounding her eyes. He slipped out of the house and headed to the barn to milk the cow before the sun took over the sky.

A half hour later, the scent of sausage filtered through the front door, along with the sound of off-key singing. He bumped open the door with the milk-heavy bucket and mustered a smile.

She quit her song mid-word and shot up from the bed, where she'd been tugging on her boot. "Why, Everett. I was just about to do that. Did I sleep too late?" She pulled a strand of hair away from her face. The dark waves he'd fingered last night called to him like a siren's song, but she'd braided and piled it on her head sooner than he wanted. Maybe it was a good thing she kept it up.

He smiled at the picture she made in the hazy sunlight. "No. I figured I could help you with chores this morning."

She dropped her button hook, straightened, and gave him a confused look.

He crossed his arm across his midsection and played with

the fabric at his elbow. "I'm going to check the chickens and gather eggs." He turned and rushed through the doorway. Biting his cheek, he headed to the coop. He'd been worse than he thought. She'd acted like he'd taken leave of his senses by merely helping with an insignificant chore.

He could beat himself up about this all day and then some, surely. But it would be better to simply give her no cause to bestow such a stymied look upon him again.

When he returned with a handful of eggs, he set them near the stove, where she was stirring gravy. "I didn't know if you wanted to use these today." Close to her, he could tell she used no special perfumes like Rachel, yet she still smelled feminine. Her scent even changed the aroma of his cabin. Her presence had effectually changed his entire life, yet he'd been living like he could keep her at bay.

She frowned at the six eggs. "That's more than they laid yesterday."

"In a few more weeks, you'll probably get a dozen a day."

He almost laughed at the utter devastation on her face. How was increased egg production a bad thing? Did she hate eggs?

But she made them every day.

Julia got a bowl and reached for them, not bothering to hide her disgusted sigh.

"I didn't mean to imply you need to cook them now. I'm sure biscuits and gravy will be plenty. I just thought you liked them for breakfast."

She shook her head. "I used to. But I'm so tired of them now."

"Then why don't you save these?"

"But why, when they'll just make more? Soon we'll be eating eggs for every meal just to use them up before they go bad."

"But they'll last almost a year in the cellar. And you'll want them come January, when we'll hardly get an egg a day."

She searched his face and her shoulders slumped. "A year? How?"

He resisted smacking his head lest she believe the gesture meant he thought she was stupid. "I'm sorry, I thought you knew." He gathered the eggs in the bowl and took her hand. He pulled on her arm, but she seemed riveted to the spot. "Come, I'll show you what to do with them."

She dragged her feet as he led her to the root cellar, so he let go of her hand. Did she not want him so near? He'd not been close to her these past weeks out of fear, but what if she was happy with that arrangement? What if he repulsed her in some way, and she would detest his attempts to be around her more? His heart sank a little, but his resolve to do right propelled him toward the underground storeroom.

Lifting the door, he led her into the dank interior. He handed her the bowl and pulled the lid off the large barrel in the corner. "This is lime and salt water. I'll teach you how to make it the next time we need it. You'll have to get your arm wet, because you have to gently put the eggs down in the bottom. I keep them in here until I get around to larding and salting them. Don't like toting tons of water in here, but I like to do the packing in lard and salt in big bunches."

He rolled up his sleeve, grabbed the eggs, and put them in.

She stood with the empty bowl, looking at the crock. "I should be the one doing this."

Too many things he had taken for granted. Too many things he'd been a fool to assume. "I'm almost done, and I'll help you with how to do the packing when the time comes. Is there anything else you need to know about what ought to go in the cellar?"

"I'm sure there is, but I don't know enough to ask. The next time Rachel's over, I'll have her show me other things to preserve, so you don't have to bother. I'm sure she can show me the larding and salting process as well."

He rubbed on his neck. It'd be too easy to let her run to Rachel for everything. "I don't mind showing you."

She turned to look at him, gnawing on her lower lip.

"Let me." A strand of hair covered an eye, and he reached out to pull it from her lashes like he had done last night.

Her eyes widened, and then she turned to run out the cellar door.

Such a simple touch couldn't have scared her that badly. If she ran at that, knowing how much her lips distracted him into thinking how they would feel against his own again would have put a fire under her feet. He peeped out the exit. She was running at full speed across the yard. Turning this relationship around wouldn't be easy if such a little thing scared her off.

Then he smelled biscuits. Burnt biscuits.

He closed the cellar and made his way to the front door.

She bounded out of the cabin, dispersing the smoke rising from the round blackened mounds by waving her hand.

He stopped chuckling when she glared icy darts at him.

"This is not funny. Now we don't have breakfast."

He shrugged and worked hard to keep a smile from forming. "You can toast bread for the gravy. I'll wait."

She flipped the baking sheet over, dumping the charcoaled lumps on the ground, and huffed back inside.

During breakfast she kept her eyes averted, like she was daydreaming, and he let her. But when she got up to clean, he grabbed his Bible off the stump and sat back down.

He cleared his throat and pushed the opposite chair away from the table with his foot. "Come sit, Julia."

She wrung her hands as she crossed over to take a seat. "I'm sorry that I didn't know how to store the eggs. I promise I'll have Rachel help me figure out what other things I don't know. You have better things to do than help me with what a woman already ought to know." She swallowed hard. "I'll do that today if you'd like."

She looked ready to bolt out the door. Like a frightened rabbit. Though no frightened rabbit had ever made him feel so terrible. He had no gun leveled at her, but from her stance, one would think he had. He let her reaction sink in. He'd really messed up this whole marriage thing. "No, really. I'll help you. But I thought we ought to have some reading time." He fingered the leather front of his Bible. "We ought to start our day with the Word. I apologize for not doing this sooner." Her posture hadn't changed. "That's all right with you, yes?"

She shrugged. "If that's what you want."

He flipped open to his bookmark. It had been too long since he'd read his Bible daily. He'd done this whole searching-for-a-wife thing with hardly any communion with God. No wonder he'd made a mess of it. He sighed.

She sat stiffly while he read James 4 aloud.

"'Therefore to him that knoweth to do good, and doeth it not, to him it is sin.'"

He grunted and shut the book.

I got it, God. I'm working on it already.

He bowed his head to pray. "Father in heaven—"

Julia's seat screeched, and he looked up as she returned to her seat and folded her hands in her lap.

"Thank you for the food and shelter you have provided us. Thank you for providing me with a wife who works hard. I know I don't deserve her. Forgive me for how I've treated her and being arrogant enough to think I know how tomorrow

166

will turn out. Please help me return to relying on you and not myself. I know you want to help me. And help me to be better about talking to you. Help us to remain humble, resist sin, and come closer to you. Help us to do as you would have us do in all areas of our life."

His heart pounded at the thought of looking at her. Would she believe any of his prayer? Would she still look like a rabbit ready to skitter off into the woods or more like she believed him a wolf disguised with flowery words? He deserved the last reaction, but the thought of seeing it made his palms sweat.

He looked up, but her head was still bowed. "Do you want to add anything, Julia?"

She shook her head vehemently.

"Amen, then."

"Amen," she whispered. She caught his eye for a second before standing and grabbing her apron. "I'd best attend the garden before the sun gets too hot."

He stood. "I'll help you."

"Oh, no need." She waved him off and disappeared out the door.

He smashed his hat on his head. He was uncomfortable too. She didn't want him around, and he couldn't blame her. Maybe he shouldn't try to be her shadow on the first day. He walked past the new house toward the fields. He'd return for lunch and work on the house afterward. With luck, they'd be able to move in at the end of the month. Would that make her happy or even more jumpy?

Chapter 13

Julia watched Everett walk toward the pasture, making sure he was indeed going somewhere other than anywhere near her. The Everett she'd seen at the Stantons' days ago had stood in front of her this morning. Maybe a bit jittery, but the same affable Everett who'd played with John, smiled at Ambrose, and teased Dex. Where had he come from so suddenly? And why did this change make her hands tremble?

He'd apologized in prayer—not to her, but to God—for how he'd treated her. She'd never prayed anything but the Lord's Prayer. His prayer was so different, like a conversation. People should not talk to almighty God like they were friends. It simply wasn't done.

Did that apology mean he'd stop shunning her? Maybe. He did offer garden help and instruction afterward. For the first month, he'd worked from dawn to dusk. And after he finished with crops, he worked on the new house or split wood. When he rolled onto his pallet after supper, he snored the second his body lay flat. How had he fed himself and kept his clothes washed during the growing season in years past? No wonder he'd searched for a spouse—he needed a helper.

Julia kneeled in the dirt. The sprouts in the back rows had gotten big enough to distinguish the weeds from the plants. Gaps in her lines indicated she hadn't differentiated so well earlier in the month. She scraped the tines of her garden fork around the leaves that weren't green beans or potatoes. She picked her way through the plants, wincing a couple of times, unsure if she'd pulled the right thing. If she knew more about gardening, digging in the dirt might have been enjoyable. But she didn't want Everett to have to tell her what she should already know.

Did she need to do something special with the plants before they got ripe? How would she know if they were ripe?

Her stomach twisted at her ineptitude and lack of knowledge. Why had Father decided to marry her off instead of allowing her to help in the store? If he hadn't set her up with Theodore, she'd not be here meddling with the mysteries of vegetation. And this was scarier. If she ordered the wrong fabric, no one died. If the garden survived her clumsy hands, would it produce enough food to get them through the winter? She laid down her implement and stared at the shack. The months she'd be cooped up inside with Everett hit her like the ceaseless whack of his maul. Could he keep his distance when the snow and the winds trapped them indoors, when evenings descended before sleep beckoned? She'd seen the look in his eye. He found her attractive. But he hadn't pushed. In fact, those looks were fleeting, only lasting a second before he turned away and busied himself.

But when might he cease busying himself with something else?

She threw her handful of weeds over the fence and sat back, hands firmly planted on her dirty knees. She didn't want to do this any longer.

But she must. She'd made the choice to make this her home.

She ripped out a dandelion. She'd never understood how much work it took to cook and keep house. She'd been spoiled by Father's shop and the restaurant down the street. Everett must have realized how ignorant and lost she was this morning—not even knowing eggs should be preserved for winter. What a failure his choice of a wife turned out to be.

She wiped the tear tickling her nose. Hopefully he wouldn't ask her to leave. She only had her looks, a tiny bit of farm experience, and Rachel's instructions to lean upon. That wasn't enough to live on her own out west, or even choose a good situation for herself.

She sat back and glanced through the wooden railings of the fence sloped around the tiny garden plot. In the field, Everett wriggled out of his shirt and wiped his face. He flipped his suspenders back over his shoulders and picked up his hoe. The sight of his bare chest caused flutterings in her that she pushed away. She wiped at the perspiration along her brow. She was dirty and sweaty and smelly and sore. And it was unseemly to sit there gawking at Everett shirtless. It was time for a bath—in a tub.

Julia went inside to splash water on her face, retied her bonnet, and packed a small bag before heading to the barn. After hooking up Dimple and Curly, she drove the team over to Everett, the sculpted muscles in his upper back constricted under a sheen of moisture as he pulled off his hat and swiped the streams of sweat off his temples. She didn't feel like talking to him in his state of undress, but she'd promised not to go anywhere without letting him know. Was he wrong to think she'd run away one day soon? She'd do almost anything to avoid talking to him now, even though it was not inappropriate for a wife to talk to a shirtless husband. Would he be relieved if she left?

He turned around in a circle, agitatedly searching for something.

"If you're looking for your shirt, don't bother, I'm about to leave. Just wanted to let you know I was going into town."

He swallowed hard, but he didn't ask the question written on his face.

She couldn't leave him thinking the worst. "I'll be back."

He nodded, but the fear and panic still expressed themselves in his widened eyes and his tense muscles. As if he let himself relax, he'd somehow release whatever it was that held her to him.

"I know you thought I'd leave that first day without a good-bye, but I won't. Even if I decided it would be best to leave, I wouldn't just disappear—I wouldn't leave you wondering."

"I'm sorry for thinking you might, but it wouldn't be the first time it's happened around here." He swiped his sweaty forehead and glanced off at the horizon to the north. "Silas Jonesey's bride left without leaving a note."

"Well, that was Mrs. Jonesey, and I'm Mrs. Cline."

A bit of his rigidness disappeared, but she could tell he wasn't quite certain. But then, if a woman really had done that to a friend of his, she could see his worry. He'd just have to find out in time that she was better at keeping her word than his friend's wife was.

"I'm going to check on the tub that the Hampdens ordered." A drive into town to check something. She gripped the reins. A foolish amount of time on an insignificant errand, but she was already geared up to go, and more important, she had to get away from her failing garden and tauntingly sparse root cellar, even if it was only for a day.

"Carl said it wouldn't be in until next month."

She took out a lace handkerchief and wiped at her neck, more because she needed something to do instead of look at him. "A girl can hope." She licked her dry lips. "I do believe I'll stop at the boardinghouse and bathe before returning." Would he balk at the time and cost of this trip when they had a creek to bathe in, even though it was almost dry and had foamy film gathering in its stagnant crooks?

"If that would make you happy."

If only a bath were all she needed to be content. But it would help. Maybe. "I'll be back before nightfall." She crammed her handkerchief back up her sleeve and gathered the reins.

"Julia?"

She stopped, but didn't look at him.

"I'll be waiting for you."

She swallowed and nodded, but shouted giddyap without answering. She was pretty certain he had that look in his eye again, and she didn't want to see it.

The breeze in her hair as she drove to town blew a tiny bit of relief upon her clammy skin, but not enough to turn her around from this pointless trip. It was impractical to spend all day traveling to take a bath, only to get dusty and sweaty on the way home. Though she hadn't made a list, she could at least attempt to purchase the things they were low on. Maybe she could delay their monthly trip into town by buying enough. But if she could bring home a tub, she wouldn't feel silly at all. Should she bathe or shop first? Maybe if the tub was in, she'd just take it home and bathe there.

She stopped the team in front of the mercantile in time to

hear the door's bell tinkle and see Mrs. Hampden shut the door and turn over the open sign.

She scrambled down the wagon wheel and rushed to the door. She couldn't have driven all the way into town on a day they closed early. She couldn't return without even inquiring about the bathtub.

She knocked several times. Mrs. Hampden couldn't have waddled far enough from the door not to hear.

The closed sign moved a bit, but she couldn't see in because of the sun. A key jiggled in the lock, and Mrs. Hampden opened the door. Her face appeared peaked and sweaty.

Julia frowned. She'd thought she'd been miserable with this heat, but she couldn't imagine being pregnant and swollen during summer. "I know you're closed, but I won't take up much time. All I wanted to do was inquire about our tub."

Mrs. Hampden nodded, but her eyes turned glassy as she stared out into the street.

"Are you all right?" She almost reached out to touch her brow to check for a fever.

Mrs. Hampden shook her head.

Julia slipped her arm under the lady's shoulder and walked her back into the stuffy interior and stopped. Maybe it would be better if she sat outside. At least there was a breeze. "Let's get you some fresh air."

"No. Lock the door if you would. Help me get up—" Mrs. Hampden squeezed her arm hard, the muscles in her face bunching into tight bundles.

Julia's heart tripped. "Oh no, you're in labor."

"Yes," she hissed.

"I need to get Rachel." She took a step back, but Mrs. Hampden squeezed even harder, her nails gouging into her flesh.

She let out a steady stream of air, followed by a calmer breath, and straightened. "These pains are coming so fast. I don't want to be alone through another one."

"Where's Mr. Hampden?"

"I don't know. He should have been back hours ago."

"I'll go find him."

"Did you come in with Everett?"

"No."

"In his wagon then?"

"Yes."

"Parked in front of the mercantile?"

What did that have to do with anything? But she wasn't going to argue with a laboring woman. "Nearby."

"Then as soon as Carl sees Everett's team, he'll rush over." She gave a faint smile that turned into a twist as she tensed again. She clamped down hard, almost collapsing them both to the floor.

Julia bore the woman's weight until Mrs. Hampden could speak again.

"Please get me upstairs before I have this baby in the middle of the store."

Anchoring the slightly taller woman's arm around her shoulder, she half shuffled, half walked Mrs. Hampden to the back of the store and up the stairs, pausing twice as Mrs. Hampden stopped breathing while her whole body tensed.

"You ought to try to breathe, Mrs. Hampden." The silence grew longer, and Mrs. Hampden grew paler. Julia jiggled her. "You'll turn blue. Breathe in."

Mrs. Hampden sucked in a breath and blinked. "Call me Kathleen."

"Well, Kathleen, you need to breathe—otherwise you're

going to faint, and I don't think I can carry you up the rest of these stairs."

"That would be a funny picture." Kathleen giggled, and thankfully her flesh regained the pink color it had lost so quickly.

Now was the time to move, not laugh. "Let's go." She rushed her as quickly as the woman could waddle, stopping only once at the top of the stairs to shout at her to breathe and to keep her on her feet. Kathleen seemed intent on doubling over and falling to the floor.

"The bedroom is to the right."

Julia helped her onto the lovely thick mattress, envy stealing in for a second before Kathleen's snarl of pain and contorted face chased away every ounce of jealousy.

She could not stay here. "I have to get Rachel."

Kathleen snagged her by the arm. "Rachel told me you'd help."

"I can't help, not all by myself."

"Carl will be here any minute now. He can go for Rach—" Her breath stuck and her eyes turned flat.

Her mother hadn't had this many pains this close together until the end. But she had vocalized much more than this. "How long have these pains been coming?"

Kathleen hissed, then relaxed. "Three hours, but Rachel said this would take all day."

"I don't think you have all day." She stood, but Kathleen wrenched her closer.

"You will stay with me." She narrowed her eyes and growled when another contraction hit.

Julia placed her trembling hand on her shoulder until the woman's rumblings died away. She wadded up the quilts behind Kathleen and ran to look out the window. Not a single person walked down the sunbaked street.

A mewling moan escaped Kathleen's chapped lips.

"Kathleen?" A male's voice boomed down below. "Everett?"

Kathleen sat up in bed and scrunched her face. "Everett wouldn't be up here helping me birth your baby, you ninny!"

Clomping footsteps hit the stairs at a run.

"When are you going to get over worrying about him? What I need is a man who'll—" A screech like that of a mountain lion staunched her words as she drew up in a ball.

Julia bit her lip. She had no idea what Everett had to do with anything, but after seeing the look on Kathleen's face as she dressed down Carl, she wasn't about to ask.

The door crashed open against the wall. Carl looked at Kathleen and then toward her. "Why aren't you helping my wife?"

She let go of the curtain. "I was looking for someone to yell at to get Rachel. But now that you're here, I can go."

"No!" Kathleen strangled the quilt beside her, her voice ascending. "He'll be no use to me, look at him."

Carl's face had turned white and glassy like his wife's, his eyes so wide they looked ready to pop.

"Go get Rachel," Kathleen spit before hunching over and moaning in escalating tones.

He turned and sped down the stairs faster than he'd come up.

Julia swallowed. She wanted to run after him. She couldn't be here. Not alone. Kathleen didn't know what she was asking—she wouldn't want her here if she did. "I can't do this. I can't."

All Kathleen did was grit her teeth and stare, but the promise of wrath blazed from her intense expression. She hollered and sunk lower into the quilts. "It's coming."

Not already! She ran to the end of the bed and tried to remove Kathleen's clothing to accommodate the birthing, but she had no hot water, towels, nothing. Kathleen writhed in tempo with her staccato howl.

Legs devoid of strength, Julia lowered herself onto the foot of the bed and stared at Kathleen and the blood. Blood everywhere, just like when she was nine.

Blood and screams. Endless screams.

Time ceased, replaced by writhing and moaning and shrieking. The baby should have come already. She was a curse. She should get up and prepare some swaddling clothes, but then she could miss it. Surely it would be there any moment, but it wasn't, and Kathleen's cries grew strangled. She gripped Kathleen's knees to steady them both, waiting in agony. What should she do? Surely anything she did would be wrong, just like her choices at the last birthing she'd attended. But what if doing nothing was the wrong choice? She had no idea what to do with a baby still tucked away inside the mother.

She swiped the tears from her eyes and whispered against Kathleen's raging, "Come on, baby. What's wrong?"

Kathleen cried all the more and nothing happened, nothing happened, nothing happened.

"What's wrong?" Rachel's firm hand crushed her shoulder, and Julia almost fainted with relief.

"My mother, my . . . my . . . Kathleen. The baby. It's right there, but it won't come." She glanced up at Kathleen, white and pale and listless. "I think Kathleen is dying."

Rachel shoved her aside and examined Kathleen. "Take some deep breaths, girl."

She didn't know whether Rachel was talking to her or Kathleen, but she worked at breathing and reached over for

Kathleen's hand. The weary woman held on, but without the fervor or a tenth of the strength she'd had an hour ago.

"The baby is turned funny." Rachel nodded toward the head of the bed. "Hold her down, this is going to hurt."

While Rachel grunted, Kathleen screamed anew and sank her fingernails into her arm.

Blood seeped from the punctures in her white skin on her wrist. Blood trickled down her arm. Blood stained the blankets. Blood marred the midwife's dress. Blood spilled out of her mother and onto the floor.

And then, once again, a blue baby boy was handed to her.

"Slap it! Get it to breathe. I gotta stop this." Rachel turned back to the bed.

Julia held out the boy. Another dead one. Her curse. The sound of her mother's voice declaring that this newborn son would regain her husband's love echoed in her skull. The feel of her cold, shivering brother, whom she'd forgotten to swaddle against the winter drafts as she watched her mother die, was as light and cool as Kathleen's baby.

She'd lost her chance to be loved when her mother passed into eternity and her father blamed her for his only son's death.

Rachel swiped the child from her arms some moments later. "What are you thinking?" She whacked the child upside down and when he gurgled slightly, she handed him back. "Get a hold of yourself. I need you to help the baby."

Julia swallowed hard and tried to concentrate on the here and now. She picked up a discarded shirt and wrapped the limp infant, though it was hotter than an oven in the bedroom. Holding him close, she rubbed and jiggled him. "Come on, cry." But there was no hope, he was too blue. Her hands shook uncontrollably, and she let him slip onto her lap lest she drop him. If Kathleen lived, how could she face the woman again when it had been her fault, her incapability, her fear that had kept her from doing something, anything? She thumped the boy's back harder, thinking she could see him coughing up something.

"Please." Kathleen's voice was a weak, low hum.

Afraid to look, Julia glanced over, but instead of a dying woman in a pool of blood, Kathleen smiled wanly at the bundle and reached out her hands.

The baby wriggled and murmured. She couldn't pick him up; her fingers wouldn't work.

Rachel swooped him off her lap and swiped her finger inside his mouth. "He's not breathed well for quite a while. Only time will tell if he'll suffer from it." She blew in his face and he mewled, quiet and pitiful.

"I . . . I didn't kill the baby?" Her voice squeaked.

Rachel placed the whimpering baby in Kathleen's ready arms. "Of course not." She gathered up the dirty sheets. "You look as if you've seen a haunt. Don't do well at the sight of blood, eh? Perhaps you should go outside and get some air."

If Rachel hadn't been there, she'd have killed the baby and Kathleen. She was worthless, just like father and Theodore said. Nothing more than a pretty face, and that wasn't worth much and would be gone in years.

She staggered out of the room and nodded at Carl, who rushed past her. She only had one place left to prove she was worth anything. She clambered up into the wagon and drove home.

Chapter 14

"Looking good, my friend." Dex entered the new cabin's main bedroom, surveying it with his hands on his hips.

Everett pounded the last nail into the bed frame. "Thanks. I couldn't have gotten to this point without you." The smell of new wood and the fact that the wind rushed in only when Dex opened the door did his heart good. "Are you here to help?"

"Not really. Daisy wandered over here, but I could if you needed something."

"Nah, you've done plenty enough for me." Everett dragged the coil of rope from the corner to the bedstead. "You don't know how long I've wanted to sleep on something besides the ground or a wood plank." He uncoiled the cordage and threaded it through the frame.

"I'd bet since you arrived in Kansas."

"That'd be a bet you'd win."

Dex grabbed the rope and fed him a bit at a time. "How long until you move in? I could help bring in the cookstove while I'm here. You could be in tonight."

His heart stuttered. "Not ready for that."

"Why not? I bet Julia'd be happy to get out of that miserable excuse for a roof over her head."

She didn't seem to be in a hurry to do anything but take on more chores and store every edible wild plant in the cellar. Perhaps this house would make her feel more secure in facing the winter. But it had to be faultless. No half-hearted gestures. This needed to be a good move. "I'm planning on making more shelving and a counter first. And more chairs."

"But why stay in that hovel? I'm sure you can add those while living here."

"Julia's not in a hurry. And I want it to be . . . well, perfect." He kept his gaze on the rope as he worked it through a tight hole. Truly, he was buying time, hoping not to have to build a second bed frame.

"What are you doing?" Everett scurried over to hold the chair Julia was standing on.

"I'm putting up wallpaper." She smeared some white gloppy stuff on top of a page of newspaper and pressed it into a corner, her chair tipping slightly to the right.

He gripped the back of the chair with both hands. "No need to do that."

Julia looked down at him, then bent over to get another paper wet in her murky white water. "Rachel said it would help keep out the drafts. How you kept this place warm in the winter is beyond me."

Frankly, he hadn't.

Should he stop her and tell her the new house was ready? Any woman would be ecstatic to move out of this leaning box. When he finally did move them, she'd probably be angry if she learned how much earlier they could have switched.

But would she be willing to move in with only one bed?

"No," he answered.

Julia stopped in midstroke and cocked her eyebrow. "No?"

Heat rushed into his face, and he shook his head. "Never mind." He needed to make another bed.

"I can stop, if you don't want me to do this." She wiped at the paste on her hands. "What do you want? Food? Is it later than I thought?" She bunched her skirts with one wet hand and rested the other on the back of the chair.

He grabbed her by the waist and set her in front of him, the smell of her clean hair but inches from his nose. "That's not what I was thinking."

"What're you thinking?"

What I'm thinking now would send you running. I don't want you to run anymore.

He let go of her waist, crossed over to the stove, and grabbed a pan. "Food's not a bad idea." His voice cracked. Stupid vocal cords. "But you don't have to continue with this chore. The new house will be done before winter arrives."

"All right, I see." She cleaned up her mess, and they made dinner together in silence.

It's not good enough just helping her, I need to know her.

He slid the warm bread onto the table. "So, Julia, how . . . how was your day?"

She scrunched one eye. "Fine."

"I mean, what did you do?"

"Oh!" She stopped dishing out food. "I cleaned the coop, put away the eggs like you told me to—" she brought up her hand to tick each task off with her fingers—"rearranged the root cellar, mucked the barn, watered the garden, cleaned the stove, and started on the wallpaper. Is that enough?"

He shook his head at her serious face. "Plenty enough."

"I should have chopped more firewood, knowing how much you stress firewood. I should have done that before wallpapering, but I'd intended to put in an hour of that after dinner."

"Why?"

"Because that's why I'm here." She placed the plates on the table.

"To do the wood chopping?"

"Well, yes, and all the other household chores. I hope I'm learning fast enough. Rachel gave me an idea of when to pick vegetables from the garden. I wrote it down so I could remember. I'm afraid . . ." She pulled at her collar. "I'm afraid I didn't plant enough. Or really that I planted enough, but ruined too many. From what Rachel said, I don't think I have enough to preserve for the winter. I'm sorry for that." Her voice dropped to little more than a whisper. "But she's helped me identify some tubers and other things growing in the wild to help me make up in stores for what I've destroyed."

He dragged his hand through his tangled hair and let his arm drop to his side. Why did this woman stand before him slumped as if beaten? Had she always stood this way? He'd averted his eyes so often when speaking to her in the past, he didn't know.

"Maybe I should have asked you sooner if what I was doing was right. . . . No, I should have, but you were . . ." She bit her lip and traced the plate's edge. "You didn't seem interested."

"No, I . . ." He set the potatoes on the table and dropped into his chair. She sat quickly and folded her hands neatly in her lap, head bowed. Her immediate obeisance bothered him. So much of how he'd treated her in the past had to be undone, and he hadn't been doing enough to show her he wanted her to stay. And he wanted her to stay regardless of how many jars of tomatoes and corn she could put away.

She peeked at him. "Are you going to pray?"

He wasn't sure he should attempt it. God said He heard anyone who called upon Him, but would He be willing to grant anything to a man who'd treated his wife so poorly that she acted like an abused animal instead of a cherished companion? "Why don't you pray this time?"

She held out her hands. "Oh no. I can't do that. You wouldn't want me to do it." She bowed her head.

He sighed. "Dear God, thank you for our food. Help me . . ." He looked at Julia, stiff in her chair. "Help us."

Julia followed Everett as he walked to the creek, guitar slung over his shoulder. He'd never played it before, but when he asked if she wanted to go with him to the creek after breakfast, she'd about said no, except he'd picked up his guitar. She hadn't heard music since she'd left Boston. Despite wanting to search for berries, she'd agreed to a small break. And if he sang while he played, then he couldn't be asking questions. Prying questions. Absurd questions.

He'd badgered her these last few days since Kathleen had given birth. Not on what she did on the homestead anymore, but about crazy things, like her favorite colors and what games she played as a child. He gave her advice on what to do each day, but then often remained around the house like a shadow, random, silly questions popping out of his mouth.

He made her uneasy. Not uneasy like Ned, but uneasy like . . . like how Theodore's eyes used to make her uneasy when they'd first met.

She played with the button on her collar. Everett's new pastime was watching her. But not like an overseer. He simply observed her. So many men had ogled her in the past, but he didn't leer, he . . . Well, it was just unsettling.

At the bank's edge, he leaned against a willow tree. She sat at the base of the one across from him.

He plucked at the strings while turning the little knobs at the top. "So, what songs do you know?"

"Oh, I don't know many songs." She fluffed her skirts around her.

"You seemed pretty excited to hear some music."

"I haven't heard music since I left home. But I've never heard much on the guitar. Just the symphony, so I wouldn't know what you could play on a guitar."

He whistled. "Just the symphony? That must have been grand."

She nodded. The sound of his tentative strumming, the haphazard melody he paid no attention to, made her heart swell with the same excitement she used to feel when the string section tuned before a concert. The promise of hearing sounds like that again convinced her that putting off chores to follow him would be worth it.

Evidently done fiddling with his instrument, he plopped down on the grass. "Did you sing at church?"

The happiness at the thought of listening to music fluttered away. God things were important to Everett. Well, at least all of a sudden. And the change in his attitude coincided with this God talk. She would have to humor him. "We went to church infrequently. Since we didn't have customers on Sundays, we did a lot of inventory and cleaning then."

"Do you remember any songs?"

"I might if I heard one."

He smiled and patted the ground next to him. "Come over here and sit by me."

"I'm fine here." She couldn't enjoy the music if she was but an arm's length away.

"But I'm not. How 'bout you get closer, so I can hear you sing?"

Oh no no no. "You don't want me to sing."

"Why not? Surely you'll catch the words after a few times through. Then you can join me."

"I don't sing well enough." Her father had let her know that often. And he wasn't wrong, judging by the looks she'd received in church the few times she attempted a hymn.

He patted the ground next to him again. "It doesn't matter. You'll catch on."

Julia moved to a closer tree, but not to where his hand lay on the ground.

He leaned back and closed his eyes, strumming the strings gingerly, as if it were a pet. He opened one eye and glanced over at her. "I'm a bit rusty." He gave her a playful smile.

Her breath caught at the fleeting grin. Then Everett settled back, eyes closed, fingers working the strings. That smile had passed quickly, but it transformed his work-weary face into a handsome one. Her heart beat with heightened rhythm. All the girls back in Boston would be jealous if they saw that smile. She averted her gaze to the sky. Billowing clouds hid the sun, lazily floating by. A flock of birds changed directions three times before settling in a tree.

She closed her eyes to listen to his guitar and the sound of water trickling behind her. Much more beautiful than a church organ. Not quite as captivating as the symphony, but close. The simple melody Everett plucked soothed her anxiety over wasting daylight. His clear tenor pierced the air, and she opened her eyes just enough to study him.

He sang with expression, head resting against the tree, eyes closed. Like he meant it.

Good thing she refused to sing—she'd ruin the sound of

his singing with hers. After a few repetitions, she could have attempted the song. If she had a different voice.

"Fairest Lord Jesus, ruler of all nature,
O Thou of God and man the Son,
Thee will I cherish, thee will I honor,
Thou my soul's glory, joy, and crown.

"Fair are the meadows, fairer still the woodlands,
Robed in the blooming garb of spring;
Jesus is fairer, Jesus is purer,
Who makes the woeful heart to sing."

After playing the song through a few times, he sighed and looked over at her. "Forgot how much I enjoyed singing. Feel like you can join in yet?"

She clasped her hands. "You don't want me to ruin your song with my sorry attempt at singing."

"God doesn't care what it sounds like, just so long as you mean it."

She wasn't sure He didn't care. And she wasn't sure she could mean it. "No, thank you. I'm enjoying listening more than I would trying to remember the words and sing."

After playing a few more chords, he laid the guitar across his lap. "What church did you attend in Boston?"

She squirmed. He was ready to pester again. Maybe it would have been better to have massacred the song with her pitiful voice. "Summer Street Church."

He stretched out his legs. "What kind of church was it?"

She tore apart the grass in her hands. "I don't know. Big? Father took us there because Mr. Kendall and Mr. Yang attended."

"Kendall and Yang?"

She shrugged. "Two men who did business with my father. Well, Kendall did. Father just wished he did business with Mr. Yang. He made sure to greet them each time we went."

"So you really didn't go that much?"

"No." Would he be mad? It's not like they attended church often here either.

"Did they teach from the Bible?"

"I didn't have a Bible to look up what they were saying, but I'm sure that's what churches do." She searched her mind for a chore that would have enough persuasive power to excuse her from this interrogation. Church could be important for him, but it wasn't for her, and she didn't want to say anything to offend him since they were finally on speaking terms.

He leaned forward over his guitar. "Did they talk much about Christ and how to know God?"

"I suppose so." Would he be angry if she admitted she didn't think you could really know God? Everett certainly talked to the air like God listened to him when he prayed over meals, but maybe that's just how he learned to pray. But even if God did listen to him, He wouldn't listen to her. "The pastor definitely harped on the things we did wrong."

"Did he touch on God's love, and how He wants to get to know you?"

She got on her knees and brushed the broken blades of grass off her front. "I'm sure he did. I better get to making lunch, if you would excuse me—"

"Julia, wait a second."

She stopped herself from standing. *Please let me go.*

"I need to apologize for something."

Apologize? Could he see how much this was bothering her?

"The way I've acted these past weeks has not reflected God's love." He picked at his hat. "Not at all, actually. I hope

188

you can forgive me." He cleared his throat. His face a slight hue of pink. "I shouldn't have been so . . . scared to talk to you. I was an idiot because—"

"It's all right, Everett." She stood and nodded to break off his discomfiture. When his mouth opened again, she rushed to cut him off. "I've got to get back to work, but feel free to enjoy your music. I'll have lunch ready by the time you get back."

She gathered her skirts and stumbled over the tree root in her haste. A few minutes passed before his guitar droned his song again, but he didn't join in with lyrics. She glanced over her shoulder. He lazily strummed, staring into the sky.

Thankful to be free from his questions, she strode home, passing the new cabin. The light color of the wood exterior gave it a shiny appearance compared to the old shack. He'd spent a lot of time on it.

She rounded the corner and frowned at her wilting garden plants. She wasn't the girl he needed. Even if she scrounged around in the prairie all day, she'd not have enough stored up for the winter to see them through. That's what he'd asked her here for, why he'd married her. He needed someone who knew how to run a farm. A girl who liked going to church. A woman who wanted to be a lover and mother. A wife who wasn't her.

She groaned as she picked up the buckets and trudged to the pond. If it would only rain, she could use the well again. If Everett prayed for anything, it ought to be for a nice storm. She struggled with the weight of the pails and the heaviness inside.

How she had longed for Everett's chatter, but now his talk ranged too close, too intimate, and his gaze made her uncomfortable. They'd only been married for a month and a half. As much as she would love to live in a nicer, larger house, perhaps it would be best if they lived in separate buildings. His gaze measured her too often lately, especially when she passed on adding to the prayers at mealtime. She couldn't ask him to allow her to live alone in the house he'd worked hard on, but she feared staying close to a man who looked at her like he did: boldly yet alluring, judging yet compassionate. But then, could she handle being alone, completely alone on the wind-blasted prairie? He was nothing like Theodore beyond coloring and build. Could her heart yield and her fears subside enough to give him a chance?

She needed time. More time.

The sound of harnesses brought her up short.

An unfamiliar team stood strapped to a shoddy wagon in front of the shack. Gooseflesh formed on her arms. Julia glanced toward the path to the creek but didn't see Everett. Breathing deeply, she forged ahead to welcome the visitor.

No one stood near the wagon. She dropped off her buckets at the garden's edge. A twinge in her gut kept her from calling out a greeting. A proper visitor would have waited near his animals or announced himself.

She stood on tiptoe and peered in the cabin's window. No one inside. She spied the shotgun on the rack above the cookstove and stepped inside to grab it. Her hands shook with its weight. She tried to figure out how to hold it to appear as if she knew what she was doing. Another thing a farmer's wife ought to know. She tested its weight a few times in her hand. Giving up, she decided to use it for a club if need be. With the firearm at her side, she slinked out onto the porch and scanned the yard. Still clear.

The barn door stood ajar. Trembling and sweat made it

difficult to hold on to the gun's stock, but she pushed herself to cross the distance. She lifted the gun to her shoulder, ready to heave it down upon an intruder like an ax. Her breathing matched the rhythm of her heart.

A hunched figure in the barn's shadowy interior stirred.

Chapter 15

The shadow unfurled and the outline of a cowboy hat popped off the specter's top and traveled to its chest.

"Afternoon, sweetheart." The voice was sickeningly sweet. "Whatcha got there?"

Julia grabbed the stock tighter. She should run. Oh, how she wanted to run, but it would expose her back. "Who are you? And what are you doing in my barn?"

The figure's swagger was familiar. Ned Parker's face showed up in a beam of light stabbing through a gap in the roof.

Her stance eased, but her heart sped up. "What are you doing here, Mr. Parker?"

He stopped in front of her and held his palms out, away from his body. "You can put that gun down. I'm no thief." His eyes narrowed.

She should lower her gun, but though he was a neighbor, her arms wouldn't cooperate.

He chuckled. "It'd be easier to stop a criminal or critter iffen you made ready to use that gun for shooting. Not for clobbering."

She lowered the shotgun and shoved the barn door wide

open. Light, much more light, was required. "Again, Mr. Parker, what are you doing in my barn?" His sneer made her skin prickle. So much like Theodore's the moment she told him she wouldn't marry him. She shuffled away and threw a glance toward the path, hoping the pale blue of Everett's shirt would appear through the leaves. Nothing but green.

Ned strolled up to her, his thumbs tucked in his leather belt. "It's Ned, sweetheart." His lips pushed up his scraggly mustache. "I'm here to borrow Everett's plow. Mine's broken." The left side of his face twitched.

His eyes wandered from hers to other parts of her body. Cold shivered up her back and pooled in the base of her skull. Could she not get away from these kinds of men? She looked out at the line of trees. Why wasn't Everett shadowing her like he had the past few days? "I'm afraid I can't give permission for you to take it."

He leaned his body against the doorjamb, his focus returned to her eyes. "That's all right. Was just getting it ready. I'll wait for Everett."

Did a plow need to get ready? If only she knew more about farm things! How long would Everett be gone? She didn't want Ned to wait around. "I can go get him for you."

"No need. What I'm really needing is something to drink."

Julia ignored the way his tongue moved across his lips. "I've got . . ." She crimped her eyes shut. She couldn't invite him in. What if he tried something? But what else could she do if he was here for something the men had already discussed? "I could bring you some tea while you wait. Everett should be along soon." And if he wasn't back by the time she'd finished serving Ned, she'd go get him.

His lips twirked. "You serving sweetened tea?"

She tipped her head down.

"Of course you are." He put his cowboy hat back on. "What other kind of tea would you serve?" He reached for her shotgun. "Let me carry that back for you."

She jerked it to her shoulder, cradling its butt in the palm of her hand. "I've got it, thank you." She didn't want his help for anything.

He shrugged. "Suit yourself. I could teach you to use that thing properly. Then when a real scoundrel came along, you'll have him in quite a predicament." He took a step closer. "Of course, just batting your lashes over them dark brown eyes could get a man in quite a predicament of another sort."

The ice crystals residing at the base of her skull shuddered out to her elbows. "This way, Mr. Parker." She turned and practically ran to the cabin. Where she'd invited him. Dumb, dumb, dumb.

She faced him as she held open the door with her back. "It's too hot to go inside. Why don't you just have a seat on the porch, and I'll bring you a cup." He hadn't sped up to match her pace, but swaggered. She slammed the door behind her, not waiting for a response.

She leaned the shotgun against the wall and banged through the pots. Light poured into the room as Ned moseyed in and sat himself at the table. She set one pan with water to boil. Another one she gripped, testing its weight. She could swing it hard if she had to. Hit him square in the face.

What was she thinking? Her nerves popped like the little roiling bubbles in the pan as she kept her face turned from where he sat watching her. He was simply an ill-mannered neighbor, even had his dirty feet on her table.

If only she hadn't felt obligated to be neighborly, she could have left him in the barn. She gulped some breaths and stared out the window. If only she hadn't been so quick to get away from Everett's pesky questions. She straightened her shirt-waist and then gathered the cups. Overreacting. Ned was unpleasant, yes, but surely he'd try nothing with a married woman.

"You don't have to be so anxious for your man to come back. I know you ain't much to him." He chuckled low and rumbly. "'Course, wouldn't suspect no man really matters to you."

She turned, eyes narrowed, and her short breaths returned. "What?"

Ned shrugged and leaned farther back. "Same as me—he needed a wife to handle chores." He tipped his head toward the bedding made neatly in the corner. "Nothing else."

She colored. She needed to put that makeshift bed away in the mornings. Her hand tightened around the spare skillet.

"But as for me, I don't get why that's all he wants you for." He stood and sauntered over to the stove. "Why'd you come running to Kansas to marry up with a no-account farmer?"

His unwavering gaze pierced hers. She had to take a step back. The tilt of his eyebrows made her heart stab her chest.

"There's only so many reasons a lady runs off to marry a stranger." He tilted his head. "One, she ain't nothing to look at, but we know that ain't your reason."

"My reasons are none of your business." Julia stepped to the other side of the stove to grab the tea canister, but knocked it over. "If you don't mind returning to your seat, I could keep track of what I'm doing."

"Or she don't got no money." He reached out to finger the lace on her shoulder. "Appears to me Daddy had plenty of money."

She stepped back, pulling her shirt from his grasp. "I've had enough of your surmising—"

"So that leaves me to thinking you're running from what you was." His gaze never left hers, like he was trying to dig out her past from the depth of her soul.

She sucked in a breath and closed her eyes. Where could she run? She'd married Everett to protect her from this! Where was he? "You're wrong, Mr. Parker."

"Then tell me why you're here." He flicked her chin up toward him, his face dark. "And why you're trembling like a trapped kitten."

She poured the hot water into two tin cups and dumped in the tea. She set his drink down at the narrow end of the table. "Your tea's ready." If she let on that his deductions were near correct, he'd use it to his advantage, so she threw back her shoulders and stared him down.

He let a slow smile creep across his face before he returned to his seat. He lowered himself into the chair and leaned back.

She sat across from him and pushed away from the table. She could still reach her cup, though she knew she'd have difficulty drinking any of it. Everett's name played over and over in her head—like her soul was beckoning him to her side. He was twice the size of Ned and better built. Everett would fight for her.

Ned took a sip and smirked. She knew that look. "Mmm-mmm. Tastes mighty fine."

She gave him a tight-lipped smile and put the cup to her mouth, but couldn't make herself taste it. Every inch of her being told her to run, but where would she go that he couldn't follow? She needed to keep her distance and convince him to leave on his own.

Minutes ticked by as Ned's perusal unnerved her. "Your kind of woman doesn't belong out here on the prairie as the wife to one man."

She focused on keeping her breathing regular. Could he really be able to guess what had made her run? No, he couldn't have gotten information about her from back east. But then, she'd not assumed a false name or kept her hometown a secret. No, he was only playing some cruel guessing game. Well, she wasn't going to participate.

He leaned across the table and waited until she met his eyes. "Just like Everett said, you don't belong with him. He regrets marrying you. Especially with the games you're playing." Again he glanced at the pallet on the floor.

Her chest moved with the rapid emptying and filling of her lungs despite her efforts to take slow, deep breaths. "Everett wouldn't have talked to you about any such thing."

He shrugged and sipped his tea, watching her over the brim as he drank.

She stifled an all-over body shiver. Could it be true? Ned had spent a lot of time with Everett soon after their wedding day with the coyote tanning. Would Everett say such a thing out loud? She fingered the tablecloth, feeling its fine embroidery. The same cloth she'd pulled out from the woman's trunk stowed under Everett's bed. He'd never given her any explanation for the items she had pulled out and displayed around the cabin. Then Rachel had told her about her sister, and Kathleen assumed Carl was jealous of Everett. Could he be regretting being tied to one woman—especially a woman who wasn't giving him any favors?

She didn't know Everett at all. He'd shared nothing about himself. But he wasn't that kind of man. He found her desirable, but the look in his eye was nothing like Ned's or Theodore's . . . or was it just different? Unsure of his true character, she had trusted Rachel wouldn't set her up with an indecent man. But what if her friend had been wrong?

But then, she'd shared none of her past with Everett. Maybe he'd done some checking of his own. Would her father inform him about what had happened if Everett asked? Did the whole town of Boston gossip about her as if she were a loose woman?

Her chair scraped the floor when she shot out of her seat. What she did know was she didn't want to hear any more from Ned. "I find this to be an inappropriate conversation. I think you ought to head outdoors."

Ned took a slow sip from his cup and watched her. "Just thought I'd tell you, figuring it has to do with you. Might help you make decisions. But to tell the truth, I agree with him. You don't belong on the prairie." He stood and walked around the table.

She put the chair between them before he reached her. She gripped the back of the chair with sweaty palms. "Well, I for one don't need you to tell me where I do or do not belong."

"It's too bad you ended up with Everett. You could have had so much more. A man who wanted you . . . in spite of what you are." Ned's eyes flashed.

"I think you've said enough, Mr. Parker." Her heart thumped erratically in her throat. Would that she had trusted her instincts and not offered him tea! She searched for anything heavy in sight, but nothing but the chair was available to keep him away. Could she make it past him to grab a heavy pot before he blocked her? "Maybe you ought to go check on that plow." Despite trying to keep her voice steady, it wavered.

"You could be mistress to a man who knows how to handle you. How to keep a woman of your—" he licked his lips, and his voice dropped—"talents happy." He leaned forward.

She stepped back and hit the wall, glaring at him as hard

as she could. He stood in the pathway to the door, and even if she could dodge around him, her short legs would be no match for his long ones in a race.

He took his time perusing her body. "You're no innocent angel, are you?" His breaths were heavy and slow.

She glanced toward the pot of boiled water, and Ned moved sideways. He'd catch her if she ran that way as well. *God, could you make Everett come home?* "I will pretend that I don't understand what you are insinuating. Leave now and—"

"You don't defend yourself." His smile widened. "I thought so." He leaned over and clasped onto her jaw. "Before God, can you deny it?"

Her teeth were clamped so hard her head ached. "Unhand me." Her breathless words quavered in the space between them. But the sound of tears in the back of her throat couldn't be masked. Would that God would send Everett to her!

Ned reached out and grabbed both of her wrists and yanked her forward. The top of the chair between them wedged into his chest. The legs of the chair slipped to each side of her legs. He pushed both her and the chair against the wall. "It's not right to keep a woman with your gifts for one man who won't even use you. But I'm"—he leaned over to put his hot breath next to her ear—"going to get what I want. One way or another."

The shiver in her body couldn't escape the confines of her flesh and grew more violent until her whole body shook. Trapped. How could this happen again?

"No," she snarled, but her command didn't change the look in his eyes. His grip tightened.

Tears threatened to crowd her vision, but she blinked heavily, needing to see. Perchance something would materialize to help her out of this situation. But nothing had nine months ago. Why would this time be any different? Her throat clogged. There was no way out.

The chair.

He would need to move the chair before he could grab more of her. This cage was good, but soon he'd remove that obstacle. Unless she did it first.

Her breathing labored. If she tried to use it as a weapon, she might be throwing away the one thing keeping her safe. Everett could be just around the corner. But if he wasn't, the chair wouldn't deter Ned for long.

Growling, she collected her quivering strength and shoved the chair into his stomach. He stumbled back, but the force wasn't enough to push him far. She hooked her foot around his ankle and yanked, taking advantage of his poor balance. He fell on his rump and cursed.

He threw the chair to the side, let out a disturbing laugh, and jerked her foot out from under her before she could run past. She hit the floor.

"I like feisty women."

She screamed and scrambled back against the wall. Would that she were dead.

Chapter 16

Pain jolted through Julia's arm sockets, and then she crashed into a wall. She swiped the hair from her eyes so she could aim a kick at Ned.

But he wasn't in front of her.

A maniacal growl filled the room, sending shivers down her spine.

Ned's body thumped against the wall three feet away. Everett's left hand twisted into Ned's plaid shirt. As soon as Ned opened his eyes, Everett's right fist cracked squarely on Ned's jaw.

Ned stumbled back, hand cupping his chin. "Wait! I ain't done nothing," he growled through clenched teeth.

"That's not what I call nothing." Everett's fists doubled.

Ned put out his arms in a blocking position. "She fell."

"That's not what it looked like." Everett's face was redder than a tomato.

"Your woman made me some tea and fell. Knocked me over." Ned straightened and glared at her. "Tell him."

He was expecting her to lie for him! She clenched her hands in the fabric of her skirt. "That's a lie!"

Ned spat at her.

Another of Everett's jabs found a home in Ned's stomach.

She wanted to cry, but she couldn't tear her eyes away from the angry scuffle. Had prayer actually worked? Had God sent Everett to her?

Ned swore and scrambled off the floor. He held out his hands and circled to the door, facing Everett as he shuffled. "My word against hers."

Everett sent a punch into Ned's cheek, sending him flying into the stove. "I take her word." He jerked Ned up by his shirt and threw him against the wall. "And as for your words, I never want you to speak to her again. You leave and don't ever come back."

Ned held out his hands. "Fine," he snarled.

"If we meet again," Everett said as he straightened, "you walk away. If you can't leave, you go to the furthest corner from my wife and you stay there."

"You can't tell me where I can and can't be."

Everett crossed the room and hoisted him against the splintery wall. "If I ever see you on my property again, it's a bullet in your gut."

Ned winced as spit hit him in the eye.

"I won't be letting you run off like I'm doing now. In town, if you so much as look at her too close, I'll pummel you." Everett shoved Ned toward the door.

Ned glanced hatefully at her before slamming the door behind him. The upper leather hinge gave way.

Before the door stopped swinging, Everett was on his knees beside her. He grabbed her shoulders. "Are you hurt?"

She shook her head. The pressure behind her eyes and forehead wanted to burst through her nose. She covered her eyes with both of her hands, shielding the tears from his sight. Hurt? Not on the outside, but the inside felt like one big bruise. Even with Ned gone, she felt like running, running and not stopping. Running with no aim. For where would she go? No place was safe.

Or was she in the right place? Would Everett be able to protect her every time? Or if she let him into her heart, would he hurt her too?

She began to shiver, then the emotions she'd restrained for months broke, and a dry heave preceded a deluge of tears. She rocked and tried to stop the rush of tears with the palms of her hands.

He gently tugged at her wrists. "Shhh. It's all right."

Resisting his pull, she kept her hands where they were. She didn't want to deal with anything right now. She wanted to stay in the dark.

Everett continued to shush her. He pushed hair behind her ear. Both of his hands moved to turn her jaw to the side. "The lout. He scratched your face good."

Her sobs stopped, and she gritted her teeth. Her face! Who cared about anything else as long as her beauty was intact to exploit, to desire, to take? She shot the evil look she'd given Ned at Everett.

He sat back and cocked his head.

"I'm sure my face is just fine. I make sure to keep it protected at all times. Don't want to have anything happen to my face! Leave me alone." She scrambled to her feet and pushed through the door. With a quick check to make sure Ned's wagon was nowhere in sight, she ran into the thicket.

———

"Julia! Julia, stop. Please!"

When she disappeared into the brush, Everett swallowed hard. His heart cramped in his chest.

Should he run after her? It seemed she didn't want him, and all his body wanted to do was collapse. Incredible amounts of energy had kicked in as soon as he'd walked around the Parkers' wagon and saw Ned and Julia fall to the floor through his open doorway. He'd been a fool to let the man off so easily the last time he was here. Maybe he'd been a fool to let him walk now. He kicked the railing and winced at the pain. Gripping a wooden post, he stared through the distant foliage.

Even if the scratch on her face was as deep as it looked, why'd she run from his protective reach with Ned barely out of the yard? He didn't know what made the woman tick. He'd studied every curve and plane that filled out her dress, every dimple and freckle on her face. Asked her every question he could think of, but he still didn't know her, not at all.

He slumped against the beam. He'd prided himself on caring for every woman the same regardless of her physical features. But he probably understood Helga better than his own wife.

Sitting on the railing, he took slow breaths to settle the rattling in his chest. His fingers raked into his hair until they caught in the gnarled mess, his forehead cradled in the palms of his hands. He closed his eyes and searched his soul.

He wanted a real marriage. Not a convenient one. Not a fake one. Not one governed like master and slave. But one like his parents had. When his dad had stepped in the door after a long day's work, the first person he'd greeted was his mother. Not because his father forced himself to do so or was stuck in a routine, but because that was all he wanted to do.

And that's what Everett wanted too. To care for her, protect her, love her. To know she spent the day waiting to step back into his arms.

He had to shuck his restraint and lay himself open. She

might stomp on his heart and crush him into tiny bits, but would he not deserve it for how he'd treated her?

He pushed himself off the post and grabbed his hat off the porch before walking toward the woods. A bit of blue through the scrub brush down by the pond broke through the green and brown. His heart beat low and hard as he threaded his way through the thicket.

He'd start slow. But he would woo his wife. No matter what personality lay behind the veneer of beauty, she was the only wife he had. And that made her worth it.

Chapter 17

Everett's footfalls sounded behind her. She wiped her tears with her sleeve, grabbed a rock, and hurled it into the pond. Why must he bother her? She'd been bothered enough today, bothered enough for a lifetime.

Not even glancing toward him, she found another rock close to where she sat and chucked it into the water. Everett's knees cracked as he settled in the grass beside her. As long as he didn't touch her, she'd endure his presence.

The frogs hidden in the grasses along the banks chirped in rhythmic pulses. Bubbles popped on the water's surface where a turtle's nose poked into the air. She hugged her knees and leaned against the tree, waiting for him to speak. Nothing he could say could unclench her stomach or make her gooseflesh go away.

The frogs croaked on.

Keeping her head down, she looked at the ground next to him. His hand lay flat on the earth inches from her skirt. A knot of purple and blue puffed his top knuckles. She blinked back tears at the sight of his bruises. He'd saved her. No matter what happened, she'd always be thankful he'd rescued her. Though she wanted to be alone, a little part of her was glad he was there.

"I'm sorry I was so upset back there." She peeked at him from under her eyelashes. His eyes were ready the second hers found his. "I'm very grateful you came and saved me from . . . from . . ." Her mind's eye faded into gray. A good thing—otherwise she'd too easily summon up a picture of her fate if Everett hadn't arrived.

"Do you want to talk about it?" His voice was hushed, barely discernible above the insect humming.

She shrugged. Yes, she wanted to talk, but not to him. Not even to Rachel. Not to anyone she knew. What would they think of her?

The same as Ned.

Everett's hand inched toward hers, but she tucked her fingers under her skirt. He took his hand back. "I won't let him come onto the property anymore. He didn't . . . Did he do anything I should—"

"No." Her voice cracked. But he would have. How could she have endured another man forcing her to fulfill his pleasure? The thought of suffering through it again made her want to curl up so tight she'd vanish. "Ned didn't anyway . . ."

Everett's face grew a bit older, the question on his face unmistakable. "If you don't want to talk, how about you lean against me instead of that tree? At least let me help you feel a bit more comfortable."

She searched his face. Nothing but kindness and sympathy. She wanted comfort, but the tree would suffice. A man's arms—any man's arms right now—would not feel pleasant. She couldn't look at him anymore.

Like Ned said, Everett thought she didn't belong on the prairie, that she needed coddling. Life here couldn't break her—she'd prove it. No more tears, no more wasting time. Too soon harvest would come and then winter.

She stood and looked down at him. "I'll prove myself worthy of the trouble you've taken to save me."

He reached out and tugged on her skirt. "Please sit, Julia."

"There's no time to sit. I've got chores." The longer she remained here idle, the more likely she'd crumble in front of him.

He squinted at her.

She turned toward home and put speed into her feet.

Everett called to her, his voice rushing closer each second. "Wait."

She kept walking, but shortly his warm hand encircled her upper arm.

"There's no reason to rush. You've just been through something awful. We could use a day of rest."

"Chickens need tending." She took another step toward the house, pulling against his grasp.

He shook his head and took her other arm. "Then I'll see to them."

"Dinner needs fixed." The conflicting desires to flee his embrace and to bury herself there fought within her. Her fists tensed into tiny balls. No, she needed to be left alone.

"I lived on canned beans and hardtack before you came. I can come up with something." A small smile graced his lips.

The concern in his eyes, however, begged her to succumb. But she didn't want to be held. Ned and the men back home had only wanted her body. Theodore had gotten it. The thought of more touching made her shiver.

She pulled her arms from his hands. An embrace was not what she needed.

Crying mixed with the sound of the grease popping in the skillet. Julia took the pan off the stove and set it on a trivet. Poking her head out the door, she listened. Yes, crying. She glanced to the far field, where Everett had begun weeding and dispatching worms once they'd returned from the pond. He shuffled down rows at an even pace, flicking his hands back and forth, gathering the pests in a bucket for the chickens. She was thankful he hadn't followed her inside and insisted she answer more questions.

Her muscles tensed. Surely some crying man wasn't out there waiting to pounce on her. On the other side of the barn, a movement caught her attention. A thick-hipped woman hobbled in the shadows, her right leg stiff and her hair a tangled mess.

"Helga?" Her breath wedged in her throat as she raced to the woman's side.

Blood oozed from Helga's mouth. "I'm sorry, but you said I may come without asking."

Julia threaded her arm underneath Helga's and braced the woman, her tiny body acting like a human crutch. "Such nonsense. Don't apologize."

Every other step, Helga sucked in air. How had she gotten hurt? Could Ned have hurt this sweet woman because of her? She was pretty sure she knew the answer, but she held her tongue. It took all of her strength to keep Helga upright as she hobbled along.

She helped Helga to the bed, but the woman resisted. "No, your quilt will be dirty."

Julia gave her a gentle push. "Sit." She grabbed the pallet blankets and shoved them behind her neighbor so she could recline, then pulled the kitchen chair over to the bedside, the chair legs thunking against the planks. "What happened?" The gash next to the woman's mouth kept pulling Julia's attention to the blood dried there. She doubted that was the only injury the woman had. "What hurts?"

The lines around Helga's eyes grew pronounced as the woman squinted. A few moments later, she let out a long stream of air. "Lots of places."

Not being able to stand the sight of blood on the woman's face, Julia patted her shoulder. "I'm getting some water."

She filled the bucket and grabbed the dipper from the well. After helping Helga take a few sips, she wetted a cloth and wiped Helga's mouth. She tried to catch the woman's gaze, but she kept her eyes closed. How could Ned wreak so much evil in one day?

Finally, Helga looked at her, the pain evident in the funny way one eyelid drooped and the other spasmed. "Can I have cloth? My hands are dirty. And my knee—" She touched the bump under her dress and hissed. "I need clean it."

Wringing out the cloth, Julia passed it into the woman's filthy hands and grabbed another before pushing back the woman's skirts. A large abrasion marred her knee and shin. With as little pressure as possible, she cleaned the wound, but Helga still tensed. She examined her neighbor's round face. "Ned did this to you?"

"No." She let out something that sounded like a chuckle. "That he didn't do. I must need add pain to myself, so I trip on tree root."

"So Ned didn't hurt you?" Helga's muscles tightened when she brushed more grit from the cut. No one could get that many scratches and bruises by tripping on a root.

The line of Helga's mouth grew thinner and wider. "That

is not what I say. Just my knee. I do that myself." She pushed hair back from her face, uncovering a greenish ring around one eye.

"What did he do?" Similar to what she'd endured at his hands that morning, no doubt.

"Not much more than other times." She leaned against the blankets and wrung the limp cloth in her hands. "But more anger this time. Enough I was afraid he would not stop, so I run out the door when he grab something."

Julia sat in the chair and held Helga's hand in both of hers. Ned's anger was surely because of her. She was responsible. If only she'd never come to Kansas . . .

Helga's head rolled to the side. "He said things about you—"

"I don't want to hear them. Don't tell me." She didn't mean to snap, so she calmed her voice. "But do tell me where you hurt."

Helga shrugged and grimaced. "My face, my knee, and my head. He pulled hair. And then my arm."

"Did he say why he hit you?"

"No," she whispered. "But often he does not tell me reason."

"Helga . . . your husband was here earlier. He, uh, made some advances toward me, and Everett punched him a few times. I'm so sorry he went home to you the way he did." She'd considered her looks to be a problem for herself, but now they caused problems for others. "It's my fault."

Helga's glittering eyes snapped open wide. "No. He is to blame for what he does. Today he had more anger, but today is not the first day he hit me."

"He has no right."

Helga smiled lazily. "He would not say that."

"We need to get you away."

"I am away. I am here."

"But you can't go back to Ned."

A sigh escaped her lips. "Yes. I think that, but I don't know how I cannot. I have only one place to go, but no way to get there. The train is too much money. Ned doesn't have enough for me to take. But I've wanted to go to my sister for so long."

"Then we'll get you there."

"I wish that I never married Ned. But it is my fault, and I should live with my punishment."

"You could not have done anything that merits such treatment."

"It is not what I done, but what I did not do. You did right marrying Everett. And you are more beautiful and young than me, so that should make him very happy. He is a man who deserves good wife."

Julia frowned. How hard had Helga hit her head? She wasn't making sense. "What does my being—"

The loose door thumped against the wall. "Julia, we need to talk—" Everett's mouth dropped open, and he strode straight to Helga. "Are you all right?" He gently pushed back a swath of bloody matted hair from her forehead. Though he did it slowly, Helga winced.

"She's got scrapes and bruises. Ned took his anger out on her."

"Why, that low-down dirty—" Everett clamped his mouth.

"We can't let her go back." Julia clasped his upper arm.

He placed his hand over hers and turned to Helga. "That's right. You'll stay here until we figure this out."

"Yes, stay." A maternal fierceness low in her stomach rose to invade her chest. Helga had to be older than Everett, but her helplessness reminded her of little Emma Stanton. "And we'll get you back to your sister."

Helga shook her head. "I check railroad schedules. Second class is seventy-five dollars. I can sleep in my seat, but need food too. Can't get so much money. Ned has twenty dollars only."

Julia looked at Everett. Should she ask him if what was left in her purse should be used to help them through the winter? She'd kept it hidden in case she needed to get away. But would he agree to giving Helga so much cash? "I have a hundred and two dollars I've kept since I arrived. . . ."

She was worried about him disagreeing with giving Helga her savings. Everett could see it in the way she bit her lip, kept her gaze from meeting his, and tucked her head in. But hers was the perfect solution. He had enough to cover Helga's passage, but wiping out his savings needed for the winter if the harvest failed was not smart.

A hundred dollars was a lot of money, and she looked guilty at the mention of it.

"Please let me give it to her." Julia's eyes glistened.

If Helga wanted to abandon her monster of a husband, he'd help any way that he could, but if Julia wanted to leave later, how would she afford it? He didn't want her to go, but he didn't want her to stay if she didn't want him. He didn't like either option, but he wanted her to be happy. If she could give such a large sum to a neighbor, he could save enough to purchase Julia a ticket to return east someday if she ever wanted to go. He prayed he would never have to watch her leave on the train that had brought her to him.

He swallowed and nodded.

Julia's attention returned to Helga. She patted her hand.

"You won't be able to eat well, but we could send you with food."

Tears pooled and cascaded over onto Helga's cheeks, which were turning a strange shade of yellow. Everett's hands clenched. He should march over to the Parkers' place right now and make Ned's face match hers.

"I can't," Helga whispered.

Julia placed a hand on each of her shoulders and spoke when Helga looked up at her. "You will and you must. How long have you wanted to return to your family?"

Everett could barely hear her say, "Almost a year."

"Then it's my gift to you." Julia shook her head. She glanced over at him. "I mean *our* gift to you." Her eyes had never looked so soft and unguarded before. Was it simply concern, or something more?

When she broke from his gaze, Everett turned to the crumpled woman on the bed. "Don't argue, Helga. You take the money and get on the next train."

Helga shook her head, closed her eyes, and leaned against the wall. He glanced at Julia, who kept wiping the woman's wet hair with an equally wet cloth. Both women held their bottom lip between their teeth.

How could Helga not jump at the chance to leave? Ned was not a good husband, but Everett hadn't known to what extent. If it hadn't been for Julia, Helga probably would never have ventured over for help. She'd always been too ashamed by how she'd abandoned Everett to ask him for anything.

Why had he not done something before now? Had his embarrassment over being jilted so many times caused him to turn a blind eye to her suffering? He clasped the injured woman's hand and squeezed it gently. "It is my wish as well

214

as Julia's for you to use the money to return to your sister. You'll not be putting us out."

The front door slammed against the wall. "But you'll be putting me out."

Everett sprung to his feet. Why hadn't Merlin barked? The gall of the man to return the same day he'd been warned off his property forever. "Leave or—"

"Or what? You'll pummel me?" The smell of alcohol permeated the room. "You did that already." Ned flicked his hand, an unsheathed knife glinted in the filtered light.

Julia let out a gasp.

"You want to kill me? Try it." Ned brandished his blade and ducked his head toward Julia. "See? You ain't enough. Now he wants my wife—again."

Everett held out his hands and watched the path of the blade Ned haphazardly waved. He had no experience in a knife fight, but Ned's uneven steps and the knife's chaotic movements gave him confidence he could disarm him.

Ned lunged, his knife's tip targeted at Everett's heart. Without thinking, Everett grabbed the man's wrist with both hands. The sight of the blade inches from his nose caused him to tighten his grasp.

"Well, you ain't gonna get her," Ned growled.

The stench of liquor made him cringe. How much whiskey had the man consumed in just a matter of hours? Ned tried to shove the blade toward Everett's face, but he locked his elbows in defense. He took a step back and used Ned's unbalanced momentum to pull him forward, keeping his focus on the rusted blade. With each angry thrust Ned attempted, Everett pulled him further around in a circle, attempting to keep the blade from hitting anyone or anything. A few turns about the room brought the drunk down to the floor.

"Drop it." Everett shook the hand holding the blade.

"Forget it," Ned slurred.

Gritting his teeth, he slammed Ned's wrist into the planks with as much force as he could muster.

The knife clattered across the floor. "Ow! Stop hurting me." Ned tried to retract his hand. "Let me go."

Everett stood, fists ready.

Ned swore and pushed off the floor.

Everett punched him—once, twice, three times.

Ned scrambled backward.

Heart beating double time, Everett noted the pain in his already bruised knuckles. He watched Ned attempt to gain his feet and decided beating up a sloppy drunk didn't sit right. If he could steer him away, the drunk man might not even remember coming.

Yet, if he didn't follow through, this morning's threat had been empty. "Your wife is under my protection for now. I suggest you go home and sleep."

Ned hiccuped. "I'll do what I want." He staggered backward.

Everett shoved him to the door.

Ned hit the frame and called him a foul name.

Straightening, Everett glared at him. "Get out. Now!"

When Ned lunged toward him, Everett threw a fist and connected with Ned's soft middle. The man groaned with the contact, snarled, then lunged again.

Ned's fingernails clawed at his neck. Wrenching off the man's weak handhold, Everett spun him around and pushed him completely out the door.

Ned fell in the dirt and struggled to stand.

"When you get up, you'd better move in the opposite direction."

"I'll go." With one knee up, Ned used it as leverage to get the rest of him upright. "But Helga comes with me."

"Helga stays." Everett grabbed his shotgun from above the doorframe. Would it convince the man to leave without a further fight?

"You have no right anymore! You got Julia whether you want her or not." His fist pounded the air every few words, and Ned stumbled with the action. "You've no right to mess with my wife. Helga's mine!"

"If only you'd heeded my earlier admonition. Need I remind you that this morning you assaulted Julia? And now you've gone and hurt your own wife beyond what any decent man will forgive." He stepped off his stoop and stood, legs spread, with the shotgun aimed at Ned's chest. "She's staying. You're leaving."

"Who're you to tell me what to do?" Ned heaved and took a step back, then retched his lunch onto the dirt.

Everett wrinkled his nose at the foul odor. Ned's pitiful position made both sympathy and revulsion course through his veins. No reason to counter the man's drunken arguments; it would do no good. When Ned wiped his mouth, Everett pointed his finger to the south. "Go."

"I'll go since you ain't fighting fair." He swayed. "But I'll be back."

"Not unless you want to test my marksmanship."

"Don't think you've seen the last of me," Ned said with a hateful leer, then lurched and stomped out of the yard.

Chapter 18

Dropping his hoe against the barn wall, Everett wiped his brow and trudged over to the well to get a long draught of water. A swell of Julia and Helga's laughter came from the cabin, and he stood still until the last chuckle died away. He gulped down his water and stared into the inky hole, where a slight underground draft rose to tease his hot face.

He couldn't stay away from Julia long. Not anymore.

However, a one-room cabin felt entirely too small for two people who couldn't trust each other with their secrets. With three? Forget it.

Though it couldn't be far past noon, he'd finished the chores. What else could he do to keep from intruding upon the women's easy camaraderie? The last five nights, he'd slept in the barn and tended every crop and animal twice over during the day.

Two more days until Helga left. Had she told Julia about how she'd stayed in the Stantons' barn while determining he fell short at farming? Never mind that the weeds had grown tougher and the hedgerows had taken over the ground while he was away those long years at war. Never mind that locusts and droughts had set him back once he'd returned.

But he couldn't blame Helga for believing Ned's farm was better than his. It was. But Ned hadn't informed his new bride he'd acquired the property from a group of brothers who'd mismanaged their finances . . . but not their fields. Ned had no chance of maintaining the farm as well as the brothers had.

Still, he couldn't fault Ned for keeping secrets. Unless he blamed himself for the same.

He sat on the rim of the well and let his head slump back against the post. He should tell Julia everything—as soon as possible.

She'd said she wouldn't leave without telling him, yet he hadn't realized how easy it would have been for her to do so. A hundred and two dollars surely could've bought her a ticket back home.

His heart wasn't going to break because she'd leave—rather because she'd stay and never love him.

But Dex had said he treated her no better than Ned treated Helga. Oh, he'd not hit her—never would—but did he truly love her if he was only worried about himself all the time?

She didn't want his touch, but why would she if she didn't feel secure? A touch without love was like the slaps Ned lavished upon Helga's face. But how could he show love without contact?

The jangle of harnesses and cadence of hoofbeats on the road raised his hackles. Surely Ned wouldn't come back so noisily, but he untied the knife at his side just in case.

At the bend in the road, William Stanton rode in alone, smiling upon seeing him. The boy waved and then steered his mount toward the well.

Everett cupped handfuls of water to his face and neck and smoothed back his hair before greeting him. "What brings you here on this surprisingly windless, miserable day?"

A Bride for Keeps

"Visiting." William slid off his mare and rubbed her neck before leading her to a shady patch of grass Blaze had yet to rip from the ground. "Ma said Julia was worried about the gash in Helga's knee. Dr. Forsythe isn't around, so Ma thought I could look at it." He shrugged as if it weren't odd for folks to ask a sixteen-year-old about their coughs, fevers, and rashes. Most people simply consulted a passed-around copy of *Gunn's Domestic Medicine* to avoid pay-ing—or feeling guilty for not paying—Dr. Forsythe. Half the time the physician's remedies of blistering and purging made them feel worse, so they only called on him in dire circumstances.

But William's strange interest in herbs had led him to be a walking medical guide if the worn copy of *Gunn's* was unavailable.

"Let me take you to her then."

"Um, before we go in, do you mind if I ask you something?" The boy's face was a little too red. Unless he had a sunburn.

"Shoot." Everett swiped at the trickles of water dripping from his hair and down his neck.

"I can't ask Ma or Pa because they're . . . well, they're the happiest couple I know. The way they tell it, even their jabs at one another are an expression of love." William pulled a face only a child witnessing his parents' kiss could. "They don't understand what it's like to love someone who doesn't exactly worship the ground you walk on."

Oh, why hadn't he been inside when William came down the road? However, he couldn't ignore the boy. He'd certainly come to the right man for advice if he loved a woman who wasn't in love with him. "Are we talking about Nancy? You're both barely sixteen."

William rolled his eyes. "People marry that young all the

220

time. And you can't say I ain't a man. I've been overseeing Pa's cattle almost singlehandedly for a year now."

"I didn't say you weren't a man, William. I'm just saying you have plenty of time to make up your mind about Nancy. Don't rush into anything." He swatted at a fly buzzing his neck. "I was in love at eighteen—and too young to realize her love was shallower than the root of a lettuce plant."

William rubbed at his temples. "It's not that I don't think Nancy loves me. I just don't know if it's enough. She's really pushing me to go to medical school." He flung out his hands and sighed. "Which I'd love to do, but I can't afford it. It's a wealthy man's vocation. Ma's been talking about saving money for me to apprentice under Dr. Forsythe, but my parents need that money, and there'd be years of fees, though I could work to pay some of them. And that's only if he'd be willing. He's never apprenticed anybody as far as I know. But I'm not even sure I should."

"Don't you want to?"

"Oh no, I want to. But then, life isn't always about wants, is it?" William crossed over to the fence and sat on the top rail, sagging it a bit. "If I marry Nancy, what kind of husband would I be if I'm gone all the time like Dr. Forsythe? He doesn't have a wife, and I'm sure everyone's glad of it. He'd want to stay home instead of attend patients. People who rely on him in emergencies would suffer while he dined with the wife and kids. Or his family would eat without him days, maybe weeks, at a time."

Everett moved to sit next to him. He folded his hands between his knees. How could he advise a boy who had his head screwed on straighter than he had his own?

What kind of husband would he be if he were gone all the time? Probably not much worse than he was now. "I can't give you any better advice than you're giving yourself. Have you prayed about it?" Here he was telling him to pray about big life decisions, when he hadn't bothered to ask the Lord His opinion on which woman to write.

"I don't feel any peace after praying about it either. I just don't know what to do." William drummed his fingers on his thighs. "But I want both, Nancy and medicine."

"Well, perhaps you can have both. Maybe it's not worth being a doctor out here. Maybe if you go east and settle in a town—"

"They'd want a college-educated doctor."

"Or you could put off the wedding. You don't have to get married the moment you find the girl." Or the moment one shows up who's willing. "But I'm afraid I don't know enough about medicine to advise you there." Not that he knew enough about women to counsel the boy on that either.

William picked at his fingernails. "Should you part with someone because you don't agree on the big things in life?"

Closing his eyes, Everett wished he'd sent William back to his father for advice. "I've always been the one left behind." He let out a derisive chuckle. "I haven't had the opportunity to consider such a thing."

"But Julia is . . . " William looked askance before continuing. "Well, she doesn't exactly seem to be in tune with you, so what keeps you working at your relationship?"

Everett turned his eyes toward heaven. Why had God summoned a sixteen-year-old to probe his failings? "I have wedding vows. You're not as bound as I, but if you find yourself in love, you'll start counting the cost of the changes necessary to keep her. Change hurts; but if she's worth marrying, she's worth the pain." Everett stood to avoid William's gaze as he uttered the rest of the damning evidence against himself. "If you can't make the changes, then your love isn't deep enough to commit yourself."

"Thanks." William rose and gestured toward the shack. "Think they'd mind if I check on Helga now? I've got a lost calf and its mother to find before dark."

Everett tried not to audibly sigh with relief. He needn't add any more shame to his weighed-down soul by listening to a boy who'd thought through marriage more than he had for any of his five brides. "Sure, we can go."

William nodded, and a strange lump shimmied under his vest.

"Hold up." Everett pointed to the boy's chest. "You got some strange disease?"

William reached in and tugged at the stubborn lump. "She must have just woken up. She refuses to stay in my pocket." He pulled out a puff of white and gray tabby the size of an apple from behind his vest. The kitten's claws strained to keep contact with his shirt. "She's like sticky weed. You don't think Julia would want to bottle-feed a kitten, do you?"

"We'll see." With big blue eyes and fur sticking straight out around the kitten's body like dandelion fluff, how could a woman refuse?

"Pa told me not to bother with this runt since Tiger has eleven others and he doesn't want that many barn cats. So it's not like you have to take this one. You could have your pick when they're weaned . . . but I couldn't just let her die." He put the cat's nose up to his. The little thing's paws trembled as it cried. "But Pa's about had it with me nursing a cat instead of getting all my chores done."

Everett held out his hands, and William handed the fluffy thing over. Within seconds of getting close to his chest, the fur ball attached itself and started climbing up his torso as if a flash flood had risen to waist level. "I think this might make a good gift. Women can't refuse cute, needy things, right?"

"Sure."

Maybe he should work on being cuter.

William handed over a little glass bottle with a makeshift rubber nipple at the top. "I just feed her warm milk whenever she gets whiny and tenderize some meat for her whenever we've got some left. She was a touch sickly before her eyes opened, but I think she's good as long as she eats."

Everett pulled her off his collar and tried to stick her in his pants pocket. She wasn't about to go in there. "I'm going to go get a box. Why don't you go on in."

In the barn, he found a tightly slatted crate and put the kitten inside, but she mewed pitifully and climbed out. "All right, I'll give you a ride to the cabin."

In the shack, Helga smiled weakly at Everett from the bed but continued answering William's questions. He seemed to find her ailments fascinating.

The kitten mewed in Everett's ear.

Julia stopped kneading dough and turned a quizzical look on him. "What's that?"

She must not see men wearing gray tabby mufflers in the summer often. He beckoned for Julia to follow him outside, so she folded the dough one more time and plopped it in the pan.

Sitting on the porch step, he patted the spot beside him, then tried to pull the cat off his shoulder. "I have a present for you. Granted, a needy present that requires bottle-feeding."

"It's adorable." Julia grabbed the kitten, its claws pulling a thread in protest. "Boy or girl?"

"Girl."

She nuzzled it. "Did William bring her?"

"Yeah. He can't care for it anymore, but I figured you could. And we could use a mouser, as long as Merlin doesn't eat it."

"What shall we name her?"

She was asking for his opinion? "William said she hangs on like sticky weed."

The kitten's arms were spread out against Julia's bodice as if it could hug her with its six-inch arm span.

"She's just frightened." She extricated the thing off her shirtwaist and tucked it up into a ball under her chin. "How about Sticky for short?"

He chuckled. "Sure, it's your decision."

"Can we can keep her inside for a while?"

"I tried putting her in a box, but for something so small she sure put up a fight." He displayed his scratched hand to prove it.

"Now look what you did, Sticky. You can't go hurting Everett. He's nice enough to let you sleep with me until you're no longer frightened."

Lucky fur ball. And he'd continue sleeping in the barn, where a cat ought to be.

He scratched the kitten behind its ears, a funny rumbling coming from its throat despite its wary eyes. "She likes you." He let his hand move off the fuzzy lump and skimmed Julia's cheek with his thumb. He dropped his hand before Julia's face registered the same wide-eyed fearful stare as the cat.

Julia stared out at the horizon, and he turned to do the same. Lately, she seemed irritated by his questions, so he held his tongue. Though being alone for the first time in nearly a week tempted him to try conversation again.

He'd learned her favorite color was blue, she was an only child, and her middle name was Anne. But she never gave him anything beyond simple answers. And she never asked him much of anything.

No wonder they hadn't gotten far in this marriage. He'd known more about Rachel's sister within two weeks of courting, and he'd willingly spilled his every thought and dream to the vain girl. A woman who'd jilted him knew more about his heart than Julia.

So he'd try a new tactic.

"I used to bring stray cats home when I was little. Mother would shake her head and feed them, and then they'd disappear in the morning to a 'good home.' I've always wondered if Father really found them a home or whether I just hastened the cats' demise."

"Well, that's not exactly a happy story." Julia's eyebrows and lips scrunched as if erasing the image of their likely fate.

He started to laugh, then couldn't stop himself despite Julia looking at him like he was a madman.

"I'm so sorry." He coughed trying to get himself under control. "Here I thought I'd share something about my past, and I came up with that." He pressed his lips together and swiped at his eyes, but laughed again.

She smiled. "I've never had a cat. Always wanted one."

He sobered up and smiled back. "Then I'm glad I get to be the one to make that dream come true." Maybe in time, he could discover some other wishes she'd been denied and provide them as well. Though he had no need for a pony, he'd keep a look out for a white horse.

"Don't exhaust yourself, Helga." Julia grabbed one of the water pails from her friend, who insisted on doing more chores on her last day than Julia could do in a week.

"I need help you."

"Of course you can help, but I want to talk too. Enjoy our last day together." Julia turned the corner.

Sticky teetered on the porch stair, then her hind feet went almost perpendicular to the ground before she fell over.

"How did you get out?" She needn't ask. With the door's broken hinge, the cat could escape as easily as varmints could get in. She shuddered. Good thing Merlin slept on the porch at night.

And a good thing the dog wasn't around now to scare her cat up a tree. Julia put down the pail and snatched up Sticky. The kitten mewed and clambered up her arm until she teetered precariously on her shoulder.

Helga cooed at the kitten as she passed by on the stairs. "Pretty, pretty kitty, you will be lost out here."

"Ah, I see she has escaped again." Everett came up behind her carrying a crate. It was the same box they'd had her in, but with the slats redone. "I put her in a pot while I fixed this, but that obviously didn't work." He passed them up the stairs and bumped through the door.

"She got out of the box?"

"Yep." He slid the crate into the corner above the pallet where Julia had slept since Helga took the bed.

Julia knelt down on the tick—the scent of which reminded her every night that Everett wasn't there—and placed the kitten inside. Along with the dirt box, there was another empty box of about the same dimensions. "What's this for?"

"I figured you could put something soft inside for her to sleep on."

Helga passed her a tin cup of milk. "Oh, I shall make it. I know how much you not like sewing."

"But I don't have any extra fabric, so Sticky will have to wait until I pick something up when I take you to the train."

She nudged the kitten's nose in the milk to encourage her to lap. Sticky resisted and drank nothing, preferring the bottle method.

"Find something in my trunk to cut up." Everett poured himself a glass of tea and downed it in a gulp.

Julia eyed him. He'd give up a usable piece of clothing for a cat?

"I best get back to work." He stooped down to pat the cat's head. "I might be late for dinner."

She caught his sleeve before he straightened. "Thank you."

He stared into her eyes for a second, but did nothing more than smile and nod.

When the door shut behind him and his boots cleared the stair, Helga *tsk*ed. "He need kiss for that."

Julia's face warmed. She busied herself with putting Sticky's little snout in the milk again. She did need to be nicer to Everett . . . but not too nice—not kissing nice.

Or was a simple kiss something she should think about giving him?

She wrapped her arms about her stomach and stared at the tabby's whiskers, frothy with milk, blinking up at the human insisting she do things her way.

"Mew." Sticky's little pink tongue quivered.

Me, she was saying. *My way.*

Julia knew what was best for the cat, but did she know what was best for herself? She had thought so until she ended up here, married and confused.

"You should kiss him when he comes back." Helga sat down with a humph and removed the boot that constricted her still-swollen ankle.

Kiss him in front of Helga? No. "How about a cake? Everyone loves cake."

Helga shook her head vehemently. "Don't stoke the fire in here more, please. I am wet all over." She pulled her shabby valise onto the bed. "I will get my needles. You get something from trunk."

Thankful that she'd dropped the kissing advice, Julia scooted across the floor before Helga started talking about rewarding Everett again. "I don't know what to sacrifice for the cat. It's not like I can easily replace Everett's wardrobe with my sewing skills, and it'd be a terrible waste." She ducked under the bed to pull out Everett's trunk, but the mystery trunk loomed in the shadowed corner. She'd forgotten about it. Most of the things in that chest had been in good shape, plus they weren't doing anything useful—just getting musty. But what if it remained untouched because Everett wanted it so?

"What is wrong under there?"

Julia grabbed the trunk full of secrets. Maybe she'd glean some information as she rifled through it. "I forgot about this trunk." Kneeling on the floor, she wiped off the dust and opened the lid. In case Helga became curious as to why a much larger woman's clothes were hidden under the bed, she didn't pull anything out. "There's a yellow dress I don't think I could easily refashion."

Helga shook her head. "Too nice for cat."

She shrugged. "Too nice for Kansas." And it would look awful on her.

"Is there something soft?"

She rummaged through the items, bypassing a shawl. That could be useful. A flannel wrapper lay in the bottom, worn, as if a favorite. "Here we go."

Helga raised her eyes at it, shook it out, but quickly nodded. "Much better for kitty."

Julia went in search of scissors, but then realized Helga had a set and had started cutting. She frowned as fabric fell away onto the bed. Would Everett be mad? "I could pull some feathers from my pillow."

"No, too nice for kitty. Enjoy your feathers. We fill with straw."

Of course. If left up to her, Sticky would be spoiled rotten within a week. The kitten scratched at the sides of the box, as if looking for a secret escape panel, tempting Julia to pick her up.

Helga cut strips from the skirt instead of an even square. "What are you doing?" She picked up a narrow piece.

"I not cut so you can't wear, just take from bottom. It is very long for you." And without any more words, she returned to her task.

Did Helga wonder about the other woman's things as much as she did? "I'll go gather the padding."

In the barn, she could hear tines scraping against wood, but she couldn't see Everett. Hoping not to disturb him, she climbed into the loft and stuffed some hay in a gunnysack.

"Can I help?"

She peeked over the edge. "Just getting hay for the cat."

"I'd rather you used straw. Hay's better for the animals to eat."

Everett scrambled up the ladder and headed toward the straw. "Over here."

Though tomorrow they'd be alone again once Helga left, Everett couldn't neglect the chance to join Julia in the hayloft, though she likely wished he wouldn't.

"Can I ask you a question?" Julia stumbled in the hay behind him.

230

Thankfully, for once, she was asking a question. "Sure." He turned and took her elbow as she tried to walk across the pile with a bit of grace.

"Whose trunk is under your bed?"

He frowned at the dusty sunbeam obscuring her face. "Mine or yours?"

She stopped moving. "The trunk engraved AGG."

His eyebrows moved with the scurrying of his brain. AGG. An extra trunk. He swallowed hard.

The extra trunk.

He coughed, more to clear his constricted throat than against the irritants floating in the haymow. "Ah, that would stand for Adelaide . . . uh, something, Gooding."

"Who?"

"A woman." He took a deep breath to calm his tremors. When she asked a question, she made it count. He'd rather tell her his favorite color was pink. But then, he'd decided only hours ago he had to tell her everything. Might as well be now.

Not that this conversation could be anything but awkward.

He pulled her over to a short pile of hay and sat.

Julia perched precariously on the edge beside him. "I've begun to wonder if I've missed something everyone else knows. Helga said something about you that didn't quite make sense. Like she'd been . . . attached to you somehow. And Carl Hampden seems to think you have feelings for his wife. And this trunk—does this Adelaide have something to do with them?"

"Yes." He dragged off his hat and flipped it around on his finger, trying not to roll it as he normally did, since a split where the brim and top met had recently appeared. "It's a long story."

Would she turn silent again once she'd heard about his

brides? He swallowed. It didn't matter how she reacted, she had the right to know. And he'd told William just a couple days ago that if a man loved a woman enough, he'd change even though it hurt. "When I first moved here, I was smitten with Rachel's sister. Never declared myself, but it was understood. I decided I needed a decent house for her, so I built my cabin so I'd—"

"You think that thing is decent?" She screwed up her face as if questioning whether he knew the definition of the word.

He grimaced. "It was when it was new."

She tucked her hands between her knees. "Sorry, I didn't mean to hit a sore spot."

"I admit the shack is run down. But only after years of neglect during the war. And I'd built it in a hurry." He released his death grip on the hat. So much for not making the split wider.

"So what happened to Rachel's sister?"

"Before the war, some fellow asked for her hand before I did, and she moved back east."

She raised an eyebrow. "But she left her trunk?"

"No, that's not hers." He sighed. "I think you know from Rachel's letters I was looking for a wife?" At her nod, he continued. "I was drowning in crop failure and needed help desperately. Droughts had made it near impossible for me to care for everything by myself, so a woman agreed to come. A Miss Gooding. I'd forgotten I shoved her trunk under the bed. She died on the train, and I didn't know what else to do with it."

"Ahh, I see." She frowned. "How sad."

He glanced over her way for a moment before returning his gaze to his hay-covered boots. "Then I requested a second bride to come, but she jilted me for another man on the way here: Carl Hampden."

Julia sucked in air.

"And then Helga came."

"Helga?" Julia's face paled.

"She stayed with Rachel for a time. But she decided my farm was too much work. She married Ned."

"Poor Helga," Julia murmured.

Yes, as humiliated as he'd felt—poor Helga. "The train's brought me nothing but trouble since it first came."

Julia crossed her arms and started to stand, but he shot out his hand to keep her from getting up. "I'm sorry. I didn't think before I spoke. I used to say that. But you're not trouble." His lips pressed together. Not exactly, anyway. Why did he excel at making bad situations worse?

She lowered herself back down, and he released her.

He picked up his hat and dusted it off. "Maybe now you'll understand my hesitation to welcome you when you arrived."

He could feel her glare shoot through his ears. "That wasn't hesitation. That was out-and-out shunning."

"I'm sorry." His neck grew hot, but he forced himself to look at her. Just yesterday they were getting along decently, laughing over a cat. Now he'd fallen victim again to her chastising frown. "The hesitation was more before you stepped off the train. That . . . the shunning, was for other reasons."

"What other reasons?" Her gaze seared into him, and he turned from it.

"You."

"Me?" Her voice rose an octave.

"Well, you see," his voice squawked. He cleared his throat. "You're beautiful beyond words. After being rejected by one very pretty gal and three plain women, I figured I had no hope with you." And he blew whatever hope he did have. "I was an idiot."

Her posture relaxed. "You were."

Well, she could have been a little slower to agree.

"So you didn't even meet this AGG?"

"No."

"So do you care what I do with the contents, then?"

Why hadn't he told her this long ago and given her the trunk? "You can do whatever you want with it. Perhaps she had some work dresses you could use."

She nodded, then stood with her gunnysack. "I can use some fabric for a cat bed, so I'll need that straw."

In silence, they walked across the loft. He took her lack of questions as her needing time to absorb that all together five women had not found him worthy of fully making him theirs.

Chapter 19

Julia drove the team slowly and silently into town. She glanced at the tough woman sitting stoically beside her. How would she get along without Helga? Granted, it had only been a week since she'd come to stay with them, but another woman under the roof had eased the tension between her and Everett. He'd halted his constant interrogation, and she'd enjoyed Helga's quiet presence.

She'd been worried Ned would come back in another drunken rage, but Helga seemed certain he wouldn't return for her, and she'd been correct. He'd not set foot on their property since Everett shooed him away at gunpoint. Did Ned not want to deal with Everett again, or did he care so little for his wife that he decided winning her back wasn't worth his rotten breath?

"So we say good-bye today."

Julia swallowed against the glumness in Helga's voice. "You will write and let us know you've made it?"

"Yes, of course. I cannot thank you enough for what you do for me." Tears shimmered on her lower lashes.

Julia stopped the team in front of the depot and reached

over to squeeze Helga's hand. "I would have wanted someone to help me if I were in your situation."

"You will never need such help."

True. She couldn't imagine Everett laying a vicious hand on her. He was gentler with his horse than most men she'd known, but would she never want to leave? Just the thought of returning to the farm without Helga made her feel uncertain. The vague, worrisome feelings stirring within made her want to flee. With her nest egg gone, she had no choice but to stay. But a small part of her . . . well, a small part didn't want to leave, which made her want to run all the more.

Helga gripped her shoulder. "Why are you having so much trouble?"

There was no need to burden the woman; Helga had enough to worry about. "I've enjoyed your company. I don't want to see you go."

Helga smiled, the tired wrinkles about her mouth bunched. "I have to, but I mean trouble loving Everett."

Loving Everett? Julia was nowhere close to loving him. It wasn't even possible. She'd never be able to trust a man, and trust was necessary for love. But why couldn't she trust Everett? She stared at the reins in her hands as if she'd find the answer there.

She'd never planned to love the man she married. Hadn't wanted to. But she couldn't tell Helga that. It would sound cruel.

And it was cruel. She groaned. She hadn't meant to be unkind, just self-protective. "It has to do with why I came here, but it isn't something I want to talk about." She would never talk about it to anyone. Ned's actions—based on his suspicion alone—confirmed how people would think about her and treat her if she provided any information to turn conjecture into certainty.

"All of us brides run away from something. But running from Everett is a mistake. I believe I know more than all of us. You were more wise not to leave him, but you are not most wise. You should trust him; he is kind."

Julia puckered her lip, trying not to let a silly thing like Everett offering Helga his hand in marriage first bother her. It didn't matter. "He's very kind, but I'm uncomfortable."

"Don't be so much. God gives you good gift."

Why hadn't He given Helga one as well? She had never talked ill of Ned once he'd left her, never complained about the gash they'd found behind her ear and the bruises her sleeves had covered. If anyone was an enduring saint, it was this stolid, persevering woman.

"And you take the gift, but you need to enjoy it."

Enjoy? The fear of the physical side of marriage barred her from relaxing in his presence.

"Trust me."

Could she trust Helga to know since she'd chosen her husband so poorly? "I'll think on it."

They climbed out of the wagon and worked their way to the window to purchase Helga's ticket. Julia stood at the bottom of the Pullman's stairs as the porter announced that all passengers should board. She gave the stout woman a hug. "I hope you have an easy journey."

"It will be much easier than yours." Helga patted her cheek and frowned.

Julia swallowed against the lump in her throat. Nothing about her life had been easy thus far, and she hadn't expected it to be any different when she'd come to Kansas.

She'd always have to be wary lest she be crushed again. If

she opened herself up, she could be hurt more than ever—to her very core.

Everett stopped mucking and listened. A distant rhythmic banging sounded close by. Gunshots? Another flurry of sounds traveled through the window. More like haphazard hammering.

Grabbing the shotgun from where it leaned against the barn wall, he slunk to the door. A week had passed since Helga left for New York, but he still worried Ned would show up on his property waving pistols and shouting curses.

In light of Ned's threats and Helga's recent departure, he'd stayed close to the house. Julia was guarded and jumpy, and both their meals and nights were strained. He could protect her from outside threats, God willing, but he couldn't figure how to protect her from the emotions churning inside her, closing her off from him again.

But then, he wasn't much better off. Images of Ned's hands wandering all over her plagued his mind, making him angry and jealous. Insanely so.

As his eyes adjusted to the bright sunlight, he listened for more of the hammering sound. A few seconds later it came— from the top of the shack. Julia swayed atop his rickety roof. Her tiny frame careened forward as she bent and grabbed something off the peak.

"What are you doing?" He ran to the house and craned his neck. "Get down this instant!"

Unmoving, she looked at him, a nail sticking out from between her lips.

"Did you not hear me? Get down." Impertinence. He never realized how much he disliked that quality before this moment. He glanced around for the ladder.

She pulled the nail from her mouth. "I'm fixing the roof. It's leaking again. When I'm done I'll get down."

"Do you even know what you're doing?" He set the shotgun on the porch and ran to the ladder. He held it tight and stared at the eaves. "Come down. If you want me to fix something, ask me." His heart sank. Why didn't she ever ask him for help? He must be worthless to her.

Her voice carried over the edge. "I said, I'm fixing it."

It had actually leaked for years, but he hadn't bothered fixing that tiny spot because the new house's roof was watertight. But why would she think this was her job? He'd been particularly attentive to household problems this past month, fixing anything he thought she wanted repaired. He didn't know the leak in the corner bothered her. He took a deep breath, settling himself to wait for her, yet sure she wouldn't come. After a few minutes, he bounced the ladder a few times, making sure of its stability, and climbed the rungs.

Careful not to disturb the ladder's seating, he crawled onto the roof. He'd do anything, if she'd just ask. Why wouldn't she?

On her hands and knees at the peak of the roof, Julia spread shingles in a disorganized fashion. She glanced over her shoulder. "I can handle it."

A bunch of shingles nailed in a crazy quiltlike pattern meandered up the left side. He clamped his lips to keep from loosing a roofing lecture. "Why didn't you ask me to do this?"

She shook her head. "You have enough things to do."

"Of course I do. Doesn't mean you should be doing dangerous things."

"It needed doing, and I'm here to work."

Why was she so bent on work? A subconscious jolt reminded him that he'd told her he'd been ordering mail-order brides because he needed a helper. He hadn't asked any of them to come for love.

And she was determined not to have any feelings for him whatsoever. He planted himself on his backside and resigned himself to watch.

She stared at him with raised eyebrows and then returned to work.

She'd almost become human with Helga around, relaxing from constant work to chat and take walks with her friend. But she was back to her old habits. He didn't want this driven woman trying to prove herself through hours of back-breaking labor. He wanted the woman who laughed, who hummed off-key, who talked to herself when she thought no one was around. She'd shown up for a while but had left as if she'd traveled away with Helga on the train.

Julia had proven she intended to stay—at least bodily. But this was not how he envisioned living with her for the rest of his days. She'd drive him insane. "I don't need you to work so hard, especially if you could get hurt."

She glanced up in between a hammer blow, but kept pounding until the nail lay flattened, nice and sideways. She sat back on her heels. "That was the deal. You provide for me. I work for you. What else do you need me to be doing?"

Warming me at night, laughing with me, sitting under the stars and dreaming up names for our future children.

I want you to live with me.

How could he tell a woman so attractive, so distant, what he desired? When he didn't answer, she returned to her task.

He picked at the dirt under his fingernails. Why couldn't he charm Julia like he had Rachel's sister?

Patricia had shadowed him at church and every time she found him in town. She clung to his every word when he visited. Her eyes told him she couldn't wait for him to whisper in her ear when he said good-night.

Until he had his house built, he'd kept those words bottled, but he'd known she'd say yes. And say yes she did—to another man. A man who hadn't waited until everything was perfect and ready for a wife. And without a word to him, she settled onto the wagon seat beside her husband and headed back east.

Everett stopped cleaning his nails and glanced at the new house. He'd finished adding the furniture two days ago. He was completely ready for a wife now.

Julia's tiny form scooted across the rooftop near the edge. Everett held out his hands for support, but she ignored the offer. He let out the breath he'd been holding when she quit backing up. "This is ridiculous."

Julia dropped her nail, but kept her eyes on the roof. "If I'm doing that poor of a job, you could tell me how to fix it rather than insult me."

He crawled over and snatched the nail. "That's not it. I mean how we're acting. We're ridiculous."

She looked up at him, her delicate eyebrows arched. How he wanted to run his finger across them and down to her cheek, her mouth, her neck. Her fake cough made him glance up from where he'd been staring. A twitch pulled at his lip. "I'm sitting here, thinking how nicely you're put together—" he rolled the nail between his index finger and thumb—"and all you're thinking about is needing this nail so you can get back to work."

She swiped the nail from his hand. "Yes, I need to get back to work. I'm more than just a pretty face, you know. Men like my looks. You like my looks. That's nothing new. Still doesn't mean I'm incapable of doing anything besides being displayed in a china cabinet."

"Actually, I don't like your looks." Her looks drove him mad, made it hard to get stuff done, to stay in his celibate cocoon, to think about anything else.

She dropped her nail, which skipped down the shingles and off the roof. "You don't like me for the work I do. You don't like me for my looks. I've got nothing." She stood, brushed off her dress, and grabbed the hammer.

He stood with her.

"Since you don't need me for anything, I'm going to go visit Rachel." She turned her body parallel to the roof's edge to slip past him.

He grabbed her by the elbows when she passed inches from him. What thoughts ran through her head, making her this skittish? "That's not what I meant." His thumbs caressed the crook of her arms. "I said I didn't like your looks . . . because they distract me."

She stiffened.

His hands slid to her wrists and then clasped her hands. "Why are you being so stubborn? You act as if I'm invisible."

She tugged against his grasp, but when he didn't let go, she looked away. "Don't think I don't notice you." Her neck turned a nice shade of pink.

So she did notice. He'd been attentive, protective, admiring, but still she pushed him away. What else could he do to prove himself trustworthy?

She whipped her head around to face him. Her eyes narrowed into tiny slits. "Why can't you stay out of my thoughts? Why can't you leave me be? I'm working as hard as I can."

He examined the hands he held and her bare ring finger. "I appreciate the work you do for me, but it's not enough."

She huffed and shook her head, her mouth constricting into a tiny line.

He tried to capture her gaze, but she wouldn't look at him. "Actually, it's not enough that way too. You work hard. I work hard. But we'd need to have a whole army of children to keep up with the work on this land. If we expected our efforts alone to be enough, we'd be fools."

"So now I'm not enough, and I'm a fool to think so? I've got to produce a shipload of children to satisfy your homestead's never-ending work needs? Well, unfortunately, that's not even possible. If you've forgotten, I'm unlikely to have children, let alone an army of them." She sniffed. "So you'll have to be satisfied with the work I do or find someone else."

"I'd never trade you for anything." If an arrow struck him in the chest, the pain radiating out from his heart couldn't be more painful. Did she really think he'd toss her aside? Where had her anger come from all of a sudden? He had to let her know he loved her. Words wouldn't pierce her heart, but maybe a kiss. The shaking in his gut and the knowledge that this wasn't the right time couldn't keep him from her any longer.

Swallowing hard, he moved a bit closer. He'd kissed her once. Wanted to a thousand times. "I don't need you to work all day long or have a hundred children to be happy. But I'd like it if we could be friendlier." His hand traveled up her arm to the strand of hair lying listlessly against her neck. He kept his gaze glued on the soft brown lock as he caressed it. "A lot friendlier."

She wasn't looking him in the eyes, yet she hadn't pulled away. Could it be that she wanted his touch but couldn't ask for it? Whatever made her so upset after Ned's attempt at harming her kept her stockaded behind a wall of fear.

"You shouldn't be afraid of me. Haven't I kept my word? And I will." His other arm coaxed her forward. "But I can't help loving you just the same." His mouth touched down on hers, her lips trembling under his. The softness, the taste. They'd become sweeter since the wedding.

Waves of pent-up desire rushed up from deep within, faster than an uncontrolled fire licking up dead grasses after a season of drought. He needed more. A bit more.

A lot more.

Her hands flattened against his shirt, but he couldn't break away. She pushed herself from his embrace with a shove. And right to the roof's edge.

Falling flat on his chest, the shingles tearing into his shirt, he tried to snatch at the last bit of green fabric disappearing over the eave. Her scream when her ruffle tore off in his hand stomped on his heart.

"Nooooo!" Their like cries ended in unison.

Chapter 20

Like a reckless boy leaping from a hayloft, Everett jumped off the roof after Julia. But the ground was closer than anticipated, and his ankle cursed him upon landing.

Still, the pain knifing up his leg was nothing compared to the agony-laced howl coming from his wife. But at least she was breathing.

Why had he lied to her about being able to control himself? He'd just stolen a kiss on an uneven roof. "I'm so sorry. I wouldn't blame you if you slapped me good. Repeatedly."

Julia didn't snap at him as he expected. Clutching her leg with one hand, she tried to sit up, but slumped back to the ground with a moan.

"Julia?" His sore ankle protested beneath him, but he shoved off it anyway and scrambled over.

Perspiration lay atop her creased eyebrows, and her mouth had thinned into a tight bundle of lines.

"What hurts?" He pulled her up into his arms.

She answered with nothing but a gasp, and then stillness.

He'd known women to faint at pain any boy would scoff at, but that didn't explain her ashen skin. He brushed a hand against her face where a rock had scraped her cheek. "Look at me."

Her eyelids obeyed halfheartedly as if awaking from a long night's slumber. "Mmm?"

"What hurts?"

She tried to push into a sitting position again. "Can't."

He threaded his arms under hers to haul her toward the shack's wall, but a yelp brought him up short.

"Stttttop . . . sssssst . . . opppp," her voice slurred, though he'd quit moving her the second she'd hollered.

A trail of blood colored the grass where her leg had dragged a few inches.

His breathing sped up. It couldn't be that bad. "Did you scrape your leg on the way down, or are you talented enough to land on every spare rock I have in the yard?"

She didn't even scowl at his ill-timed joke. But at least her eyes remained open.

"William's actually pretty good at stitching if you need it." Everett propped her against his bent leg so he could maneuver to look without dropping her. "One of my steers slashed himself real good once. After William was done with him, I could have sworn he'd figured out a way to sew up animals from the inside out—couldn't even see the gash once he'd finished." He stretched over to straighten her leg, and blood bloomed against her skirt.

He muttered words he didn't want her to hear as his shaky fingers pulled up the layers of skirting. "Hold still."

Her stockings were pristine until he exposed the gash— and then the bone, a sickening white protrusion in a pool of blood.

"That's . . . that's . . ." Julia heaved.

He dropped the wad of fabric and turned her upper body so

she could keep from getting sick on herself. His own stomach was barely under control.

He'd seen broken bones jutting from a man's flesh a few times during the war.

But he never again saw that soldier with all of his limbs intact.

If he ever saw him again.

The tears obscuring his vision swelled faster than the crimson spreading across her skirt.

He had offered to let her slap him—but she ought to smack him into kingdom come.

If she didn't arrive there first.

———————

Julia turned her head toward the front of the cabin. White flashes followed her vision's progress until she found the groaning door. Rachel's stout form entered and flew to the bedside.

"Oh, Julia!" Rachel landed on her knees beside her. "How did this happen?"

Julia groaned and held her cold hand against her throbbing temple. "Everett?" The raw side of her face hurt when she moved her mouth, but that pain was minuscule compared to her leg.

"He's gone to Salt Flatts. Dex was out somewhere in the pasture, so I sent Everett for the doctor. Figured it'd be faster. I didn't know where William was." Rachel pulled the tendrils of hair from the scrape near her eye. Each strand stung as if Rachel were pulling out thorns. "Maybe I should have gone myself and sent Everett back to you." Rachel squeezed her hand. "I'll get water."

"Everett cleaned—" though the vocal reverberations inside

her skull hurt, she powered through—"cleaned it. Whiskey." She rolled her head in the direction of the jug sitting on the stool.

Rachel scooped up the jug, rag, and bowl and knelt beside her. She soaked the rag.

"No," her voice croaked. "Drink." The pain and fire in her leg cried for relief.

Rachel slid across the mattress. Her backside bumped against Julia's knee. Twinkling stars danced in patterns Julia couldn't track.

"Oh dear. I'm making it worse. Let me have a look at your leg." Rachel stood.

A bit of petticoat stuck in the wound as Rachel pulled the fabric away. Hot pricks of pain crawled through her already screaming flesh.

Rachel's eyes grew huge, and her hand shook as it floated up to cover her mouth. "Oh!" She closed her eyes. "I . . . I don't know what to do."

Was there any hope if Rachel was at a loss? The searing pain made Julia wish life would end today anyway. The glimpse of bone protruding at the shin and the lightning strike of pain when she'd first seen the injury had made her lose her lunch. She'd have fainted if Everett hadn't gathered her in his arms and shouted in her face.

"Everett cleaned it." And she had screamed almost the entire time. When her voice turned raw from overuse, the yells became moans. After he'd finished cleaning her leg he apologized over and over as he set it in a splint and waited for the applied pressure to stop the bleeding.

The pain was old now, as if she'd always lived with it, like she would always have to live with it. "Don't need to clean it again." The pain swelled into her head and burst forth with fresh tears.

Rachel gingerly set her skirt back around her legs. "Everett's coming, honey." She grabbed the whiskey and filled the cup to the brim. "There now, the doctor will be here real soon." She glanced toward the door. "Please, Lord, let them hurry."

Julia floated into darkness accompanied by the sound of Rachel's pleading.

Blaze slid to a stop in front of the homestead, and Everett jumped off his sweaty horse and rushed over to the doctor's mount. The nag sagged under the large man's weight. "Let me get your bag." He grabbed the black leather portmanteau and left Dr. Forsythe to follow after him.

Inside, Rachel kneeled beside the bed, her head cradled in her arms by Julia's side.

Julia's face was pale, her eyes were closed.

"She's not . . . she's not . . ." Everett dropped the bag on the table and rushed to touch her face.

Rachel's hand rubbed his back. "No, Everett. She's passed out."

Dr. Forsythe's rotund form hefted its way to the bedside. "Make room, please."

Rachel jumped back, and Everett clung to Julia's hand as the man did a quick check of her face and pulse before moving to her leg.

The sweaty physician settled himself and moved aside the torn dress. He peered down his spectacles at the splint Everett had thrown together before racing to the Stantons and on to Salt Flatts.

"You did well enough for something this extreme." He opened his bag. "Just so happens I've been reading the material I picked up about Lister's antiseptic principle in regard to compound fractures." He pulled out a bottle and gauze. "Seems successful enough, but I've yet to try it. A bit impractical, but with a mortality rate of eighty percent of my own cases with fractures like these, it can't hurt to attempt it."

Rachel whimpered.

Everett's whole body tensed. Eighty percent! How could the man say such a thing? His taste buds relived the sweetness of Julia's lips. He might have very well killed her for that second of pleasure. He slid down the wall until his rear hit the floor, dragging her limp and clammy hand to the bottom with him.

Julia moaned.

Rachel knelt beside him as the doctor huffed and bustled about Julia's injury. "We best pray, Everett."

He nodded and listened to her prayer but couldn't form words to add to her petition. Julia might never want him, but he prayed God would want her and save her, not just from death and decay, but from an eternity without His love. Since the day at the pond, he knew Julia didn't have a relationship with God. He'd figured he'd have time to talk to her about it once she opened up. If God would turn this horrid mistake into the path that would lead her to understand God loved her, he could let her go. His desires had put her in jeopardy. He could, he would, lay them down. If she would only survive . . .

"I need you up here, boy. Hold her down."

For a few seconds, his tears thwarted his vision, keeping him from detaining her thrashing limbs. Her cries murdered his heart, and he choked on her screams.

Falling, falling, falling, splash. Julia sputtered and clawed to keep herself above the water's surface. "Help! Help!" She yanked the arm that plunged in near her face. "Help!"

"Shhhh." A deep soothing voice hushed her. She knew that voice. She pulled the muscular arm and tried to see through the water. Worried steel gray eyes swam before her.

"It's me, Julia. You need to stop moving. You're going to disturb your leg." His tone was forceful. "You cannot disturb your leg."

Her leg. Her leg was on fire.

"You're burning up. I've got to get more water."

A door slammed, leaving her alone. Alone in a fire, reaching inch by inch to her middle. She didn't want to feel that fire anymore. Make it go away!

Freezing water trickled down the sides of her head and into her ears. Her ears ached with the cold. They throbbed with the cold.

"Don't leave me, love. Don't leave me."

Despite being inside a vat of boiling water, shivers ran along every limb of her body. Up and down, over and across, and back again. All she could do was tread water. She wanted out!

The pot. Senseless to stay in the pot. She clawed for the rim, but grabbed immaterial fluff. Where was the rim? She couldn't pull herself out without the rim. "Help me!"

"I don't know what else to do," a shaky voice answered. "I don't know what else to do."

"Can no one . . ." The insides of her mouth were melting. She tried to make her tongue work, but it was burned to a crisp. She had no tongue. Could she make the leftover ashes form words? "Can no one save me?"

"I can't."

A waterfall of cold pricks landed on her neck. The sound of a steam engine chugging and weeping and chugging and weeping neared her. She had to get out of the boiler car.

"I can't do anything. God, it's now or never. Let it not be never."

Her hands were quickly sheathed with ice-cold gloves and squeezed. Pain shot up through her wrists.

"Pray with me, darling. You're here right now. Listen. Ask God to stop it. He loves you. Call out to the Father to rescue you. I'm inadequate."

Was someone weeping? Why didn't God tell the babbling man to stop sniffling and rescue her from the fiery waves?

"So inadequate."

Her father didn't love her. No one had loved her. Why would God love her? The heat from the cauldron she was in proved He did not.

"God does not love me," she cried.

But she wanted love. She wanted love.

She gave up, exhausted, and slid back into the boiling water. And it burned.

Chapter 21

Flames of fire no longer seared her leg, but they pierced through her eyelids. She covered her face with a clammy hand and groaned.

"Julia?"

She turned to Everett's voice and squinted. His shadow moved, and intense light filled the room. She winced, the action shooting pain from her temples to her ears. "Ugh."

"Are you awake?"

She moved her head slowly from side to side, but the pain sloshed as if she were shaking her head like a dog shakes a rag bone. "Light." Her throat felt scratchy and dry. "Water."

"I'll get you a drink."

She searched for a blanket to pull up over her head, but the quilt covering her was securely anchored across her chest. She turned her head away from the brightness. "No light." Her voice slurred, and she struggled to make her brain correct her speech. "Please."

"Of course, I'll recover the windows. I can change your bandage later."

Windows? There were more than one? Where was she? She

moved her hands and rubbed the fluffy tick below her that smelled of sunshine. Not the straw tick that smelled of must.

Moments later soothing darkness fell, and she tried to pry open her eyes. Everett's arm slipped behind her neck, and the rim of a cool tin cup pressed against her lower lip. She downed the contents. "More."

He assisted her again, and she fell back onto the pillow. Every part of her body ached, all the way to the bones. The room tilted, and she closed her eyes against the nausea swelling in her chest.

His warm hand brushed across her forehead. "You feel cooler."

The throbbing behind her skull made her wish sleep would return directly.

"Lord, I pray that this isn't just a calm in the storm. Let this fever be gone for good. Wake her up so I can talk to her, so I can tell her how sorry I am."

Praying again. Why didn't he just tell her? "Tell me you're sorry."

His hand brushed hair off her temple, soft and gentle, yet still painful. "Are you really awake?"

"Mmm-hmm."

"Thank you, Jesus."

Jesus had nothing to do with her being awake—hadn't she opened her eyes herself? Well, before she closed them again against the windows. "Where am I?"

"With me in the cabin."

"How many windows?"

"Three all together."

"Put in new ones?"

"No, this is the new cabin."

She wanted to see. Pushing against the mattress, she worked

to set herself upright, despite her head exploding. "Why am I . . ." Though she'd moved her leg only a fraction of an inch, she remembered exactly why she was confined to bed. Though her lower limb no longer felt on fire, the pain resembled a slashed burn wound.

Everett's hands settled against her shoulders and pushed her back down. All the effort to sit upright had only resulted in an inch or two in elevation. She gave up. It was too hard, and she'd already augmented her pain simply by waking up.

"Take it easy, darling. Just because you woke up doesn't mean you're getting out of bed for a while."

"How long was I asleep?"

"Two weeks."

That must be why her backside hurt so much. She moved slowly, trying to turn a bit onto her side, but her leg was a leaden weight that shot sparks whenever she put pressure on it.

Everett braced her back with a wad of softness. "Better?"

She hummed in assent, but she kept her eyes shut until the pain of his jostling left her.

His eyes stared down at her, dark, anxious pools of blue.

"I'll be fine." Maybe it was a lie, but she had to ease his anguish.

"Will you?" He picked up her hand and rubbed her fingers with his thumb.

She felt as if she could die any minute, if pain were an indicator. "What has the doctor said about my leg?"

"I have a list of things to check for each day—that's why I opened the windows, so I could see better." He cleared his throat. "He's not very optimistic. But no matter what happens, I want you to know that I will be here beside you."

Julia took a long look at him before setting her face on

a cooler part of her pillowcase. She couldn't shun this man forever; she could see he fancied her. And how many women had she known back home, stuck in loveless marriages, who would have been content if their husbands had simply found them attractive? She might even have been swayed into agreeing to her father's marriage arrangement with Theodore if her intended had looked at her with a quarter of the care shining from Everett's eyes.

"I'm so sorry about the roof. I didn't mean to push you into anything. . . . I know I gave you my word to keep my hands to myself, but I . . ." He raked his hands through his hair. "I've no excuse. I just need to make sure you know that I'm grateful that you married me, and having you with me is enough. It was more than any of the other . . ." He blew out an unsteady breath. "Well, simply . . . I don't deserve you."

She closed her eyes against seeing the emotions play across his face. If he knew her past, every detail, he'd take those words right back. She pulled her hands in tight against her and curled up as much as her leg allowed. He'd told her his secret and she ought to tell him hers, but she couldn't. A decent man was on the verge of loving her, and despite the fact that love would complicate everything, she didn't want to toss it away.

"Are you asleep?"

She worked to keep her breathing even and slow. Let him believe her asleep; she hadn't the emotional strength to face her feelings. What could she say that would make him feel better anyway? That she was sorry she was terrified of a man's touch? He'd want to know why.

He tucked her blankets in tighter. "Rest well, darling. But more important, wake up again." A whisper of a kiss caressed her brow.

The satiny touch of his lips sent a tickling sensation down to her toes, and she curled up tighter. Perhaps with time she could endure his intimate embrace; he'd proven to be honorable and trustworthy even when he had pushed. But then she'd have to face being with child. The fear of losing one after another and becoming a vacuous shell like her mother was something that would never get better with time. Would she ever feel enough for him to endure what her mother had?

"Ugh, Sticky." Julia tried to catch the spool of thread before it flew off the bed, but failed. She wrapped up her embroidery panel before the kitten could catch her claws in the mess of thread on the back side of her project. Rachel said the back should look as pretty as the front.

Rachel was either lying or had skills beyond a normal woman. Not that Julia had ever inspected the back of anyone else's needlework, but who cared if the back looked like a thread cyclone?

"Come here." She pulled the cat off her knees and petted it, trying to avoid its playful paws. "Too bad you've outgrown your box, or I'd put you in there."

Sticky finally settled down, her purr rhythmic and unending, like the cicadas' song that had grown louder overnight.

The door bumped open, startling her.

"I'm sorry, did I wake you?" Everett didn't look remorseful with that smile on his face.

"No, just trying to keep my thread away from Sticky's paws."

Everett slid a dish of food onto the table that filled the air with garlic and some other smell she didn't recognize and then came to sit next to her.

Had he finished his chores so quickly again? "Who brought food this time?"

"Mrs. Nogales. I didn't quite understand what she called it, but the smell makes me hungry."

"Why didn't she come in?"

"Her English is worse than Helga's, though she said something that sounded like she was praying for you."

Prayer. No one had ever prayed for her before, yet someone seemed to come over every day to do just that. Thankfully they didn't expect her to pray aloud with them. She'd tried to ask God for a few things since being stuck in bed, but gave up. Everyone else's words were better and surely more effective than hers. If they were effective at all. "I've never heard of Mrs. Nogales."

He shrugged. "She and her family actually live on the other side of town."

"And they came all the way out here?"

"Just the mother and one of the sons. Seems they intended to buy a horse from someone down the river." He reached down to pull off his boots. Hours before sunset.

"Wait."

He stopped.

She couldn't take another evening of endless reading and embroidery. But there wasn't much else to do but chat. And she'd talked, but the more she told him, the more he probed.

She didn't want to talk tonight. She'd considered telling Everett about Theodore last night when she couldn't sleep, so bed weary she couldn't get comfortable despite her heavy eyes. But when she'd managed to doze off, terrible dreams visited her. Reliving the past. Watching Everett leave her future.

She put the cat down and sat up. "Please help me walk around."

"You can't walk yet." His face looked as panicked as if she'd asked him to dump her in a vat of boiling grease.

"All right, limp around." She pushed her splinted leg off the bed and forced herself not to wince at the tingles that shot up from her toes.

He raised an eyebrow at her.

Her face must have betrayed her pain. "It still hurts, but I know it's better. And it's not going to work properly anymore if I don't move it around some. My leg feels like it's dying."

He jammed his heel back into his boot and put his hands on her shoulders. "Only if we go slow and I basically carry your weight."

"Fine. All this loafing has made my body sluggish." As long as she could move—anything besides lying down—she'd even kiss him. Could she work up the nerve? No, she couldn't kiss a man first. What was she thinking? "And my brain doesn't seem to be working right either."

"Do I need to pick something more stimulating to read?"

"Does Rachel have more books?" He'd read her more than a dozen already.

"Several more cases. She keeps them in the back of the barn. Not sure how many more novels she has, but I saw several sermon collections last time I looked."

Just what she wanted—a preacher pointing out her every fault for hours and hours on end. "Maybe she's got something on gardening?"

"Good idea." He smiled as he hooked his arm under her shoulder.

How far could she walk before he'd drag her back into bed? As they hobbled down the stairs to the yard, her stomach growled. He had to be hungry too.

"Maybe just to the barn and back." Sticky weaved in and out of her legs. Not a smart cat.

"Sure, that sounds like enough exercise to me." He held her tight and started forward.

"No, let me try to actually walk." She tried to loosen his grip on her arm.

"Don't put pressure on your leg."

She tested a bit of weight on her foot, gritting her teeth. "I have to someday."

"When Dr. Forsythe says."

"What about when William says?" Normally, Everett agreed with William's advice, but not on this. It was as if the second she was free to move, he feared losing her.

Maybe they wouldn't have time to talk as much, but the farm needed him. "You'll be relieved once I can get up and do things. You're behind because of me."

"Not on anything important." He clomped along beside her, smelling vaguely like leather and hay.

She dragged her leg. "You needed a wife to help you farm, and this past month I've hindered you more than helped." She had put her weight on her foot for five steps, but the pain had increased twentyfold. She wouldn't tell him that though. He might banish her to bed for a week again.

"I want to make sure you stay well. I could lose the farm for all I care."

What man risked his farm for a woman who was more a companion than a wife? He must think it his Christian duty to say so. "Well, I don't want you to lose the place because of me." They reached the barn's edge, and she leaned against the side. "Let me rest a bit."

Moving quickly, he rolled a thick log toward her. "Sit."

With his help, she sank down onto the tiny stool, thankful she'd arrived at the barn wall before she collapsed. Even William would insist on strict bed rest if that had happened.

Everett lowered himself against the wall and sighed. "Such a pretty day. I'm glad you got outside to enjoy it."

She glanced at the soft blue sky, but winced at the sun peeking through the clouds. Thankfully Everett wasn't watching her. She needed to look restful, as if walking out here had been a good plan. But the throbbing up and down her leg was hard to ignore.

"I know you don't want to discuss your parents, but can you tell me why you left your father?"

Should she admit to the pain to avoid this question—again? No, she might as well give him just enough so he'd quit asking. Hopefully. "He doesn't know where I am. And it needs to stay that way."

"Of course." Everett pushed up from his slouch against the wall. "But can you tell me why?"

She flinched against a scorching twinge. "He pressured me to marry a business partner entirely for his gain, not mine. That's when I realized he loved me as little as my mother had." How could a father overlook a man's indecency toward his daughter—no matter how much he could profit?

"Do you think I'm like your father? Only worried about my gain?" He kept his gaze on his hands as if afraid to hear the answer. A vulnerable question. Since her fever had broken, he'd repeatedly exposed himself to her criticism—like he was asking for it—apologizing for every real or imaginary sin he believed he'd committed against her.

"No, I don't think you're like him." Everett was trying to give her his heart, though she'd yet to give him anything of worth.

"Good. Have I told you I didn't know Rachel asked you here on my behalf?"

More confessions. How many more could he own up to before she couldn't stand the guilt of her own unacknowledged sins? "I gathered as much."

"Well, I just wanted you to know that I'm glad she did." He winked.

He wanted her to smile, but Julia couldn't. He was falling in love with her if he wasn't already, and that made her feel even worse for having a hesitant heart.

Chapter 22

Sighing, Julia clenched her fist to keep from knocking the doctor's probing hand away so she could scratch her itchy leg. The man sure took his sweet time. While Rachel made the evening meal for the third time in a row, Everett hovered over the doctor's shoulder.

Her leg had been better more than a week now. She had told Everett, but he wouldn't believe her until the doctor said so himself. Eight full days passed before Everett tracked down the busy man, and another three for him to come. Evidently, a rash of cholera was keeping the county doctor busy.

"My leg feels better. It does. I know it's healed." Why must he tarry so long? "Besides feeling a bit numb along the scar line, it couldn't feel better."

Dr. Forsythe laid her leg back onto the new rope bedstead. "I think you're right. And one lucky girl." He gathered the dingy bandages and splint material. "I thought Lister's idea of using acid was either sheer idiocy or wild genius. I kept expecting you to call me for an amputation." He patted her arm. "Good thing I heard about his methods before leaving Boston. Most likely saved your leg and your life."

She shuddered at the vision of her right leg missing. Perhaps that's why Everett had hardly left her side during her recuperation. If she had gotten through the infection and fever, yet lost her leg, he'd have been bound forever to a crippled woman, even more of a burden. She released a sigh.

"I wondered if I'd doomed you to life with a useless, painful limb, but it healed by first intention without even an appearance of laudable pus like Lister predicted." He took a long look at her leg and hesitated before covering it with the fold of her nightdress as if burying a treasure. "Though you could have simply beaten the odds."

"It was a miracle, Doc." Rachel put her hand on his shoulder. "Lots of prayers to the Lord were offered at this bedside."

Everett nodded behind Rachel, his eyes closed.

Julia frowned. Everett had told her how the doctor assumed she would die or need an amputation. Did their prayers work, or was she simply lucky, as the doctor said?

The doctor's lower lip protruded a bit, but he gave a sharp nod. "I suppose the Almighty can do better work than me." He patted her shoulder. "If you received His special attention, then you'd have to be extraordinary." Taking a long look at her skirt as if he could see through the fabric to her scarred leg, he fiddled with his satchel's handle. "I have no more to do here. You might feel the effects of this injury for years to come, especially on days the weather changes drastically. I do believe I'll keep using Lister's methods to see if they hold out."

Julia shook her head. There was nothing extraordinary about her; maybe the advancement of medical practices had healed her. God shouldn't have worked a miracle just for her. She wasn't worth it. He would be as ashamed of her past as she was—and how she was treating her husband now.

Dr. Forsythe turned to shake Everett's hand but was pulled

into an embrace. The man's fat sides bulged over Everett's tightened arms. After stepping back from the bear hug, the doctor cleared his throat. "Well, so long, Mr. and Mrs. Cline. I have more visits in the direction of Fossil Creek." A big yawn split his mouth open wide.

Rachel handed him a loaf of bread. "You get some rest, Doctor."

Dr. Forsythe stared at Rachel. "I don't intend to take lectures from a woman in your state. The bags under your eyes are as large as my own, I'm sure. You should be getting more sleep."

Her hand slid to her swollen abdomen. "I try."

The doctor took his leave, and Julia swung her legs to the mattress's edge and breathed in deeply. Her arms pushed against the bed frame, but Everett's hands on her shoulders stopped her progress. She growled at him. "I'm fine. The doctor took away the bandages and declared me a miracle. Please let me stand. I can't stay in this bed any longer."

"I don't want you to hurt yourself. You need to take things slow."

She groaned. "If we take this as slow as you want, I'll be here another month. My leg's been better for several days now, but I submitted. Now please, let me move to that chair over there. I've yet to enjoy any of the new furniture." At his half-cocked brow, she pleaded. "The doctor gave me no restrictions. I just want to sit, not turn cartwheels."

He held out his hand. "All right, but I don't want you to fall. You've lost your strength."

She could not argue with that and allowed him to guide her as she took a few feeble steps to the chair with the fancy embroidered cushion. Her embroidery decorated all four chairs. The embarrassing progress of her needlepoint skills graced their seats. She might not have gotten any better at patience during her bed rest, but her needlework had improved. Of all the silly things to be wasting time doing.

Everett sat in the chair beside her and placed a small kiss at the crown of her head, breathing in deeply. "You smell lovely," he whispered.

Thankfully, Rachel was busy cooking and couldn't see her flamed face. Memories of the rag bath he'd helped her with last night brought warmth to her cheeks. He'd bought lavender water especially for her on his last trip to town. Tilting her head toward Rachel, she shushed him. Prudish of her, considering the care he'd performed while her leg healed, but things had not changed between them that way.

The ordeal had brought them closer, but for him to flirt boldly in front of Rachel made her cringe. Only a girl of ill repute would encourage such public behavior. But was it different if they were married? In front of a good friend? She'd not thought ill of Rachel when Dex had leaned in for a kiss, but for her . . . She reached for her brooch, but it wasn't at her neck.

A sly smile played at his lips before he left the new cabin through its wonderful, properly hung front door.

"Oh, he frustrates me!" She strangled the arms of her chair.

Rachel turned from the stove. "How so?"

Her thumbs rubbed the smooth woodwork of the armrest. Impressive. "I don't know. Just does. He's underfoot all the time. And this is the first time I've been out of bed for him to actually have a chance at being underfoot."

Rachel snickered.

"Don't you laugh! I had to answer unending questions, explain my embroidery, listen to him read sermons . . . He pestered me more than Sticky."

"My, aren't we crabby."

"I'm not crabby, I'm . . ." Fine. She was crabby.

"Maybe a nap is in order. Think I ought to help you back into bed." Rachel wiped her hands on her towel.

"No, please no." She closed her eyes for a few seconds, then lifted her gaze to meet Rachel's. "I'm all right. A bit testy, yes. But you don't know how it is to be in bed for weeks." She grimaced. "Embroidering chair cushions."

Rachel's mouth skewed to the side. "I think you should hop in bed and make a few more."

"What?" She gripped the chair's arms tighter, but the twitch in Rachel's mouth gave her away. She relaxed. "Don't tease about such a thing. I just got out of bed."

Rachel clucked and returned to the pan on the stove. "And I thought Dex was a whiny baby when he's sick."

Julia took several deep breaths through her nose and let them out her mouth. Her body shook with tension. Wouldn't anyone be irritable after so long in bed? She'd been sure that once she got up, she'd be happy. But she'd only made it to the chair. Rachel's busy hands made her antsy to help, but her legs wouldn't hold her for any length of time. How many days of idleness would pass before she could get up and do something? She scrambled around her mind for positive thoughts.

"Thanks for those prayers, by the way." Deep down, the knowledge that those prayers had saved her life fought to be recognized. The pain during her fevers had left her desirous of death, but now she was glad she'd survived. Was she ready to meet the God behind the power of those prayers? The quivering in her stomach said no.

"I said prayers sure enough." Rachel turned to her and brandished a wet serving spoon at her. "But I think Everett down on his knees was more effectual. How could God ignore the persistence of that man?" She dished out two bowls of chicken soup. "I don't think I've seen a clearer picture of praying without ceasing. When your fever was high, your hallucinations terrified you. I think he stayed up three straight nights early on, nursing you and praying." Rachel's extended belly came into view as she walked around the table setting dishes.

Julia frowned. "And you here too, with children at home and a babe depending on your well-being."

"Don't worry yourself over things that have turned out just fine."

"The doctor said you should rest more." She flexed her feet, trying to banish the tingling sensation slithering from her toes to her knees. "I'm glad I've gotten out of that bed before you have to be confined to yours."

Rachel snorted. "Out here, we don't have the luxury of a confinement." She rubbed her lower back. "What a treat that would be." She smiled at her. "If you want to let me laze around in bed for a few days and corral my children, I won't complain much."

"Consider it done. As long as my guard dog deems me well enough to walk by that time. He might let me stand by, oh . . . how long do you have?"

"Probably a couple weeks."

"Hopefully I'll be promoted to moving on my own by then." She sighed. "He thinks I'm worthless."

"Whatever gave you that crazy idea?"

Her stomach called out to the steamy food piled on the table, so she inched her chair closer. "Anytime I offered to attempt housework in my splint, he'd refuse. Told me it was no big deal. Then I tried telling him I could fend for myself for a day so he could get work done in the fields, but he said everything was taken care of." She shook her head. "I've been released from the state of being a burden now, but I'm wondering if I'm actually useful. Evidently, he can do both our jobs with ease."

Rachel's laughter hit the rooftop. "Foolish girl. People have been stopping by this whole time helping with the outside chores—why do you think you've had so many visitors? They came in to cheer you with their words and then worked in the fields and barn to encourage Everett."

Julia furrowed her brow. No one had ever done that much for her back home. She didn't really know anyone here except the Stantons. Why would strangers take their precious time to help her? She'd find out who had spent time doing Everett's farm chores and bake them something for their sacrifice.

"And of course, Everett was going to be in here every possible second of the day. You gave him quite a scare. Not only being crazy enough to walk along the roof of a leaning shanty, fall, and give yourself one of the worst wounds you can acquire, but also having a fever so high we were sure you were going to set the sheets afire." Rachel set glasses of fresh milk on the table. "The man is trying to protect you from yourself."

Julia bit her lip to keep from telling her how she really fell off the roof.

"And might I add, you're not taking advantage of Everett's devotion. The time will come when you have to return to your daily work, but for now, enjoy the attention your husband wants to dole out." With a flourish, Rachel flipped napkins on the table and bent to kiss her on the head. "Get out of that nasty mood and be content. Make him happy. He is desperately trying to make you so." She grabbed her shawl and left.

Julia stared at the bowl across from her. Could she shake

herself from her petulance and please him? She knew what would make him happy. Her breaths quickened of their own accord. Could she do that?

————◆◆————

While Everett slurped the broth from his chicken and noodles, Julia swished her spoon in her still-full bowl. The lump in her throat kept her from consuming food or conversing.

"Was dinner not to your liking?" Everett peered at her bowl.

Because of her need to eat, she squelched the desire to push the food away. She required strength, and a lot of it, to get back on her feet. She brought a spoonful to her mouth. "I'm just savoring the meal."

Frowning, Everett watched her for a second before taking his bowl to the basin. "Don't savor too long. It isn't as delicious cold."

Chewing, she lamented that her own soup was not near as tasty as Rachel's. She'd bet Everett would miss Rachel's cooking terribly. She would.

Grabbing his chair, Everett scooted nearer. He straddled the seat and crossed his arms on the chair's back, his chin propped on his right forearm.

Taking another bite, she avoided his intense gaze. She swallowed, gave in, and peeked.

He smiled. A slow smile.

She ladled another spoonful. That smile did weird things to her stomach. She shouldn't have dawdled with the food. "So, now that I'm up and about, I can start household chores again, freeing you for the work I know has to be piling up."

"I'm a bit behind, but not too much. I've had help."

She wiped at her mouth and shoveled in another bite. It was the first time he'd mentioned that others had helped him. Why had he kept that from her? She ran a finger along the neckline of her nightgown. What a silly thing to get riled over. She needed fresh air; she was going stir crazy.

"But don't you worry about household chores yet. Take the time to gain strength before you shoulder a workload."

She choked a bit, requiring several sips of water. "Take some time?" Cough. "I don't want any more of it. I'm tired of time."

"I'm sure you're restless, but you shouldn't throw yourself back into work because you think that's what I need. I can help you with the household chores."

"I know you can, but the best way you can help is to allow me to exercise." She didn't want to be relegated to a chair to embroider more superfluous items. Her leg still tingled oddly though an hour had passed since she'd gotten out of bed. "Let me work through the pain while doing something useful."

"Just promise me you won't overdo it."

"Promise." Hopefully that would convince him to let her go at her own pace. Maybe she'd do too much, but her body would advise her to go slower if she did.

Gulping down the rest of the food, she sneaked glances from the corner of her eyes and found his dark, gentle gaze fixed on her. He was trying to get closer—to burrow into her heart. She knew what that would entail. But did she want to push him away? Her throat tightened, making it hard to get the food into her stomach.

She shifted in her seat to take the pressure off a tender spot. Obviously, he'd had the chance to feel closer to her through her ordeal, but not until the last month had she been aware of his ministrations. He'd been careful and gentle, but she'd avoided his gaze, thinking about the minutes and seconds left until she could get up from under his care and stand on her own two feet. She pushed the empty bowl away.

Everett swept it up as if nothing gave him more pleasure than to wash her dirty dish. "I've got a surprise for you," he said over his shoulder.

Her posture slumped. "You've done plenty for me." And she hadn't given him anything he wanted in return. Isn't that what he'd implied minutes before she fell? He didn't want her to work—he wanted her.

He shook his head. "Not enough." A quick smile brightened his face. "I'll go get it." Everett banged out the door, and his footsteps thumped on the steps.

A wave of dizziness caused her to close her eyes for a second. She gripped the table, willing her light-headedness to pass before he returned and demanded she get back into bed.

A hollow metal sound clanked on the porch. Everett shoved his hip against the door and backed in, the shadow of a large object behind him. A bathtub. The thought of soaking her achy body in warm water brushed her feelings of inadequacy aside. How long would it take to fill?

He set the shiny metal tub in the corner beside the cookstove and surveyed the oversized trough with his hands on his hips. "Won't this be something? I haven't yet used it." He grabbed the pot that had boiled while they ate. "This morning I placed several buckets of water off the porch in the sun. I think with the boiling water, it will be ready for you in no time."

"Thank you," she whispered. Only a few minutes. Tension ebbed from her shoulders. She could already feel the water's soothing effects.

The first few pails of water hit the tub's metal floor. How wonderful to bathe indoors again. The new cabin was built much tighter—no wide gaps between the floor slats, no crumbled chink leaving holes in the walls. She had expected nothing more than feet soaks throughout the winter since the old shack had been drafty. But now she could bathe whenever she wanted. Nothing in her father's entire store held the worth of this simple tub.

"All right." Everett stuck his hand into the water and swished around drops of rose water from a bottle she'd never seen before. "It's ready for you."

He helped her stand, and she steadied herself before walking across the planks. A few little white stars danced on the edge of her vision, but nothing would deter her.

When his hands reached for the sides of her nightgown, she automatically clamped her arms across her chest.

He dropped his hands. "I'm sorry. I thought I could help."

He'd changed her during her time of bed rest, but the idea of him undressing her while she was no longer sick . . . She trembled. "I can get it."

His hands moved to steady her. "Are you sure?" His voice was soft.

"Yes . . . and you should leave," she whispered. Her soul cringed at her words, but she couldn't face him right now. She didn't feel right. But would she ever feel right?

The utter silence tore at her. Tension radiated through his hands and settled on her shoulders. She'd hurt him. But she couldn't fix it. Not now. Tears gathered in the corners of her eyes. She just wanted to be alone.

"All right." His voice drew out the two syllables almost in a question. He dropped his hands. Seconds later, his feet scraped across the floor and out the door.

She hurriedly undressed and sank into the water. The heat soothed her body, but not her mind. She scrubbed with a brush and a sweet-smelling soap bar—a luxury over the soft lye they normally used. He'd probably bought this along with the perfumed water. How much had he spent on her?

Everett's savings account was small, and paying for Helga's departure had taken all of her savings. She had to repay him. But could she offer him what he wanted? If he knew Theodore had already ripped away her virtue, he wouldn't want her anymore. He'd despise her. The feel of his arms she'd unwillingly dreamed about in her delirium would turn rough and uncaring, just like Theodore's.

But Everett didn't know what had happened in Massachusetts, and that made her feel dirty.

After scrubbing until her skin felt raw, she lathered again. Her right leg ached a bit more than the left with the heat of the water, but she stayed in, scouring.

Chapter 23

A scream from the bedroom jolted Everett from his seat. Dex sat whittling.

Everett mussed his hair, cringing as a throaty feminine growl rumbled through the walls. "This doesn't bother you?"

Dex looked toward the door and sighed. "Yes and no. She's done this so many times. Believe you me, this is tame in comparison with the first two." He swept curls of wood off his lap. "But she insists a man ain't supposed to be in there." His fingers returned to carving. "Silly rule if you ask me. Men are the reason for it."

"So you've never been in there? You just endure it out here?" Another scream rent the stuffy air in the cabin, causing his skin to prickle.

"I've been in once. With Ambrose. No midwife or female around at the time." He shrugged. "Let's just say her tongue was loosened by the experience. She wasn't too fond of me at that moment." A small smile formed on his lips. "Rachel's normally good at holding her own. But that day, she was dazzling."

"Don't you want to be in there?" Though it was Dex's wife

and not his, not knowing what was happening behind that door made him jittery.

Dex shook his head. "She don't want me, so I ain't pushing. Nor fretting." He poked his blade at Everett. "Why don't you stop worrying for me?"

Rachel's voice screamed, "Dex!" followed by other unintelligible words.

Everett pushed himself against the back of his chair. "I couldn't do it." He leaned forward, hoping Julia would come out and order him to do something. "I won't be able to sit calmly outside while my wife calls for me."

Dex's eyebrows rose.

"Not like I'll be experiencing that anytime in the near future." He huffed. "I'm just rambling."

Dex's knife went back to its even slicing tempo. "I don't mean to say I don't want to be in there, but at this time in a woman's life, you let her have what she wants. I'll know if she yells my name in a way I shouldn't ignore, but with Emma, I thought I was answering a beckon only to get a sound tongue-lashing for coming in and getting in the way." He chuckled. "No, I'll stay right here as of yet."

A groan and a cry from the bedroom tore at Everett's heartstrings, but he took his cue from Dex and sat still in his chair.

He'd borne Julia's anguish through her fever and broken leg. Borne the suffering as if it were his own. And it was his own; he'd been the cause of it. He didn't know whether he or she suffered more—her leg and body, his heart and guilt—all had been on fire and writhing. But God saw them through. Every previous desire for his marriage had been selfish, so he threw himself into praying and nursing with no one but Julia in mind.

If only God had seen fit during her suffering to birth her

276

anew. But she was confused and wary when he spoke of how the Lord saw her through the agony. His ascribing her recovery to God made her uneasy, as did any talk of his faith.

God would have to save her and heal her past hurts before his marital situation would turn around. His past kindnesses and romantic attentions had not been enough.

Between Rachel's cries he prayed for two births: the easy birth of a Stanton baby and the rebirth of Julia's soul. Sudden quiet snapped him from his prayers. Julia's tense, worried voice, though hushed, captured his ears.

Should they wait or rush in to assist? Surely he'd be useless to the women in the other room. Dex sat, gripping the edge of his seat, but remained cemented to his chair. So Everett held on to the arms of his and prayed for a healthy wee one.

The infant's blue face gulped soundlessly. The air rushed from Julia's lungs as she dropped onto the side of the bed, firmly cradling the little girl.

"You can do it, Julia. You need to do it."

Mimicking Rachel's actions with the Hampden baby, she swiped the baby's mouth, then patted and rubbed vigorously until the little girl took in a shuddering breath, followed by a muffled cry. The vestiges of panic disappeared from every muscle in her body, and she suddenly felt as weary as Rachel probably felt.

She wrapped the child and took even, deep breaths. "You've got a girl, Rachel. A beautiful girl." She ran her finger down the baby's plump cheek before handing the bundle to her mother, who promptly suckled the infant.

Rachel yawned while taking her first peep at her daughter. "So tired."

Julia shook her head. "Ten hours of hard work when you should be sleeping would make a body so."

"Oh, that was nothing." Rachel wiped at the whitish-blue fingers curled around hers. "William took twenty."

Julia didn't want to think about how crazy she would have gone helping Rachel through a whole day of labor. "Have you picked a name?"

"Suppose we ought to have Dex come in and talk about that." Rachel smiled. "Let me finish feeding her, then you can wash her up."

Julia tensed. "I haven't bathed a baby before."

"It's not difficult. Take a rag with warm water and wipe her off so she's not so messy." She jiggled the baby since she'd stopped nursing. "Just keep the towel on the parts you aren't washing to keep her from catching cold."

Staring at the tiny form curled on top of her mother, Julia bit her lip. "I can't believe you'd entrust her to me. I don't know why you even wanted me here after what happened with Kathleen. . . ."

Rachel smiled lazily, not taking her eyes off her infant daughter. "I knew I'd be here for the whole thing, so you wouldn't be alone, and William could be called in if anything major went wrong. But the longer you stay afraid of birthing, the worse things will be when your time comes. You've got maternal instincts somewhere in there. You got her to breathe, didn't you? They'll show up for a simple bath."

"I hope so. I won't use them otherwise." She slumped onto the mattress beside mother and baby.

Rachel clucked. "Come now, you've only been married four months. I didn't get pregnant with William until we were wed for a little more than a year. Be patient. It will happen if the good Lord wills. On His timetable, not yours."

"Well, that's not exactly it." Heat crept into her face, and Rachel arched her brows. The color in her cheeks must be high. "There're other reasons I'll never have children."

Rachel remained quiet as she rewrapped her sleeping daughter, but her eyes made Julia want to voice every secret, every confusion, every hope, every fear.

But how could she tell her everything? "Now's not the time to engage in such a discussion."

"Oh, yes it is." Rachel glanced around the room and whispered, "This will be one of the few times we have alone. As soon as you step through that door, the family will no longer consider this room sacred ground. We won't be able to speak about delicate matters for some time."

Julia smoothed the baby's matted hair, amazed she lay sleeping so soon after coming into the world. "Are all babies this quiet?"

"No, Ambrose cried for eight hours straight, but don't let this babe's first day fool you. Emma slept her first day away, and then she showed her true colors." Rachel groaned. "I need your help again. Just lay her in the bassinet."

Julia helped clean Rachel after the birth, guided her into a new gown, and fixed the bedding. She headed for the baby's cradle. "I'll take her to Dex. I bet he's quite anxious by now."

"Julia." Rachel grabbed her arm. "Talk to me."

Sighing, she looked toward the window, but didn't really see through it. A vision of her mother's last seconds on earth, lying in a bed surrounded by the blood of her last failed attempt at childbirth, and the cold blue face of her last sibling in her arms haunted Julia. "It's just that Mother had so much difficulty having children. I shouldn't awaken the desire for them."

"That doesn't mean it will be the same for you."

Tears pushed at the back of her eyes. "No, it doesn't, but it seems likely. My grandmother only birthed two live children. Plus, I don't think Everett and I will ever be . . . that close."

Rachel snorted.

She frowned. "What's that mean?"

"Means I've never seen Everett so smitten in my life."

But would Everett still feel anything for her if he knew everything? She crossed the room and took her time wrapping her arms about the baby. "I'm not sure his feelings are anything beyond attraction to a pretty face. And guilt."

"Why would he feel guilty?"

How had she let that slip? She sat on the bed next to Rachel. "Um, it was Everett's fault I fell off the roof."

Rachel's eyebrows fell until her eyes were tiny slits. "There's no way that man carried you up to the roof and threw you off."

"No, I was up there on my own. But when he kissed me—"

"So he kissed you?" Rachel's face was smug.

"Yes. He scared me so much I backed up and fell off." She rubbed her leg where it still felt numb.

"I'm sure the accident would bother him, but you have absolutely nothing to be afraid of. The man's in love with you. For more than your looks." Rachel chuckled. "You weren't anything nice to look at after that tumble off the roof, and that didn't faze him."

Tightness gripped her chest. She hugged the baby closer and looked at Rachel through her tears. "But I'm afraid. Afraid I'm just a pretty face like everyone says. That he . . . that he's only feeling what he feels because I'm nice-looking and under his roof, but when he discovers the real me . . . what happ—" She shook her head. "To be used for a while and then cast off . . ." She sniffed and wiped at her tears. "I couldn't handle it."

Rachel's thumb rubbed circles on her elbow. "I know Everett, honey. He isn't solely interested in your looks. I'm sure your gorgeous face enthralls him, but to be attracted to one's spouse is a good thing. And as for being used, that's not at all what it feels like when a man in love with you holds you in his arms. Where would you get such an idea?"

"I don't know." She couldn't tell Rachel that she knew exactly what it felt like. It probably wasn't the same with a man who loved the woman he caressed, but the control Theodore had wielded was not something she could easily forget. She needed to erase every memory of the time Theodore had forced her into his arms and bury the feelings so they couldn't ruin her life anymore. But how many times had she tried and failed?

And could she be certain Everett would still care about her if he learned about Theodore . . . about everything?

And Everett might love her, but what if she couldn't love him? "If I don't yet love him . . ."

"Love will come, honey. I doubt the Lord brought you two together in such a convoluted manner to make you unhappy for the rest of your lives, but you're bent on being miserable. Why not go forward and see how the heavenly Father wants to bless you? It's not good to be together yet separate."

The baby wriggled in Julia's arms. "I better go tell your daddy you're here."

Rachel nodded. "I suppose you should. I'll pray for you. But you shouldn't be letting your past define who you are or how much you're worth. Look to God and through the eyes of Everett. That's where you'll find your worth."

Julia stared at the peaceful girl in her lap. Maybe Everett would find her worth something. But God? She didn't have anything of value to capture His attention. Could a heavenly Father think more highly of her than her own father did?

Julia took a deep breath and considered the little charge in her hands in need of a bath and Rachel, eyes closed, resting. There wasn't time to fix her whole life right now; it was time to be productive.

The bedroom door opened and Everett leaned forward, as did Dex. Julia walked out, her face grim, a bundle of cloths in her arms. Did she hold a dead infant? They had been quiet too long, and no newborn cry announced the presence of a living child.

Everett reached over and gripped Dex's arm, letting him know he was there.

Julia pulled the blanket away from a baby's face. Her mouth twitched into a tiny smile. "Rachel needs you to help her decide on a name for your little girl."

Dex shot up from his chair. "Do you mean . . . you mean she's all right?" He glanced toward the bedroom door.

"Both of them are fine. Tired, but beautiful."

Pulling back the blankets and exposing thick black hair, Dex caressed his daughter's head, pressed a light kiss to her forehead, then rushed through the couple's bedroom door.

Julia took a deep breath and spoke to the baby. "It's time we got you clean."

Everett jumped from his chair. How could he help? "Do you need hot water?"

She smiled. "That water right there will do. This cabin's like an oven anyway. I'm sure the water's warm enough."

Moving to the window, he unlatched it. "I'll let the heat out."

"No. Wait." Julia glanced at the baby. Would that be a good

idea? "Maybe we should wait until I've bathed her. Rachel said something about keeping her covered so she doesn't chill."

Everett let go of the latch. "All right."

"Where are the kids?" They'd be excited to see their baby sister, but then again, they might get in the way of the bath. She didn't need an audience watching her fumble through a simple procedure.

"We sent them to play in the barn hours ago." Everett grabbed the bucket of water and held it up in question.

Where should she do this? Grabbing a few rags and towels, she created a nest on the kitchen table. "Put the water here. I'm just supposed to wipe her to get the blood and white stuff off."

"Glad you know what you're doing."

She turned to give him a crazy look, but he was too close. She recognized the smell of his sweat, which did weird things to her heart, knowing such intimate details about the man. Yet she still felt so far from him. Not from a lack of trying on his part. Could she let down her guard, allow him in a bit? "I have no idea what I'm doing."

He locked eyes with her for a few seconds before returning his attention to the baby.

Gingerly, she unwrapped a body part, then washed and re-wrapped it before uncovering a new spot. He moved closer. Was he as afraid that her trembling hands would hurt the baby as she was? Why must he make her more nervous with his nearness, watching over everything she did? He was not helping.

"Seems you're quite capable." The hot air of his words caressed her neck, causing a shiver to rush down her spine.

The baby had not awoken once, just flinched and pulled in her limbs when treated to the damp rag. Julia wrapped the infant and picked her up. She should return her to her mother.

Everett's breath tickled her ear. "Maybe we should try having one?"

She clasped the baby to keep from dropping her. Everett's eyes were the color of wet steel. Had he overheard her conversation with Rachel? Tightening her grip, she pulled in a shaky breath. Her vision glazed over. What if she overcame her fear of intimacy but was unable to give him a child? Julia stared at Everett, unable to form a response.

His face went blank. He took a step back, made a faint bow, and left the cabin.

Her heart's thumping stole her concentration as she attempted to clean up the bathing mess. The way his face drooped tugged at her emotions. She continued to hurt him though she wanted to make him happy, but how could she do so adequately when she wasn't happy with herself? If he knew of her past, what was so dark inside, would he still love her?

"I don't think so," she whispered to the baby.

Chapter 24

Everett helped Julia down from the wagon, letting his hands linger at her waist longer than necessary. Of course, she probably didn't notice through all the fabric and boning. She looked him in the eyes before she ducked her head and headed into the Stantons' cabin. The incessant crying of little Rebecca ripped through the lifeless late-summer air. On her first day of life, she'd lulled him into believing babies were sleeping angels, but the many times they'd visited these past two weeks swiftly changed his mind.

John burst from the house, hands clasped around his ears. He ran toward Everett. "Save me! Take me fishing. Anything."

The sun directly overhead was busy pouring buckets of heat. "There's no shade at the pond and probably no fish crazy enough to surface."

"But there's no screaming there. Just fish. And they don't make a sound."

If Everett went with John, he'd be comfortable. He'd know what to do—cast, wait, catch. Yet his wife's presence in the cabin drew him. He couldn't observe her fluid movements or listen to her melodious voice from the pond. But he didn't know what to do with her in the least. She'd been friendlier since the baby was born, but she'd also increased the amount of choring she did. He couldn't make her understand she didn't have to make up for months of bed rest—that they should relax and enjoy each other's company.

"Please." John folded his hands in front of him. Another scream wafted out the door.

He must be lovesick to contemplate returning to the cabin on purpose. He patted John's head. "Let me make sure it's all right with your ma and pa."

"Oh, it is. It is! Ma just told me to find somewhere else to be."

Everett suppressed a chuckle. "I'm still going to make sure."

John shrugged his shoulders and then ran to the barn. He turned around to yell, "I'm getting the fishing stuff ready."

Everett walked into the cabin and let his eyes adjust to the interior. The screams reverberated off the walls. He shook his head, amazed that the noise of such a tiny thing could be so loud. Rachel stood in the middle of the kitchen, twisting back and forth, bouncing the baby at the same time. She gave him a weary frown. "Sorry, she's not in a mood for entertaining company."

He pulled off his hat. "Not here to be entertained."

Julia was already attacking a pile of dirty dishes. She had finished her own chores that morning at high speed to rush here and do more. He was proud of how hard she worked, though at home he wished she'd let up a bit. Compared to her, he looked like a loafer for trying to sneak in a few minutes of conversation. He wished he could pull her away right now, but his friend needed her help more than he needed Julia's time. "John's wondering if I would take him to the pond."

Rachel swiped at the hair in her face. "What did you say?"

Everett raised his voice to match little Rebecca's. "John wants to go to the pond."

Rachel grimaced. "Julia, would you mind holding Rebecca for a few minutes?"

Julia wiped her hands on a towel and took the infant with no hesitation. He was sure at least a frown would have crossed his face if he'd been handed that squalling bundle. She'd make an excellent mother. If only that day would come.

Rachel led him out the door, but she kept walking toward the fence. He strolled behind her, taking his time so she'd have the longest break she wanted for answering such a simple question.

"Feels nice to get out sometimes. I don't think any of the others were near this bad." She leaned against the paddock's post, sucked in a huge parcel of air, and let it out slowly. "Thank goodness the boys are old enough they don't need my full attention. I'd let her cry, but then she just screams. Without stopping. Never heard a child scream so long."

"Is there something wrong?" He twisted his hat in his hands, certain he could offer no assistance besides what he already did—allowing Julia every spare minute to help.

Rachel chewed on her fingernails. "My mother's heart says no. Just . . . I don't know. She's difficult. Hopefully it won't last long."

"I'll pray it won't." He leaned against the railing. "John asked if I could take him to the pond. Thought I'd ask to make sure."

She waved her hand. "That's fine. It's Ambrose's turn to occupy Emma, and John was underfoot."

"Then I'll take him." He crammed his hat back on his head.

"Everett?" Rachel's hesitant voice stopped him. He pivoted and waited.

"How's it going with Julia?" She pulled at a splinter of wood on the post.

How was it going? Bad, good, who knew? One second, she drove him to distraction being but a few feet away from him, acting like she wanted to be as far away as possible. The next, she'd give him a look that made him feel weak down into his toes. But the few times he'd leaned in for a kiss after receiving one of those looks, she'd scurried away. "I don't know. You probably know better than me."

"How's that?"

He shrugged. "Women talk."

She stared at her knuckles, but made no move to dismiss him or return to the house.

Why hadn't she chosen somewhere in the shade to hem-haw? "Do you want to say something to me?" He wiped his brow with his handkerchief.

She sucked in her lips and looked skyward. "I'm not supposed to meddle."

"That didn't stop you in setting this whole thing up, so out with it." Actually, if she knew anything about Julia's feelings in the matter, he'd take whatever information she could provide.

"Julia's scared."

"Scared of what?" He'd nursed her with gentle hands while she was bedridden. Would she have confided in Rachel about whatever it was that made her fear men so? Was it as bad as he thought? Had she told Rachel how she'd fallen from the roof?

"Scared that you'll hurt her more."

He cringed. "But the roof was an accident!"

Rachel's smile turned lopsided. "Yes, I'm sure it was. She's not worried about getting hurt physically. She's worried you'll break her heart, I think. Use her and cast her aside."

"I don't understand." He never wanted her to leave.

"You love her, right?"

Everett jammed his hands into his pockets. He felt wrong to admit it to someone other than Julia for the first time. But then that kind of information would probably make her uncomfortable at the moment. "Yes," he whispered.

"For more than her physical beauty?"

He squinted at Rachel, trying to gauge what her question meant exactly. It hurt him to think she might think he solely lusted after Julia—but hadn't he, from the first moment he saw his bride, been stuck on her surface features? He closed his eyes as if it would help him search within. When he thought of her now, a picture didn't form in his mind, just the feeling of her. How he wished he could be closer, know her, be with her. Love her. He swallowed the lump in his throat. "Yes."

Rachel's weary eyes shone a bit. "Good. Tell her."

"I don't know how, beyond what I already do. She skitters away any time I try to tell her how I feel." He tossed up his hands. "I know I messed up in the beginning. I was a fool, but—"

"Yes, definitely a fool."

Great, everyone thought him an imbecile.

"She's built a wall around herself, just like you did—to protect yourself from the possibility she'd run away and hurt you. Something in her past is keeping her away, something inside. And walls that strong don't let love—"

"But what is it?" His cheeks burned. The thought that she would confide in Rachel instead of him humiliated him. "What happened that makes her so unwilling to respond?"

She shook her head. "I don't know. She's guarded against me too." She chewed on her nails and looked over the harvested hay field. "But you've got to tear them down, though right now she doesn't think she wants them torn down. What did it take to bust through your walls?"

Dex calling him out on his sin and the near death of his wife.

Dear God, make her wall not as stubborn and thick as mine!

"If you can get through to her, Everett, I promise you there's a woman there who wants to be cared for, who wants to be worthy of your love."

"But I can't make her feel worthy and whole, only God can do that. I'll let her down if she looks solely to me for that."

Her lips pursed. "You're right. I'll pray harder for God to get into the situation. I think she just might be ready to hear about His love for her, and if she feels your love, she might put two and two together."

He sighed. He still didn't know what to do. Talking about destroying walls didn't help him know how to proceed. Choosing the wrong strategy could drive her further away.

Rachel grabbed one of his hands with both of hers and squeezed. "You'll figure it out with God's help. But if I don't get back inside and relieve her, she might just run away before you get the chance." She darted off, leaving her words to bounce around in his mind.

She might just run away.

Would he ever stop worrying about that?

Sweat escaped Everett's hat and trickled into his ears. He wiped his face with his handkerchief and pulled his line in. "John, I'm about to be a roast goose. Why don't we head in?"

"Aw. Do we have to?" John wiggled his line.

"It's so hot the fish aren't even biting. Why don't we do something else? We ought to find your pa." He had some questions for Dex, though he didn't relish having to ask them.

"All right. Maybe he'll let us help him work." John scurried up the bank, his feet blackened with dirt.

"He can always use help picking bugs in the garden." Everett grabbed the boy's suspenders to help him over the steep edge.

John stuck out his tongue. "Forgot he was doing that. Maybe we can find something else to do?"

Everett ruffled John's dusty hair. "You need a bath. Maybe you ought to take one."

"Maybe I might just pick bugs."

He laughed. "Like being dirty that much, eh?"

"Race ya!" John sprinted to the field where Dex and William were stooped, checking plants one by one.

Not about to run, Everett called after the boy, "Get us some water. Then come help."

Like a flock of birds in flight changing their collective minds, John veered toward the well.

Everett moseyed over to the field. Thankfully, William's head bobbed toward the far end, nowhere near his father. John rushed back with a jug of water.

Dex took a big gulp before handing over the water. "You two done playing?"

"Sure, Pa." John's voice couldn't hide his reluctance. Everett hid his smile by taking a swig.

Dex tweaked his son's ear. "Why don't you go help Will, then?"

John pivoted on bare feet.

"Hold on, boy!" Dex pointed to the canteen. "Will needs water too."

Pulling a goofy face, John snagged the water before racing toward his older brother.

Knees creaking, Everett stooped next to the row of plants Dex was working on. "The speed of that boy's feet is only matched by his mouth."

Dex snickered. "Don't I know it."

"Fun kid though. You're awful lucky to have them all."

"Yep." Dex threw a thick hornworm into a bucket.

Everett scanned the underside of the leaves for the green caterpillars with bright yellow slashes across their back. "Bet it takes a lot to keep them all happy." He added a bug to Dex's pile of wriggling insects. "What makes Rachel happy?"

Dex moved ahead a pace. "Doing what she wants me to do."

"Like what?"

"Like me mucking out the chicken coop though that's her job, so she can read the paper."

"But what about wives? More in general, I mean."

Dex stopped his picking and stared at him. When Everett broke eye contact, Dex humphed. "As I see it, the Bible says to love your wife like Christ loved the church. The Divine giving up everything. He laid His life at the feet of unworthy sinners. That's the ultimate sacrifice—giving up your worthy life for the undeserving who want nothing to do with you. So, how much easier is my situation—to give up my wants for a woman who loves me? Not near the same sacrifice."

Grabbing another worm off a leaf, Everett moved down a few feet. Was there anything left for him to give up?

Dex threw another pest in the pail. "Besides, the more I make Rachel happy, the more I see her strive to make me happy. It's when I'm looking out for myself that our marital harmony hits a bad note. When I balk at doing something

Rachel wants, I remind myself God doesn't even ask me to love her with the same magnitude He required of His Son. So I buck up and do as she asks. Unless of course it's immoral, but that's not the kind of thing I'm talking about, just selfish things I don't want to give up."

Everett spent a few minutes checking several plants down the rows, double-checking around the nibbled leaves before moving to the next. Dex's advice seemed sound, but how could he give himself to a woman who asked nothing of him? He kept his hands busy feeling for worms. "But how do you make a woman happy with you to begin with?"

The constant hum of John's chatter forty yards away filled the otherwise silent fields. Everett stopped and took a side glance at Dex, who pulled his mustache into his mouth with his lips. One eyebrow pushed his forehead into a mess of wrinkles. "What did you not get about my little sermon there?"

Everett tossed a worm. "Uh, I understood the speech. Sounds right. But I mean more like, how do you get a woman to . . . to love you in the first place?" Admitting he'd failed to capture the attention of a woman who'd lived under his roof for more than four months filled his chest with shame.

"Well, have you taken care of what I said last time? Do you talk to her?"

Looking straight at Dex, he crossed his arms across his chest. "I've tried. A lot. I would think you could see that. I didn't like what you said. Hated it, in fact. I wasn't acting like the kind of man I want to be, but I think I've messed this up for good." He reached down and snapped a worm between his fingers. Rachel's speech about tearing down Julia's walls with love nibbled at the edge of his mind. "How do you make a woman understand you love her?"

Dex's goofy grin showed up. "Like that."

"Like what?"

"You say, 'I . . .'" Dex leaned forward. "Wait for it." He put his hand behind his ear and pushed it forward. ". . . love you."

Everett huffed. "You're very funny."

"Well, have you tried that?"

"I think so." Everett threw a chewed-up leaf in with the worms.

"Think?" Dex shook his head. "What happened after you *think* you said it?"

"She fell off the roof."

A fit of coughing hardly covered Dex's laughter. He shook his head and returned his attention to the plants in front of him. "I think I'll stop giving you advice right here and now."

Could no one help him? "God help me."

"Yes, my friend." Dex's voice was underlaid with amusement. "God help you."

Chapter 25

Julia attempted to rub her back while balancing on the bouncing wagon seat. A violent bump over an upturned rock sent her scurrying for a handhold.

Everett's welcome vocal hum relating his fishing adventures with John entertained her. She smiled at his pleasure in the child. He'd make a good father. . . . Julia's heart constricted. She'd stolen that chance away from him. She never wanted to hold a dead baby again, not after having the pleasure of holding little Rebecca, screaming and all. Her brother's lifeless body still weighed heavy in her arms. But then, she'd only been nine. If she'd known how to get an infant to breathe, if the midwife hadn't been busy staunching the flow of blood . . .

No. She couldn't blame herself for her ignorance. And Mother had lost more than one child, most before they were supposed to be born. What were the odds it would be any different for her?

"And so he took the worm off and bit into it." Everett's laugh turned into a sputter. "His face was really something. Almost made me want to take a bite to see what caused such terrible disfiguration."

How different the rides back and forth to the Stantons had become from that initial one in late March. Everett's jaw was still sharp and square, but unhinged now. And the dark evening shade of his eyes stole her breath. She'd never seen anyone whose eyes neared the color gray.

"He said the thing tasted like dirt and . . ." Everett took his focus off the oxen to look at her, but his voice died off. His Adam's apple bobbed.

Quickly, she assessed herself, staring at him with a muscle-stretching grin. Straightening in her seat, she relaxed her mouth and looked out over the prairie. "I had a good time with Rachel. Despite Becca's crying. Thankfully she takes naps. Rachel napped too, so I cleaned everything I could quietly."

She stretched the fingers of one hand against the fingers of the other and yawned. "Got tons of cleaning at home to do, but it feels good to help, considering how much Rachel did for me while I was bedridden. And how much she taught me about farm chores when I first arrived."

"I'm sure Rachel is grateful. Without ladies taking care of the house, we farmers would be less successful, less relaxed." He reached over and squeezed her hand. "Thank you."

She squeezed back, but didn't let go. Birds flying overhead twittered as they passed, filling the silence that descended. Her heart encouraged her hand to lie there. Why couldn't he hold her hand? She'd been giving quite a bit of thought to letting him kiss her, but she kept shying away from it anytime he seemed to think about it. So she'd have to start slower— with hand-holding.

The feel of his roughened palm swallowing her thin fingers made her feel connected, relaxed . . . like she belonged.

"Julia . . . " His thumb lazily caressed the back of her hand, and she could feel the bloom of heat filling her cheeks.

"I know the day on the roof was a disaster, but I was trying to tell you something rather important that I hope you didn't miss."

Dots of white, yellow, and purple flowers poked their faces between the tall grasses dancing in the light breeze. She couldn't meet his eyes, knowing what he was going to say, and not sure she could say it back.

"I want you to know that I love you more now than then."

She swallowed hard a few times, testing the words in her head, but she couldn't force them off her tongue. She couldn't toy with him.

"And even if your heart never lets you love me back, I'll still love you."

The sway of the wagon kept the awkward silence from being terribly uncomfortable. She took his hand in both of hers and squeezed her thanks, holding on to his hand as if she'd slide off the seat without that anchor. He dropped her hand and pulled her closer, the tension of the moment dissolved under the security of his arm wrapped around her. Asking nothing, offering everything.

They stopped in front of their pine cabin. She glanced over at the old one and smiled. Of course, before Kansas she'd never lived in anything as small and sparse as this new cabin, but compared to the one they had lived in for two months, the new house was bounds better. Just like their relationship, from horrible to good. He talked to her and helped without her having to ask. How many women had that? Not her mother.

Everett stood next to the wagon with two hands extended. She tentatively grabbed both of his shoulders, instead of one to steady herself.

On the ground, he seemed reluctant to let her go, like the

last several wagon rides. She squeezed his arms and let her hands drop before she turned toward the well.

His hand snagged her elbow, and he pulled her to him. Her breath catching, she questioned him with her eyes. Would he kiss her? Any day now, he'd take another step toward becoming more than just the friendly man she lived with, and she needed to let him. He wasn't out to take and not give. She had to give back, but the brush of fear in her stomach fought against the anticipation in her heart.

"What . . . what can I help you do?" His voice resembled a frog's. His clammy palm slid to her wrist.

She searched his face. Why had he stepped away? "I need water for dinner tonight. I hope you don't mind leftover stew. I'm tired from the work this morning, so I don't have the desire to do much more."

His left hand joined his right, holding and caressing her knuckles. Her heart beat with each stroke. "Would you like me to cook dinner?"

Her mouth skewed awry. "I've heard plenty of your hardtack and bean stories. Should I really take you up on the offer?" But did she really care what dinner was? She'd welcome anything that got her to sleep faster.

He bit his lip, and then his eyes shone. "Yes."

She smiled. "Well, then you best get to it. Stew would be easy, but you'd need to start now to get dinner done in time." She should work on the other chores that needed doing before night fell. "I'll tend the garden then."

"Do you want to tend the garden?" His hands disappeared behind his back.

What did *want* have to do with anything? "I suppose I do. It needs to be done."

"Why not . . . rest?"

A tempting suggestion, but she laughed it off. "No time for that."

He shook his head slowly, as if he were entertaining a different thought with each turn of his head. "Is there anything you've wanted to do? Something that would make you happy? Read? Paint? Sing?"

Without thinking, she blurted, "Sleep."

His toothy smile broke through his face. "Then take a nap."

"That's silly." A midafternoon nap next to a cookstove adding heat to the already hot day did not sound enjoyable. "You're cooking."

"I am, but I'll cook outside."

That would be inconvenient for him. "No, that's not necessary."

He grabbed her by the shoulders and turned her to the cabin. "A good day for a nap—too hot for much else. I have a feeling summer is going to drag its heat into fall."

"This is ludicrous. This is your busiest time of year."

His head came so close his breath stroked her neck. "I want you to." His whispered words tickled her ear. "If I weren't cooking, I might join you."

A tingle shot up her back, but she shied away from the confusing feeling. Since the accident, they'd slept together side by side in the huge bed he'd built. He'd not had time to build another bed during her illness. After all that time sharing, asking him to make another bed seemed childish. But they'd never slept next to each other during the day. "I think I ought to be doing something useful instead."

"You do that every day. At the very least, sprawl out on the bed and read something. You should at least rest your leg. You've been doing double duty this week. I'll manage the chores for the afternoon." He left her at the doorstep and strode away. On a mission.

She walked into the kitchen and fingered the dirty dishes on the counter. Her heavy eyelids begged her to give in. She moved the plates into the water basin but refrained from washing them.

An unbidden yawn surfaced. Never would she be able to sleep during the day without feeling lazy for doing so. But she had permission, so she'd take that nap. Just not a long one.

But her mind wouldn't settle. She'd never been so worried about hurting a man who had feelings for her.

How long until admiration and caring become affection?

And was the stirring of love enough to get her past her darkest fear?

———◆———

Wiping at sweat along his hairline, Everett found another stray feather in his hair. He flicked the downy plume away and returned to turning the chicken on the makeshift spit. The smell of smoke and meat made his stomach gurgle. He preferred to eat dinner earlier than this, but Julia was sleeping soundly, so he whistled a slow tune and didn't rush. With his knife, he pricked the meat. Almost done. The pot of boiling green beans was close to ready as well.

Ladies liked picnics, right? He tiptoed into the house and grabbed a blanket and his Bible off the trunk and peeked into the bedroom. Julia stirred a bit, so he froze. She murmured and her eyelids flickered, cheeks rosy. He held his ground.

She bolted upright and blinked hard several times. "Everett?" Her throat sounded full of rocks.

"Good evening, Julia." He ambled over to the bed and offered his hand. "You ready for dinner?"

"Did I sleep that long?" Her eyelids kept opening and shutting.

Her long eyelashes begged to be kissed, but he refrained and pulled her to stand. "Yes. But that's what you were supposed to do."

"But . . . no." She put her hand to her forehead. "If I slept that long, I'll just lie awake all night."

A tightness in his chest clenched the rest of his body. All kinds of images popped unbidden into his mind. He'd had enough trouble sleeping next to her. He dropped her hand, needing to put distance between them. He called to her as he nearly ran out the door. "Come, dinner's outside. Bring the guitar, would ya?"

To take advantage of the beautiful view to the south, he spread the blanket beside the bed of flowers Julia had arranged near the house. The horizon was just starting to show signs of the approaching sunset as pink and orange hues tinted the sky.

He grabbed the browned chicken from the fire spit, set it in a tin pie plate, drained the vegetables, and returned to the blanket. Julia had already settled herself, sitting with her head tilted back, eyes closed. Her hair was a mess and her bare toes poked from beneath her skirts. His throat constricted. Like that first day he'd seen her after she'd awoken in the Stantons' barn. That day he'd run from her. Now, he wanted her to run to him.

She opened one eye and glanced at the chicken. "Who's that?"

"The mean little hen." He took his fork and pulled apart the meat to hasten cooling. "I think she deserved it."

"You went through a lot of trouble."

"Not much." He said a quick blessing over the food and handed her a fork. "Hope you don't mind, but since I'm doing dishes, we'll eat out of the same pan. Less cleanup for me."

Huffing, she speared a long green bean. "Maybe I should start taking such shortcuts."

Around a mouthful of chicken, he mumbled, "Sure. You oughta. No need to stand on formality with me."

She took a delicate bite. "This is good! Why didn't you do this when you were a bachelor instead of eating biscuits and beans?"

He laughed. "If I did this every time I was hungry I wouldn't have much of a flock left."

"Right." She chewed slowly before taking another mouthful.

Eating his meal in a comfortable silence, he listened to the drone of cicadas while watching the colors of the sky grow richer. And he sneaked glances at the fine figure of a lady next to him, but she kept her gaze pinned ahead.

When finished, he opened the Bible. He'd been out of the habit of reading God's Word when she first came, and he didn't realize how much he had missed hearing from God every day. During her fever and recovery, he'd read aloud to her, beginning in Genesis. Those long lists of names and numbers in the Old Testament had put her to sleep. Thankfully, William had ordered just that to promote healing. He flipped the pages to 1 Samuel. Finally out of the long lists of names and tallies and into more histories, the reading seemed to keep her interest.

She'd listened every night since her fever broke, but never said much of anything. When she had uttered in her delirium that God did not love her, his heart had fractured. She was good at taking a hammer to his chest and splintering it into a million pieces. He prayed God would use His Word to make crevices in the wall she'd wrapped around herself since she'd succeeded in keeping him out. Perhaps God would have better luck.

He cleared his throat and read.

"And it came to pass, when they were come, that he looked on Eliab and said, Surely the Lord's anointed is before him.

"But the Lord said unto Samuel, Look not on his countenance, or on the height of his stature; because I have refused him: for the Lord seeth not as man seeth; for man looketh on the outward appearance, but the Lord looketh on the heart. . . .

"And Samuel said unto Jesse, Are here all thy children? And he said, There remaineth yet the youngest, and behold, he keepeth the sheep. And Samuel said unto Jesse, Send and fetch him: for we will not sit down till he come hither.

"And he sent, and brought him in. Now he was ruddy, and withal of a beautiful countenance, and goodly to look to. And the Lord said, Arise, anoint him: for this is he.

"Then Samuel took the horn of—"

"Wait." Julia grabbed his arm.

He lowered the Bible. "Yes?"

"I don't understand."

"Don't understand what?" Scanning the text he had read, the story sounded straightforward.

"It said God didn't want the first son. That He looked at the heart and not on the man's pretty features, but the Book says the last son God chose was beautiful and fine featured." She bit her lip. "Sounds like He's choosing what He said He doesn't choose."

Glancing through the text, Everett could see how it sounded like God rejected one handsome man for another. "Well, it says He sees the heart, but the text only describes the looks of the two men. I suppose being in the same family, he was bound to be as nice looking as the first one."

She thumped her chin in her hands.

"God saw something in the first one that wasn't as pleasing as what He saw in David." Everett stopped a moment and tried to arrange his words for clarity. It was the first time she'd made a comment. He didn't want her to stop now. "I guess He ignores looks, be they ruddy and beautiful. Or not. It's what's inside that matters."

"What is He looking for?"

"Remember a few days ago when we read that God sought 'a man after his own heart'? He meant David."

"So He only wants to bless those that are like God?" She dropped her head. "No one's perfect."

Everett's heart wobbled. *God, help me to help her understand. Your Word has brought this opportunity to share, and I need your wisdom to take full advantage of it. If I can't show my love to my wife every way that's possible, at least give her your love. Give her the peace that comes from you, to comfort her in the stressful relationship I've put us in here on earth.*

She sighed and turned away.

Clearing his throat, Everett plunged forward. "No. We're not perfect. I know my own heart isn't perfect. I don't think I could get anywhere near the description David was worthy of receiving."

"Then there's no hope for us."

His head shook of its own accord. "David wasn't perfect either. In fact, as king, not only did he steal a man's wife and have an affair, but he killed her husband so he could keep her once she was found to be with child."

"Well, that doesn't sound much like 'after God's own heart.'" Her features appeared confused, but something glimmered in her eye, like a fleck of hope.

"No, it doesn't, does it?" He twiddled his thumbs. "But God still saw the man's faith and desire to know God and be what He wanted him to be. David messed up, but his desire to obey was evident in his heart. That's most likely why God knew he'd be the best king. Despite wrongdoing, David's heart strove to be right."

"So how do you know if your heart is good enough?"

Everett paused, his heart beating in his ears. How did he know God wanted him? A memorized verse shot into his thoughts, and he flipped to the book of Romans to make sure he quoted it correctly.

"I guess we can never know." She made a move to stand. "Just wait until we're dead, I suppose."

Snagging her sleeve, he pulled her back down. "Give me a second." His finger scurried across the words until he located the spot. He held the Bible close so he could see in the dim light and read aloud.

> "That if thou shalt confess with thy mouth the Lord Jesus, and shalt believe in thine heart that God hath raised him from the dead, thou shalt be saved. For with the heart man believeth unto righteousness; and with the mouth confession is made unto salvation."

He laid the book aside and turned so he could judge her expression. "That's what the New Testament says, so that's what our instructions are today. David's heart was right with God. And these are our directions to get a right heart—believe Jesus died for your wrongdoings and conquered death on your behalf. That simple confession, if it's backed with real belief and trust, makes your heart right with God. This is the kind of heart God seeks. Someone who believes His commands and entrusts his life to God."

Julia pulled her knees to her chest and wrapped her arms around them. He detected a glistening in the corner of her eye. His arms ached to drop the Bible and pull her into his chest, but he didn't want to stifle the conversation.

"But there's nothing in my heart worthy of wanting. All I have is my beauty. It's all I've ever had of worth. And the Bible says God doesn't even want that."

Brushing away her solitary tear, he cupped her face. "You are the most beautiful creature I've ever seen. Just one gift God gave you that I enjoy. More than I ought. But He's right. The inside of a person is what counts. None of us are good on the inside, but once you take the step to believe and become right with God, He takes an initial willing heart and makes it better every day."

Scooting closer, he took her other hand in his. "If you want to, you can trust Him with your heart. He can save you from the wrong you have inside if you believe." He closed his eyes, as if his concentration could compel her to make a decision.

"Well, if my looks are worthless and my insides are worthless, then there's really no hope besides trusting that He's willing to save me for no apparent reason. Right?" She sniffed.

He paused and considered her words. "You're right, there is no hope apart from Him. Hope only comes from God and throwing ourselves onto His promises, having to rely on the fact that He speaks the truth. But He does have a reason to save us: He loves us."

She nodded and propped her chin on her knee. Her frown twisted his insides.

After a bit of silence, he couldn't remain quiet anymore. "Do you want to do that? Confess and believe?" His heart teetered.

"But what if there's something truly bad on the inside?"

"Nothing's too bad." He shook his head. "Remember David committed adultery and murder. Surely you haven't done anything like that."

Her eyes darkened, and her arms tightened around herself. *Could she?* No, not his Julia. But she was hiding something. Something that terrible could explain a lot of her reactions. Did he even want to hear? He reached for her hand, to comfort her as much as himself. His mouth was dry, but he pushed out the right words. "Whatever you've done, He'll forgive. He promises to."

She turned to him. "But—what—about—" a body-wracking sob interrupted each word—"you?"

He took her into his arms and held her for a long time as her sobbing ebbed and flowed. The few times she tried to talk, the words tripped over one another and only brought more tears. When she seemed spent, he nestled his cheek in her hair. Her body stiffened in his arms. *Please, God, don't let her revert back to silence.* "I believe in Christ the way He asks us to. I'm His child, and He gives me commands, just like a father does. He tells me I have to forgive others just like He has forgiven me. So yes, I will forgive you. Is there something you need to tell me?"

"But it's too bad," she whispered.

Figuring she hadn't murdered, that left David's story of adultery to have caused her emotional letdown. He braced himself for something that would hurt to his very center. "I won't lie and say for certain what you've done won't hurt me, but the past doesn't matter to me unless it's standing in your way. Get rid of the guilt by telling God about it. He'll forgive your sins, and I should do no less."

She loosened her arms from his waist, but he only gripped tighter.

"Don't pull away, love. Let it out."

She spoke into his chest. "I've been defiled. Another man has taken what you as my husband alone should have."

Wincing, he held her firmly. The hurt he'd expected couldn't compare to the sinking feeling he experienced in his chest. His arms trembled around her, and he blinked hard and fast.

"My father promised him my hand, but when I learned he was marrying me only for the business my father would give him, I refused," she choked out. "He wouldn't take no for an answer."

Flashes of fury bolted from Everett's heart, toward his hands and head and back again. He labored to keep his hold on her loose while desiring to crush the man. A trip to Massachusetts for a manhunt burst into his thoughts. But that wouldn't help his wife hurting in his arms right here, right now.

And to think how she'd almost relived her nightmare with Ned. So that was where her fear of men came from. He couldn't blame her for the wrong done to both of them.

"Honey, there is nothing to forgive you for." He leaned her head back and brushed the hair from her face. "But I'll tell you how that feels—awful. But there is no possible way my pain could match yours. I want to kill him for hurting you. I'm so sorry that happened. But it doesn't change how I feel about you. I love you."

"You're not—" she hiccupped—"not repulsed by me?"

"No." He couldn't keep the huge grin off his face. "I can't fathom anything about you that would repulse me."

"So God feels the same way about—"

"He hates sin, all sin. But that wasn't your sin, although you've reaped the effects of that man's wrongdoing. But still, I'm sure you have done wrong things in your life. Those are the things that you have to turn away from and ask forgiveness for. Do you want to do that?"

"I suppose I should. I've always believed the story of Jesus dying on a cross and coming back to life. I heard about that when we went to church every now and then. But I never trusted Him for anything, and I don't pray. How do I know He'll accept me when I've never really cared what He thought?"

Everett shrugged. "Because He promised He would. Faith is leaning completely on the promise of someone to do what he pledges. If God said He'll forgive us, and we believe He is a God who can do anything, then we have to believe He'll do what He said."

She chewed on her fingernails, and he prayed through the silence. The sun sank behind the rolling hills, and he sighed. It was good she asked questions. Perhaps she would ask more on a later day. He prayed in time she would trust God.

"So how do I do this?"

His eyes snapped open, jolting him from prayer. "Huh?"

Julia waved her hands beside her face. "The confessing thing? Do I have to do something special?"

"No. You just pray." A smile teased his lips, but he kept it from taking over. This was serious, despite her cute flailing limbs. "It's simply talking to God. Remember, it's what's in the heart He looks at. As long as the heart holds true what the mouth says, He'll hear you."

"Fine." She moved to bended knees and arranged her skirts. Like a little girl at the side of a bed for her nighttime prayers, she folded her hands before her and whispered, "God, I have nothing of worth. My heart isn't even good, but Everett says you'll take it that way and make something better of me. I suppose I have to trust that you will. I want you to want me. I want my heart to be wanted, not my face. You say that's what you desire. Please save me."

309

She settled back on her heels, and her lower lip quivered. "Was that right?"

"Yes," he croaked. His beautiful wife was one of God's own.

Without thinking, he leaned over and brushed his mouth against hers. He lost his breath when her face tilted up instead of away. Did he dare press another kiss to the same spot?

She didn't move when his hands encircled her upper arms, and he touched her lips again. A tiny bit of returned pressure made his heart soar. Could it be true? Could God answer both of his prayers in only a matter of seconds? One with God and one with him? With her fear and guilt gone, was her heart free to love him? A heat from the center of his being radiated to the far reaches of his body, and he pulled her in tighter. A small hand cupped the back of his elbow. She was kissing him back!

His fingers turned liquid and he let go of her, his hands thumped against the blanket to keep himself from melting into her lap. And then he couldn't hold back, breathing her in like air.

She pushed away. "No." A tear rolled down her cheek. "I can't."

His breathing labored, he wished he could hide in a hole. Her eyes were terrified. "I'm sorry." His voice cracked.

She rubbed her arms and looked away from him.

His whole body trembled with the feelings he had naïvely given in to. He stood and rubbed his neck. He couldn't force out the words to apologize again. Had this evil man not only stolen her innocence but also his hope of ever fully showing his wife how much he loved her?

Lord, I praise you for saving my Julia's soul. Never would I have thought it would have been so quick and simple, but

310

you knew what it would take to capture her. I'm glad you have her in your arms. Keep her safe there, for my arms are not capable. I went headlong into this relationship without your approval. I chose without your help and guidance.

Julia remained quiet, keeping her gaze averted toward the darkening horizon.

What a good gift you've turned her into: a believing, hard-working, beautiful wife. Help me not to want anything beyond that. To keep my hands to myself.

Her body quivered too, but he surmised the shivering was more from fear than the fervor that trembled through him. The sun sank as fast as his hope.

Was I wrong to believe you'd bless me beyond what I deserve?

He'd asked too much of God. She'd been hurt too deeply, and he was not desirable enough to overcome the panic one man's touch had created within her.

She'd never love him.

$\mathscr{C}$hapter 26

Over at the house, Everett was feeding bits of leftover meat to Sticky and Merlin, but Julia stayed on the blanket outside. Her fingers found her lips. They felt different, from the inside out. His kiss hadn't scared her, but the sensations hadn't stayed where they should have. Drawn to the feel, her lips had responded, and then her body had reacted. She had wanted to kiss him longer to make that feeling last. But a buzz inside her heart set off an alarm.

Slouching forward, she hung her head. Feeling such things in the arms of her husband was good, right? Or was her sensuous reaction wrong? What kind of girl felt such things? She dug her hands into her hair. Everett had held her in his arms, not Theodore.

Would that man's cruel grasp never let go?

She bit her lip and gazed in the direction of the Stanton cabin. If only Rachel, with her no-nonsense advice, could tell her what to do. But Rachel had never experienced anything but love in a man's embrace.

Glancing at her feet, she saw that the Bible Everett had left lay fluttering in the breeze. *God*. Her lips pursed in amusement. Simple, really.

I . . .

Hmmm. Did she have to start formally like the preacher did? She hadn't earlier, and Everett rarely did.

I need help.

That about covered it. Sucking in air, her chest expanded, confident God would answer her prayer. Rachel, Everett, and every pastor she'd heard believed prayer received answers. Now that God had saved her, surely He would answer a simple request.

She placed her bare feet in the grass, swishing her toes through the cool blades. Her lips still tingled, reminding her of his kiss and the heat that had flowed through her body. She pulled a few dandelion heads and ripped away their minuscule petals one by one, painting her fingers yellow. Why had she pulled away from him? It wasn't like he hadn't kissed her before. Although, thankfully, this time she was firmly seated on the ground.

The feel of Theodore's first kiss pushed its way up through her memory. She hadn't pulled away from that one even an inch. Her stomach soured. Why must memories of that odious man surface when she thought of Everett? Beyond looks, the men were so different. She shouldn't keep comparing the two—because Everett actually loved her.

He walked from the front of the house to the well. She could just make out his form in the dim light. His shoulders slumped. Her reaction must have hurt him terribly.

She replayed the kiss again—the pull of his scent, the trembling of their bodies, the wash of warmth that spread to her outer limbs. Not the unpleasant feelings like those that overwhelmed her when she revisited Theodore's kiss.

Her husband's kisses were warm, gentle, tender—and yearning. So why hadn't she given in when she'd wanted to?

The moon in the dark blue sky shone bright, low and large in the heavens. The expanse lit with twinkling white. Head tilted, she took in the awe-inspiring sight of planets and stars. What had kept her from trusting the obvious Creator behind such a lovely world? What kept her from accepting the love Everett offered now?

Knowing that I shouldn't have what I don't deserve.

She stared at the stars, shimmering and blurred by tears. And yet, God and Everett offered themselves to her anyway.

Thank you, Lord. Please help me get over my fears so I can show the man I don't deserve how happy I am that he chose me in spite of what I asked of him.

Panic had kept her from something she had wanted before Theodore killed her dreams: to be cherished by a man and adored by her own children—or to be held in her husband's gentle arms if the dream of little ones was never realized.

With God's help, she'd chase that dream again.

"Can I help you?" Emerging from the mercantile's back room, Kathleen gave a tired smile. "Oh, hello, Julia. What brings you in?"

Julia fingered the lace in her hand. None of the spools matched the lace tucked away in Adelaide's dusty trunk. Should she buy enough to redo her new nightgown's trimming, or just make do with a hodgepodge? Would Everett even notice? She sighed. "I'm just trying to figure out how much lace I need to buy. But I'd love to see the baby again."

Kathleen smiled and swept past the counter. "Carl's changing him, but I'm sure he'll come out with him soon. Can I gather supplies for you while you're deciding?"

"No. I came in just for this."

Kathleen cocked her head. "You drove into town for lace? Everett was here for supplies three days ago." She pulled down a few dusty spools from a high shelf. "What are you working on?"

Julia's cheeks heated. "Um . . . just a . . ."

"Another new dress?" Kathleen frowned.

She shook her head. Goodness knows she had more dresses than any woman in the county. "I'm working on . . . uh, my . . . nigh—nice mittens." She bit her lip, trying to maintain a serious face. How would she explain that?

"Mittens?" Kathleen's brows jiggled. "With lace?"

Julia closed her eyes and sighed. Looks like she'd be making mittens so her foolish brain wouldn't turn her into a liar. Why couldn't she have said *nightgown*? It's not like that was an unusual garment. Only she knew why she was making it fancy. "Well, I was thinking that I could make some uh . . . thick quilted mittens for baking."

"Are your towels or aprons not working well enough?"

"I just thought it might be nice. Who knows? Maybe people will find them . . . interesting, especially if they're pretty."

"Hmm. If you have a hankering to, make some extras, and I'll put them on display at the front counter."

"Sure." Julia nodded and scratched her head. No one would buy such a thing, but at least Kathleen seemed to have accepted the crazy idea.

"Everett drove you into town for mitten lace? Are you sure he doesn't need anything?"

"He didn't come with me." Hopefully he wouldn't return from the fields before she got home and discover she'd left.

"But he's outside with your team."

Julia fumbled the lace. "I'm afraid you're mistaken. He didn't—"

315

The mercantile's bell jingled, and Kathleen touched her arm before stepping around the overflowing shelf of sewing notions.

"Good afternoon, Everett."

Julia bit her lip and wished she could disappear. He'd be sore at her for leaving since she'd promised not to go anywhere without telling him first. But she hadn't the gumption to tell him why she wanted trimming now instead of waiting for his next trip. Had he galloped after her all the way into town like last time?

"Is Julia in here?" His voice sounded a bit raspy.

Her stomach sank lower. Could she do nothing right where he was concerned?

"Yes, right around here."

Julia slid out from behind the shelf, wadded up the lace she'd been fingering, and thrust it toward Kathleen. "I'll take five yards of this."

"Five? That's a lot of mittens."

Julia suppressed a laugh, but felt the pink in her cheeks. Mittens indeed. "I might need it for other projects as well." She glided over to Everett and shakily took his clammy hand.

He squeezed hard. "I'm sorry I've disturbed your shopping."

"No, of course not." But why was he here? Had he not enough faith in her to believe she'd not really leave him without some kind of warning?

Carl stepped out of the back, his infant son tucked against his side. "Are you all right up here, Kathleen?"

"Yes, unless you want to take care of Mr. Cline."

He shrugged. "Not if you don't need me to."

Everett's surprised gaze shot over to Carl, then back to Kathleen.

Carl walked around the counter and leaned against the pickle barrel. He lifted his eyebrow, looking in Everett's direction. "You've met Junior, right?" The baby's bright eyes blinked against the sun streaming through the front windows. Julia itched to shield the boy's eyes, but he looked happy enough.

"No, I believe he's been napping each time I've come around."

"Well, take a look." He hefted the baby up and cradled him against his chest. "He's already got bottom teeth." The baby gnawed on Carl's probing finger. "See, two little nubbins. He's got my cleft here, the prominent brow bone, the lips. No mistaking him for anybody else's son, huh?"

Julia's heart grew warm at the man's obvious pride. The boy surely did look a lot like his father—along with the sparse hair, overbite, and mottled skin.

Carl pulled Kathleen over with his free arm and bussed the top of her head. "She couldn't have birthed me a finer son."

Everett reached over and took the baby's chubby fist and shook it. "Pleased to meet you, Junior."

Junior got a serious look on his face and turned red. Julia tried not to giggle at the baby's extreme look of concentration.

"Ah, excuse us." Carl lifted the baby into the air above his head and brought him down to touch noses. "Come on, stinky britches. Let's change you again."

Kathleen smiled at the two of them disappearing into the back. Then she turned to Everett. "He's so enamored with him—especially the fact that he's his spitting image."

"No longer worried about me, then?"

Kathleen brightened, and her lips twitched. "Nope. Finally. The dense man."

"Good." Everett nodded, then sneaked a glance back at Julia before tugging his hand free and toying with the pipes arranged next to the tobacco on the front counter.

Julia laid a hand on his bicep. "Was there something you needed? I'm sorry I didn't ask, and I'm sorry I worried you."

"Excuse me, but I need to check on this price." Kathleen swiped up the bundle of lace on which she'd already pinned a receipt and escaped in the direction of coos and manly chuckles.

Julia clasped his sleeve and lowered her voice. "I should have told you where I was going."

"Oh, I wasn't worried about that." He sneaked a glance back out the window.

"Then you came in for something? A pipe?" She let her fingers slide down along his thick forearm.

He tried to set the dark wooden pipe back in its place, but it clattered back onto the counter. "No, never smoked in my life." After three attempts, the pipe stayed upright. He pulled at his collar. "It's just that I saw Ned's team pass after you left. . . ."

The store door banged open, and an irritated humph sounded behind them. The hair on her neck bristled.

She whirled around and met Ned's black gaze. Everett stepped closer to her side and placed his hand on her shoulder. She couldn't help the shiver that trembled through her whole body. Everett squeezed her for reassurance, but still she fought the urge to duck behind him. They hadn't seen Ned since Everett threw him off the property. Surely he wouldn't start trouble in town. Would he flaunt Everett's demands, believing he wouldn't fight him in public?

Ned stared at them both for a few seconds, his expression full of hatred now instead of lust. He made a sucking noise, then aimed a brown slurry of spit at the brass pot near the door's frame. He spit again before turning. The door slammed hard behind him, bouncing twice before settling in a closed position.

"Wonder what he wanted?"

Julia jumped at Kathleen's annoyed voice.

"Nothing he can have." Everett's grip on her shoulder slacked, and he gently pushed her back toward the lace counter. "Pick out whatever else you need. I'll be escorting you home."

She rubbed her arms, attempting to dispel the prickly feeling under her sleeve. She hadn't thought about the possibility of meeting up with Ned alone when she'd ridden in. If Everett hadn't seen him pass the homestead . . .

She looked over at his stony face. He'd put distance between them, pretending to be fascinated with an oil lamp this time. His behavior had definitely backslidden to that of their first month of married life since their last kiss. Acted as if he didn't care how she spent her day, left in the mornings with hardly a word, skipped meals, and left her to her own devices. The only thing different was he continued to read Scripture after supper.

But she needed him. And he needed her.

She looked at the jumbled piles of bobbin and needle lace. "Kathleen's already prepared what I needed."

"All right." He nodded and strode toward the front door. "I'll ready the team."

She took a deliberate breath and felt the uneven patter of her heart. Maybe this venture had turned out better than she'd hoped, even with the run-in with Ned. An hour and a half alone with her husband beside her. A few days ago, he'd gone to town at the last minute and hadn't taken her, claiming he didn't want to interrupt her plans. But she knew he'd done so to avoid conversation—and sitting next to her that long.

And so she would sit next to him now, close. Real close.

"I'm ready to go, Kathleen." She grabbed an armful of apples to make Everett a cake. "And I was wondering if you and Carl might want to come out to the homestead and have dinner sometime. I know it's quite a way to drive, but I'd love to spend some time talking to you about things other than flour and sugar."

"I'd love to, but let me talk to Carl. It'd have to be late, considering he doesn't like to close the shop early."

"Maybe a Sunday?"

Kathleen smiled. "That would be better. How about two Sundays from now, after church?"

"Sounds good. I can't wait to have you over." She gathered her things and left the store, but her smile died. Everett was sitting atop Blaze behind the wagon. He tipped his hat to her, and she hoisted herself up onto the wooden seat and yanked up her reins. He couldn't sequester himself from her forever. A distant husband wouldn't make a good dinner guest two weeks from now.

His impatient pace on the way home required her focus to remain on Dimple and Curly so she wouldn't fall behind.

Well, she too was growing impatient. But she'd fix that.

The next night after dinner, Everett couldn't help but notice Julia kept looking out of the corner of her eye at him when she thought he wasn't looking. And he shouldn't be looking. She had put on a lacy nightgown she'd fitted to her tiny frame.

The sweltering summer temperatures had crept into September, so he stripped to his drawers and undershirt. He brought the quilt up to his chest despite the heat, poked his feet out as he stretched on the far side of the mattress, and finally curled up facing the wall.

She hummed to herself as she brushed her hair. He flung his arm across his ear.

The bed bowed with her weight, but she didn't lie down. "Do you mind if I pray at bedtime? Since you pray at dinner, I thought maybe I ought to take on an evening prayer."

Her question made him feel ridiculous, lying balled up like a defiant child. Here he was hardening his heart, and she was growing in God. He rolled onto his back and clasped his hands on his chest. The trembling in his fingers betrayed his desire for her, making it tough to talk with her in bed, but he couldn't return to his taciturn ways without destroying all hope for a good relationship. He longed for a godly wife. How could he expect her to mature in her faith if he demonstrated the opposite? "Sure."

Bowing her head, she remained silent. After a few moments, her breathy voice beseeched God. "Lord, help us to know how to live together. Thank you for saving me and providing me with a good home. Give us rest to accomplish the goals we have in the morning. Amen."

"Amen."

The lamplight succumbed to Julia's breath. Her shadowy outline appeared, barely discernible in the dark room. He sighed. He should be demonstrating God's love to her, but engaging her in lighthearted conversation hurt too much. His physical desire for her wasn't yet locked up tight. He needed more time to get under control.

The blanket jerked around as she searched in the dark for the top of the quilt. She would twist it into knots like usual, so he reached over to flip the covers down. The weight of her backside fell upon his hand, his pinkie finger crooked at an odd angle. "Ow!" He clamped his hand to his chest. "That smarts."

Her minty breath wafted inches from his face. "I'm sorry. I didn't know your hand was there."

"Obviously." He stretched his fingers.

Her hand caught his and pulled it to her. "Let me kiss it. Where did I hurt you?"

"Nowhere." He tried to tug his hand away, but she kept a tight grasp.

"If you don't tell me, I'll just have to find the spot myself." He sat up. "No thank you."

"I'm sorry, I just thought—"

"Kissing hurts away might have worked when I was a kid, but it's useless now." Her hand found his knee, and he swiped it off. He couldn't let her lips touch his skin, even for a childish kiss. He didn't trust himself right now. She was too close, too enticing. He pushed out of bed.

"What are you doing?"

"Leaving." He stomped his right heel down into his boot.

"I'm sorry, Everett. Please. I won't offer any more kisses."

"Good." He wrenched his left foot into the other boot.

"Stay, Everett."

Shaking his head, he walked out and down the steps.

"What's wrong?" Her voice warbled from the porch. "Must you run? Please, let's talk."

She stood at the porch railing, her white gown glowing in the moonlight. He growled to the maker of the stars above him, "This isn't working!" He spun on his heel and raced to the barn. A nudge in his heart told him he was making this train wreck of a relationship worse.

Go back. Go listen.

He swiped the prodding aside and stomped toward a dark stall full of hay.

Her heart thumped in her throat. Agitated and downright angry he was. For nothing. Simply nothing. She took a step down the stairs, intent on finding him and chastising him for his childish behavior.

Merlin stepped in front of her at the bottom of the step and whined. Boy did she feel like whining herself.

God, I don't understand. I wouldn't act like this.

The thought of how she'd pushed him away at every single advance and the look in his eye as he told her of the four women before her who'd rejected him rushed from the confines of her memory.

Her heart slowed and her fists unclenched. She crossed her arms and glared at the barn. They needed to talk. She needed to tell him.

The barn door stood open, and the full moon made the outline of stalls and sleeping animals visible. As she stepped inside the barn, the cicada humming receded, and the sound of sputtering and mumbling filled her ears.

Taking a step back, she clenched her hand against her stomach. Walking in on a man weeping was certainly wrong, but her name being sputtered between moans drew her forward. Her feet crunched on the hay-littered floor as she followed the sounds to the last stall. The window across the way let in enough light for her to see Everett on his knees, hands clasping a wad of hay.

"What you ask me to do is too difficult, Lord. I can't do it. It's absurd." His ragged breath sounded from the stall. "I was wrong to bring her here. But what would you have me do? I want to get away . . . but my vows hold me, and my heart enslaves me. But your expectations . . . your expectations are too much."

Her heart drooped like a withered plant after drought and neglect. Had she read him wrong? She covered her mouth with a trembling hand and slid to her knees while he stammered incoherent sentences. If he left her, she'd never get over the hurt. And to know he loved her once would make the pain so much more acute.

She was too late.

Blinking hard to get her tears under control, she readied to push herself off the ground.

"But I can't, Father. I can't leave her." His erratic breathing evened. "Help me rid myself of these feelings. I love her, I do, it's just too hard." He slumped against the stall's side. "Sleeping next to her is killing me." He hiccuped.

Her heart sang. What did he say?

"I can't be her companion. I can't be what she's forcing me to be. She won't have me, yet she tortures me. Make my agony stop, Lord! Rip out these feelings so I can be the friend she wants me to be. Every day that I wake up beside her, I want her more."

A loud, shuddering breath escaped her lips.

His silhouette tensed.

Her skin prickled, and her heart felt light. She crawled toward him.

He began to rise, but she reached for his shoulders, keeping him on his knees in front of her.

Coughs and swallows preceded his whisper. "I'm sorry. You weren't supposed to hear that. Don't fear I'll pressure you. I won't. I've promised."

She scooted next to him. "I'm not sorry I overheard. It's time we ended this sham of a marriage."

He rocked back on his heels and stood as quick as lightning. She scrambled to stand, grabbing the hand clenched over his chest. He hung his head. "I suppose it is."

She clasped his tense arm with both of her hands. "What you were praying for just then would require a miracle." She peered up at him, but his face turned toward the window, his neck taut. "I don't want to see God do such a mighty work."

With her finger, she drew lazy lines on his tensed arm. The muscles flexed under her touch. "It's wrong for you to be sleeping next to me a foot or two away. That ought to stop. Every night, since you kissed me last, I struggle to fall asleep, wondering what another one of those kisses would feel like if you rolled over and took me into your arms."

He stiffened more, and she let her hand travel up his chest, the muscle solid and reassuring. He clamped her arm against his racing heart, staying her movements. "Don't toy with me, Julia."

"Why didn't you want me to kiss you a few minutes ago?"

He sucked in a breath. "Because I feared I'd kiss you back, and I can't watch you turn away from me in disgust again."

"That's all I've done, isn't it?" Her posture slumped.

"And I shouldn't kiss a woman who doesn't love me."

He deserved better than her; she now realized what a gift God had given her. "I shouldn't have married you—"

He released her and stepped away.

She grabbed a fistful of his shirt. "Wait. I only mean I shouldn't have married you when I did." Reaching up, she straightened his collar. "I let my fear of men cloud my discernment, but I love you for respecting my impossible expectations and for loving me despite how I've treated you."

"What are you saying?" He bent his head, his eyes roving

back and forth as if he could read her thoughts by taking in every inch of her face.

How could she have ever toyed with this man? And how had she ever doubted what her attachment to him really was? "Yes, Everett, I love you. Very much."

Cupping her face, his thumbs trembled as he smoothed the skin at her jawline. "I'm not sure I can keep from kissing you right now." He swallowed hard. "May I?"

Her heart hammered in her throat as she nodded. "I promise not to pull away."

One roughened hand whispered across her neck, and the fingers of his other combed themselves into her hair. "Good," he whispered. The moonlight from the window illumined the flash of fire behind his eyes. His kiss was slow and tender as he tucked her in close. She closed her eyes, awash in the comfort and love of the man who adored her. A few seconds later, he pulled back, shivering.

At least she thought he was, since her body shook of its own volition.

"Just wanted to see if I could be the first to break a kiss for once." His voice was husky.

His boyish smirk made her smile. "I now see why you didn't like it."

"Beloved, are you certain you love me?" He tucked a strand of hair behind her ear, his eyes softer than the moonlight. "I don't want you to ever think I want you tucked into my side for anything baser than the fact that you are my other half. The only woman I dream of, the one I need beside me. The girl I'll spend the rest of my life getting to know so well, no one will believe our marriage started off so rough."

"Yes, I'm certain." She wrapped her arms around his waist and pressed her head against his chest. The warmth of tears flooded her eyes. "And I know you'll love me no matter what because you loved me before I was any good to you."

She didn't deserve him at all. "What can I do to erase these last miserable months from your memory?"

A low chuckle vibrated against her cheek. "They weren't that miserable."

She leaned back to look at him. "Yes they were. You just told God as much."

"All right, more than miserable." He smiled as he swept a tear from the corner of her eye. "But you just told me you loved me, and those words have already wiped away the hardship. I would have gone through anything to have you say that to me."

"Then let's add some more good memories to today, shall we?"

"What do you have in mind, love?"

She stood on tiptoe to meet his smiling lips, starting a kiss she refused to be the first one to break. Time and the need to breathe disappeared in the security of his embrace.

Why had she ever pulled away?

Epilogue

Julia sucked in a mighty breath before it was too late. Rachel leaned over and clasped her uncontrollably quivering knees. "Almost there."

Growling, she pushed.

"One more."

Through gritted teeth, she spit word daggers at her friend. "You told me that a hundred pushes—"

"Save your breath, girl."

Her vision turned black, and then a thousand stars obliterated the darkness. She gulped for air.

"There. I told you. Do it again."

With one last shove, the pressure slipped away and the pain dissolved. She didn't have to ask if the baby was alive. A cry pierced the air, and her legs fell limp to the ticking. A sigh escaped, and she lay back onto the pillows, exhausted.

She'd lost two little ones early on, but this one was here, actually here. Anticipating the anguish of losing children hadn't truly prepared her for it. New empathy had allowed her to forgive her mother for how she'd been treated as a child.

But she was determined not to let her lost children affect her treatment of the one crying in Rachel's arms.

Rachel's beaming face swam before her. "A boy. A big, loud boy." She wiped the damp hair from her forehead and smiled. "And you told me you wouldn't be having any children."

The bedroom door flew open, and Everett's tall form filled the doorway. His eyes locked onto hers.

Rachel moved away to the corner, hushing and cooing to the swaddled baby in her arms.

Everett knelt beside her and grabbed her hand. "How are you?"

She sighed. "We have a son."

"I can hear." The baby's wails nearly drowned out his words, but she still heard the pleasure behind them.

"You should be happy." She mustered up a smile. "A strong boy to help with the workload."

"So that's why you wanted this baby so bad." His face sported a lopsided grin. "Needed someone to take over chores so you could be lazy."

Her head moved back and forth across the pillow. "You said I'd be a fool to think we could do the farm work alone. The Lord knows I tried."

He covered a laugh with a cough before letting his fingers slip into her hair. "Glad you worked so hard making our home ready for my son."

Laughing, Rachel placed a freshly washed bundle of baby in the crook of his arm. "I'm afraid you've added to your workload with this tiny thing. Doubled if not tripled. A long, roundabout process to scale down your responsibilities."

Julia sat up against the headboard and caressed her son's velvety cheek. He turned toward her fingers, and Rachel gave her a few minutes of instruction on feeding the baby before she left the room.

Feeling no fatigue, she placed her thumb in the babe's grasp.

"He's the most beautiful thing I've ever seen." Everett's voice broke.

She raised her eyebrows. "You once said that about me." Their son's big blue eyes stared up at her as if she were the most marvelous thing in the world. She caressed his folded velvety ear. "He's usurped me already."

Everett's hands planted themselves on each side of her lap, forcing her gaze off the perfection in her arms.

"I suppose I've looked better." She took in his dark, vivid blue eyes.

"No." Everett's voice was rough and low. "No you haven't."

Acknowledgments

I am indebted to so many people for helping me on my journey to publication, and I've most likely not thanked any of them enough for their generosity, time, and expertise.

To my husband, who listens to my rambling story ideas and the woes of making characters do what I want—even though I often keep him up late at night to do so. I'm grateful he enjoys being my fight coordinator and weapons and outdoor expert.

To the original Scribes 203 group, Anne Greene, Charlie Marquardt, Diana Sharples, and Glenn Haggerty Jr., who had to deal with a very green writer, yet saw my potential and hacked my words to pieces so I could grow. If it wasn't for your kind but thorough help in learning the craft, I'd not yet be where I am.

To my critique partner, Naomi Rawlings. Not only is she exactly who I need to kick my stories to the next level, but she is a friend I treasure.

To two of my very best friends, Andrea Strong and Karen Riekeman, who believed in me before reading my manuscript and still believed in me afterward, their confidence in me is incredibly encouraging.

To my agent, Natasha Kern, and my editors, Raela Schoen-herr and Sarah Long, and the other people behind the scenes at Bethany House who championed my manuscript and helped me achieve my dream of holding this book in my hands: I'm very, very grateful.

To authors who give of their time to judge prepublished contests, I know how much work that is and am thankful you do so. I especially want to thank the ones that came out of anonymity to encourage me. And to contest coordinators and organizations that provide contests and industry professionals serving as final judges who make them worthwhile, this book most likely wouldn't be published if it hadn't been for your time. And to Seekerville, which posts monthly contest updates that spurred me to put this manuscript in One. Last. Time.

And to my poor children, who have to put up with a writing mommy, I thank them for not caring that the house is often a disaster. I'm glad that ditching housekeeping to write doesn't make me a poor mommy in their eyes. And to my husband, who deals with it.

And to my God, who loves me for reasons unfathomable. May I grow to be a better servant with the gifts you've given me.

Melissa Jagears, an ESL teacher by trade, is a stay-at-home mother on a tiny Kansas farm with a fixer-upper house. She's a member of ACFW and CROWN fiction marketing. Her passion is to help Christian believers mature in their faith and judge rightly. *A Bride for Keeps* is her first novel. Find her online at www.melissajagears.com, Facebook, Pinterest, and Goodreads.